"Ashley E. Sweeney minces few words as she unravels Ruby Fortune's fate on the early Arizona frontier. Wild west performer, drug addict, ardent lover, mother, and murderer, Ruby's story is gritty and unabashedly raw. She quickly learns she is sometimes no match for the trials that come her way, but she survives as only she knows how—with her strength, her wit, and her gun. Spellbinding from beginning to end."

—JAN CLEERE, New Mexico-Arizona Book Award winner of *Military Wives of Arizona*

"Ruby's is a thrilling ride across the hard land of Arizona in the early 1900s as one woman takes on and tames the West. Sweeney's third novel is a courageous stunner."

—GRETCHEN CHERINGTON, author of *Poetic License*

"Smart, savage, and bold as brass, Ruby Fortune's strength and sense of survival explode from the pages of this portrait painted by master storyteller, Ashley E. Sweeney, using the harsh, historical Arizona Territory as her palette. Through captivating and unsettling events, Ruby's independent spirit, ingenuity, and sheer guts held me hostage from the first vivid page to the last."

—LAURIE BUCHANAN, award-winning author of the Sean McPherson novels

"Ruby is a difficult woman, in the best way possible. She shoots, she kills, she enjoys lustful sex. She survives. She protects her children and the people she loves. Literature is filled with men like this. But there are very few Rubies. Reading her story, I reveled in her life-force. She is a newly described American archetype."

—SHELLEY BLANTON-STROUD, award-winning author of *Copy Boy*

"Ruby Fortune doesn't harden her heart or break apart at the cruel hands of domestic abuse, but gains compassion and strength in her ultimate journey to wholeness by fighting for dignity and self-worth, loving fiercely those close and deserving, and by welcoming all to her table and more. A bright and resilient gem of a woman in an unforgiving land."

—DEBRA THOMAS, award-winning author of *Luz*

"Gritty, honest, and real. Sure to be on everyone's TBR list."

—NANCY E. TURNER, award-winning author of *Light Changes Everything*

"Ruby Fortune defines grit and grace—she is the heroine we need in these times. Riveting and beautifully told."

—SUSAN TWEIT, award-winning author of *Bless the Birds*

"Ada is every pioneer woman who accomplished more than she ever thought possible."

—*BOOKLIST*

". . . this book captivated me. With its rich sensory details and the varied humanity of its characters, this book is a must-read for fans of historical fiction, and for anyone looking for insight into a period that carved and honed people down to their core."

—*SEATTLE BOOK REVIEW*

". . . .a fascinating historical novel, aimed at anyone interested in the struggles of pioneers, especially the Donner-Reed Party. I will certainly look for more novels by this author."

—*READER'S FAVORITE*

"Sweeney immerses the reader in the time and place, giving a brilliant picture of daily trail life, particularly from a woman's perspective....Stronger still is Ada's character development. Always scrappy and resourceful, Ada develops a grit and determination on the trail that serves her well....Sweeney deftly gives readers a feel for the horrible choices some members of the Donner Party had to make and is careful to preserve the humanity that is too often removed from histories...."

—*HISTORICAL NOVELS REVIEW*

"So well researched, one can almost feel the cold of winter and the stifling pain inflicted upon the heart and soul of these courageous pioneers."

—K.S. JONES, award-winning author
of *Shadow of the Hawk*

". . . a gripping story of loss, survival, and female strength. Sweeney does such a masterful job of evoking the journey, from the shifting challenges of the landscape the emigrants move through to the emotional complications of being dependent for survival on people who were strangers months or even just weeks before. The epic sweep, the vast scale, of the trek is vividly felt, but so are the smallest of details."

—Society Nineteen Journal, 5/5 stars

"With faultlessly authentic period detail and relentless, riveting twists of fate, *Answer Creek* puts the reader right on the Oregon-California Trail in every sensory and emotional aspect-imaginable. This compassionate but utterly realistic telling of the story gently crushes the sensationalized versions and releases something that feels much closer to truth. Ada is hope personified—it takes wing, soars, crashes—and survives."

—Ellen Notbohm, award-winning author
of *The River by Starlight*

"If there can be beauty in horror, Sweeney has managed it in the writing of this book. Doom hovers on every page— in the sunsets of the western sky, in emaciated cattle, in boots worn down to shreds—yet the human spirit radiantly perseveres in the form of young Ada Weeks, who is determined to find love despite an avalanche of losses and sorrows. Her harrowing physical and psychological journey grips the reader in a tightly woven web of suspense. Impeccably researched, Answer Creek is a triumphant re-telling of a mythic American tragedy."

—Laurel Davis Huber, author of *The Velveteen Daughter*,
winner of the Langum Prize for American Historical Fiction

For *Eliza Waite*

✳ **2017 Nancy Pearl Book Award**

✳ **2017 The WILLA Literary Award:**
Finalist in Historical Fiction

✳ **2017 International Book Awards:**
Finalist in Fiction: Historical

✳ **2016 Best Book Award Finalist in Fiction:**
Historical

✳ **2015-2016 Sarton Women's Book Award:**
Shortlist in Historical Fiction

"Cast off by her family and living in the shadow of unthinkable tragedy, Eliza Waite finds the courage to leave her remote island home to join the sea of miners, fortune hunters, con men, and prostitutes in the Klondike during the spring of 1898. Ashley Sweeney's exquisite descriptions, electrifying plot twists, and hardy yet vulnerable characters will captivate historical fiction fans and leave them yearning for more. *Eliza Waite* is a stunning debut!"
—KRISTEN HARNISCH, award-winning author
of *The Vintner's Daughter* and *The California Wife*

"Meticulously researched, *Eliza Waite* transports us to the Klondike Gold Rush, where a resourceful young widow searches a more elusive prize: happiness in a re-forged life.
—PAMELA SCHOENEWALDT, *USA Today* best-selling
author of *When We Were Strangers*

"This book hooked me from the first page. Just beautiful."
—FOR THE LOVE OF BOOKS

"Sweeney's debut novel is a beautifully written work of historical fiction tracing one woman's life in the wilds of nineteenth-century America. Readers will be immersed in Eliza's world, which Sweeney has so authentically and skillfully rendered."

—BOOKLIST

"I can confidently say that *Eliza Waite* will easily be in my top 10 books of the year for 2016. The writing is so stark and beautiful, the story so compelling. I couldn't put this book down, and I couldn't stop thinking about it when I finished reading."

—A SOUTHERN GIRL READS BLOG

"*Eliza Waite* is carefully crafted, beautifully edited, and masterfully formatted. And all of the old-school baking recipes are an unexpected plus. I highly recommend this story, especially for women. It truly helps give a context for the suffering and struggles of women throughout our American history. Five stars."

—READER'S FAVORITE

"Sweeney has written a brilliant piece of historical fiction whose lead female character has it all. She is a woman who refused to bow to the cruelties of a misogynistic society, only less damnable than her own family. This is a woman who reached down inside and found herself. She is a character who deserves, no, is due the right of having a book named after her. And so it is."

—THE ANCHORAGE PRESS

HARDLAND

HARDLAND

A NOVEL

ASHLEY E. SWEENEY

SHE WRITES PRESS

Published 2022
Printed in the United States of America
Print ISBN: 978-1-64742-233-2
E-ISBN: 978-1-64742-234-9
Library of Congress Control Number: 2022907465

For information, address:
She Writes Press
1569 Solano Ave #546
Berkeley, CA 94707

Interior design by Tabitha Lahr
Map design by Anders Rodin

She Writes Press is a division of SparkPoint Studio, LLC.

All company and/or product names may be trade names, logos, trademarks, and/or registered trademarks and are the property of their respective owners.

This is a work of fiction. Names, characters, places, and incidents either are the product of the author's imagination or are used fictitiously. Any resemblance to actual persons, living or dead, is entirely coincidental.

Other works by Ashley E. Sweeney:

Answer Creek
Eliza Waite

In memory of and gratitude to
Anne Vaughan Spilsbury
who taught me the walls will hold as many as are invited,
and there will always be room for more.

The world breaks everyone, and afterward,
some are strong at the broken places.
—ERNEST HEMINGWAY

ARIZONA
TERRITORY
1905

ROADS
RIVERS
RAILS

FLAGSTAFF
JEROME
PRESCOTT
PHOENIX
GLOBE
ORACLE
JERICHO
YUMA
TUCSON
TOMBSTONE
BISBEE

N
W   E
S

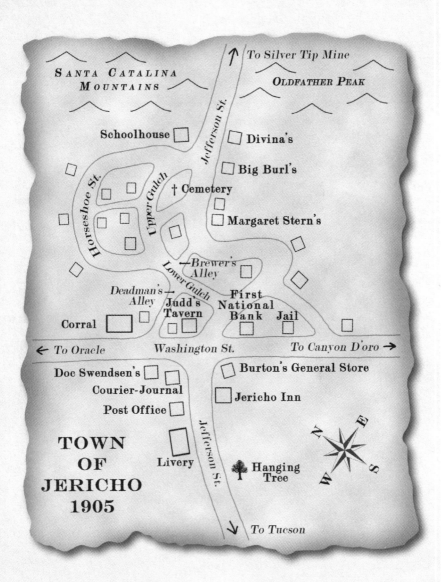

In the beginning, God created the heavens and the earth, or so I've been told. Well, He must've had His knickers in a knot when He conjured up this corner of Arizona Territory because it's nothing but dust and cactus and snakes—and some of the rattiest men you'll meet this side of Kingdom Come.

Let's just say you grow scales, like a lizard, to survive here. I should know, or my name's not Ruby Fortune.

Jericho's not unlike any other jack-rough mining town cantilevered on the side of a mountain like a tilting house of cards. Cowboys, land agents, and ladies face up on a mattress. Lawmen and outlaws. Con men and swindlers by the wagon load. Not a day goes by without a gunfight or a knifing, all washed down with rotten beer. The hanging tree? Used far too many times for my liking, sometimes without so much as a goddamn trial. No question about it—no one comes to these parts on holiday. For land or freedom or gold, yes. Or to escape something or someone you'd rather soon forget back in Tennessee or Arkansas, or wherever you come from, your pants or your wit or your dick too short.

It's a rough life here, too. I've been beaten on more occasions than you'd probably care to know. Broken bones, split lips, blackened eyes. And welts so unmistakable you can see the outline of a man's hand long afterward. I've got scars you can see, sure enough, and a heap more you can't. And that's not the half of it. Been swindled and cheated and deceived, time and again. Sometimes I curse that I'm a woman—although most times not.

I've done my share of wrongs and I'm not proud of it. Killed a man, for one. But did I have a choice? Do I have regrets about it? No. That I had to purge this world of my boys' pa so we could get on with the living of it, that takes it out of a body. We're all wounded because of it, me and my boys, Clayton, Fletcher, Virgil, and Sam. Most of all Sam. That I live with every day, a pain so deep in my soul I'd need a cleaver to cut it out.

Will I ever be forgiven? That's up for debate, although I'd do it again. God and the devil both lay claim to me, and they've each got their reasons. One minute, The Lord God Almighty Himself is perched on my shoulder and I whistle through my teeth. But then, quick as I can jerk a trigger, the devil's got his claws into me, hissing in my ear, and I just can't shake him.

Way I see it, I'm either on the chuck-holed road to Heaven or the slick road to Hell.

Hear me out. Then you pick.

SEPTEMBER 7, 1899
JERICHO, ARIZONA TERRITORY

Wind growls at the corners of Ruby Fortune's mouth as she leaves the flatland and zigzags up a sharp, rocky incline toward Silver Tip Mine, four miles east of Jericho in the Santa Catalina Mountains north of Tucson. Ruby's neck is still sore, the tail of a sickly yellow bruise circling her throat. He could have killed her. As she shoves her kerchief over her nose and mouth to avoid dust, strips of hair whip her cheeks, glance off her eyes. Pulling her wide-brimmed hat low, Ruby flings tangled hair behind her shoulder. It's as futile as harnessing air.

Ruby has borrowed Doc Swendsen's best mare today before she changes her mind. The horse path up Oldfather Peak is slower than the ore road, but less dangerous—don't want to be crushed by a twenty-mule hitch careening down the mountain, hell bent for leather, drivers cussing like cowboys that a woman is riding up into their domain.

"C'mon, Maisie. 'Atta girl." Ruby clicks her tongue. She needs to rein in her shaky nerves today. She's had two shots of whiskey and it isn't noon yet.

The mare's deft hooves crunch on hardpan and clatter up loose gravel as Ruby winds her way around cactus thickets, thorny ironwood, and sun-whitened bones of the dead: big horn sheep, mule deer, bobcat, desert hare. Millions of years ago, the earth heaved up so quickly that there wasn't time to smooth the edges, so chain after chain of mountains rise from the cracked desert floor like islands in a sea, here at the rough edge of the world.

Crossing a dry riverbed, ocotillo line the snaky pathway, their spindly stalks casting oblong shadows across the trail. Stark white billows bank up against the jagged Santa Catalinas as Ruby gains altitude. It's August now, February's moody twin. It won't be long before lightning rips the sky and thunder gallops behind, rumbling savagely the length of the mountain chain. Ruby trains one eye on the sky and the other on the trail. Monsoons can make a body nervous.

The boys are with Divina today, Virgil, Fletcher, and Clayton, almost like triplets at eight, nine, and ten. And little Sam—now there's a worry. Only four, he wasn't a big talker before Ruby shot the boys' pa. Sam hasn't uttered a word since that day. It's been what? Two weeks? She's still alive, and her boys too, and she wouldn't have been if she hadn't pulled the trigger.

A shy half-mile from the mine, Ruby's skirt catches on a white-thorned acacia bush, tugging her backward for a moment. She whacks the branch away with blood-red leather gloves. There are still traces of an old burn here, but the desert is, if anything, resilient. Ruby hears a snort. Just ahead, past a copse of scraggy mesquite creped with mistletoe, a squadron of javelina snuffles across the trail, chuffing snouts close to the ground. The mare whinnies.

Horses have navigated this terrain since Francisco Vasquez de Coronado brought horses north from New Spain in the 1540s. Conquistadors, priests, and *vaqueros* have roamed these Apache hills for centuries. And then the floodgates opened: trappers and hunters, soldiers and settlers navigating well-worn trails long before Ruby took to the saddle. None wants to cross a javelina on a bad day. Ruby uses her damp shirtsleeve to wipe sweat from her brow as she waits for the javelinas to pass. She pats the mare and feeds her a lump of sugar. When Ruby was learning her *ABC*s, her father fed her lumps of sugar, too, like a favorite horse. "Word by word, Ruby," she hears her long-dead father say. Still good advice as she spools out the exchange she's going to have in a quarter-hour's time. She has to get it right. Her heart taps a steady *rap rap rap* at her ribcage as she draws in more dust than breath, even with her face covered. Could God Almighty turn off this wind, just once?

Sitting straight as the saguaro up ahead, Ruby rides up the last incline and skirts a deep cleft in the trail. Ruby is not so worried about falling into a crack in the earth and finding herself in China. It's Hell she's more nervous about. Now that Willie Fortune is buried in Jericho Cemetery, others—including the man she is riding to see—might rather it had been her funeral. It's scandal enough as it is, a mother of four shooting her husband in broad daylight and walking away. Today, Ruby's loaded derringer is fastened to the belt that circles her boy-like waist. One can never be too prepared.

SAME DAY

Ruby reaches Silver Tip Mine and dismounts, raising a cloud of copper-red dust. Her boots, clothes, hat—all of it—are a burnt shade of dirt. She arranges her good brown skirt and tugs at the bottom hem of her cream-colored suede vest with her gloves. Her father gifted the gloves to her on her fourteenth birthday, a few days before his heart up and exploded. She's twelve years past fourteen now and certainly wiser than the day she first unwrapped them in Big Burl's marvelous carnival tent in Amarillo.

Ruby rises to her full height—five foot two in stocking feet, and a hair taller in spurred red boots. She takes in a deep breath. There's more than silver buried here at the northern edge of the Santa Catalina Mountains. She knows. Stories too, there are, just waiting to be let out.

Ruby hitches Swendsen's mare to a post adjacent to the large corral. More than twenty mules loiter in the corral in this morning's already sweltering heat. Horses, Ruby is comfortable with, not mules. She doesn't dislike them, she just doesn't know them. She's heard they're smarter than horses and easier to train, and a much better bet when it comes to packing and hauling, seeing as they eat less and can withstand the heat. Plus, mules can see all four feet at once, something a horse can't do. Ruby's gaze lingers on the braying mules for a moment, the word *surefooted* crossing her thoughts.

"*Dobro jutro!*"

Greek? Slavic? Ruby doesn't know one foreign tongue from another. She nods and says good morning back to the men and then cranes her head around camp. Her neck is still tender. No, she's not going to cover the bruise that rings her neck. Let them see what Willie Fortune did to her.

At the mine entrance, trammers push heavy-laden ore carts. A four-man crew shovels ore to side carts, dust exploding from their tools like buckshot. A pair of burros pulls one cart off to the loading dock while another pair takes its place to heave the next load. A hundred yards to the right of the opening, a steam engine belches air. A mechanized hoist grinds as a small metal cage emerges from the bowels of the earth. Men exit the cage, faces and carbide lamps caked black.

Then, a whistle. Cornishmen, Slavs, Italians, coloreds; tall, bandy, fat, trim. Rough lot, the miners, oilskin coats swishing behind them and hats pulled low, calling to each other by names they weren't baptized by: Big Nose Dan, Texas Joe, One-Eyed Swede. The cage opens again and down they go, timbermen, drillers, swampers, and muckers, sinking more than a thousand feet into the earth. They are not going to China, or Hell. It's silver they're after, ten-hour shifts drilling rock, blasting dynamite, timbering chutes, extracting ore—hot work, cold work, wet work, dry work, depending on the day or the job or the shaft or if they've crossed the big boss. They risk it all—misfired dynamite, deadly gases, random fires, all-too-often cave-ins—for three dollars a day, two dollars more than any ordinary laborer. No wonder the camp is packed, the whole world come to Jericho.

Ruby wends her way through a maze of bunkhouses and outbuildings and sidesteps a refuse pile. *Watch for snakes, Ruby. Always watch for snakes.* And where is the damn mine office? She nods to a Chinaman smoking at the rear of the mess tent and strides past unmarked tent after unmarked tent until she comes out not far from where she started. There she spies a shack with a less-than-handsome sign over the door: SILVER TIP MINE, Est. 1897.

Ruby rattles the brass door handle and enters, her confidence leaking like a sieve. "Mr. Bugg."

A rustling of papers.

"Well, well, well." A tall, lanky man with a shock of dark hair pushes back his chair and stands. His vest hangs unbuttoned, a dirtied shirt underneath. Has he shaved in the last month? Doubtful. He steps from behind his desk.

Ruby stands her ground.

Jimmy Bugg leans back against the desk, his rear perched on the edge. He doesn't say anything as he glares at her. He crosses his arms, fingers ink-stained, fingernails crusted with dirt.

Ruby can't imagine being touched by him. "Came up as soon as I was able."

"Alone?"

"I am."

"Maybe not the best choice, under the circumstances."

"And by that, you mean?" Ruby fingers her derringer. "Come now, Mr. Bugg. You've likely been peering out your window counting the minutes before I arrived."

"You're not wearing black."

"Not today."

"After only two weeks, Mrs. Fortune? I would think the grieving widow would want to at least pretend to be in mourning before she comes barging up here looking for trouble."

"I'm not looking for trouble." *Steady, Ruby.* "But I'm not reeking of regret." Ruby takes in a breath and delivers the line she's been practicing for days in front of the plate glass mirror in her parlor. "I've come to claim my share of Silver Tip Mine."

Bugg scoffs. "A lady mine owner? That's—might I say—opportunistic, coming from you. Willie's barely cold and you're here to weasel your way into mine ownership?"

"Partner, Mr. Bugg. Got the proof right here." Ruby stabs a piece of paper held mid-air.

Upon the death of Willard G. Fortune, Jr., his quarter-share of Silver Tip Mine passes to his wife, Ruby B. Fortune, of Jericho, Territory of Arizona.

"Even after you murdered him?" Bugg asks. "Down-right laughable." Bugg clatters back behind his desk and sits. He doesn't offer Ruby a seat. "Why anyone bothers to marry is beyond me. Never had the inclination myself." He lowers his head and resumes work on a hefty stack of papers. "You're wasting my time here."

"I'll stand here for as long as it takes."

Bugg slams his dirty hands on the top of the desk. He stands again. A line of perspiration runs down his jagged face. He might have been handsome once, but those days have long fled. "For what? I'm not giving you an inch."

"I'd rethink that, if I were you," Ruby says. She pulls her derringer from her waistband and points it at Bugg. "I know how to use it."

"I'm next, then? Will you stop at nothing to get this mine?"

Ruby trains the derringer at Bugg's chest, watching his hands for any sign of movement.

"Put your piece down and we'll have a conversation," he says.

Ruby waits a few seconds and lowers the gun. She pulls up a chair to Bugg's desk. "That's more like it, Mr. Bugg."

Bugg sits again and Ruby keeps a keen eye on his hand. One move and she'll shoot him. All those days practicing as a little girl and then on the traveling circuit, no, none of it was for waste. She wasn't once a sharpshooting wonder for nothing.

"What is it that you really want, Mrs. Fortune? I can't picture you working this mine."

"I'm not afraid to get my feet wet, tear my dress, spoil my gloves." Ruby pulls off her gloves and smacks them on his desk. "Or shoot you."

"Whoa, now. I said, let's *talk*." Bugg peers at Ruby's slender hand. "Your wedding band?"

Ruby fingers the large ruby. Someday, she'll sell it. "I've come to offer you my share in the mine. For the right price."

"Ah, now we come to the heart of it. Getting rich off the recently departed. Very clever, Mrs. Fortune."

"I'll get what's coming to me, Mr. Bugg. I have four sons and aim to care for them the best way I know how."

"There are other ways," Bugg snorts.

Two other men burst into the shack.

"Assays at $12.57, boss," the first one says.

"Highway robb . . ." The second man stops mid-word.

"About time you two showed up." Bugg stands. "Mrs. Fortune here . . ."—Bugg motions to Ruby, now standing again and squeezed between three large men—". . . has come to sell us her share of the mine. What do you say, boys? Twenty dollars?"

The one who relayed the assay information snickers and reaches inside his vest. He pulls out a leather billfold and extracts a crumpled bill. "Got it right here, boss." He turns to Ruby. "Here you go, little lady."

"Little lady?" Ruby reaches for her derringer again. "This claim is worth at least forty thousand dollars. Split four ways, that's ten thousand each. Pay me what I'm owed and I'll be on my way."

"And if we don't?" Bugg asks.

"Are you threatening me?" Ruby's eyes narrow. "If there's any shred of trouble up here, the sheriff will have your heads."

"I suggest you pay the little lady right away."

Ruby wheels around to see Sheldon Sloane, Jericho's sheriff, in the doorway, his craggy face beneath a Stetson. He pauses before he steps inside.

"Sheldon?" Ruby gasps. "What . . ."

"I'll trouble you to unload your six-shooters, gentlemen." He ducks as he passes through the doorway, his white shirt damp beneath a buttoned black vest. Sheldon, too, is covered with dirt, from his belt to his trousers to his boots. He takes off his hat and runs his hand through long, unkempt hair.

Bugg shrugs and empties his cylinder into his palm. He tosses the rounds onto the table.

Sheldon turns to Bugg's partners. "You, too."

Bugg nods to his partners. They empty their chambers and pocket the ammunition.

"Getting a little too warm in here," Bugg says. He barges out of the shack, muttering, his partners in tow.

Sheldon turns to Ruby. "And you." He towers over Ruby, six-foot four and change, lean, with rough hands and strong eyes.

Ruby replaces her derringer in her hip holster without unloading. She gathers her gloves and glares up at Sheldon. "'Little lady?' Honestly, Sheldon. I was handling this fine on my own."

"No doubt."

"You tailing me?"

"Swendsen told me you borrowed the mare. I guessed you might be heading this way. I have a little business up here myself so I followed you. Just to be sure."

Ruby swats Sheldon's arm away. She steps out of the shack. It's coming on dark at midday.

Sheldon faces the mine partners. "As I was saying, gentlemen, we'll come to an equitable arrangement today, and, in return, I won't be looking into the case of another colored man gone missing. That makes three by my count, so you might say my attention is now piqued. I'd swear,"— Sheldon taps on Bugg's chest—"you send coloreds into shafts you'd never send one of your other men. Even Slavs."

"Boss?" The other mine owners exchange glances.

"So it is true," Sheldon says.

Bugg slams his thigh. "Sonofabitch." He scowls at his mine partners.

"How much did you say, Mrs. Fortune?" Sheldon asks.

"Ten thousand even. You gentlemen won't see hide nor hair of me at this mine again. If we come to—what did Sheldon say?—an equitable arrangement."

Bugg disappears for several minutes back into the shack and reappears holding a thick envelope. He hands it to Ruby.

She opens the packet. "A deed? Come now, Mr. Bugg. I'm looking for cash."

"Think we have that kind of cash here? Who do you think we are, fools? Meet me at First National at eleven tomorrow," Bugg says. "We can settle up there."

"And I'm supposed to believe you'll be there? I don't."

Sheldon nods, his square jaw set. "If you're not there, Bugg, I'll take up that case," he says. "Wouldn't be good for business, you behind bars and these two cheats in charge."

He cocks his head toward the other mine partners. "There's something funny going on up here. I can smell it."

A corkscrew of lightning torches the lip of the Catalinas. It won't be long before they're knee-high in Noah's flood.

"I'll be there." Bugg spits. He motions to his partners. "If you'll excuse us now, Sheriff, Mrs. *Fortune*. We've got a business to run."

Thunder rumbles as Sheldon guides Ruby back to Swendsen's horse, his hand on her waist. "Hurry now, Ruby. There's a gully washer coming. I'll follow you back."

Ruby reaches to untie the mare. Sheldon's hand covers hers as he works out the knot. He leads the mare away from the fencepost and offers Ruby a hand up to the saddle.

"Mark my words, you'll have the cash by noon tomorrow," he says. "Ten thousand even. You can turn around and buy that inn of yours within the hour."

"From your lips to God's ears. If He's listening."

Ruby spurs the mare and points her downhill toward the flatland, this time on the quicker route. Sheldon rides beside Ruby as they negotiate the rutted ore road toward Jericho. Roiling clouds swirl overhead and cast unnerving shadows on the trail. Ruby shushes the mare and spurs her on. They don't have much time. Another crack of lightning hits the Catalinas, followed three seconds later by deafening thunder.

"He's listening alright," Sheldon yells. "It's you that has to believe it." Large droplets *splat* on the dry desert floor, the beginning of the deluge. Sheldon spurs his horse, faster now, and motions for Ruby to speed up.

"Never had much use for God before, Sheldon," Ruby yells back, as she comes abreast of him. "But I don't mind being proved wrong in this case."

"You've got nothing to worry about, Ruby. They'll never see through it. It's foolproof."

SEPTEMBER 8, 1899
JERICHO, ARIZONA TERRITORY

With the taste of money in her mouth, Ruby barrels up the wide steps of Jericho First National Bank at five minutes to eleven on a scorching Friday morning. She's wearing black today, top to toe, for appearance's sake. Where is Sheldon? She cranes her neck.

Town teems with freighters, ore wagons, horses, mules. Jangles. Shouts. Hoots. Whistles, some so loud your ears could burst. And what the devil?

"Clayton! Fletcher!" Ruby sees her sons, dark-haired Clayton and strawberry blond Fletcher, running down Jefferson Street toward Tom Tillis's livery. That livery is no place for boys, especially at their ages, ten and nine. And they're supposed to be home with Virgil and Sam this morning. Ruby didn't let them play hooky to waste it at a gambling den.

The boys disappear down the alley. The livery is the heartbeat of Jericho, if you don't count saloons. Stable a horse. Rent a dray. Hire a hearse. Order a plow. Contract a blacksmith. Buy kerosene—or hooch. Fill up your pockets or lose it all on cockfights and dogfights, Sundays when the parson's not looking. No place for boys.

Sheldon bounds up the bank steps two at a time. His dark trousers, shirt, and vest are spotless, as if he had a laundress, or a wife. His badge, shined just this morning, contrasts to his worn and scuffed boots. A laundress might not notice that. A wife would.

"Did you see Clayton? Fletcher?" Ruby asks.

Sheldon shakes his head. His sandy-grey hair is still damp under his hat.

"They're going to be the death of me." *Death of me*, she thinks. *Could have been me*. "Headed to Tillis's, of all places."

"Don't worry your head over that, Ruby. Boys will be boys."

"And you know this how, Mr. Sheriff?"

"*Ruby*." Sheldon shakes his head.

Ruby glowers at him. "*Sheldon*."

"God, you're maddening." Sheldon guides Ruby's elbow as they enter the bank's wide doors and cross the large foyer toward the bank manager's office. "We don't want to be late to this dance, darlin'."

Jimmy Bugg stands and worries his hat as Ruby and Sheldon enter. No sign of the other partners. Sheldon closes the bank manager's door and rests with his back against it.

Ruby sits and adjusts her mourning dress. Off come her black gloves, but not her hat. Facing the bank manager, Ruby turns on forced charm. It's gotten her places her mouth or her sex alone doesn't get her. "Sir," she says, "I believe we're here to complete a rather large transaction." She throws a champion's grin at the bank manager. "And, as I understand it, you will get one percent."

"Mr. Bugg," the bank manager says. "You are here of your own accord, I take it?"

Sheldon shoots Bugg a sly eye.

"I . . . am," Bugg stammers.

The banker continues. "And you understand that you are acquiring Mrs. Fortune's quarter share of Silver Tip Mine for ten thousand dollars."

Bugg gulps. "That is correct."

Ruby smiles at Bugg. "I'm glad we could come to an agreement on this, Mr. Bugg. I could have sold my share to anyone, a barkeep, a madam . . ."

Bugg blanches.

"So, as you can see, I am doing you a favor," Ruby says. "Keeping it in the family, you might say."

After a full hour, the documents signed, Ruby shakes the banker's hand and nods to Bugg. Sheldon opens the door for Ruby, who steps out of the bank manager's office, the deed to the local roadhouse in her name.

Outside, on the semi-circular bank steps, Ruby pulls on her gloves and adjusts her narrow-brimmed hat. She looks for her sons, but can't see them in a sea of heads crowding Jericho at noontime. Ruby'll have a word with Clayton and Fletcher about this. And Tom Tillis.

Sheldon looms over Ruby. He bends down toward her ear. "You've got yourself a roadhouse," he says. "Like I told you. Nothing amiss, little missy."

"'Little . . .'" Ruby moves to the side of the steps as two rough-looking men approach the landing.

"A minute, Ruby." Sheldon follows the strangers into the bank.

Ruby checks her watch, pinned to her bodice. Noon, straight up. Across Jefferson Street, the schoolmistress heads into the post office, a tidy square brick structure with three marble steps up to its double door. The town bum, Wink, shuffles toward the livery. On the east side of the post office, Dog Webber locks the door of the *Jericho Courier-Journal* and pockets the key. The newshawk heads across Washington Street toward Judd's Tavern, his hat jammed low. Just past the newspaper office, there's a lineup at Doc Swendsen's surgery at the noon hour, and it's no secret most of them have the clap. Behind Judd's, another line forms at the bottom of a narrow stairway, where many likely caught it.

Where is Sheldon? Ruby will wait a minute, no more. She taps her foot. *Has it been a minute?* She needs to check on Virgil and Sam.

Sheldon emerges from the bank, shaking his head.

"And?" Ruby asks.

"Not this time."

Ruby starts down the stairs, her satchel close to her thigh.

Jimmy Bugg barrels out of the bank and down the stairs. He doesn't acknowledge Ruby or Sheldon.

Ruby scowls. "Can't trust that louse as far as I can spit him."

Sheldon smiles, as rare as snow in July. "Bugg doesn't have sense enough to spit downwind, Ruby. You got him. Got him good."

"Didn't I?"

"So what are you going to call that inn of yours?"

Ruby is quick to answer. "Hell's Roadhouse, of course."

Sheldon snorts.

"Honestly, Sheldon, what did you think I would call it? The Lily Flower?" Her face sours. "Not like I got it legally."

"Not another word about it. You got what's coming to you. Your money bought that mine, and don't you forget that. Willie Fortune got what was coming to him, and you've got your investment back. Fair and square in my book. In this corner of Pinal County, I decide which side of the law the coin falls."

Ruby squints in the midday sun. "How about Jericho Roadhouse?"

"Maybe too rough. Jericho Inn?"

"That's it. Short and to the point."

"Like you. Short. To the point."

"Don't mess with me, Sheldon."

"I know better than to do that, ma'am." He tips his Stetson. "You're a better shot than me. So who's going to help whip that place into shape? By my estimation, you'll need ten men . . ."

"Forget men, Sheldon. A turn around the dance floor now and again, maybe. But I don't need help. Not that kind. And, if you're wondering, I'm not sharing sheets or changing my name again for anyone. Or any reason."

"But . . ."

"Not even for you, Sheriff."

"I might rethink that, if I were you, Ruby."

Ruby tilts her head. "Are *you* threatening me now?"

He bites a smile.

"Damn you, Sheldon." She hits his arm, hard.

"Why're you so upset? I'd think you'd be ready to pop a cork."

"Got a gnawing hole, here." Ruby points to her stomach.

"Some people call that an ulcer."

"Maybe so. I wake up nights in a sweat."

Sheldon nods, his mouth set in a fine line. "I've killed a few men in my day, too, Ruby. You'd think it would get easier. It doesn't." He tips his hat again as he strides down the steps. "I have no doubt you'll make that inn of yours the best damn place to lay your head in all of Arizona Territory. Even if you're stubborn enough to do it all yourself." He darts across the street, his long legs kicking up dust.

Is Virgil really alone with Sam? Ruby ducks up Lower Gulch, a hairpin curve where neighbors live atop each another. Can't whisper, sneeze, or fart here without someone overhearing. Cutting right on Brewer's Alley, Ruby steps over a drunk sprawled in the gutter outside The Empire. He's face up, crotch a shade darker than his britches. She snakes up Jefferson Street, past the bakery and the tailor and the barbershop and the schoolmarm's house, one curve giving way to the next even-steeper curve, row after row of flat adobes and wooden shacks pieced together with no more than baling twine.

Everything so long familiar looks different to Ruby today. Seven thousand dollars later, she owns an inn, which leaves three thousand to spare. *A new-fangled stove. Fresh-from-Sears & Roebuck linens. A sofa as big as Arizona Territory,* make that two. *Beds. Rugs. Curtains. Soap. And dishes! Cutlery! Glasses! And food,* she thinks. *Enough to fill the largest table in Arizona Territory . . .*

The derelict roadhouse she just purchased—with Sheldon's help, damn that a woman can't get a loan on her own—was once a going concern when Ruby was a girl, but it's been abandoned for years, a broken-down sign at the curb that reads faintly, Traveler's Rest. Being an innkeeper is Ruby's ticket in this town if she doesn't want to find herself upstairs at Judd's. There aren't many other options for a woman alone in Arizona Territory. Her mother learned the hard way.

At the far end of Jefferson, Ruby stops to catch her breath at the graveyard, full up with fellas who couldn't shoot straight or found themselves at the exact wrong place at the exact wrong time. Or died too young, or too old. Or, like her pop, with a heart that exploded into a million pieces and shattered her in the process.

Across from the cemetery—before barbed wire holds you back—Ruby's and Divina's houses sit side by side like old companions. Other than love, and lots of it, her sturdy house in Jericho is all Ruby got from her pop, George Burlingame Barstow, when he up and died. Divina Sunday, on the other hand, George Burlingame Barstow's right-hand gal, got nothing in return. Town ends there, right after Divina's, where the incline rises sharply like Divina's chin does when she isn't pleased.

Well, Ruby is none too pleased with Clayton and Fletcher right now, either. But there's no sign of them. Just Virgil sitting on the steps watching Sam play in the dirt. At first glance, there doesn't seem to be any harm done, but that doesn't mean Clayton and Fletcher won't get a talking to.

Ruby scoops up Sam and ruffles Virgil's hair. "Got some news for you."

Virgil squirms away. "Quit it, Ma."

"Can't ruffle your hair now?" Ruby grabs Virgil in a mama bear hug. "You too old for that now, too?"

Sam looks like he might laugh. *If only he would.*

Now Clayton and Fletcher round the last curve of the block and chase each other into the yard.

"I've got a mind to tan you boys," Ruby says. "But we don't have a minute to waste."

"What's going on, Ma?" Clayton says. He needles Fletcher in the back and Fletcher yelps.

"Knock it off, boys. And listen to me. You're not going back to school today."

Fletcher jumps in the air and pumps his fist.

"But you're not playing hooky for no reason. Go on, root out some boxes. We're moving down to town."

WILLIE FORTUNE PUNCTURES RUBY'S dreams, his fists clenched above her. She screams, tensing her shoulders, her backside, her thighs. *No, Willie, no!* Bruises flower from her pale skin, the edges raw.

Then she's in the kitchen, running from a belt. *Don't talk back to me, little missy.* Ruby crouches in a corner, her hands shielding her face, her eye already oozing. *Take that, thwack. And that.* She cowers, the cold metal barrel of a gun now pointed at her temple. *Stop, Willie! Stop!*

She runs, falls, gets up again, clawing up an incline. *Faster, Ruby, faster.* Willie grabs her by the hair and drags her. *Whore, just like your mother.*

Once, on the ground, one hand crushed by Willie Fortune's steel-toed boot, Ruby reaches for her pistol. One bullet, she thinks, just one bullet. Her fists tighten around the pearl handle. But then Willie kneels beside her, pounding his fists into the floor and saying sorry for the hundredth (or was it the thousandth?) time. You shouldn't shoot a man while he's apologizing, should you?

Tonight, nestled in tight quarters off the kitchen of the ramshackle roadhouse, Ruby wakes with a start—*bang!*—her nightdress soaked. Air hangs still, heavy. Has it really only been two weeks?

One breath at a time, Ruby forces her racing heart to slow as she wipes sweat from her forehead with her sleeve. *He's not here, Ruby. Willie is dead, and won't be back, ever, except to scare you out of your wits and cheat you of sleep.* Gone now are black eyes and broken bones and threats of a thousand welts flowering from purple to yellow to a sickening grey around the edges in places that are hardest to heal.

The welt on Ruby's neck is all that's left of Willie Fortune's clamped fist now. But, no matter how hard she tries, Ruby can't help thinking Willie Fortune isn't done with her yet.

TWENTY YEARS EARLIER
SUMMER 1879
LUBBOCK, TEXAS

Ruby trains her skinny arm toward the target and knocks another pock-holed can off the wooden crate onto sandy ground. She has hit seven out of nine cans so far today, a sight better than yesterday, when she only hit four of ten and was in a pouty mood all day.

"That's better, Ruby." Big Burl reaches from behind to steady her hand.

Ruby feels the warmth of her father's breath in her ear. She raises the pistol. "It's heavy, Pop."

"It's not a toy, Ruby. One more try now." Big Burl steps back and crosses his thick arms over his barrel chest.

Ruby aims, shoots, misses. She grimaces and drops her arm. She rubs her forearm with her other hand.

Big Burl wraps Ruby in a grizzly bear embrace. He smells of leather and whiskey. "No long faces, Ruby," Big Burl says. "Practice, practice, practice. One day, you'll be wheeling around the ring and not miss a one. You're a nat-ural." He ruffles Ruby's blonde hair, hitches up his trousers over his large mid-section, and tweaks his hat. "Off you go, then. Save me a seat at supper."

Ruby meanders toward Divina's tent. She chases a toad, picks up a penny. At the corral, she stops to pet Major, Pop's favorite horse, a white stallion worth more than all the other horses combined, or that's what her pop says. Ruby slips Major a carrot from her pocket and nuzzles his face. Down two wagons, cut across, down two more. At the costume wagon, Ruby lifts the flap, waltzes in, and flops on a cot.

"Well, if it isn't Little Miss Pip." Divina's needle flies through cotton and velvet and suede as she mends costumes and headdresses, a never-ending job in the ever-changing carnival business.

Ruby sucks on a carrot and tries to bend her skinny legs and arms into a pretzel shape, like she's seen the con-tortionist do. Three times she attempts to hook her leg around the back of her neck. She grunts and pounds the mattress. "I can't do it."

Divina sets her needlework down and grabs for the side of the wagon to heft herself up. "Here, let me. Sit up." Divina bends Ruby's neck forward and grasps her leg.

"Ow!"

"Well, then, we'll just have to try again tomorrow."

"That's what Pop said."

"How many today?

"Seven, but it shoulda been eight. I nicked the last one and it went all wobbly." Ruby shakes her body from left to right.

"Practice, practice, practice. Only way you'll get better, Ruby."

"How come you and Pop always say the same thing?"

Divina smiles. "Because we know what's best for you, me and your pop."

Jean Parker Perdue, Divina's given name is. She's a big woman—always has been—folds and folds of flesh that cascade from her chin to what should be her ankles. Her dark hair is pulled back in a bun, accentuating her thick neck. She wears a black dressing gown and a small pince-nez on her prominent nose. Her blue eyes spark from beneath manicured eyebrows.

Young Jean watched her mother read tarot cards on their back porch in upstate Illinois every night for extra cash, a halo of cigarette smoke and mosquitoes circling her head, and men in and out of her mother's tiny bedroom. When her mother abandoned Jean and left her with a crotchety maiden aunt downstate, Jean took in sewing to help pay rent. She was never asked to a dance or courted or kissed. So it was no surprise to anyone (and heartily encouraged by her aunt) when Jean hooked up with a handsome shyster come through town who needed a button sewn on.

Jean wouldn't be the first or last to run off with the only prospect in sight. Her lover's suits were always washed and pressed, and never a button missing. A year later, they still hadn't married. He spun one excuse after another, but soon, he promised, soon. It wasn't long before Jean got wind that her suitor had other intentions. On a hot Texas night, her knight in not-so-shining armor never came back to the Golden Hotel, where they were lodging after attending the breath-taking Triple B Traveling Carnival and Wild West Show.

The next morning, the proprietor kicked Jean out of the hotel without breakfast. The bill wasn't paid, the proprietor said, sorry, ma'am. Business is business. Flat broke and hungry, Jean approached the owner of the carnival outfit as the show was shutting down for the day. Stopped in her tracks, Jean was love-struck when she laid eyes on George

Burlingame Barstow. She found her tongue and asked the showman—he was as large as she was, or maybe larger, and much more handsome close up than in the carnival ring yesterday—to take her on, good with a needle she was, after all. It wasn't long before Jean put her mother's tarot readings to good use, too, and started reading palms. She was never Jean after that; the name Divina was born in a hot dusty town in west Texas that was forgettable, except for that.

Divina followed George Burlingame Barstow like moth to flame for years on the traveling circuit all over the west as he plowed into town after town commanding nickels and respect. Divina loved Big Burl with a heart exploding. Big Burl loved Divina in every way except the way Divina wanted to be loved.

Divina sits on the cot where Ruby is sprawled out and pats the girl's tummy. "Five days old you were, when your pop brought you up from Tucson. First time I saw you, you were madder than a cut snake. All legs and arms. And a soaking diaper. Your pop didn't know what to do with you." Divina smiles. "Most babies are fat, like me."

"Was I always skinny?"

"Skinnier than a pole cat. I don't know where you put away all that pie."

Ruby jumps up from the cot. "I'm gonna go get some."

"It's not even suppertime," Divina says. "But I bet if you go to the back of the mess tent, you might get lucky."

Ruby stretches and leaps off the cot. "See ya, Divina."

Ruby wends her way to the back of the mess tent and watches shadows creep up the side of the canvas. Big Sue comes out from the tent and stands, back against a tent pole, and lights a cigarette. That women smoke or drink or swear (or even spit) doesn't surprise Ruby any more than the sun working its way up over the horizon every morning.

"Well, if it isn't Miss Ruby," the cook says, as if seeing Ruby there is any surprise. "You'll be wanting more pie?"

Ruby nods, "Yes'm," and quick as the toad Ruby had chased minutes before, in front of her there's a plate heaped with blackberry pie and a big-person fork.

"I do believe you could eat a whole pie," Big Sue says. She blows smoke rings in the air. "But where you put it is beyond me. You weigh less than a mouse."

Between mouthfuls, Ruby nods again. "Yes'm."

Stick comes up beside Ruby. "I'll take a slice too, if you're offering." Big Sue smacks Stick's arm, but not before he gets a peck in on her cheek. Stick is the tallest man Ruby's ever seen, and taller still when he's on stilts. He bends over and pinches Ruby's bottom under her dress. Then he plucks a nickel from Ruby's ear. "Well, what did you have hiding there, young lady? I do believe you're a nickel richer."

Ruby smiles through blackberry teeth. She reaches for the nickel.

"Not until you plant a big one here on Stick's cheek." He lowers his head so Ruby can kiss him through a mass of whiskers.

"There's a good girl," he says. "Now you run along. Big Sue and I got some business we got to attend to, don't we, sweetie?"

Ruby hands her plate to Big Sue and nods, crushing the nickel in her palm. With this she can buy popcorn or a bag of peanuts.

"Don't let anyone pinch that nickel, you hear?" Stick says to Ruby.

Ruby ambles though the carnival grounds and swipes a bag of peanuts from the concession wagon. The door was unlocked, so why not? She's still hungry, and now has Stick's nickel for popcorn in her pocket for tomorrow. Ruby sits on a stack of lumber, her legs dangling, and watches the set-up crew hammer up the grandstand, a big U-shaped arena where two days from now crowds will erupt in earsplitting applause. When she finishes the peanuts, she curls into a ball and uses her arms for a pillow. She closes her eyes then, hammers clanging and men shouting and animals making the most god-awful noises a girl ever heard.

FIFTY CENTS FOR YOU, SIR, and yes, the same for the missus. A quarter for the kids, and here, take a program. That'll be another nickel, sir. Right this way. Popcorn?

Barkers stand at the entrance to the carnival show, voices louder than a thousand dogs. Come one and come all, now's your chance. Three days only! A new show every day! Step right up, there you go, young sir, little missy, what a fine looking family you are! The photograph booth is just beyond the entrance, first tent on the right. Yes, sir, that's correct. Just two bits for a portrait of your lovely wife and the young'uns. I can see it now on the piano, your beautiful missus looking like the first bloom of spring. In you go, then. Next!

Families scramble up planked steps and root around like rats to find suitable places to sit, spreading blankets on splintery boards to save a spot. Flags fly on stanchions set fifty-feet apart, reds and blues and yellows fluttering in the breeze above the high-sided arena. At the closed end of the showground, hidden by a large *trompe d'oeil* desert scene, a large pen houses twenty horses. Smaller pens hold sheep and calves, and in a large cage, a dull-eyed bear. The cowboy band sets up in a box just to the right of the entrance—better to sit a ways away, if you're there early enough. Those trumpets can get inside your head.

There go the Mexicans, a dozen of them, and a posse of white men dressed in full regalia, parading around like they are native as dirt, painted chests and beaded clothing, deerskin moccasins and feathers. No one seems to notice or care. It comes with the territory, gamblers and gunslingers and swindlers and tramps. What's a little artful deception? No one's the worse for it.

And there, in the center of it all, clad in beaded buckskin and velvet and fur, his *Concho*-jangling boots thigh high and dark curled hair to his shoulders (and a huge gut in between) is Ruby's pop, the legendary Big Burl. Feathers sprout two feet into the air from the brim of his enormous hat. It can be hot as Hades and Big Burl wears the same get-up every show. There's a reputation at stake here.

"Ladies and Gentlemen!" he crows. "Have we got a show of shows for you today!" There's humor and offhand comments and a rundown of acts, peppered with cheers and waving of handkerchiefs. And then the Grand Entry, the whole costumed entourage making one big sweep of the carnival grounds.

"On your mark, get set, go!" Big Burl's voice rumbles across the fairgrounds. In the center of the arena, large poles sprout from dirt. In the first act, cowboys outdo one another in feats of horsemanship: bronco riding and rope handling and barrel races. After the first intermission, gunslingers take to the arena, their litany of tricks a mile longer than the cowboy's. Ever see someone shoot a coin out of another man's hand? Or extinguish a lit cigar hanging out of another's mouth with a single bullet? Knock an apple off a trained dog's head? Or (the kids love this one), aim straight through a chicken's neck and then watch the poor thing dance around the arena without its head? The crowd roars in applause.

Between acts, Ruby loves to watch other kids, she doesn't have many to play with in the carnival. A little boy tugs on his father's sleeve. "Look, Pop! Lemonade!" An older boy jerks on his father's other sleeve. "Games! Just a nickel, Pop. You should do it, try to hit that colored in the head! You got three chances! Can I do it, too? Please?"

Ruby wanders from tent to tent, coins clinking at the entrance. She peeks in through the back of the contortionist tent just in time to see the woman wrap her legs up around her neck like a pretzel. *How does she do that?* She skips the dwarves today, stops for a minute to listen to the musicians. At Divina's tent, a line snakes around the back of the tent. Ruby hears Divina's low voice from inside the tent and wonders what she's saying. Maybe someday, she'll read Ruby's palm.

After the long second intermission, the audience cheers for the shooting contests. It's louder than before, deafening almost, the thunder of firearms and drumbeat of hooves. A girl wonder rides a horse three times her size and shoots glass balls with a flashy show piece, once hitting ninety-eight out of a hundred. Smell of gunpowder everywhere. Ruby wants to be her.

In come the fancy riders, western women in jingle-jangles and bared legs between split skirts and boots. They ride haywire around the arena, barely missing one another as they pluck hats and hankies off the ground while lunging off the sides of their mounts.

And then there's the finale, and, as if it couldn't get any louder, the arena erupts into applause as the so-called noble savages chase women and children in a wagon careening around the arena. In come the cowboys, rescuers all, who pretend-shoot the marauders one by one. Down they go, good for ticket sales.

When Big Burl steps into the fray and fires his rifle into the air, the crowd quiets for one second, and then, as the entire ensemble takes their final bows, the crowd erupts in cheers.

"RUBY!" BIG BURL TAPS RUBY on the shoulder. Ruby sits up in a daze, peanut shells exploding from her dress. Her father and Divina are standing over her.

"We looked everywhere for you," Divina says. "Catching a cat nap, were you, after all that pie?"

"I was just dreaming . . ."

Big Burl lifts Ruby up and tosses her into the air. "It's not like you to miss supper."

"I missed supper?" Ruby's eyes fill with tears. Her lip quivers.

"Let's see if we can rustle up a plate for you." Big Burl hefts Ruby to his shoulders and she grabs onto his long hair. "Hold on, Ruby!" he bellows.

From this vantage point, Ruby can see the whole carnival. Through a maze of tents, lumber, and animal dung, Big Burl deposits Ruby at the back of the mess tent, where she just had pie a few hours earlier. Her tummy grumbles.

"Sue!" Big Burl's voice rumbles through the tent opening.

Big Sue pops out from the tent, her hands soaking. "Saved you a plate, Miss Ruby," she says. Sue disappears in the folds of the tent and returns with a plate heaped with roast and potatoes and gravy. "Sit right here," she says, pointing to a stool just outside the tent flap. "I'll check on you in a few minutes."

"Dig in, Ruby," Big Burl says. "And see as you're back to the tent before dark, you hear me?"

Ruby nods, her mouth already full.

"I'll keep an eye on her, Burl," Divina says. "How's that, Ruby? Good?"

Ruby nods again.

"We've got to fatten you up, Pip. Go on, finish it all." Divina sits on a campstool next to Ruby, her skirt puddling on the ground.

"Where are we?" Ruby asks, between mouthfuls. "Still in Colorado?"

"Right here." Divina reaches for a tent stake and draws a map in the dirt. "Lubbock, Texas."

Lubbock is the halfway mark, all of Colorado and most of Texas behind them, as they journey southwest toward Odessa, a hundred and thirty-odd miles over rough country. Unlike Buffalo Bill Cody, who travels all year round, Big Burl's entourage travels the "The Golden Circuit" for shy of four months, starting each May in Globe to get the kinks out and then meandering clockwise from Arizona Territory into Colorado and then deep into Texas over scrubland and *malapais* and sand dunes, in towns big and small, even stopping in backwaters like Cuckleburr and Foolsville, anywhere there's a nickel to be made. When they use up all their goodwill in one town, they move on, stripping down and loading freighters in a quarter of the time it takes to set up.

After Texas, it's on to New Mexico Territory, the hottest place Ruby has ever passed water. In Las Cruces, her pee hisses on the ground and evaporates before she finishes her squat. After rip-roaring shows in Albuquerque, Silver City is next, and then into familiar territory, all eighteen wagons of the outfit rumbling into Bisbee and Tubac before the last hurrah in Tucson, where the entourage showers local kids with pennies as they leave town. There, performers part company for other jobs: ranching or mining or other shows until May rolls around again and Burl expects them back again, ready to go in Globe.

"When will we be back home?" Ruby asks Divina.

"Not for awhile, Pip. Texas is a big place, and then we have all of New Mexico. But don't you worry, we'll be back in Jericho in time for school."

Ruby doesn't much like school; she can't sit still. All the readings and recitations and arithmetic come to her fine enough, but why be inside when the sun is shining? When there are bottles to shoot and ponies to run? Ruby's dresses are always ripped or stained, much to Divina's displeasure. And Ruby's knees, well, they never heal up. In absence of a mother, Divina washes and dresses Ruby's wounds and covers her own heart in bandages again when Burl takes up with a local Apache woman every winter.

So one year turns into another, and another, and another, and at the end of the season, it's always home to Jericho. Not that anyone much crows about Jericho. But when it's the town you lay claim to, the one you're born in or find yourself in or stay because, well, just because, you fight for it—and everyone in it—until your last dying breath, or until the walls come tumbling down.

SUMMER 1887
AMARILLO, TEXAS

Ruby is wedged up against the wall of the costume wagon, sandwiched between the Jarrett brothers, Lorne behind her and Leroy facing her. They're in Amarillo, Texas, after a second sold out show. Ruby leans back against Lorne. "I like you better, baby girl," he whispers in her ear. "But Leroy won the coin toss this time."

After Leroy's had his turn, Lorne pumps Ruby until he's spent. "Oh, Ruby," he says over and over. Ruby feels another well of warmth filling her groin and, this time, a tight tingling explodes deep inside. She arches her back and groans as a stream of warm liquid runs down her bare legs.

Leroy sinks to the ground, his back against the wagon and his long legs splayed out. Lorne joins him. They both look at Ruby, her gold hair mussed and red boots wet. At first, Ruby couldn't tell the twins apart, but now she can tell. Lorne has a birthmark just below his left eye. It looks like a tear. They say they're nineteen, but Ruby doubts it. No one tells the truth around here, she learned that from her pop.

Ruby hides a smile. "So that's what all the fuss is about." She pulls up her damp bloomers, rearranges her skirt, and runs her hands through her hair. "Move over." Ruby kicks at the boys' legs. She sits between them, smoking, her head on Lorne's shoulder and hand on Leroy's knee. "Got any hooch?"

Leroy unfolds himself and pecks Ruby on the forehead. "Back in a minute." He hoists his britches and lopes off to the supply tent.

Lorne takes Ruby's rough hand and rubs it. "You alright, baby girl?"

"Mmm-hmm."

Lorne strokes Ruby's hair. "How old you say you are?"

"Not telling."

Leroy appears from the shadows dangling a jug. "What aren't you telling?"

"Not telling," Ruby says. She stubs out her cigarette. "How many girls you do like that?" She takes a swig from the jug and wipes her mouth.

The brothers glance at each other.

"Not telling," Leroy says.

"Although most of them don't seem to like it as much as you," Lorne says.

"Again?" Ruby asks.

"Now?" Leroy asks.

"Yes, now. I'm not talking about going to Sunday School."

"It might be a little while, miss," Lorne answers. "You see . . ."

"Why?" Ruby says. "I'm ready." She starts to get up, but Lorne pulls her back down.

Lorne hands Ruby the jug again. "Seems likes there's some parts your momma left out."

"Leave my momma out of it."

From the corner of her eye, Ruby sees a group of men round the costume wagon. Their faces are shadowed, but she recognizes the boots.

"There she is, fellas," one of the men says.

"Where?" says the largest of the three. Ruby would know that voice anywhere. It's her pop's assistant, that smooth Chicagoan who joined the troupe at the beginning of the season. He's a natty dresser and a looker. Ruby can't help but notice. Handles gate receipts. Books big names. Proceeds have never been better, and Big Burl says Ruby is going to be an even bigger star, now that Willie Fortune is marketing the show.

"What have we here?" Willie Fortune asks. "The Jarrett brothers at it again?" He takes a swipe at Leroy's boots with his steel toe as he loosens his belt.

"Knock it off, Willie," Leroy says.

Lorne protects Ruby with his arm.

"You've got no business here, Willie Fortune," Ruby says.

"Seems you are my business. Better I do this than your pop," Willie says, as he swings the belt buckle at Lorne's face. The buckle broadsides Lorne's cheek and chin and leaves a bloody gash. Leroy wrenches free and scrambles up. He runs.

"Stop it, Willie!" Ruby says. "What did Lorne ever do to you?" She reaches over to see to Lorne, who is bleeding from the ear and nose.

"Got what was coming to him," Willie says. "Taking advantage of young girls."

"They weren't taking advantage of anyone," Ruby said. "I asked."

"You did, did you? Get up, Ruby."

"No."

"No one says no to Willie Fortune."

Lorne turns over toward Ruby, coughs up blood. He reaches to touch Ruby's face. "I'm sorry, baby girl."

Willie kicks Lorne in the mouth. "You'll regret this." Lorne's eyes loll back into his head.

Leroy circles back from behind the costume wagon and kneels by his brother. "Wake up, damn it."

"I'll tell my pop about what you've done," Ruby says.

"He won't hear you, Ruby. That's what I come to tell you. Your pop's dead."

"Liar."

Divina rushes from around the back of the costume wagon and crouches at Ruby's side. "What in tarnation do you think you're doing, Willie Fortune?" she screams. "There's a better way to tell a girl her pop's up and gone." Divina grabs hold of Ruby and pulls her to her breast.

"Just sealing the deal, Miss Divina. Went to Big Burl just today to ask for Ruby's hand. Shook on it."

Divina strokes Ruby's face and hair. "I'm so sorry, Ruby. About your pop."

Ruby stares into the night sky, her eyes dulled. "Pop?"

Divina turns to Willie. "Not something you're known for. Truth telling, that is."

"It's true, every word of it," Willie answers.

"Get out of here," Divina bellows.

Ruby still hasn't moved.

"Pop?" Ruby says. "Pop!"

"Won't do you any good calling for him now," Willie says.

"I said, get out!" Divina thrashes at Willie.

Willie Fortune repositions his hat. "As you wish, your majesty." He steps around Divina and bends close to Ruby's face. He pecks Ruby on the cheek. "You're my girl now, don't forget it."

Ruby hits his arm, hard.

He cocks his head toward his henchmen, Red and Slim. "I like them rough." The men laugh. He swaggers away, flanked by his cronies. "What do you think, boys? I can see it splashed all over the banners." He spreads his large hands out. "'Ruby Fortune, Girl Wonder.' We'll get our money's worth out of that name."

Divina bends over Ruby.

"What happened?" Ruby asks.

"Shh, now, Pip. There will be time enough to tell you."

"I want to know!"

"It was his heart, Ruby. Gave up, no warning." Divina takes Ruby in her arms. "We lost a damn fine man today. I don't think I'll ever get over that he's gone." She rocks Ruby then, the girl reduced to wracking sobs.

Gone, this is a word that Ruby can't grasp. Her pop? Gone? What will she do now, no mother and now, no pop? Of all she has lost, one thing she has found, and in the cruelest way: nothing will be the same ever, never, again.

"WE GOT OFF ON THE WRONG foot last night, Ruby," Willie says. He takes off his large-brimmed hat and sits at the edge of the cot in Divina's tent, where Ruby has slept fitfully. Dressed in good brown trousers, a crisp white shirt, and trim paisley vest, Willie fingers a large gold watch chain that loops from his vest pocket. He puts the watch away and strokes Ruby's cheek. "I aim to make it right by you." His long, brown hair curls at his chin and his trim mustache twitches as he talks. Ruby is tempted to touch it.

Ruby turns her head away. Her head, her bones—even her hair—ache. Is her pop really gone? She fidgets on the small cot, at once hot, then cold. She can't stop crying. A large wad of rags is sandwiched between Ruby's thighs where blood seeps. Her thin nightdress is soaked. She can't get up to change while Willie is here. And she can't go back to her own tent because Big Burl is laid out there.

Willie wipes a tear from Ruby's face. He cups Ruby's chin and kisses her forehead. "You know you're the prettiest girl in all of Texas, don't you?"

Ruby juts her chin out of his grasp. Her long curly blonde hair is matted to her blotched face and her large brown eyes rimmed in red. "Don't you go getting all sweet on me. Me and Divina have our own plans."

"You do?"

"Mmm-hmm."

"Women aren't meant to be alone."

"Just because you say it, doesn't mean it's true." Ruby adjusts the rags, which are becoming increasingly more pungent.

"And you, only sixteen."

"Fourteen, you mean."

He whistles. "Could have fooled me." He runs his fingers through Ruby's tangled hair. "Thing is, your pop and I shook on it. Just yesterday."

"I don't believe you. And neither does Divina." Ruby closes her eyes. She pictures her father, velvet, fur, *Conchos*, and the lustiest laugh in Arizona Territory. She won't hear his voice again, all those campfire stories, all those rides on his broad shoulders, *Hold on, Ruby! Hold on!*

Willie touches Ruby's shoulder, his hand warm. Ruby pushes it away. "I didn't say you could touch me. Go find yourself another girl."

"Your pop knew what was best for you, Ruby. You might say Divina and I don't see eye to eye. But it's true, Ruby. I swear. Your pop gave me his blessing."

Ruby sits up and moves away from Willie. "I still don't believe you."

A minute later, "Well, blast it," Ruby says, sniffling. She wipes her nose on the bed sheet. "Why did he have to up and die on me?"

"I'll take care of you, Ruby." Willie bends over and takes her into his arms. "Starting today." He reaches into his vest pocket and takes out a small flask. "Here, take this. It will make you feel better." Willie tips the flask into Ruby's mouth. "Good for what ails you."

Ruby screws her face up. Within seconds, a warm rush envelops Ruby's throat.

"You'll get used to it."

Ruby is silent for a minute, her body relaxing.

"And you'll never want for anything, Ruby. Dresses, jewelry, shoes. Leave everything to me."

Ruby stares at Willie Fortune's angular face. Is there a better-looking man on the planet? "I'd rather have a pony."

"Done. Today. Your pick of any of them."

"You're not pulling my leg?"

"Two, if you like. Before we sell off the rest of the entourage. You see, without your pop, there's no more Triple B."

"What do you mean, no more Triple B?"

"Your pop was highly leveraged, Ruby. I don't expect you to understand, but there's nothing left. He owed everybody. We'll have to sell everything—horses, wagons, supplies, all of it—to pay off his debts. It's every man for himself now, time to pack up and move on." Willie runs his hand down to Ruby's slim shoulders. "From now on, God as our witness, we'll be man and wife."

"Wife? I thought you said you'd take care of me. No one said anything about wife."

"It's for the best, Ruby." Willie kisses Ruby's neck, moves to her budding breasts, and down to her flat stomach. There is no urgency. Ruby thinks to push him off, but she's drowsy. And it feels good. Over and over, he murmurs, *There's a yellow rose in Texas I'm going down to see . . .*

Willie's tongue traces a line south of Ruby's navel. When his mouth reaches the blonde mass at the parting of her thighs, Ruby gasps. Her hands rush to the rags. "Not now, Willie."

"I've got to go now, anyhow. It's going to be a hell of a day." He squeezes Ruby's thin arm.

"What about my pop?"

"From the sound of it, there'll be a large contingent going to, where the hell is he from? Jericho? To bury him. After that, you and I need to see about getting on with another show. You're worth a lot of money, Ruby. You're my Girl Wonder."

Ruby stares at Willie Fortune and weighs her options. "You take me, Divina comes too." She sticks out her hand.

"Deal." Willie shakes Ruby's hand and bends to kiss her forehead again.

"Do you have more of that stuff?"

"Plenty. Here, take another slug."

Ruby shifts to her side. She needs to change the rags but she won't do that in front of Willie. Not yet. "Don't forget the ponies." Ruby's voice is slurred and she's seeing double now. All she wants to do is sleep. "Two ponies. You said, Willie. We have a deal."

SUMMER 1888
ON THE TRAVELING CIRCUIT

The first season after Big Burl's sudden departure from the world, Ruby and Willie join the Reginald "Doc" Davis show; but it isn't long before Willie's mishandling of gate receipts gets them booted. It's on to another traveling show after that. That first season, they are in so many shows, Ruby can hardly keep count. She should have inherited Big Burl's show, but it's obvious now that Willie Fortune ran the show into the ground, damn you! Damn you! she screams at him.

When she gets into these screaming jags, Willie gives Ruby laudanum to calm her down. Ruby is up to four teaspoons per day of the brownish-red liquid and it's all she can do to keep her act up. She can't function without it. Last month, they pulled up stakes again and traveled through scrubland, sparsely-treed bosque territory, pebbly *malapais*, and wide, fertile bottoms all over Hell and gone in search of another outfit, Divina keeping watch over Ruby, and Willie's friends Slim and Red trailing Willie like dogs.

They have signed on with Johnny "Captain Jack" Grinnell's show now. Divina asks for two bits a day, seeing as she's more nimble with a needle than any other seamstress. A day doesn't go by before Divina has heaps of new costumes to repair, ragged sleeves of a cowboy or sequins off the big boss's vest. Rips in trousers and buttons—so many buttons—on coats. And beads and feathers galore. How Divina gets through all those repairs in record time is another of her secrets.

So far, there's been no scandal on Willie's account. Ruby breathes a sigh of relief. It's hard to get close to anyone when you move around so much, but she's taken a shine to a young sharpshooter, Esther Lemon. Keeps Ruby sharp, Esther does. They practice together, afternoons, the loser paying up. Ruby never loses. Plus, Ruby's got someone to empathize with. Esther is Johnny Grinnell's girl, and she's not much past sixteen. There are secrets to be shared, and not just about firearms. Massage. Pennyroyal. Fellatio.

The next summer, Willie gives Ruby a ring. Willie and Ruby have been living as man and wife for a year now since Big Burl's heart gave out. Common law marriage is legal in Texas, where Willie and Ruby first hitched up. After seven years living as man and wife it's as good as God Himself put His stamp of approval on it. And you don't even have to go to church, which is the best end of the bargain. Ruby has six years to go before husband means husband but it *looks feels seems* like Willie Fortune is her husband, for good or for ill.

"Don't want anyone thinking you're anyone else's girl," Willie says. "I see the way Grinnell looks at you."

So much for love. Ruby twirls the penny-sized ruby on the fourth finger of her left hand. She doesn't know how to say thank you and wonders if she's ever thanked Willie for anything. Not that she's never thankful. He's handsome and charming and brings in more cash Ruby ever thought possible. Their tent is a veritable traveling hotel room, complete with copper tub. And what he can do to her in bed. Ruby wonders where Willie learned to take a woman to such heights and then drop her down again and then up, up, up, flying, like a new-fangled roller coaster, but made of desire. She doesn't care where he learned it, as long as they can do it every day. Or twice a day.

And with Willie, there's never a shortage of laudanum. Has Ruby ever thanked Willie for that? One thing Ruby is grateful for is the stirrings in her womb. She'll tell him tonight, in bed, after the coupling. Ruby is starting to show now, and doesn't want anyone suspecting or commenting before she gets the chance to tell Willie properly. Won't he love a baby? Especially if it's a boy?

Day in, day out, more crowds. The traveling show has camped in Durango today, five hundred men, women, and children packed into the hastily constructed arena.

"Now's the time you've all been waiting for," Willie Fortune barks to an adoring throng.

Who wouldn't be attracted to Willie Fortune? Slick dresser, smooth talker, thin hips and slim legs. Handsome beyond handsome (and knows it), with a smile to light up every town in Colorado. And those boots! Turquoise with steel tips, can you imagine? Ruby sees all manner of women smiling at Willie, and he knows how to woo them.

"Who here thinks they can match Ruby Fortune shot for shot?" Willie hollers. "She's the best shot in the West, so think twice whether you're up for the challenge." He surveys the crowd and picks his target before the man even raises his hand. "Winner takes home fifty dollars!" The crowd erupts. Willie turns slowly to assess the horde. "You there!" he points to a tall man in a blue vest in the third row of the bleachers. It's Slim. He always picks Slim, keeps money in the show.

Slim swaggers to the table and chooses a piece. It's all part of the show: guns, whips, knives, ropes. Ruby keeps pace with Slim in the shoot off, her eye quick and her hand quicker. She's done this trick more than a thousand times and ten times out of ten she wins. In Bisbee, Slim edged her for the prize, and Willie yelled so loud God probably woke up from the ruckus.

"You're worthless, Ruby! Worthless!"

Worthless worthless worthless. The words pounded inside her head. She almost believed it.

Tonight, late (thank God she beat Slim today), Ruby lowers her robe and stands naked in the flickering light of the oil lamp. She's filled out in all the right places. "Willie?"

Willie sits on a stool and removes his boots. "Shut it." He doesn't raise his head.

Ruby moves to stand behind him and runs her fingers in his hair. "I've got a secret."

"I said, shut it. I have things on my mind."

Ruby swats his head.

Willie whips around, his fists clenched. "I'm warning you, Ruby."

The next day, Ruby can't keep breakfast down so she skips the dinner meal before the show. She loses her concentration *worthless worthless worthless* for a split second and misses the final target. A gasp emanates from the crowd.

"Let's let the little lady have another chance, shall we?" Willie glares at Ruby. He whispers in her ear as he passes her. "See that you don't miss, Ruby."

Ruby steadies her hand and nails the last target. The crowd cheers. She exhales sharply. After the competition, and fifty dollars pocketed by Willie, Ruby ambles at the periphery to watch the rest of the show. She's nauseous and unsteady on her feet. The heat saps all her energy, anyway. All eyes are rapt on the spectacle. Doesn't matter what show you attach yourself to, the finale is always the same, everyone in the stands cheering like they've just won the goddamn lottery.

Later, while undressing back in their tent, Willie lets loose on Ruby. "What the hell was that about?" he fumes.

"I tried to tell you last night."

"Tell me what?"

"I'm in the family way."

"You better not be." Willie smacks Ruby across the mouth.

Ruby swipes at her lips and tastes blood. "Who the hell do you think you are, cuffing your wife?" She dabs at her mouth with a handkerchief.

"Jesus, Ruby. You should know better. This will tank gate receipts. You'll be in the saddle until you fall off. Lady sharpshooters don't grow on trees." He thrashes around the tent. "As if I don't have enough to do, now I'll have to take out a notice in all the papers, do the interviews. Hire another girl. Or two. Maybe steal that Annie Oakley right from under Bill Cody. Show him. And show you now that you've gone and gotten yourself knocked up."

"And who got me knocked up?" Ruby ducks to avoid another clap to the side of the head. "And what's all the fuss about? You've still got Esther. She's as good as I am."

"She's nowhere as good as you are. And nowhere near as pretty. That nose could point the way to Texas all by itself. Don't go getting any ideas about missing even a day." Willie comes up to Ruby and stabs her nose with his forefinger. "Until I find another girl, you'll do what you have to do. The whole show depends on it. And there'll be no more laudanum."

"You can't."

"I can, and will. You've gotten sloppy, Ruby."

Ruby beats on Willie's chest. "Give it to me!" Her hair is matted from the heat, her eyes crazed. A large welt swells on her upper lip.

"No more, Ruby. Look at you. You're a disgrace."

Ruby fidgets all night, never finding a comfortable position. When she is sure Willie is asleep, she rifles through his trunk. No laudanum. Her hands tremble.

Ruby turns to others in the entourage for the bitter brown drug. She does it on the sly, away from Willie's hawkish eyes. Slim has a stash in his tent; she meets him there twice a day. It's all she can think about, when will she get to Slim's tent next. Ruby can shoot just fine, even better when she's juiced. She just can't have Willie finding out. She trades at first with trinkets and loose coins. When she runs out of options, she offers sexual favors, Slim's warm cock in her mouth.

A month later, after a catastrophic show where Ruby misses the final mark, despite being given two extra chances, Willie stomps into their tent. Ruby's morning sickness still hasn't abated and she's weak from the heat. Where is Slim? She's looked everywhere for him and she's got the shakes.

"That lying, cheating sonofabitch." Willie is fuming. "Double-crossed me, he did. No man's going to do that to Willie Fortune."

"Who? The big boss?"

"No, Slim. Of all people. I loaned him half a grand and now he's gone."

Ruby tenses. Gone? Slim is gone?

"Red, too. So much for loyalty." Willie throws his pistol down on the bed, hitting Ruby on the knee. "We'll have to default on that loan, Ruby."

"What loan?"

"Borrowed a thousand dollars from the big boss to front Slim. Slim knew he'd have to pay a sharp interest. But now Slim's gone and I got the big boss's henchmen breathing down my neck." He sits on the trunk and rubs his knees. "With you in that condition, money's not coming in like it used to. Give me the ring, Ruby."

The color drains from Ruby's face. She slips the ring from her finger into her pocket. "I can't find it."

"What do you mean, you can't find it? I saw it on your finger this morning."

"Maybe it was pinched. There are rat bags in this outfit. Slim being one of them, as it turns out." Her hands tremble. What will she have to do now for laudanum?

Willie turns his head in a flash of anger. "Do you know how much I paid for that ring?" He stands and advances on Ruby. He cups her chin a bit too tightly. "Find it." He juts her chin to the left a little too harshly, picks up his pistol, and leaves the tent flap swinging as he leaves.

Ruby reaches into her pocket, curls her fingers around the ring. It's hers, not Willie's, bruises be damned. A rush of cold blood jolts her. What can she do? Where can she go? She rises from the cot. Light is draining fast from the day and she needs to find someone—anyone—with laudanum. She's past caring how she has to pay for it. She'll sell the ring if she has to.

Over the next days and weeks, fear creeps in, unbidden. Before now, Ruby has been fearless, if you don't count the time about the rowboat.

"IN YOU GO, RUBY," BIG BURL had said. "Big Burl don't raise 'fraidy cats."

Ruby had never seen a lake before, or a boat. They were somewhere in Colorado, although Ruby can't remember where. She remembers it was hot (it was always hot).

"C'mon, Ruby. You got to trust me."

After considerable cajoling, Ruby stepped into the rowboat, not knowing if it would float. She settled her behind on a narrow wooden thwart at the front of the rowboat and reached for both sides to steady her as her pop lumbered in and rowed away from the shore with wide, slapping oars, him singing and Ruby's breath trapped in her lungs so long they hurt. When she finally exhaled, all her bottled-up dread came out in a rush of relief. That a boat could float on top of the water—and with Big Burl in it—was the first of many wonders Ruby can remember.

In the middle of the lake, Ruby joined in with Big Burl's songs, "Oh, Susannah" and "Goodbye, Liza Jane," their voices carrying across the water. When Ruby and Big Burl got back to shore, Divina splashed into shallow water to steady the boat. Ruby grabbed the side of the rowboat as Big Burl lumbered out. Big Burl lifted Ruby over the gunwale then and plopped her down next to Divina as he pulled the boat onto shore.

"And how did you like that, Pip?" Divina asked.

"I loved it more than anything, except maybe my birthday."

"That's my girl," Big Burl said, as he swept Ruby up in his arms and tossed her into the air. "You're the best thing that ever happened to me." Ruby felt weightless, so happy her heart could burst.

Never again did Ruby see a lake as large. The closest she came to seeing anything as vast is the desert, and she knew without asking that she'd never need a boat there. If a puddle lasts ten minutes after a monsoon, it's a record. Any other "lakes" are mirages, and dry as dirt.

But George "Big Burl" Burlingame Barstow was no mirage. Larger than life, he was. He turned the lights on in every place he stepped foot in when the Triple B Traveling Carnival and Wild West Show came through town, back in its heyday. Showman, horseman, and crack shot, Big Burl. And the best pop any girl could ask for. Wasn't a day went by that Big Burl didn't say Ruby was the best thing that ever happened to him. Then again, he was the world's greatest storyteller or liar, Ruby never figured out which, though she chose to believe him every time. And now, she misses her pop more than sun on a rainy day.

RUBY GAUGES WILLIE'S MOODS: blowhard, she pretends to be agreeable; hell bent for revenge, she tiptoes at the edges of his temper. She kowtows to Willie's whims to forestall the back of his hand. But then a certain comment, or a certain look—and sometimes, for no apparent reason at all, down comes his fist like lightning and her back takes a blow, a mirror image of a large man's hand imprinted there, edges ragged and tender. And does it hurt, inside and out. *Why, why, why does he hit me? What have I done? Something? Nothing?* She wonders who stares back in the mirror, eyes dulled and hollow.

Ruby gets better at play-acting to avoid beatings. But it's not failsafe. Whatever ignites Willie Fortune's belly runs in a direct line to his hands before it reaches his head. And it's become so frequent, it's hard to get through a day unscathed. Of his heart, Ruby is convinced now he doesn't have one. If he's got it in him to wallop her, there's nothing to stop him short of a bullet.

But now she's carrying his child. If there was a way out before, there's no exit now, is there?

A few months after the first lip-splitting incident, Ruby claws up an incline behind the tent city, her mouth filled with grit and dried blood. Her head throbs and her bones ache. How long has she been out here? She's seven months along now, her good dress ripped. A bloody trickle runs down her legs. Ruby cradles her midsection, as if holding it from the outside will protect what's within. The last thing she remembers is Willie's arm coming down hard on her head with the full force of an ax swing as she inched through the *arroyo*.

Wasn't it bad enough to find Willie in bed with her friend? As she lifted the tent flap, Ruby had stopped short. "What the hell?" Her mind was swimming with laudanum, bought with bills she swiped from Willie's billfold while he slept. Laudanum can't be good for the baby, can it? But a day off it, and she's jittery, irritable. It's got to be better for Baby Willie if she's not so anxious, right?

Willie bounded off the cot, his prick swinging. "Get out!"

Esther Lemon? Captain Jack's girl?

"This is *my* tent, damn it." Ruby stood still as a stone, taking in the accoutrements of the tent, as if in a photograph. No one, save Big Burl himself, ever outfitted a tent as lavishly as Willie Fortune. Underfoot, a Persian rug, centered under the massive feather bed. A clothes tree overloaded with belts, trousers, vests, and shirts. Next to Willie's desk and chair, the remnants of a woman's clothing, and a trail of water from Ruby's copper tub to her bed.

Willie covered himself with a blanket and advanced on Ruby. "I said, get out," he yelled, shoving Ruby out of the tent. She half ran around to the backside of the outfit, away from the other carnival tents, and stood there, numbed. *Damn you, Esther, in my tent and in my bed.* Not a minute later, Willie rounded the corner and pushed Ruby, hard. She fell forward, hands clenched on her enlarged stomach.

"Who do you think you are, Willie Fortune? Whoring around again?"

Willie kicked dirt into Ruby's face. "Who did I find whoring on the night your pop died? Answer me that. Teapot calling the kettle black, Ruby. I should've known better. Women are only good for one thing. Once you're hitched, all the fun goes out of it. Especially when you're the size of a goddamn whale."

"Is that what this is all about, Willie? You liked me fine when I wasn't knocked up. Making you all that dough."

Ruby scrambled to get up, but Willie clamped her down with his boot. He reached down and grabbed her hair. Prickly pear gouged Ruby's bare legs and a sharp rock scraped her shins as Willie dragged her down the incline. A faint trail of blood leached out behind her.

"Willie! Stop it!"

"Shut it. Walking in on a man like that and not saying you're sorry." At the bottom of the rise, Willie let go of Ruby's hair and stepped into the shade of a small shrub to light a cigarette.

Ruby clambered to her knees and crawled away from Willie to avoid more blows. "Say sorry to you? You've got that backwards, Willie Fortune." Ruby would regret talking back, or not getting far enough away before she said it. Willie threw the cigarette to the ground and arced his arm over his head. When the blow hit, Ruby wobbled under the impact and dropped back into the dirt, her head cracked open like a melon.

A MONTH LATER
ON THE TRAVELING CIRCUIT

A torrent of blood, gut-twisting pain. And then the small still body, blue as ice. Ruby clutches the child, brings him to her breast as if to warm him. Not a cry, not a breath, even. Ruby clasps his tiny body, down *drown* down, and sinks unconscious. *Did I do this to him? Or did Willie?*

Divina calls to Ruby from somewhere, like from underwater. Ruby cannot think or feel. *Am I dead, too?* Divina nurses Ruby through the night—*shh, shh, Pip*—and into the following day, hovering, rarely leaving Ruby's side, cheating herself of sleep to care for the girl like a mother. Ruby winks in and out of sleep, too tired to care.

"Divina! Let me in!"

Ruby would know that voice even if she were half asleep. "I don't want to see him."

"No, Willie Fortune, you cannot come in this tent!" Divina yells from her perch next to Ruby's cot. "Don't bother coming back."

On the second day after the stillbirth, Ruby hasn't stopped bleeding.

"We need to get to burying him," Divina says. "Soon."

Even though she's rummy, Ruby knows time is not on her side here. "Where is he?"

"Right here, Pip."

Ruby eyes the tiny casket beside her in Divina's tent.

"We'll bury him next to your pop," Divina says. "You can visit him there every day because we're staying this time. In Jericho."

"How?"

"We'll make ends meet somehow, take in mending and ironing, let out extra rooms. We've got the two houses between us." Divina takes Ruby's cold hand in her own. "Just tell me you won't go back to that bastard. Ever."

Ruby nods. Can she even get up?

"When you're ready, put a few things together. Just what you need. I'll be right back. I need to put in our notice with the big boss." Divina waddles from the tent.

Ruby's belly is sore. She wedges new rags into her crotch and sits at the edge of the bed. The room spins. She grabs the bed until the spell passes. When she feels strong enough, she gets up slowly. Blood trickles down her thigh. Behind a stack of trunks, Ruby roots for her battered red valise. In it, she throws undergarments, a couple of blouses, and three good skirts. Just what you need, Divina said. *A stack of rags. Laudanum.*

"Where the hell you think you're going?"

Ruby freezes. Willie stands in the doorway, blocking any chance of escape. Has he been watching? Damn right, he has, unspeakable louse. Ruby takes in a deep breath and crosses her arms across her chest.

"Jericho."

"No, you ain't," Willie seethes.

"I am, Willie."

"You'll do what I say, and I say you'll be in that saddle again tomorrow."

"No." Ruby shuts the valise with a snap. "I'm going home, and you can't stop me."

Willie narrows his eyes and moves toward Ruby. "Watch me."

Ruby grabs a wooden hanger and thrusts it out toward Willie. "Not another step."

"I make the decisions around here, little missy."

"You'd deny a mother the opportunity to bury her baby?"

"Wasn't even alive."

Ruby sets her mouth. "He was, too. Ten minutes I had with him," she lies. "Maybe fifteen. His eyes . . ."

"What color were they?"

"Blue, like yours."

"A boy?"

"Mmm-hmm."

Willie lowers his eyes. "He got a name?"

"Baby Willie, of course."

That nails it. Ruby knew it would.

"I'll get you a ticket." Is Willie crying as he leaves Divina's tent?

Ruby creeps into the tent she shares with Willie and empties the remainder of Willie's cash box. Let him think someone else did it. Ruby smiles in spite of grief and pain. He owes her. More than this.

Divina has wrapped Baby Willie in enough extra fabric inside the tiny coffin that he shouldn't begin to smell, not yet. Willie sees them off on the stage, and Ruby is grateful for every mile between them now. Ruby and Divina share one bench riding backwards, a small pine box between them on the rough seat as they rumble out of New Mexico

Territory toward Jericho. An armed deputy rides shot-gun to the driver. Must be bullion aboard, always bullion aboard. And today, something far more precious.

IN THE CRAMPED COACH, two rough-looking men attempt to get some shut-eye on the opposite bench. They take turns glaring at Ruby and Divina if the women say a word. Silence, and stifling heat, their shared companion.

When she's sure the men are asleep, Ruby whispers to Divina. "Where did the old Willie go? The one I fell in love with?"

"Was there ever an 'old Willie?'" Divina answers. "Or did you see something that wasn't there?"

Ruby doesn't answer right away.

"After all this, you better not go back to that louse. Ever," Divina says.

"Do I have a choice?" Ruby's hand has not left the top of the tiny box between them.

"Heart harder than your head, sometimes. Of course, you have a choice. Every woman has a choice. But one of those is giving up everything you've got to get to where you're going next."

Ruby falls silent as the coach bumps over wearisome terrain between ever-more infrequent springs and creeks. Her rear goes numb, her legs tingle. As the stage slopes downward from a thin gap between high hills, the coach lurches to the right. Ruby grasps for the roof handle as they rumble and pitch through the tableland toward the valley floor.

Ruby fans her face. Can it be any hotter in here? The stage approaches a watering hole and grinds to a stop.

Divina needs a hand to stand in the rickety coach. The coach driver opens the door of the rig and assists her down.

He then offers a hand to Ruby. She glances over her shoulder and wonders if she should leave Baby Willie alone in the stage. She won't range too far, just stretch her legs. She's had so little water that she doesn't need to pass it here. And she hasn't been hungry since Baby Willie left the world.

Wind and dust and heat blast Ruby's face so she ties a kerchief around her nose and mouth and shades her face and eyes with her wide-brimmed brown hat. Their gruff coach mates walk toward the pump while a ranch hand unharnesses the horses. The stage driver and his deputy retreat to the ranch house for vittles. It'll be an hour stop, no more, time enough to eat, take a leak, trade horses. Ruby needs to change her sopping rags.

"Shall we?" Divina asks.

"I can't leave Baby Willie alone."

"Bring him."

"You go ahead."

"You're sure?"

"Not sure of much right now. Just hoping something will change."

"Hoping doesn't make it true," Divina says. "I should know."

"Damn it, Divina." Ruby is no longer whispering.

The ranch hand's ears perk up as he bends over the jangling harnesses.

"Why pour a bucket on the only thing I've got right now?" Ruby shouts, her anger rising above the dirt, above her sorrow and fear.

Divina trudges toward the ranch house, a thousand yards of fabric trailing behind her. She waves her hands in the air and shakes her head without turning around.

Ruby pulls down her kerchief and yells toward the ranch house. "I've got a voice and I damn well know how to use it." She doesn't care who can hear her, ranch hands or fellow travelers or coach drivers. Not even the rancher, whose wife rings a bell on the front porch to call in the hands for the noon meal. A few of them stare at the small blonde woman ranting by the stage. By the looks of her, it's good to be a hundred yards away.

Divina stops at the bottom of the ranch house steps and turns back toward Ruby. "I'm listening."

"What if I didn't have hope? What then?"

Twenty sets of eyes are trained on Ruby by now, including the rancher who has joined his wife and the cowhands on the porch.

"Tell me, Divina. I've got a dead baby. No husband. No money. No job. No Pop." She stomps and raises a cloud of dirt. "So if I want hope, don't you go taking it away from me. Otherwise, what's the goddamn point?"

DISHEVELED AFTER THE TWO-DAY stage ride racing past drought land and badlands and old Indian territory (and a wicked sandstorm that caused the stage to pause for three-quarters of an hour and did Ruby have to pass water bad by then), Ruby and Divina arrive in the Sonoran Desert, saguaro, spiky yucca, ocotillo, and cholla like old acquaintances pointing them home. At the crossroads of the coach road and the long hill up to Jericho, Ruby and Divina step out of the creaky stage into the hot and bruised sky of a late afternoon. The burly driver hefts their dusty traveling bags from the top of the carriage and pitches them on the ground.

Divina tips the driver and the women trudge up Jefferson Street toward the center of town, balancing bags and the small coffin between them. Even though he's wrapped in yards of gauze, the tiny corpse smells of blood and rot.

Neither of the women says a word. They've made their peace with each other through silence.

Jericho is quiet, coming on four o'clock. An hour from now, town will be abuzz, men and women clotting the streets, the tavern, coming going coming going to meals and jobs and beds, with empty pockets, empty hearts. Ruby and Divina break at the outhouse behind Judd's. Ruby changes her rags and stuffs putrid ones in her satchel. She stashes her bag under the stairs beneath an old horse blanket. "Yours too, Divina. We'll come back for them later." If Ruby's reputation hasn't preceded her, the name on the suitcase shouts it out in bold gold letters: Ruby Fortune, Girl Wonder. Everyone in the West knows that name by now. Plus, who would get away with stealing a bright red suitcase like that—with gold lettering, no less—without someone noticing?

No one sees Ruby or Divina, not even Willa, Old Judd's lady friend, who always slinks around the saloon like a cat. Willa is never without a bruise. "Clumsy," she always says. *Clumsy, my arse*, Ruby thinks.

Divina swipes a shovel from up against the outhouse and the women wind their way up the hairpin streets of Jericho toward the cemetery. Ruby is unsteady on her feet, her mouth parched. She hasn't eaten in twenty-four hours. Did a curtain part at the vicarage? Or was that a mirage? And whose face is that, from the second story of the ochre-colored house at the crest of the hill? Or was there a face at all?

When they reach the graveyard, Divina inches the gate open and Ruby passes through, her arms now clenched around the pine box. Ruby stumbles to her pop's headstone like one walking blind. She sinks to the ground. No, she can't bury the baby. No, no, no, no, no, no.

Divina digs a small pit just feet from Big Burl's grave. When the hole is deep enough, she nudges Ruby and, between them, they lower the casket into the ground. It looks so small against the whole earth. Ruby crumples on the dirt, wracked with dry sobs.

"I'm here, Pip."

Ruby wipes her snotty nose and looks up at Divina. "Not one minute we had together. One goddamn minute." One look at his tiny face and Ruby had known Baby Willie was dead. He came too soon. When he never drew a shuddering breath, it was like life was sucked out of Ruby, too.

Divina drapes her fleshy arm around Ruby's thin shoulders. "Only time will mend that broken heart of yours. Although I doubt it'll be your last." Divina helps Ruby to stand then. Ruby's legs feel like jelly. She pushes away from Divina and raves like a madwoman, hands, arms, feet. *Noooooooo!* You can hear her the length of Jericho, she screams that loud.

Divina reaches, waits, reaches again, and takes Ruby into her arms. She guides Ruby through the dusty cemetery, sidestepping loose gravel and sun-beaten wooden crosses. At the gate, Ruby stops and looks over her shoulder. A low wail emanates from her throat. "I can't leave him here."

"There's nothing more to be done, Pip. He's with your pop now."

The tired sun rides low in the tawny sky, tendrils of wild colors streaming behind. Divina fills the outdoor tub for Ruby, one kettle at a time. Ruby sits on a bench outside Divina's familiar house, her mind drained, as Divina makes her way, back, forth, back, forth, with steaming pots of water. By the time the tub is full, the sun has disappeared behind the western bank of mountains, fifty miles away.

Ruby's heart is somewhere farther, like Hell.

SAME NIGHT

"In you go now." Divina touches Ruby's shoulder as she enters the bathhouse. The brazen night sky replaces what would be a ceiling, if the bathhouse had one. Ruby undresses and lowers herself into the steaming tub, water scalding her ankles and her backside. When she can just barely stand the heat, she stretches out the full length of the tub and slowly acclimates to the water. Ruby sinks her head under water. Maybe she'll never come up. That would solve it.

Ruby can't count the number of baths she's had in the same tub. Divina's house and Big Burl's house have sat side by side since before Ruby came into the world. The lines always blurred as to which house Ruby belonged. She belonged to both of them equally.

All the traveling, setting up and tearing down, dust and freighters and cheaters took it out of Big Burl. As much as he loved center stage, Big Burl took refuge in his squat adobe at the far end of Jericho. Winters, he spent ensconced in twelve-inch walls with a fire blazing, Divina next door and an Apache woman in his bed. And Ruby never far away. Everything a man could need was only minutes away down the long, snaky hill: bank, tavern, livery, general store. Big Burl didn't have much use for the church, although he sent Ruby there with Divina on Sundays.

As a child, Ruby spent long hours at her own house, playing with the ponies out back. But most days she shuttled between the two houses. Divina had trunks and trunks of fabric and trims that she fashioned into magical costumes for Ruby—pirate and cowgirl and snake charmer. Ruby would parade back and forth like an actress, making up stories about stowaways and wranglers and circus performers and corralling stray cats into her routines.

Evenings, Big Burl would sit on Divina's wide porch drinking to the sunset, which had a habit of outperforming itself every night. All the while, Big Burl's Apache woman would be outside cooking or doing beadwork or smoking. You'd think it might be confusing for Ruby, Big Burl having two women in Jericho, one for one thing and another for the rest. But it didn't bother Ruby one bit. She had two mothers, that's just the way it was. When she scraped her knee, she went to Divina. When she was hungry, she went to Onawa.

Onawa was a grand storyteller, spinning tales about everything under the sun: creation, animals, plants, people. Ruby would sit, dirty and happy, at Onawa's feet, listening, while Onawa stirred the contents of a huge pot over an open fire.

Before time, one story began, *there was nothing—no earth, no sky, no sun, no moon, only darkness everywhere.*

Onawa raised her arms above her shoulders and cupped her hands, moving them back and forth.

Out of darkness came sliver of light.

Ruby's spine tingled.

On sliver sat Great Creator.

Ruby didn't know what a Great Creator was, but she pictured him bigger than her pop.

As Great Creator looked into darkness—Onawa's eyes opened wide as tin cans then—*he cast his hands. . .*

Onawa's arms moved rhythmically side to side.

. . . and to the east, he created yellow streaks of dawn.

Ruby's eyes were wide now, too, picturing a sky turned yellow from black.

To the west, Great Creator painted sky with wild strips of color.

Ruby imagined colors whirling in the sky, burned onto the waning day like sunset.

Creator rubbed his hands together then—Onawa rubbed her palms together frantically, transported somewhere far, far from Jericho.

Ruby didn't have the heart to tell Onawa that the pot was boiling over onto the ground. Ruby scooted away from the scalding liquid without taking her eyes off the older woman. What would happen next? If she rubbed her hands together, would something grand happen? Ruby mimicked Onawa and rubbed her dirty hands together. Her palms became warm.

. . . and behold! On shining cloud sat a little girl—here, Onawa pointed at Ruby—*who would become ruler over all the Earth.*

Onawa laughed and clucked her tongue. No matter how many times Ruby tried to cluck her tongue like Onawa, she never could. Her head was full of clouds and colors and her hands were raw. Ruler of all the earth! Imagine!

Later, nights, Ruby would sit on Divina's generous lap and fall asleep there. How she got to her own bed in her own house was always a mystery, like another of Divina's limitless tricks.

The year they buried Big Burl, Ruby was in the same tub, grieving. From underwater, Ruby heard sharp words. She popped up and shook her head to get water out of her ears.

"He's dead, I tell you. Heart gave out."

Unintelligible words, a rise and fall of voices, and then a loud wail.

"No, it's not your house! Don't you be coming back, do you hear me?"

More conversation, another wail. Then a loud slam of a door.

Ruby soaked until the water turned tepid and then cool. She watched constellations blink and wink overhead as she drifted into a dark, dreamless sleep.

A loud knock on the bathhouse door startled her.

Ruby dragged herself from the tub and toweled off. She unlatched the bathhouse door and let Divina shoulder her weight as they went inside. Divina poured Ruby a liberal shot of whiskey and a double for herself. They drank in silence, their comfortable space, Ruby nodding when Divina offered her a second shot.

"Onawa?" Ruby asked, finally. "Pop's lady friend? The one who told stories?"

Divina bristled. "She won't be coming back."

"So you got what you wanted, in the end. The tail end of Onawa heading out of Jericho for good."

"I never got what I really wanted, Pip."

TONIGHT, DIVINA PULLS THE COVERLET over Ruby and sits on the edge of the divan. She strokes Ruby's hair. "You're not the only one walking around with a heart in splinters. I'm as broken up as you about Baby Willie. But there will be others."

"Don't talk of babies."

A coyote howls in the distance. Ruby's spine bristles. Did she bury her son just this afternoon? In a maw of earth? Did they dig the hole deep enough? Is the coyote . . . no, no, no, Ruby moans again.

Ruby melts into Divina's arms.

"I've had my share of black eyes, too, Pip, even if you can't see them. Your pop was the master of that. Never lifted a hand to me, mind you, but put more black eyes on my heart than any man living. Those are the kind that never heal."

RUBY DRAGS HERSELF TO THE cemetery every morning to keep Baby Willie company. A week after she lowered him into the earth—not much past dawn, before the sun has shown up for the day—Ruby arrives at the cemetery to find the grave disturbed. Paw marks pierce the dirt around the gravesite, as if a thief has been here and left in a rush, leaving the ground trampled and damp. Ruby cries out and sinks to her knees. She reaches her hands into the earth, her shoulders at ground level. She screams into the void, her hands catching on the edge of the splintered coffin.

Ruby stays there all day, dry heaving into her balled fist. At dusk, she staggers into town, ignoring catcalls from drunks and drifters. Disappears into the back of Judd's and emerges with her eyes glazed. Everyone in Jericho, down to the newspaperman (who'd rather lose an eyetooth than let a story get by), as well as the sheriff—the latest preacher even—gives Ruby a wide berth.

Lost a baby, someone whispers. Mighty young, isn't she? Said she has a husband, but that's probably all talk, usually is. She's Big Burl's girl, right? That Girl Wonder? Think so. She's gone mad, I tell you. Too bad her pa up and died on her. Girl like that needs her pa. Reckon he didn't have two nickels to leave her, though. I remember her from school, used to be the cutest thing in Jericho. Wouldn't recognize her now, such a shame. Think she's one of Judd's girls? She's there most afternoons. Maybe, hard to say. Probably. How else could she support herself? Heard her mother was a good time girl, wouldn't be surprised if she's one now. Titter, twitter, talk, talk, talk.

Ruby ignores it. Her days have no reason except for the bottle. Her mind swims with obtuse thoughts, like she's dreaming awake. Lies, she tells herself, that's the only thing that gets a body through. Can't face the truth. Or put stock in faith. What has faith ever done except give a body false hope? Redemption? What a load of hogwash. All a body can do is tell stories over and over until the ending comes out better. It's the only way to keep on getting up the next morning, or else it isn't worth it, getting up at all.

And so months turn to dust turn to void. Ruby lives in a constant haze as Divina nurses her with liquor and love. Every day, Ruby seeks out Old Judd at the tavern. Her pop said you can always trust a barman, even more than a priest. Ruby doesn't ask where he gets his supply of laudanum because it doesn't matter. No price is too high because the law is changing. Soon you won't be able to get laudanum at all without a prescription. Damn doctors. And then what will they ask for it? A king's ransom?

Somehow, Ruby will find a way to keep her habit. No one can take that away from her. It's her life, damn it. She has enough laudanum for this month stashed in the bureau drawer next to her narrow bed in Divina's spare room. She sleeps off nights and days, a spoonful of laudanum only three blessed steps away. She's not ready to go back to Big Burl's house next door. Not yet.

So Ruby doesn't rejoin Willie for the rest of that season, and would never have considered the traveling life again for a thousand dollars or a thousand rounds of applause if Willie hadn't shown up one day in Jericho, hat in hand and more winsome than ever, promising to God and all creation to make a new start.

SIX YEARS LATER
SPRING 1895
LAS CRUCES, NEW MEXICO TERRITORY

Ruby stands nearly naked as Divina snakes soft turquoise suede across Ruby's narrow back. Divina's mouth is filled with pins. She measures with her hands, snips fabric with a large pair of shears, and begins to pin the suede.

"Don't you go and poke me," Ruby says.

Divina laughs, pins flying from her mouth. "Poke you?"

Now Ruby laughs, too. "How many times you been poked, Divina?"

Divina bursts into a deep, rumbling laugh. "Not enough."

Ruby peels the turquoise suede off her shoulders and tosses it into Divina's sewing heap. "I could use a good poke just about now. If I could just ward off babies every time, that is. There's nothing I like better."

DIVINA SITS AT HER JUMBLED dressing table and washes face paint off with a dingy washcloth. She spies Ruby through the mirror and spins around. "Not again, Pip."

Ruby rushes into Divina's arms, her face stained.

"Why you put up with him another minute is beyond me. Think everyone doesn't know how he treats you? Worse than a dog, Pip. You've got to get out from under his thumb."

"And where would I go? A mother with three children, and another on the way? Tell me that, Divina. You think Willie Fortune wouldn't come after me with his finger on the trigger?"

"You're making one poor choice to hide another."

"You know?"

"Hard to keep secrets from me. I see it in your eyes. You're on the juice again."

A trickle starts from Ruby's groin and runs down her leg. She clutches her thighs. "Damn it."

Would life have been different if Big Burl had taken Divina as his wife? Would Divina have been able to curb his drinking and smoking? Gotten him to a doctor in time? Would the two of them have stepped in to stop Willie's thrashings? Talked sense into him? Or sent him on the rails back to Chicago? What would Ruby's life look like if Big Burl were still living and breathing?

But she'll never get her pop back. Her wish list is, if anything, practical. Except for the dream to go to San Francisco one day, the carrot before the horse, dangling just out of reach. She and Divina have talked about it for years.

When the Southern Pacific arrived in Tucson in the spring of 1880, it turned the town upside down. Used to be, supplies from San Francisco were shipped around the southern tip of Baja California and up the Sea of Cortez before being loaded onto flat-bottomed boats plying up the sandbar-filled Colorado River to Yuma and from there to Tucson by wagon, sixty days one way. Now you can be in San Francisco the day after tomorrow by rail. Year by year, the thought of going to San Francisco burns brighter. Ruby and Divina will get there one day, one way or another. But certainly not anytime soon.

Samuel Finis Fortune comes into the world screaming, like Ruby did, a voice as big as two territories stitched together. He's four days old now, and sleeping, thank the Lord, if there is one. Ruby pulls the screen off the top of the cradle and pats Sam's back as it rises and falls with each breath. Ruby is weak from having lost so much blood during the delivery. It's a wonder she didn't die of it, like her momma. That's why Ruby named her fifth son, *finis*, for the last one. She has to avoid Willie Fortune if she wants to be spared another difficult birth or her own death. That might be easier than she thinks, now that Willie is sharing the sheets with other women in the traveling show. Ruby has gotten smart about claiming headaches and crotch rot to steer him away. She can't go through this again. And she's got to wean herself from the juice. A mother of four boys can't function with a head full of cotton. Let alone headline a major Wild West show.

Willie comes up behind Ruby. "He's a puny one, ain't he? At least he's not deformed, like Virgil."

"Leave Virgil out of it," Ruby says. "Look at Clayton and Fletcher. They're not puny anymore, and they started out like this." She pulls Sam's thin blanket over his sleeping body and replaces the screen. Don't want scorpions falling from the ceiling. "Got to give a body time, Willie." Ruby is thinking of herself when she says that, not Sam. "Thought you would've learned that by now." She sucks in a breath. Maybe she's said too much.

"How about a little fun?"

"I'm not up to it, Willie."

"Aren't you, now?" Willie plucks Ruby's six-shooter show pistol off the nightstand. "Always wanted to practice on live targets. Like you do. Might have a little fun in another way."

Ruby moves to the bedroom door, her robe loosely tied. "Who?"

"I'm thinking . . . Virgil."

Ruby stiffens. "Not Virgil."

"Why not? He's deformed already." Willie cocks the pistol and mimics shooting off a round.

"You won't do any such thing, Willie Fortune." Ruby smooths her robe down to minimize her shaking hands. She tries to keep her voice steady. "He can't help that he's got the palsy. Go pick on someone else."

Willie smacks Ruby across the mouth. She raises her hand to wipe away blood and saliva.

"Get dressed," Willie says. "I think I'll have a little fun with you instead." He holds the pistol to her head.

"You wouldn't."

"Watch me."

Willie pushes Ruby up against the back of the camp wagon, a makeshift target behind her.

"Momma!" Fletcher yells from the doorway, where he stands with Clayton.

"Shut your trap," Willie barks. "You a sissy?"

Ruby doesn't see Virgil. The baby is still sleeping, or should be anyway, if this racket doesn't raise him. Her heart is making a racket enough on its own.

"Don't you worry, Fletch," Ruby says. "Your pa wouldn't dare shoot me."

If Ruby moves even an inch, it'll be her undoing. She can't risk being shot for her own foolishness. She can only hope Willie's hand is as steady as hers. Ruby's eyes narrow as she faces her husband, three yards away. If she is going to be shot in cold blood, in broad daylight, and in front of her sons, Ruby is going to look straight into Willie's eyes as he takes aim.

At the first crack of the pistol, Ruby stands as still as a human can who is still breathing. The shot *zings* to the right of her ear. The second shot pierces the target above her head.

Ruby breathes shallowly so as not to move a single muscle. *Six, there are only six shots.* She keeps her eyes trained on the barrel of the gun. Even though her body is still as a statue, her mind flies. What will become of the boys if Willie finds his target smack in the middle of her forehead? *Zing.* Who will fix their suppers and dry their tears? *Ping.* And where will they end up, four motherless boys with a bastard for a father? *Ting.*

The last shot grazes her hair. A half-inch off, she'd be dead. But she's not. If Ruby wanted to die, it would be easy. Just a few extra teaspoons.

RUBY'S HANDS SHAKE. SHE'S been three days without laudanum, her skin clammy and crawling with invisible insects. She's got the runs, too.

"Sing me a song, Momma." Fletcher buries his head in Ruby's lap. He's five now, the perfect age. Clayton wouldn't dream of snuggling anymore, although he's but a year older. Ruby ruffles Fletcher's reddish-blond hair. She begins singing softly. By the time she finishes the last stanza, Fletcher's eyes have fluttered closed.

Ruby's bowels are loose again so she shifts Fletcher off her lap and onto his cot. His hair falls over his beautiful face, his mouth slack. She runs to the privy and sits in the dark, sweating. Her heart pounds. She knows the symptoms; she's tried to rid herself of the habit more than once, but she never seems to stick with it. Willie's moods. Constant demands. The goddamn heat. Any excuse. She wipes herself with old newsprint and shuffles back to the boys' tent. It's hot enough to sleep outside tonight, on cots dragged outside the tents or on the ground in old gunnysacks. But Ruby doesn't have the fire in her tonight. She can almost taste the laudanum. Maybe she'll take a half-teaspoon, take the edge off. But she's come this far, three days. That's the longest she's ever been off the juice for years. If she can just make it to four days . . .

Ruby tucks in the blankets around Clayton and scoots Virgil's leg from outside the covers back under them. Such a shame that Virgil's right leg is a full two inches shorter than his left. He tries to keep up with his older brothers, but they make fun of him. Ruby watches the boys' soft breathing and returns to her tent next door. The baby stirs and squirms. She rubs castor oil on his smooth tummy and he goes quiet again.

Willie is out and Ruby stretches out on their bed, fighting sleep. She can't be awake when Willie gets back in case he's got a hot dick in his trousers. It's too soon after the baby, but that's never bothered him before, blood or no blood. But she can't sleep; her skin itches from the inside out, like a swarm of bees.

Ruby bolts up and rummages in her trunk. With shaking hands, she lifts the dark bottle and pours a half-teaspoon. Heaven within reach. She inhales the familiar aroma and brings the teaspoon up to her nose. Her hand is unsteady. She parts her lips and sends her tongue, lizard-like, toward the spoon. *No, Ruby, no. Not again.* She touches the tip of her tongue on the edge of the spoon and wills herself to stop. Lowering her hand, she irons out her breathing. She pours the liquid back in the bottle. A few drops run down the lip. She replaces the cap without lapping up the drops, replaces the bottle in the guts of the trunk, and climbs back into bed, her hands still trembling. *I can do this. I can do this.*

Ruby wakes with a start. Willie is thrashing around the tent, naked from the waist down. He still wears his hat as he descends on her. She is weak after Sam's birth but it is not worth the struggle. She hopes it's too early to conceive again.

Afterwards, her mind roves. She wonders in what dungeon of Hell a person can expect fortune to change. Ruby knows she's got to take matters into her own hands. But when? And where? And how?

The baby stirs again, and Ruby climbs over Willie to nurse Sam. She rocks back and forth, his tiny bud-like mouth suckling. He shudders and sighs before falling back into blessed sleep. Before she goes back to bed, she peeks into the boys' tent next door. She pats Clayton and strokes Virgil's forehead. She doesn't pick favorites, but at this moment, her heart sighs. She bends over Fletcher, skimming his cheek with her lips. He is the dearest child, never a cross word or out of line. Perfect, if a boy could be labeled. *If only all boys could be like Fletcher*, she thinks, *all would be right with the world.*

SUMMER 1897
YUMA, ARIZONA TERRITORY

It's over in a flash; the stray bullet glances off Willie Fortune's leg and leaves him a cripple. The Yuma morning
burns hotter than summer in Hades, heat shimmering
off every surface and the pump handle too hot to touch.
Ruby fetches a cloth to cover the handle and works it up
and down until her arm aches. After all that trouble, only
half a bucket. Nothing good happens the rest of the day if
the morning starts off wrong, and the sun so hot it could
melt your skin off. Better to stay in bed until tomorrow or
face the wrath of chance, especially in a place where the
scorched earth burns the soles clean off your boots before
you've walked twenty yards.

The gunslinger who maimed Willie is fired that night
while Willie lies writhing in his tent. The bullet hit Willie's
femur and it took a half bottle of whiskey—most of it
guzzled by Willie himself—for the doc to fetch it out. He's
sleeping now.

Ruby keeps one eye on Willie as she cleans her pistol. She lays her derringer on a white cloth along with her cleaning tools: barrel patches, wiping cloth, short barrel rod, and small can of Nye's sperm oil. She admires the pearl-handled grip and shiny barrel, small and easily concealed. "Use it when man or animal gets too close for your liking," her pop had said. "But too far, you can't hit the side of a barn with it. You've got two shots, Ruby, one to miss; one not to." With that, he placed the over-under double barrel Remington Model 95 in her hand. She was twelve. Since then, Ruby has worn the pistol in her waistband or in its holster strapped above her boot.

Ruby cradles the pistol in the palm of her hand, loosens the barrel lock, and swings the barrel open. She slides the ejector and removes the two cartridges.

Willie is snoring now.

Ruby cocks the hammer to expose the firing mechanism. With the wiping cloth, she applies two drops of sperm oil into the action. With the rod firmly in her right hand and the pistol in her left, Ruby pushes a cloth patch through the barrel until it comes out clean. She lightly soaks another patch in oil and pushes it through each barrel until it's spotless.

Ruby oils the gun, dabbing excess lubricant. She closes the breach and cocks it, aiming squarely at Willie. She pulls the hammer and squeezes the trigger, once, twice. Willie doesn't flinch. Ruby opens the barrel and loads with two live rounds.

"That you, Ruby?" Willie stirs.

"Mmm-hmm." *I could've shot him.*

Willie attempts to sit up, grimaces. "Come here, little missy."

"Not in the mood, Willie." *I should've shot him.*

"I'm not talking about that, woman. It's an entirely different matter." Willie reaches for a stack of papers and waves them toward Ruby.

"What now?"

"A contract."

"Not another one."

"Would you shut it? I'm buying up a share of Silver Tip Mine outside Jericho. I've had enough of this circuit."

Has Ruby heard right? Jericho? She grabs the papers and stares at Willie's signature, one that she's copied a hundred times before. Every time she forges his name, she's reminded how ladylike his signature is, unlike every other aspect of him. Like he won a penmanship prize or something.

"Where'd you get the cash?" Ruby asks.

"I've been putting it by. Waiting for my big chance."

"I thought we didn't have a can to piss in," Ruby says. "The way you go through it." She's safe today because Willie's confined to bed.

"My pa never gave me a nickel, Ruby. Every cent I made with my own two hands."

"You mean I made for you. Gate receipts. 'Girl Wonder.'"

"You wouldn't been anything without me."

"No?" Ruby counters. "I thought you said your pop sent you to lawyering school. Or was that another one of your lies?" Ruby's emboldened today.

"He did, and I loathed it. When I told him I wasn't meant for lawyering, he laid into me. For the thousandth time. Nothing I ever did was good enough for him, so I finally said to hell with it. Got on a train and never looked back."

"What about your sister? Don't you have a responsibility for her?"

"I don't owe anyone anything."

"What will happen to her after your pop goes?"

"She'll get it all, the house, the property, everything. My father won't leave me a dime now. I could challenge it, of course."

"You'd defraud your own sister?"

"She'd get an allowance. Like you."

"Like what? Enough to buy a pair of stockings every month?"

"Shut it, Ruby," Willie yells. "I'm ready to haul myself out of this bed and give you a walloping."

"Is that how you end every conversation?" Ruby yells back. "With your cock or your fist?"

Willie struggles to get up, but falls back on the pillows. "You're asking for it, Ruby." His eyes seethe. "I can't stand the sight of you anymore. You've gotten fat."

"Always my fault, is that what you're saying? Every time you wallop me, it's my fault?" Ruby shakes her head. "You used to talk sweet to me, Willie. Won me over like a bowling pin. Now all I get are fists."

"Once we're in Jericho, there'll be no need of that."

"And I'm supposed to trust you? You're about out of chances, Willie." Ruby thinks of her derringer. "Leopards don't change their spots, you know."

WILLIE AND RUBY SETTLE INTO Big Burl's house, the one Ruby grew up in. Ruby has few complaints. She is home and Divina is right next door, just like the old days when they all wintered in Jericho and days bled into one another with laughter and love.

Using money Ruby made in the traveling shows, Willie purchases a quarter share in the Silver Tip Mine outside Jericho. Ruby wonders if it's not more than a cover for more disreputable pursuits. All over the west, rumors of fraudulent mineral strikes fill the papers. Rich soil, owners hawk. Balmy climate. And the best damn glory holes in the west. Salting mines is the oldest trick in the book, making mines look profitable by adding gold or silver to samples.

Boom-and-bust towns spring up like pigweed, enticing gullible prospectors and then cheating them out of every last nickel. Willie's bound to have his hand in dirty business like this. Falsifying claims. Running opium. Like it says in Jeremiah (one of the only Bible verses Ruby knows by heart), leopards *do not will not ever never* change their spots.

"BASTARD!" RUBY CHASES WILLIE up Jefferson Street, peppering his heels with buckshot as he runs. "Do I have to shoot you home again? And in broad daylight?" Willie's long legs outrun Ruby, but she still trails him with bullets. Drunk again. Whoring. Last night, a bar brawl that took three men to wrestle him down, or so the sheriff said. This is the fourth time this month that Ruby has had to bail Willie out of the town jail.

The very next day, Sheriff Sheldon Sloane separates Ruby and Willie on the street, Ruby is yelling so loud. Sheldon pushes Willie to the ground and grasps Ruby's arm. "Put down your piece."

"I will not," Ruby says.

Sheldon wrenches the derringer from Ruby's hand.

She glares at him.

Two men help Willie up.

"Don't need a woman cuckolding me in the street," Willie says. He spits toward Ruby.

"You deserve it, Willie!" Ruby yells.

A small crowd gathers, forming a semi-circle around Ruby, Willie, and Sheldon.

"Get on with you," Sheldon says. "This is between Willie and his missus and me."

Ruby fights to disentangle herself from Sheldon's grasp. "More like between me and Willie."

Sheldon leans down and talks under his breath into

Ruby's ear. "From what I've heard, you might be the best shot in the whole territory, Mrs. Fortune, but I'd watch out for that husband of yours if I were you. He's bad seed." He releases Ruby and hands her derringer back.

Lately, Willie's been suspiciously well-behaved. Ruby knows something is up. Lining his pockets? Woman on the side? Both? Nothing new there. But since returning to Jericho, at least the thrashings have stopped, like Willie said.

"Ready or not!" Fletcher yells. Sam mimics his brother. "Weady oh not!" Sam says. Clayton runs behind the flapping sheets to hide while Fletcher finishes counting to ten. Virgil watches from the stoop, his left leg dangling. He's adjusting to his new spectacles, which make his eyes look twice their size. Two-year-old Sam stands in the wooden-slat playpen in nothing but a diaper.

Ruby hangs laundry from between two posts behind the house. The lines, usually stretched taut, sag under the weight of bedding, clothing, diapers, and rags. In the billowing sea of dingy whites, Ruby pegs out her turquoise blouse. She fingers the elaborate embroidery on the yoke; it's a little worse for wear after all these years. Her mind wanders. Her hair flows behind her as she rounds the end of the arena ready for a second pass, the show hand rapidly replacing glass balls on wooden tripods. She can almost hear the roar of the crowd in Prescott as she whips out her pistol and shatters glass balls, one after another, *crack crack crack*.

"Ma!" Virgil yells.

Ruby snaps back to see Sam toddling outside the playpen, barefoot on the hardpan.

"Sam!" She scoops him up and brings his rear end up to her nose. "Another change, little mister." Ruby steps around Virgil, who is now picking at his nails. Clayton and Fletcher run like banshees through the sheets.

"Boys!" she says. "Watch Virge for a minute while I go in to change your brother." Ruby doesn't wait for an answer. She strides across the yard in her soiled skirt. Gone are the days of deerskin and feathers and crowds.

Ruby sets Sam on the parlor floor and unpins his soggy diaper. "When are we going to learn, little mister? To tell momma when you have to go?"

"Have to yo."

"Go, Sam, not yo."

"Yo."

Ruby smiles. When she emerges into the sun again, Sam hoisted on her hip, Virgil is in the playpen clambering to get out.

"Clayton! Fletcher! Right here!"

Two heads poke out from now dirtied sheets.

"Git out of there! Can't leave for a minute without some sort of trouble." Ruby shoos the boys away and plops Sam in the playpen with Virgil. "You two play together now."

"Have to yo!" Sam yells.

"Not again, Sam," Virgil says. "Ma! Get me out of here!"

Ruby hoists Virgil out of the playpen and turns to the wash basket, still overflowing with wet laundry.

"Woman!"

Ruby looks up, two clothespins in her mouth.

Willie fills the doorframe. He checks his watch. "No dinner on yet? It's five minutes past twelve." He snaps his pocket watch closed.

Virgil clings to Ruby's skirt. Ruby hadn't been expecting Willie for dinner today, thought he was up at Silver Tip all day. Meetings, or so he said. She drops a clean blouse in the dirt. "Time got away from me, I guess." She shoos Virgil away, leaves the laundry half pegged, and hurries past the playpen. She'll have to conjure up a miracle to get dinner on in less than five minutes. As she nears the stoop, Willie pulls her arm.

"Looks like I'll have to whet my appetite another way," he says.

"Damn it, Willie, not now." Clayton and Fletcher are still playing hide and seek in the laundry, leaving dusty handprints. "Boys!" she yells.

"The boys will take care of themselves," Willie says.

"Clayton! Fletcher! Listen to your pop," Willie says. "Watch your brothers for a minute, will you? Your momma and I will be back in the wink of an eye." He throws a handful of coins into the dirt. Clayton hits Fletcher as he scrambles in the dirt.

"Have to yo!" Sam tries to unpin his diaper.

"Shut it, Sam," Clayton says. "Or maybe Virgil can change you."

Virgil puts distance between his brothers and himself, his bad leg trailing. "Maybe you can, meanie."

"Come along, little missy," Willie says to Ruby. "Don't have all day."

"Have to yo!" Sam's diaper is now off and he squats on the ground.

Ruby looks back over her shoulder. Divina is on her porch next door. She shakes her head at Ruby. Ruby raises her shoulders and her hands. Sometimes she wishes Divina would mind her own business instead of hers. Ruby takes one last look at the boys before following Willie into the house. All those sheets, now needing doing again.

"No rough housing, you hear me?" she yells over her shoulder. Divina is still on the porch with a disapproving look. She can say what she thinks without words. It stings.

Willie grabs Ruby's arm and muscles her toward the divan. "Did you hear me?"

"Do you have to be so rough?"

"Shut it, woman." Willie throws his hat onto a nearby chair and unbuttons his trousers. "Pull up your skirt!" In less than two minutes, he is done. He tugs at his trousers, pulls on his hat, and leaves the house without saying a word.

Where has all that tender lovemaking gone? The words and songs and whispers that made her spine tingle? The slow touch on her inner arm or inner thigh? That roller coaster of wanting and desire? The warm western nights that dripped like honey straight from the bee? Gone, they are. Gone, gone, gone. And Ruby is left now to clean up more messes.

THE NEXT WEEK, RUBY SITS BY the dry creek under cloudless cobalt sky, the chitter of a desert thrasher her only company. Willie is in Tucson today to bid on a new business, a hotel, right on Congress Street. Just when they were saving. If buying a run-down hotel isn't a money hole, Ruby doesn't know what is.

Hell, take all the time you need, she thinks. *And a whole heap more while you're at it. A month, maybe longer. Or move to Tucson, why don't you, Willie Fortune, come home on weekends or holidays or never.* That she could get used to.

She's stripped down to chemise and drawers, her waist-long hair unraveled from curl. She breathes in desert air and thinks back to the story Onawa told her when she was a small girl about being the ruler of the world. So why doesn't Ruby feel like she's in charge of anything now? Nothing is in her control. She is flat broke. Her boys are wild. And she can't have another baby—Ruby's monthlies have become so severe that if she could rip her womb out, she would. God's got a way of telling a body when it's worn through.

Willie explodes through the door the next night and it's only a matter of minutes before Ruby has a split lip again. *So much for promises.* Next, it's a twisted arm where Ruby can't lift her arm above her shoulder for days. Then it's a flowering bruise the color of horse manure on her upper arm. For that, and a lifetime of other bruises, Willie doesn't spend a night in jail. Never. Hell never. Never-and-a-day never does any man spend a night in the lockup for messing with his missus in Arizona Territory.

Late one night, when Willie is no doubt down at the cribs on Deadman's Alley, Ruby runs her hands over her slim body, the curve of her breasts, the hollow at her pelvis. She shivers. When was the last time Willie called her beautiful? Or anything resembling love? Or brought her rings or flowers or the things women crave, even if they're too stubborn to admit it? Why has Ruby let Willie Fortune rule her life, every inch and every minute of it? And for so long? And done nothing about it?

Each blow has raised Ruby's simmer point. She's almost at full boil.

TWO YEARS LATER
SUMMER 1899
JERICHO, ARIZONA TERRITORY

"Take that, you little shit." Willie whips off his belt and coils it. Sam cowers in a corner of the kitchen. "Don't you go sassing at your ma." Sam yelps at the first blow and ducks between Willie's legs and out the back door.

"What the hell, Willie?" Ruby strains to grab Willie's belt but misses. He coils it up again and stands between Ruby and the door. Ruby's feet are planted firm. "Swine."

"You calling me names?"

"Damn it, Willie, the boy's just hungry. Do you have to go and wallop him over it? Or yell all the time. I'm tired of this, Willie. I'm tired of you." Willie's not even two days back from Tucson and Ruby has welts fresh on her back. She caught a glimpse of her shoulder blades in the mirror this morning. It hurt to put on her chemise.

Willie grunts. He lowers the belt and scratches his underarms. He's still in his long johns. His hair sprouts from his scalp and his face is full of whiskers.

"You stink, Willie. Go get cleaned up. It's nearly ten." Ruby skirts Willie and pushes out the back door. No Sam.

A glint of sun slices Ruby's eyes. What is it? She squints, her brow knotted.

It's time . . .

Is it always this way? You feel a jolt? A voice? Like someone from somewhere—dead or imagined—gives you the nod?

. . . long past time.

And there's no going back to what was, even two minutes before?

The door creaks behind her as she re-enters the kitchen.

It's time, Ruby, long past time.

Into the bedroom, the words follow her. She backs up against the bureau, her hands behind her back. The curtains hang limp in the sultry air. "I want a divorce."

"What?" Willie whips around, his eyes slits. He's got his trousers on, and an undershirt. He hasn't bothered to wash up.

"You heard me, Willie."

"Bitch." Willie advances on Ruby.

Ruby feels for her pistol on the dresser top. *Steady, Ruby.* It's always loaded, both barrels, like her pop taught her, one to miss, one not to. She knocks over a photograph as she turns around, the pistol aimed at Willie's chest. Her breathing is ragged.

"You take one more step toward me and I'll finish you, Willie Fortune. Whupping Sam just now just because he's hungry, that's the last straw. Four years old, he is, Willie. Four! If you know what's best for you, you won't come near me or the boys or Jericho again."

Willie glares at Ruby. "You threatening me?"

"The plain truth." Ruby concentrates, her hand steady as if she were in the arena in front of five hundred paying customers, a glass ball in her sights. *See that you don't miss, Ruby.*

"We could get it back, you and me. You know it, Ruby." Willie slowly raises his hand and reaches toward her.

Ruby doesn't flinch. "That time has long past, Willie. What you do in Tucson isn't for delicate ears. And whatever it is you boys do up at that good-for-nothing mine. People talk. And I do your laundry, you know. There are others. There have always been others."

"Think you know it all, don't you. You don't know much. Not even graduated from the eighth grade."

"And whose fault is that?" Ruby's breath comes on fast and shallow. She thinks of the thousand times she's been center stage at the traveling carnival. There is no room for error. Her palm sweats but she retains a solid bead on Willie's chest, her finger still on the trigger. "I know a heap more than you when it comes to common decency. So I'm asking you to leave. No, I'm telling you to leave. And don't come back."

Willie lunges and slaps at the pistol. She is too quick for him and angles the pistol toward the ceiling. A shot goes off. Willie grasps Ruby's throat and tightens his grip, his eyes bulging as he shoves her up against the bureau.

Ruby gasps for breath, the air sucked out of her, her outstretched arm and derringer still pointed at the ceiling. Dark spots dance in front of her eyes and she feels faint. Willie reaches for the gun with his free hand. In that split second before she blacks out, Ruby swings her arm around and pulls the trigger, point blank. The curtains tremble as the sound echoes off the bedroom walls.

Willie stiffens, his eyes shrunk to cactus thorns. His hands tighten around Ruby's neck and then go slack. He stumbles back against the edge of their bed, his chest wide open. Blood peppers the white bedspread as Willie slumps against the bedstead.

"Goddamn whore," he splutters. "If it weren't for me,

you'd be . . ." His voice trails off as his eyes roll back. He melts off the edge of the bed onto the floor.

Blood pours from the open wound, but Ruby does not go to him. She stares at Willie Fortune as his chest heaves and then goes still as a gravestone.

Ruby looks down at her shaking hand. "If it weren't for you, Willie, I'd be . . . free." A blast of blood fills her chest. Ruby doesn't kneel, just stands there, catching her tattered breath, until she's sure Willie's not feigning it.

Should she be filled with remorse? Horror? Fear? She doesn't feel anything. Ruby replaces the pistol on the dresser. She catches a glimpse of herself in the mirror. Her neck is beet red where Willie strangled her. She sweeps her hair behind her ears and turns toward the door.

Sam stands in the doorframe, his face the color of day-old dough.

"Sam!" Ruby reaches for him. He flinches and runs.

"Sam! Wait!" Ruby yells. She runs from the bedroom to the kitchen.

"What the devil?" Fletcher says. He's eating pie for breakfast. "I heard a . . ."

"Don't go in there," Ruby says. "I shot your pa. He's dead."

"What the hell?" Fletcher drops the piecrust and pushes past Ruby.

"I said, don't go in there, young man."

Fletcher hovers between kitchen and parlor, as much as between loyalties. "Did you have to kill him?"

"Get the sheriff."

Ruby runs to the back door and bangs out the kitchen door. "Sam! Sam! Come back!"

Ten minutes later Sheldon Sloane storms in the front door, Fletcher trailing behind. Ruby is in the back yard, wringing her hands. "I can't find Sam."

"A boy can't get too far in this town without someone bringing him home by his ear," the sheriff says.

Fletcher brushes past Ruby and slams her hip as they meet at the back door.

"See that you find Sam," Ruby says.

"Why?"

"I mean it, Fletcher. Find him. You and Clayton, both."

Fletcher scowls.

When did he get to be so surly?

Sheldon ducks into the bedroom and returns to the kitchen minutes later. He sits across from Ruby, hat in hand. "What happened?"

"If you're asking, I'm not sorry. Even if it means . . ."

"It means you're rid of the bastard," Sheldon says. "I can't tell you the number of times I wanted to throw that good-for-nothing in the clink for as much as spitting on the sidewalk. Everyone knew how he treated you, Ruby. You can't hide every bruise."

"I told him I wanted a divorce."

"And what next?"

"Had his hands around my neck." Ruby touches her neck and realizes her hands shake. "I couldn't breathe. He was choking me, Sheldon. I swear he would have killed me if I hadn't . . ."

"You won't face a day for this, Ruby. It's an open and shut case of self-defense. Especially since there were no witnesses."

Ruby draws in a shuddering breath. "Sam was there."

"You mean to say Sam saw . . ."

"When I turned to the door, he was there."

"And you didn't see him?"

"Not until after."

"Rest easy, Ruby. No judge is going to take the word of a shaver over his momma. Or me."

Sheldon stands. Ruby follows suit, but Sheldon holds Ruby back with his arm. "I'll take care of this. You go put on tea. Or maybe pour something stronger. Make it a double."

Doc Swendsen strides into the house without knocking.

"Just heard the news," Swendsen says. "Came to help." He's mid-height and wiry, with oversized hands and feet. His face is pleasant enough, although he rarely smiles. His bottom teeth are rotten.

"There's been a dust up, Doc. You might say Ruby has done us all a favor here. Way I see it, Willie Fortune dead is worth more than he was ever worth alive. Give me a hand, will you?"

Ruby can't help noticing the physician's surgical kit. He won't need a bone hammer or Hey saw or tourniquet strap today. Heck, he won't even need a stethoscope.

Swendsen trips over the corner of a Persian rug as he passes through to the bedroom. He steadies himself on an overstuffed chair. Is he that clumsy? Or drinking already midday? His shirt is untucked in the back, his trousers worn. Ruby has never seen him without a hat and wonders if he's balding in the back. She's not all that sure he's a good doctor, but he's all Jericho's got.

"Sheldon?" Ruby asks. She tugs at the sleeve of his long black coat.

Sheldon turns toward her. "Ruby?"

"I need your advice."

"And?"

Ruby looks toward the bedroom. She lowers her voice. "Would rather not discuss it now with Doc here. Come by after supper?"

"No need to ask twice."

Fletcher crashes through the back door, Clayton just behind. In his arms, Clay carries Sam, limp as a dishrag. Tearstains run down Sam's dirty face; his eyes rimmed red as blood. Ruby gathers Sam in her arms and cradles him, whispering and sobbing, tears not for Willie, and certainly not for her, but for all her boys, most of all for him.

"WHERE DO I SIGN?" RUBY asks. She holds her pen tighter than a whip.

"Right here." Sheldon taps his fingers near a large X at the bottom of the document. "Brilliant, Ruby."

Ruby nods.

"With Willie's signature, a quarter of the Silver Tip Mine is yours."

"Can't say as I calculated it. But as soon as I saw Willie lying there, I knew I had to come up with something." Ruby taps the pen on the desk. "But I'm worried sick this won't seem legal. We weren't married in the proper sense, in a church or by a judge."

"In the eyes of the law, you were married as much as the next woman. Common law. Not legal in Arizona Territory, but who's to know. If you come from Colorado or Texas, common law is legal there and we have to recognize it here." Sheldon stands over Ruby. She can smell his aftershave. "Where did you and Willie hook up, anyway?"

"Texas. Week after my pop died. But it's just that . . ."

"Justice served, plain and simple. We didn't stay up all night writing this damn document for you to back out now. You took up with Willie Fortune in Texas. Lived with him how many years?"

"Twelve."

"And bore him four sons."

"Five."

"Five sons. And made him a fortune. I'll bet my last dollar he was nobody before he met you and your pop.

You made that man. And he bought the mine with your money, Ruby. Think about that."

Ruby nods. "Here's where I really need your help, Sheldon."

"There's more?"

"Without a will, I wouldn't get a nickel. But I can't bank it. That's where you come in."

Ruby dips the pen in the inkwell. *Steady, Ruby.* She signs with a large, flowery scrawl: Willard G. Fortune, Jr. If she hadn't signed his name so many times before, she might have stopped halfway, but she finishes with a flourish like it was her own legal signature. "There. Done." She shoves the will toward Sheldon. "I've got my boys to think about."

Sheldon waits for the ink to dry and holds the document up. "Good and legal now, Mrs. Fortune. I'm happy to bank it for you. Call it an arrangement of sorts."

"An arrangement?"

"Not what you're thinking, although the prospect is inviting."

"And how do I know I can trust you?"

Sheldon sits next to Ruby, their knees almost touching. "You can." He takes her hand. She doesn't draw it away.

"I don't have much choice," Ruby says. "Except hide it in my bureau drawer. Or under my mattress."

"You wouldn't be the first. But then you're prey to thieves. Or fire. You worked too long and hard for your capital to fall into the wrong hands. Or go up in smoke."

Ruby stands. She checks the clock on the mantel, 4:35 a.m. on what promises to be another blazing day in Jericho. "You better get moving on, Sheriff. Don't want anyone seeing you leave my place at this hour. I've got enough goddamn trouble heaped up in my soul to add any more to it."

"Best be wearing black for the next few weeks, Ruby. For appearance sake."

"I'd rather wear a party dress, and you know it."

"Don't make it worse."

"If you insist. Though I don't know how I'll stand it. I won't mourn that man for a minute."

Sheldon's voice is measured. "You know I'm right on this."

"Damn you, Sheldon. You're right on everything. Doesn't that get tiring?"

Sheldon stuffs a smile beneath his moustache.

"The black bombazine it is," Ruby says. "And a veil and a hanky. I can play the grieving widow. But why bother? I can hear them already, the wolves, all the old biddies, the preacher, not to mention those good-for-nothings at the mine. The whole town'll be talking before sunup." A sneer twists her lip. "You know I'm right on this. We women get the bad end of the stick every time, Sheldon. Every goddamn time."

That night, Ruby lights an oil lamp and settles on the davenport in the sitting room, a quilt wrapped around her legs and midsection. Divina has the boys overnight next door. Ruby watches shadows play on the ceiling and nurses a tall whiskey.

Sheldon, as promised, guards the porch. Every few minutes, he walks the length of the wooden veranda, a *clump clomp clump* of his boots on the floorboards. A halo of smoke wafts from his cigarette. He doesn't sit. A while later, he knocks on the door. "Everything alright?"

"As good as can be, I expect."

"'Night, Ruby."

"'Night, Sheldon."

Ruby changes into her nightclothes in the bedroom she shared with Willie Fortune. As she lifts the nightdress over her head, she tries not to look at the bed, now stripped to the mattress with a huge red stain bleeding down the side. She'll never sleep in that room again. She drops her clothes in a hamper and returns to the davenport, glad that Sheldon is only steps away. So far, there has not been any ruckus from Willie's mine partners. The funeral is tomorrow.

Will her plan hold up? Yes. It's foolproof; Sheldon said so himself. Ruby sips whiskey and her mind meanders.

Bang! Bangbangbang! Ruby wakes in a terror, her eyes wide. Has she nodded off? Where is Sheldon? She darts from the couch and crouches. The night is quiet as death. Her blood freezes. Is Sheldon bleeding out on the porch? And Willie's friends here for her now? Ruby shimmies along the floor, her stomach grazing the worn carpet. Where is her pistol? Is it still in her room? Or did Sheldon confiscate it? Ruby's heart booms in her chest. In a whiskey haze, she sees Sheldon still at his post, his back to her, smoking.

Was it a dream, then? *Slow, Ruby, slow, breathe.* She crawls back to the couch and burrows under the quilt. She reaches for the whiskey. *Relax, Ruby.* Sip. *On the plan.* Sip. *Stick to it.* Sip. *Wait a week, maybe two, no more. Borrow a horse. Ride up to the mine. Get your fair share, Willie be damned.* Sip. Sip. Sip.

In the meantime, a betting man could lay down his last dollar Ruby won't attend Willie's funeral tomorrow, although she'd like to see the bastard lowered into the ground. One can never be too sure.

IN ANY GIVEN WEEK, JERICHO sees dozens of new faces, some on wanted posters, some savvy enough to have eluded the law. This week, town is teeming with new ones, including newspapermen from Tucson, The Honorable John "Judge" Towson, and more than a few grifters who caught tail wind of the scandal. A husband-killer gets press.

Ruby sits on a hard bench in the anteroom of the sheriff's office while the judge and the sheriff confer inside Sheldon's office. Outside, a throng of newspapermen clamors for the verdict. Dog Webber, Jericho's own newshawk, is at the front of the pack.

Sweat drips down the neck of Ruby's black high-collared mourning dress. She has had too many occasions to wear it and hates it more each time. She looks and feels like an overstuffed fudge cake, frills and all. Why did she ever think those yards of bombazine look fashionable? Or comfortable? On any day of the week, Ruby would rather wear a split skirt, blouse, and vest and get on with it.

Ruby worries her hands over lace trim and shuffles her feet to get air moving under the long hem. It's been ten minutes and she's antsy already. A verdict in her favor and she'll walk free today. A conviction, and she'll find herself behind bars and who knows when she'll see her boys again. She fingers her collar.

Jimmy Bugg presses up to the window and Ruby's stomach hits the floor. Willie's mine partner is no friend of hers. Bugg sneers at Ruby and she turns her head away. She checks her pocket watch. It's been fifteen minutes now.

The door of Sheldon's office creaks open. Ruby has never been so glad to see him. His face reveals the decision and Ruby exhales. Has she been holding her breath all this time?

"No case, Ruby. Inquiry took less time than a man takes to dump." Sheldon reads from an official paper:

The shot fired by Mrs. Willard Fortune, Jr. was a clear case of self-defense and perfectly justified. She is exonerated from all blame in said matter.

"Signed Hon. John Towson, Jericho, A.T." Sheldon hands the document to Ruby and strides toward the door. "Wait here while I knock off this mob and then I'll see you home. Best that I take the porch again tonight. A day or two, this will all die down. Mark my words, a week from now, no one will miss Willie Fortune. It'll be front-page news of the *Courier-Journal*, you can be certain of that, but Willie'll be lucky if he even makes page eight of *The Tucson Citizen*. He was a nobody, Ruby."

SIX YEARS LATER
FEBRUARY 6, 1905
JERICHO, ARIZONA TERRITORY

Every Monday, after Charley Paulson's creaky wagon whisks away boarders, Ruby sets a fire under the giant iron kettle back behind the inn and pumps water from the well until her arms ache. Jericho rises up abruptly just past her hotel, and from there to the foothills it's as rough a town as any with a hodge-podge of dwellings built one atop the other, like they're on stilts. Any day, all of Jericho could tumble into a heap, and don't think Ruby hasn't thought about that.

Ruby ducks in and out of guest rooms and leaves doors wide open to air out the quarters. She strips beds and gathers up armloads of soiled bedding and towels for the week's washing. Road agents, miners, cowhands, and the odd drifter who has enough cash can book one of the spartan rooms on the first floor for a dollar a night or six for the week, meals included. No ladies—of any kind—are allowed in ground floor rooms. The sheets are messy enough as is.

"Wink!" Ruby calls to the older man she lets stay in the shed out back in exchange for help around the inn.

"Damn good lodgings," he says as he spreads his arms wide toward the Catalinas. He's not short, but not tall, with dirt in the creases around his eyes. Under the armpits, there are gaps in his coat. Where there might have been a remnant of a shirt that, too, is ripped, leaving a shock of grey hair between man and sky. "'Night's candles are burnt out and jocund day stands tiptoe on the misty mountain tops,'" Wink recites.

Must be Shakespeare, Ruby thinks. *Again.*

"*Romeo and Juliet.* Act 3, Scene 5," Wink says.

"And 'jocund' means?"

"Delightful. Like you, Miss Ruby."

Ruby snorts. "Not likely, Wink. I wager a thousand men from here to the River Styx would take issue with that. Mistress of heaven, I am not."

Wink steps toward Ruby, his clothes bordering on rank. The smell alone could fell an ox. But his boots gleam in the morning sun.

"Washing day?" he asks.

And could I wash yours, just once, Wink?

"Doesn't take a hawk to see you're needing some help around here, woman help, Miss Ruby." He gestures toward the washing. "And maybe raise your prices. I checked your rate sheet. You won't get rich on what you charge. And free liquor."

"Free whiskey is good for business, but, then again, it's not good for business. Some people can really put hooch away."

"If someone wants a whiskey bad enough, he can pony up another nickel per shot."

"I'll think on it, Wink." She watches the older man walk toward the town dump behind the sheriff's office. *Harmless old coot, but I sure like having you around.*

As the water warms, Ruby soaks dirtied bed sheets. She sweeps her hair into a low bun, yellow hair poking out every which way. She reties her apron and stokes flames under the rusty kettle. Using a long wooden paddle, Ruby raises linens, beats them, and dips them back into the soaking pot. Three times she does this. Just as the water boils, she swirls in lye soap and briskly stirs the laundry. Sweat drips from her brow. With the back of her sleeve, Ruby wipes perspiration and pushes hair away from her face. Yes, a laundress would be nice.

When Ruby opened the inn in 1900, she was twenty-seven. At thirty-two, she doesn't look much different, short and thin and blonde and flat-chested, although her arms are stronger now. She's making do at the inn, although there are always repairs.

Lists, lists, there are always lists, too. Between stirring and resting, Ruby makes mental notes. Tea, she needs. And sugar. The basics she can afford, nothing more. She takes a swig of tepid tea and throws the dregs onto the dirt. One by one, Ruby lifts heavy sheets from the soaking pot with the long paddle and transfers the sopping load to her cold tub. Twice she rinses the load before hanging sheets to dry on a line strung between the house and a metal pole staked into the ground behind the inn.

After bed linens, it's towels—heavier still—and today, the added burden of trying to salvage a pair of curtains that a guest mistook for what? A washcloth? If she had all week, Ruby could wait until tomorrow to tackle family laundry. But who has tomorrow? Dirty clothing mounds on the porch as Ruby empties the soaking pot and starts over with kettle after kettle of boiling water. In go undergarments and thin wash bodices, blouses and boys' shirts. Once the whites are finished, Ruby attacks skirts and trousers. By now, the soaking pot is a dark shade of brown and the cold tub just a shade lighter.

Ruby props up the sagging clothesline with a stick so hems of linens don't touch dirt. Peg up, count to a hundred, and underthings dry as your back is turned. Into baskets they go, a heap of them. Peg up, peel down, up, down, up, empty pant legs, flapping blouses, split skirts.

As the last of the laundry dries in the beating sun—*no rest for the weary*, Divina says—Ruby returns to guest rooms to dust furniture and scrub floors. From one of the second-floor rooms, Ruby spies Harvey Burton delivering her weekly supplies. He bounds up the back stoop into the kitchen. Ruby stops and throws her dirty rag into a wash bucket and goes to the kitchen to get perishables put away. She nearly collides with Burton as he rounds the corner out of Ruby's bedroom, his hands stuffed into his pockets.

"What the hell?" Ruby asks. "What were you doing in my bedroom?"

"I was no more in your bedroom than you've been in mine. Didn't get tea in this week and thought you'd want to know. Was looking for you, is all."

"No tea?"

"You heard me."

Ruby hastens to put away anything that might spoil and leaves tin cans, glass bottles, and sealed boxes on the counter until later.

It only took one meeting to dislike Harvey Burton when he and his wife, Mae, first came to Jericho. Ruby had been poring over the generous shelves at Burton's General Store when Harvey asked if "the little lady" needed any assistance. Ruby is long past tired of being called that. Yes, she's short, petite, blonde, no fault of her own. But there's no shred of "lady" in her, never has been. Every time someone calls her "the little lady," her hackles go up.

Ruby's not that fond of Mae, either, for an entirely different reason. Mae gave Virgil the side eye the first time she met him, and Ruby hasn't forgotten, or forgiven. Virgil can't help that he has a significant limp. But with only one general store in town, an innkeeper can't be making enemies. No one said they had to be friends.

When the linens are crisp and dry, Ruby retraces her steps through the roadhouse, arms laden, and remakes all the beds. She nestles her nose into freshly laundered linens and inhales the echo of sunshine. Last, Ruby heads into the small bedroom off the roomy parlor where her boys sleep on two bunks squeezed into a space once used as a storage closet. She tucks fresh sheets on top of tick mattresses and layers two thin blankets on top. By the time she's done, she's wicked thirsty.

Ruby goes through a set of double doors off the parlor into the communal dining room, the heart of the roadhouse. Every night, the table is full and noisy, with enough food to feed Jericho twice over. Mismatched chairs scrape up the table, come one, come all. Ruby never turns anyone away.

The kitchen is at the back end of the hotel, and in it, a six-hole cast iron stove, complete with firebox, hot water reservoir, baking oven, warming pit. The cookware closet overflows, tin ware stacked on shelves, hung on hooks. On the counter, there's an oversized sink with a window overlooking the Santa Catalinas. Smack in the center of the room, a large table, and, just beyond, a squeaking screen door that opens to a weathered porch and patchy garden where Ruby grows potatoes, lettuces, beans, and melons. The root cellar, bathhouse, and outhouse are adjacent to the back of the inn, with a rough shed out at the back of the lot where Wink sleeps off most nights surrounded by old tools and dust motes and a braided horsehair lasso he swears keeps snakes away.

Ruby gulps a glass of tepid water that tastes faintly of dirt. She slathers a slice of sourdough with butter and rummages for the saltcellar—damn if she forgot to add salt to her grocery list. Ruby stands with her back against the dry sink and gnaws the heel of bread. After sloshing down another half-glass of water, Ruby walks the short block to Burton's General Store to buy salt. Hopefully, they haven't run out of that.

Ruby strides past shelves of dry goods, groceries, sundries, and tobacco. Two steps ahead of the matron behind her, Ruby grabs the last 10-lb. bag of salt and mutters a prayer of relief. If she had wanted produce today, she would have been sorely out of luck.

Later in the afternoon, Ruby cracks an egg inside the lip of a small blue enamel bowl with one hand and whisks it smooth. She sets it aside and mixes flour and water and lard and a hefty pinch of salt in another bowl and rolls out the crust for two pies. Out comes the pastry brush to slather egg mixture on the fluted crusts. A cockroach scuttles across the countertop and she swats it with the end of her dishtowel. As she pulls the oven door open, Ruby scorches her fingertips. Big Sue used to put hot embers on her fingertips and pour water over them to draw out the heat. Ruby plunges her fingers into the vat of lard instead to take the heat out and sucks on her fingers as she closes the oven door with her hip.

From the corner of her eye, Ruby watches Sam play in the dirt outside the open kitchen door. He is never far from the dog. He throws a stick over and over and pats Roger every time the pup retrieves it. When Sam leans down toward Roger's ear, Ruby wonders if Sam talks to him. Sam hasn't said a word aloud to anyone for six years now, not since Ruby shot his pa.

Ruby half-heartedly flips through a magazine as she watches Sam. When she calls Sam in for supper, he's dirty in all the boy crevices, so she has him strip down and dumps a bucket of water over his head on the back stoop, nearly naked. Roger gets a dousing, too.

A new houseful will arrive tomorrow, and after that, Ruby is in for another week of hard work, up at five to get coffee on and bake biscuits, and then fry potatoes, eggs, and bacon. Breakfast bell's at eight, and after the washing up, bake six loaves of bread and begin the makings for dinner, served at noon sharp. After boiled beef, turnips, beans, or whatever's on the menu that day, there's always pie. Then it's the long run up to cold supper: cold meats, hash, bread and butter, more pie.

That's the only slice of time Ruby has to herself, the mid-afternoon. She clears her mind with brisk walks. There are plenty of hills in Jericho and plenty of proverbial hills muddling her mind: never enough cash for upkeep, never enough help to do it all. And no time for anything else. It all grates on her, as if she's a potato under the knife and all that's left is a lumpy, sallow bulge waiting for the boiling pot.

Ruby will take it up with Divina; she's as good as a real mother and her words are always spot on. Other than Divina, Ruby doesn't have a close friend in Jericho, except for Sheldon, but Ruby can't risk encouraging him. Dog Webber has it out for her, doesn't he? Or does he have it out for everyone in Jericho? Enough of what goes on at Ruby's hotel finds its way into the *Courier-Journal*. So no, not him. The doctor? Too private. A tavern owner? No, although her pop did say they were good listeners. Forget about talking to Mae Burton. And not the new parson's wife; she looks like a frightened child. The schoolmistress? That one seems like a clamped book, even if she is one of the only other women in town who isn't married or shares a bed for a living. *But I* could *use a friend . . .*

Ruby pulls up a stool to the worn kitchen table and scribbles out a quick postcard instead. She owes Vi a letter—a long letter—but a postcard will have to serve tonight. Other than Divina, Vi is Ruby's only thread to Big Burl. Ruby was born at Vi's boarding house in Tucson after all, and it's there that her momma bled to death after her birth. Vi is the only person Ruby can think of to ask.

Vi—

I'm needing help bad here at the inn. Got any girls in the family way? Can't promise more than room and board. Don't worry, I'd send the girl back, after. Leave all the other details to me.

—Ruby

After a quick cold supper, Ruby checks guest rooms for the last time before tomorrow's guests arrive. She straightens bed linens, plumps up pillows, tosses a blanket over the crest rail of a high-back chair. She runs her fingers over the lace on the bedstead and centers the washbasin. She pulls back curtains, secures them behind a hook, and moves on to the next room.

Before bed, Ruby checks on Wink out in the shed. Tonight, he's snoring atop a burlap sack, his hat over his head. He didn't come to claim his plate after supper. Maybe whiskey was dinner. Is the man ever sober? Ruby doubts it. Crazy as popcorn on a hot skillet, people call him. But they should know better. In the end, it's the poets who have the most to say. What you've got to do is peel away the surface, ask the real questions. What do they want? What do they need? Who do they love, and why? What else matters, in the end?

FEBRUARY 7, 1905
JERICHO, ARIZONA TERRITORY

Come morning, Wink shuffles toward Ruby, his gait uneven. His dark felt hat is askew, a soiled brown grosgrain ribbon circling the crown and a wide brim shading his always-whiskered face. He puts down his rucksack and pulls a shiny pocket watch from his grimy vest. "Morning, Miss Ruby. Young Sam."

Ruby stands on the porch and taps her red boot upside down against the stoop to check for scorpions. You get one in your boot and you're done for. "Whatcha find today?"

"This and that." He rummages in his rucksack and pulls out a few pieces of broken pottery. "Apache, maybe. And look here." Wink reaches into the bag again and holds up a pair of men's trousers.

"No ladies' duds? Damn it."

Wink laughs. "Not today, Miss Ruby."

"Better luck next time. Care to come to supper? I've got a full house tonight, but I'm making your favorite, liver and onions."

"That'd be mighty fine, Miss Ruby."

"Six sharp. Maybe in those trousers. And," she adds carefully, "why don't you use the bath while you're at it? I'll fill the tub out back for you at five, if you like." Ruby cocks her head toward the shack adjacent to the roadhouse that houses a six-foot claw foot bathtub. At just over five feet, Ruby can stretch out full length in it. Men, as a rule, aren't as lucky.

"Mighty obliged. No school today, Sam?"

Sam shakes his head.

"Closed today," Ruby says. "Miss Stern sent word. There was a dust up in the school yard last night."

"What the devil?"

"Sheriff's looking into it. Found a dead chicken on the front stoop. Made a right mess of it, too."

"Well, if that doesn't cap all," Wink says. "I wonder what this world is coming to."

"My money's on a slighted suitor. The schoolmarm isn't exactly—what was the word?—jocund."

Wink tips his hat. Sunlight peeks though a bullet hole in the crown. "Until five then, Miss Ruby. There's a bottle with my name on it to keep me company 'til then."

"We're off, Sam," Ruby says. "See if anyone misses us." She stamps her boots. "C'mon, Roger, that's a good boy." The dog scampers up.

Sam scuffles on the hardpan next to his mother, his dirty hand swinging close to Ruby's calloused one, but not touching. Sam comes up to Ruby's chest, skinny and big feet, like Willie and all Ruby's boys. She ruffles his long blond hair. He'll be needing a trim soon. Roger tags along, his tongue lolling.

The midwinter sky is cloudless, no hint of rain. It's near seventy degrees in February. A thin breeze rustles through dry mesquite and desert broom as Ruby and Sam

head up the foothills toward the natural pools near the old
Esperanza Mine. Most of the mines in the Santa Catalina
mining district went belly-up in the early aughts, although
Silver Tip is still a going concern. *Maybe because there's more
going on up there than meets the eye.* Sun stabs Ruby's eyes. She
stops and squints. For as far as she can see, saguaro punch
the sky, gnarled arms raised in praise.

"That cactus there? The tall one with the arms?"

Sam nods.

"Apaches think saguaro are dead relatives come back
to life. Don't know if that's true or not."

Sam screws up his face like a true skeptic.

"Why the face? If you can't trust your momma, there's
no one on this earth you can trust."

*I don't doubt that they're our ancestors, but hell if I'll ever say
that aloud.*

"See that big one over there? The one with six arms? If
I reckon right, he'd be more than a hundred by now. They
don't even start to grow arms until they're sixty."

Sam kneels in mica-flecked earth and paws the dirt.
Ruby kicks at brush to check for snakes, although most
of them should be in hibernation now. She sits on a flat-
topped boulder and takes a swig from her canteen. Roger
finds a slice of shade and curls up beside the huge rock.
Ruby reaches down to pat Roger's coat and pours a dribble
into the pup's mouth. Most of it leeches into the desert
and disappears as fast as it hits the ground. A quick flash
of light mirrors off a piece of broken glass. Ruby bends to
pick it up and puts it in her pocket. Drips of perspiration
run down her cheeks and land in her mouth. What she'd
do to be sitting by that lake, the one in Colorado, the one
her pop said was as large as a sea.

Sam swipes long hair away from his shoulders and
shades brown eyes with his big-knuckled hand. He continues

to scrape through rubble and uncovers a shard of pottery. He extracts it, examines it, and puts it in his pocket.

"Bet you'll get a nickel for that one," Ruby says.

Sam collects nickels thanks to Wink, who buys treasures from him and sells them at the livery. Sam will be rich someday, at this rate. On Fridays, Sam takes one nickel to Burton's General Store and treats himself to Cracker Jack or a Tootsie Roll, sometimes a Coca-Cola. And one time, a postcard, because he liked the picture on the front, of the Statue of Liberty.

In his room—the one he shares with brothers Virgil and Fletcher—he lines his nickels on the bed rail against the wall. When Ruby peeks in on Sam at night (*does Fletcher make those strange noises under his blanket every night?*), she sees Sam finger all the coins he's gotten from Indian treasures.

The history of Arizona Territory is long, or short, depending on who's telling. If you're Apache or O'odham or Yaqui, you've ranged this arid terrain since the beginning of time, hunting for game and struggling to coax lentils, onions, and *garvanzas* from barren soil. Your peoples have bled and died for every reason under the sun, including at the unlucky end of a gun. If you made it out alive, you and your kinfolk are all on reserves now, thanks to the U.S. Army.

The way the U.S. Army spins it, the "Indian Problem" in Arizona Territory was short work as they trespassed on traditional lands. But, try as they did, the army failed to tame the landscape, leaving tailings of their efforts half built and lots of dead Indians behind. Fort after fort is abandoned now like old playthings: Bowie, Lowell, Rucker, Grant.

There's much Ruby will need to tell Sam about the Indian troubles. But not yet.

"Up we go, Sam."

Ruby and Sam keep to the trail southeast of Jericho toward the natural pools higher up at the mouth of the canyon. Sam ambles along behind and stoops to pick up other treasures that he shoves in his bulging pockets. They cross a damp creek bed as they gain altitude. Ocotillo arms make gnarly shadows over the streambeds, as if they're seeking water, too.

You'd never guess there'd be a whiff of water in this dry, broken country. For nine months of the year, streams in the flat *bajada* run parched, rivers, even, San Pedro, Rilitto, Santa Cruz. Three months of the year, and again during summer monsoons, a trickle makes way for a bona fide creek, and *arroyos* rush with water.

When they reach the head of the canyon, mountain water wells up in small rock-walled pools, filling inch by inch with tepid water warmed by the sun.

"Next month, Sam, we'll be swimming."

From an indeterminate distance, a gunshot cracks. Sam stiffens. Ruby's hand instinctively goes to her pistol. She spins around. Boulders line the pools in every direction. If someone were after them there, Sam and Ruby would be cornered. Ruby can't see who fired the round or from where. She scampers up a boulder and shades her eyes. "Nothing to worry about, kid. Not this time." She signs "n" and "o" in the new sign language she's learning from an old *Ladies Home Journal* that a guest left behind, a fist with thumb tucked between third and fourth fingers for the "n" and an open fist with a hole for the "o."

Sam relaxes his shoulders. He nods. Still he hasn't picked up any of the sign language, or, if he has, he isn't using it. *If only he would.*

Ruby stands with her feet apart on the scalded earth, her hands at her hips. "You should've seen me, Sam, not much older than you, in a fringe skirt and vest. I worked my way up from sheep roper to barrel rider to lady sharp-shooter, best job in the outfit. They started me on bottles first, and then other targets—apples from a dog's head, that sort of thing. By the time I was Virgil's age, earlier even, twelve or thirteen, I reckon, I was the center stage event before the second intermission, wing shooting from horseback. *Ranchero* style." Ruby spins and mimics shooting multiple targets. "What I could have done with six arms, like that old saguaro back there." She mimics shooting, *ka-boom*.

Sam face darkens.

Ruby inhales sharply, slapped back by the image of Sam in the doorway when she shot Willie. "Damn it. Not again. I am so sorry, Sam." She reaches for him and squats to his eye level. "You don't know how sore I am you had to see it." She signs "sorry," a fist at her chest rotated twice clockwise.

Sam pulls away and turns back toward Jericho.

"Sam?"

The boy keeps walking, shuffling over dirt and sagebrush and burnt stubs of grass clotted together. Ruby crumbles inside. Again. She can't change the fact Sam witnessed his father's death. She can wish the story different, but it's always the same, with Sam at the doorframe, terrified.

Ruby mops her forehead with a handkerchief. Her drawers are damp and her armpits stink. By now, the sun is deep onto the day. She's got to get back soon to run the tub for Wink and get supper on. Twelve tonight, plus Wink, makes thirteen. She can always squeeze in one more chair. Ruby banks on Wink cleaning up nicely, although it's a crapshoot. Will he remember to soap up? Shave?

Ruby stops and shades her eyes. "Hold up, Sam." Ruby catches up with Sam and walks beside him, not looking at him. She drapes her arm around Sam's thin shoulders. A heavy silence sags between them. Ruby smells her own sweat mingled with Sam's.

"Gotta love this place. But it does have its disadvantages." Ruby shakes her now-empty canteen. A roadrunner lopes by. She watches as it runs, right left right, scampering through desert brush with purpose.

"Did you know in New York City they've got water coming out of faucets now?" she asks. "Faucets! We're lucky to have well water that tastes like, well, you know. You would think God Almighty might send just an inch of rain here every afternoon as an offering. But no." She signs "n" and "o" again. *Please, Sam, please work with me here.* "Sometimes I swear He's forgotten this place."

Ruby wipes sweat away again with the back of her sleeve. "And then there's this heat. In New York City, the mercury rarely tops ninety. Ninety! Even in summer. But who would want to live in a city when they've got all this?" Ruby sweeps her arms around. "Can't catch a rabbit there, or see the stars. Can't soak in desert pools or pick nuggets off the ground."

Ruby laughs. "Do I sound like I'm all puffed up about this place? Well, maybe I am. Don't let anyone tell you Jericho isn't the best place for a body, this side of Hell, anyway, Sam. Just breathe in that air. It's good for whatever ails you. Try to find a better place to live. I dare you."

Sam shrugs Ruby off again and resumes his course back toward Jericho, Roger lapping at his heels. Ruby strides to keep up with them. *Damn these short legs.* Other than the calls of desert thrashers, mother and son walk in silence. Twin dust devils rise a hundred yards ahead as the sunburnt adobes of Jericho come into view. Twice Jericho has burned—once when Ruby was a little girl, and another time when, blessedly, she was away on the traveling circuit with Willie. Brick and stucco have replaced wood, for those who could afford it. Most of the buildings now are squat, except for the church and the roadhouse that rise above the desert floor like sentinels. Both are still wood.

As they round the yard behind Jericho Inn, Ruby heads to the pump. "Here, Sam. Douse your head."

He fumbles with his hand, trying to make the sign for "n" and "o" and then tucks his dirty hands behind his back.

"Take all the time you need, Sam. I'll bet every last nugget up at the Silver Tip Mine that you'll pick up this sign language right quick. And when the time is right, you'll find that voice of yours again, but not a second before."

15

FEBRUARY 8, 1905
JERICHO, ARIZONA TERRITORY

"Miss Stern?"

The schoolteacher stops, her back straight. She has a half-foot on Ruby, but is equally thin. She lowers her pointed nose into her handkerchief and coughs. "Mrs. Fortune?"

"Ruby, please." Ruby moves closer, maybe too close.

Margaret Stern steps back. Her black hair is pulled back into a severe bun.

"Any more trouble up at the schoolhouse?"

The schoolteacher shakes her head and clips off her one-word answer. "No."

An old mule-drawn wagon advances on the women. Dust swirls around the mules' feet and with each step a larger cloud kicks up. As the rig gets closer, the women move quickly to the side of Jefferson Street to avoid choking on more dirt than necessary. Old Judd, the driver, steers the mules a tad too close to the women for comfort, enveloping them in dirt and dust and debris.

"Watch it, Judd!" Ruby yells.

"Sorry, ladies," he barks. He continues down the street in a rush of brown and veers into the alley next to the livery.

"He's not sorry," Ruby says.

"That's harsh, Mrs. Fortune."

"I've been called every name in the book, Miss Stern. 'Harsh' is the least of my worries. Judd's not the nicest fella on the block."

Margaret looks past Ruby, as if she would rather be anywhere else than on a dusty street in Arizona Territory talking to a much-maligned innkeeper.

Ruby presses on. There must be a way to have a conversation with this woman. As she gropes for an opening, Sam comes from behind and shies up to Ruby. He shields his face from Miss Stern and dangles his readers from a strap. He hoists his lunch pail from one arm to the other. Ruby tousles his blond head.

"Virgil has been offered a position at the post office," Ruby says. "Just two months before he was set to graduate."

Miss Stern nods. "Now, that's a most promising career for a boy like Virgil. I'm afraid he doesn't have many choices. As for Sam here, he does quite well, under the circumstances."

"What do you mean, 'under the circumstances?' Sam doesn't talk, is all."

"And what would you call that, then? Not talking?"

"He's not mute, Miss Stern. He was learning to talk when . . ."

"Please don't talk of such indelicate matters, Mrs. Fortune. Sam tries to keep up with his peers, and that's admirable. We can't have too many expectations from feeble-minded children."

"Sam is not feeble-minded!" Ruby struggles not to raise her voice. "He's as normal as any boy. And, I might add, he is learning that new American Sign Language. Have you read of it?"

"For the deaf and dumb?"

"You might rethink that phrasing, Miss Stern."

Wink shuffles by, tips his hat. A riff of dirt cascades off the brim. "Morning, ladies. 'All that glisters is not gold.' That's from . . ."

"Morning, Wink," Ruby interrupts.

"My pleasure, Miss Ruby. And how's my partner?" He bends to Sam's eye level. "After school?" he asks.

Sam nods.

"Sam here is a clever boy," Wink continues. "We understand one another just fine, don't we? Who needs words?" The older man winks at the young boy and tips his beribboned hat. "Miss Ruby. Miss Stern. And young Sam." He ambles across the road toward the livery.

"See you at supper?" Ruby yells.

"Must you yell?" Miss Stern asks.

Old Judd rounds the corner from the alley.

"Bastard!" Ruby barks at him.

Margaret Stern stiffens. "That's no talk for a boy to hear."

Ruby snorts. "That's tame, Miss Stern. Everyday talk in traveling shows."

"I wouldn't know," Margaret replies.

"Well, you don't know what you're missing." Ruby smiles. "The horses, the trick riders, the sharpshooters, all of it. Makes a body all tingly thinking about it . . ."

Margaret clicks her pocket watch shut. "Come along now, Sam. Time for school. Good day, Mrs. Fortune."

Ruby pecks Sam on the cheek and he blushes. She signs "I love you," her thumb, pointer finger, and pinky up and third and fourth fingers down, in a subtle wave.

As Ruby crosses Jefferson, Wink stumbles on the road in front of the livery. Two men accost him as he scrambles to stand. One kicks dirt into his eyes as the other lunges for Wink's pockets.

"Mercy!" Ruby rushes across the street, dodging another set of wagons. "Wink!"

"Hand it over, you old swillpot," one of the roughs says. "We know your pockets are full."

"Take this." The other man kicks Wink in the mid-section just as he has regained his footing. Wink goes down again. "Old man not worth a shit."

Ruby muscles her way through the gathered crowd. "Piss off! Both of you!" The men back away. She kneels next to Wink. "You alright?"

Tom Tillis bursts out the front of the livery. "Get off my property," he yells after the ruffians. "And don't come back."

The roughs slink away as the throng dissipates. Tillis strides to where Wink crouches on the ground. Wink shakes off dirt and attempts to rise again. Ruby holds his elbow to steady him and Tillis helps him stand.

"Mighty obliged, Miss Ruby, Tom."

"Can you make it back to the inn?" Ruby asks. "I'll be back in a minute."

Wink nods. He holds his side as he shuffles across Jefferson.

Ruby turns to the livery owner. "Got my order in?" She checks back over her shoulder to see if Wink is getting along.

Tillis slides open the livery door. "After you, Miz Fortune."

The way he says it, Ruby hears "misfortune."

It's a *jingle jangle* of noise as soon as they enter the livery. Ruby's eyes adjust to the darkness. Tools. A clutter of machinery. Shadows of tack, and the warm, leathery smell of saddles, harnesses, reins. Ruby breathes in sweet smells of hay, oil, wood, and manure. In the distance, she hears a man yelling. A loud thud. A horse whinnies its displeasure.

"Be right back." Tom Tillis wipes greasy hands on a tired rag.

Ruby has never heard Tom Tillis string more than two or three words together. She waits at the grimy counter and peers around the muddle of tack and tools to the rear of the establishment, where Tom has disappeared. There's talk that Tillis runs cheap liquor through the livery, and illegal cock fights Sunday nights. Boxing matches, too, on holidays. There's always a steady stream of customers, Wink first among them.

Tillis reappears from the back of the building with a jug of kerosene. "Anything else, Miz Fortune?"

"Got any whiskey?"

"Freighter comes in day after tomorrow," Tillis says.

Did Tom Tillis just utter a full sentence? *Maybe*, Ruby thinks, *you've just got to get a man going on a subject he's interested in before the dam breaks loose. Liquor is a good start.* And if Ruby can save money on whiskey, why not? Less for Harvey and Mae Burton's coffers at the general store.

"Can't miss a freighter," Ruby says. "I don't know why the dead aren't raised when wagons that size come through town, all those mules raising a ruckus."

Ruby hefts the kerosene and hastens back to Jericho Inn. No sign of Wink, probably headed to Judd's by now. As she enters the kitchen, she sees the hind end of Harvey Burton heading back to his store next door. Her weekly delivery is stacked on the kitchen table: flour, sugar, potatoes, lard. Pickles, tinned meats, coffee, raisins. A receipt, to add to a growing stack of them. And milk, sweating in this morning heat.

Ice is another matter. Now, wouldn't that be something. An icebox in Jericho. Meat wouldn't turn green before cooking and milk could last more than a day. Old Judd keeps beer cool with wet gunnysacks and sawdust. Burton does the same for dairy products. Ruby's lucky her milk doesn't sour, but when you have a houseful of boys, there's no threat of that happening. She's lucky if her supply lasts a day. Ruby places the milk jug in a dark cupboard and covers it with a cool towel. The tea she steeped this morning is cooling on the kitchen counter, if you call a sultry eighty degrees cool. Ruby pours a generous mugful and sits at the table. With enough sugar in it, it's almost as good as laudanum. Almost. Better than anything she's ever known is the few hours she steals away with The Preacher, once a month, at the full moon. That's when the miners come to town to spend their wad, wallet and otherwise.

The day The Preacher showed up at her back door back in '04 was like lightning hit. A jolt passed through Ruby's body so urgently she thought she was having a fit. Her groin was on fire before he said his first word, that kind face with eyes that bored right through her and a smile as wide as piano.

"CAN I BOTHER YOU for a cup of water?"

Ruby turned to see a large dark-skinned man at the kitchen door. She dried her hands on her apron. "Of course, wait there."

Ruby poured a large glass of water from a pitcher and opened the screen. "Here you go, Mr. . ."

"Go by The Preacher," the man said, as he took the glass from Ruby and swallowed it in one long gulp. He wiped his mouth with the back of his sleeve, his bulky forearm tensing. "I'm mighty obliged, ma'am."

Ruby stood rooted in the doorway. Now this was a damn fine-looking man, even if he could use a bath. She pictured him naked in her bathhouse, his arms, his legs, his torso, his . . .

"You wouldn't be hungry, too?" she asked. Ruby was viscerally hungry for something else. *How can I make him stay?*

The man stammered. "Why, that's awfully kind of you, ma'am. It has been awhile since my last meal. But I couldn't impose on you."

Of all the doors in Jericho, why hers? *Oh, hell, Ruby, don't ask questions. Just talk.*

"Oh, hell about imposing. Sit here and I'll make a plate up." Ruby took the last of the supper fixings, the ones she usually reserved for Wink, and heaped on a slice of Ruby Pie. She balanced the plate as she re-opened the screen door. The man had not yet sat. She handed it to the stranger, their fingers brushing. Ruby's drawers were clammy.

"Please, sit."

The stranger ate quietly, murmuring *mmm-hmm, yes, ma'am, mmm-hmm.* Ruby stood in the doorway, watching the sky bleed red.

When the man finished, he stood again. "What's a woman making the best damn pie in all creation doing in a town like this?" He proffered the plate, and their fingers brushed again.

"That's a long story, Preacher Man."

"Know of any work around here?"

"The Silver Tip is always hiring." Ruby craned her neck toward the Santa Catalinas. "Good wages, too."

"I'd stay in this town just for another slice of that pie."

Ruby touched the man's sleeve. "You come back anytime. I've always got pie."

The Preacher is all Ruby can think about most days, and every night, too, as she settles into her narrow bed alone. If only he were here, his hands, his hair, his face, that sweet mole on his cheek, those long, strong, stocky legs around her. Two weeks, he'll knock at her window, three raps followed by one loud one. Ruby has the date circled in red on her calendar.

The first night they squirreled in Ruby's room was all her doing. It was the third time The Preacher had come for pie on a miner's holiday. That night, even before The Preacher had time to ask, Ruby yanked him into the kitchen and kissed him. Without a word, she led him to her bedroom and closed the door. He stood without moving as Ruby unbuttoned her blouse. She let slip to the floor her blouse and camisole, and stood before him naked from the waist up. She then slipped off her skirt and undid the drawstring on her bloomers. Still he did not move.

"I don't know if I can do this, ma'am."

"You damn well can. And will." Ruby took The Preacher's large hand and put it to her breast.

"I never . . ."

"Shush up." Ruby didn't break eye contact as she undressed the man and led him to her bed, and there they made love in the wild creases of the night.

They nestled in silence until Ruby broke the spell. She reached toward The Preacher's kind face and held his cheek in the cup of her hand. "How did you come by the name Preacher, anyhow?"

The Preacher ran his fingers through Ruby's hair. "Maybe eight I was when my pap first called me that." He cocked his head for a second. "Maybe earlier. Mam, too, and then all the others, and after awhile, I hardly knew my own name."

"Which is?"

"Percival George Washington, Jr."

"That's a mouthful."

"Don't I know it. But ask me about Scripture." He shifted to cradle Ruby. "I bet you won't stump me."

"List the Ten Commandments."

"In order? 'I am the Lord Thy God, Thou shalt have no other gods before me; Thou shalt not make unto thee any graven image; Thou shalt not take the name of the Lord Thy God in vain . . .'"

"Well, I broke that one a long time ago."

"Don't you know your Scripture, Ruby?"

"Never had much use for it. Seems God Himself dealt me a rotten hand."

"Like no husband?"

"Oh, I had a husband alright. Bad blood, that one. Lied like a dog. Swindled his partners. Sold opium under cover. Knocked me senseless more times than I can count. Worse thing, though, is he whupped my boys." Ruby tensed. "Not just whupped them. Beat them senseless. Maybe Clayton and even Fletcher deserved the belt, but Virgil? Sam? In the end, that's what made me do it, Willie thrashing Sam."

"Did what?"

Ruby disentangled herself and propped her head with her hand. She faced The Preacher, hair and sheets disheveled. "I killed him."

Percival George Washington, Jr. whistled. "Well, I'll be damned."

"You ever do anything you aren't proud of, Preacher Man?"

"Ah, Ruby Girl, that's a question no man can answer in the negative."

Ruby burrowed her nose into The Preacher's chest and inhaled his warm, musky smell.

"Want to tell me more?" he asked.

"Everything. And nothing."

"Can't order you to tell me. But I'm listening."

They talked until dawn, and would have talked longer, but Ruby knew from the start if he was found with her, he'd be strung up in a minute, so she bundled him out the back door before anyone else awoke. When he comes to town now, The Preacher stays put in Ruby's room with the door fastened shut and curtains drawn closed. Ruby comes to him after the washing up is done, long after the sky shifts from orange to salmon to amethyst to grey, chameleon-like. The risk is worth it, loving this fine, the likes Ruby has never known, tender and tough rolled into one, and closest to heaven she'll ever come and she knows it.

RUBY REFILLS HER MUG AND nudges open the front door. Tonight, brewing clouds. Slanting rain. Chance of snow, even. The mercury has plummeted. And now a raging stream has turned Jefferson Street into a gully washer caroming toward the coach road. Stray dogs disappear down side streets like thieves. Even though it's not the worst that Ruby's seen, it's foolhardy to attempt to cross Jefferson during a flash flood. Animals, grown men even, have been swept to their deaths in the trying of it.

The only person out tonight is Dog Webber, editor of the *Courier-Journal*. Webber picks his way across the side street, his trousers wet to the calf and a hand on his hat. He's quick and wiry, not tall, but fast. He disappears into Judd's Tavern, his second home.

Webber's *Courier-Journal* was one of the first newspapers in Arizona Territory to feature photographs to accompany news stories. Maverick, that newspaperman. And sharp as a whip. Some say Dog was reared by wild animals, that's how he got his name. Others say he came from Kentucky after killing a man. It's not a fragile country, the farther west you go. Everyone's got a story. Story is he sold *The Wickenburg Miner* for pennies on the dollar back in '93 after a nasty dustup. Seems someone didn't like an editorial he wrote about ex-slaves having rights like the common man and Webber got out of town faster than a cat with his tail afire instead of staring down a worse fate. What he got was Jericho, which he calls "Hellicho."

Ruby sits in a rocker on the wide front porch of Jericho Inn, the mutt Roger at her feet. The rain hasn't abated at all. She scrapes her plate, the last crumbs of piecrust caught up with her fingers. She pets Roger and he licks her hand clean. She could exist on pie. Big Sue could attest to that, Ruby showing up every night for second helpings when the carnival traveled through the Colorado and Texas and the desert southwest, eighteen wagons rolling on toward the next nickel. Her tummy used to protrude over her skirt, like her lip would do, especially when she was mad, which was more often than a scorpion stings. She has tried to tamp down her anger over the years, but oh boy can it rear up in a hurry.

Ruby's still got a sweet tooth, too, but you'd never know it from the looks of her. Weighs a hundred pounds with clothes on, slip of a thing. She's famous for her Ruby Pie, although it's never the same pie twice, a mixture of nuts and currants and dried fruit mixed up with enough brown sugar your teeth could rot.

After President Roosevelt raved about it in '03 on one of his swings through the western territories, Dog Webber asked for the recipe and aimed to print it in the *Courier-Journal*. But Ruby thought better of it, seeing as she never knows how it will turn out. Too much brown sugar, the filling is grainy. No currants? Not as tart. Stove too hot, you're going to have a burnt crust once in a while.

For three days and two nights, Jericho treated the president like American royalty. Tom Tillis pulled out all the stops, outfitted his best buggy, and took the president all over the mining district himself, at no charge.

Rumors ran wild about why Roosevelt was in town. No one came to Jericho without good reason, and more times than not, it wasn't for polite conversation. Truth is, at the height of the rush, there was nowhere else in hundreds of miles with opportunity quite like Arizona Territory's Catalina Mining District. Gold, silver, copper, and every color, shape, and size of hard rock gems in between. Ruby knew exactly why the president had come calling, even if the papers painted it differently. The lure was just too great. Like a woman, but with hard edges.

Roosevelt called Jericho "swimming," although Ruby thought that an odd moniker for a place dry as a desert. What pleased her most was Roosevelt asked for an extra slice of her pie. "The best I've ever tasted," he said, as he proffered his plate. Who's to argue with someone who's been to the far corners of the earth? Europe, Egypt, the Holy Land, Cuba? Roosevelt could have stayed in Oracle where Buffalo Bill Cody stays when he's in town, but there was the President of the United States in goddamn Jericho asking for a second slice of Ruby Pie.

"So how can you be sure it will turn out, if you don't have a recipe?" Dog asked.

"My secret," Ruby said. "Not in the habit of using recipes anyhow, Dog. Except special ones, Divina's Lemon Tarts, Big Sue's Indian Pudding, ones I've clipped out of magazines. I just use what I've got, nothing more, nothing less. And hope every time that it turns out."

Ruby copied out the recipe for Roosevelt in her neat hand, sweeps of letters and fancy curlicues in the right places. Roosevelt said he'd have the chefs at The White House make it for him—*every night*, he said—and Ruby swelled at the saying of it.

"Though it won't be half as good as eating it right here in Jericho," Roosevelt said. "Which is why I'll be back." He pocketed the recipe and tapped his chest pocket.

RUBY PIE

2-1/2 c. shelled pecans or other
nuts, currants, and dried fruit
5 T. melted butter
1½ c. brown sugar
1 T. flour
2 t. vanilla
½ t. salt
3 large eggs, whisked

Set pecans over warm piecrust. Whisk melted butter,
brown sugar, and flour until thick. Add vanilla, salt,
and eggs. Pour over nuts. Bake until golden and bubbly.
Serve warm or cold.

Ruby hasn't shared the recipe since, not even to Dog Webber. Over the years, it's become one of her best weapons. Keeps travelers coming back. Which means she can get to needed repairs, one pie at a time.

First up is re-drilling the well. Bad water Ruby can disguise with lemons. But the dirty dishwater she's pulling of late is downright unpalatable and lemons scarce. Ten feet down she might need to go, maybe twelve. It's a crapshoot finding water in the desert. So what if it means a few more steps to haul water. If it tastes better, and the well is more reliable, it's worth the extra work involved. Someday, she'll have faucets like The Mountain View Hotel in Oracle or in New York. *Someday*, that's one of her favorite words.

Next, a new paint job, off-white, cream almost, not the dingy brown the previous owners thought sensible, or maybe it was white and dust took over and never let go. It'll take who-knows-how-many gallons of paint brought up from Tucson to paint the roadhouse, and it's not happening this year, not on her budget.

The back porch is in the direst need of shoring up. Just this morning, Ruby heard a coyote digging under the entryway. When she hollered, the animal darted away, its skinny rear loping off into the desert. She got a shot off with her rifle, more to send it on its way than to hit it. Not that she's shy about shooting coyotes, mind you, she just didn't want to deal with the mess. She's shot her share of coyotes and mad dogs. Big cats, too. But never stray kittens. Other people might drown them or shut them up under the house where they screech their way to the other side of breathing but Ruby's got a soft spot for them as long as they never come into the hotel, no matter what Virgil says.

And then there's the matter of a piano. Every hotel lobby from St. Louis to San Francisco has a piano. Even if a piano sat there in all its glory, topped with a frill of lace, oil lamp, tintype, and gee-gaw, it would shout in no uncertain terms that Ruby Fortune, innkeeper, can compete with any other hotel in this corner of the world.

But that's months—and many more pies—away. Ruby gets up and heads back to the kitchen, the middle of another week of drudgery: cook, clean, wash, repeat. A heap of dishes spills over the sink and onto the drain board. Ruby is bone-tired tonight, can hardly keep her eyes open. She throws a dishtowel over the dirty plates, cups, flatware, and pots and closes the kitchen closet with her hip. *Don't worry your knuckles, Ruby. Tomorrow and its drudge, drudge, drudgery will come quick enough.*

She falls into bed, exhausted, red boots still on.

FEBRUARY 19, 1905
JERICHO, ARIZONA TERRITORY

"If you won't listen to any sense, here, go on." Divina hands Ruby a rusty spade. "Never returned it to Judd." She settles her gnarled hands on Ruby's shoulders. "If you won't sell that ring, this is the only option I can see making any sense. If it were me, though, I'd sell it for a pretty price and add it to our San Francisco fund."

"Don't tempt me, Divina. I don't want another thing from that man, no matter what it would buy me."

Divina steers Ruby toward the back door. Divina moves slower now, on account of her rheumatism. "You're the only one who can bury your own bad demons, Pip. Let someone else do it for you, and they'll botch the job. Go on. Way past time, if you ask me. But still, I'd sell it."

Ruby drags the spade behind her, *ka-lunk, ka-lunk*, the desert floor scoured white. Her boots slap the parched ground, crushing an anthill. She'll put Willie Fortune behind her once and for all with a few shovelfuls of dirt. *Bastard.*

Last night, Ruby woke up screaming again, covered in sweat, another nightmare, with Willie Fortune coming at her. She got up before dawn and ravaged her room for any sign of Willie. She had long ago divested of anything of his: boots, vests, firearms. The ruby ring is the last vestige she has of his, the thing she once thought she'd sell for laudanum. She doesn't want a thing to do with it.

The thin hem of sky is ragged with low-lying clouds, the day unraveling fast. When Ruby is out of Divina's eyesight—can one ever be out of eyesight in the Sonoran Desert?—she wipes sweat from her forehead with her forearm and rests for a moment, the worn shovel her crutch. If she expends any more energy, the day will suck her dry. The last time she used this shovel, she buried her baby.

Ruby grabs the shaft of Old Judd's old spade with one hand. Her other hand grasps the warm handle. She attacks the burnt desert floor with vigor, at first making nothing more than a dent. After several stabs, she displaces gold-flecked dirt in a growing pile beside her.

After a number of tries, the edge of the shovel hits something hard. Ruby peers into the hole, bends down, reaches in. She fingers a small fossil. One side is rough; the opposite face smooth. She brings it up close to her eyes to examine it. There is no doubt. It is a shell, whorled so tightly its concentric bands wrap around its core. Never has Ruby seen anything but a snail shell.

Why a seashell is buried here, in the Sonoran Desert, is beyond Ruby. Maybe the desert had once been an ocean so deep, so wide, that no matter how tall you were—even taller than the tall man in the carnival—you couldn't see to the far side. But then Ruby begins to doubt herself. This she will tell no one, unless she risks her hide being ridden out of town on account of insanity. Women can be institutionalized for far less: swearing, throwing fits, languishing in bed. Ruby is already guilty on those counts, among others; no need to add to the list ranting like a crazed woman about a desert left bare by the sea. Ruby pockets the shell and paws at the edges of the hole. There are no more riches to spare.

When Ruby is certain that the hole is deep enough not to be defiled or discovered, she throws the ruby into the pocket of earth. She dribbles dirt back into the hole. Then, as if in a fury, she scoops the rest of the pile into the hole, stands, and stomps on the ground. "Bastard." Ruby kicks rocks and brush over the site. Only she knows where it is buried, at the base of a saguaro with a dozen rotting arms. But she will never come to salvage the ring, no matter how hard up.

Maybe, over millennia, the ruby will slowly disintegrate into particles so fine it will meld into the desert like so much pain. But Ruby doubts it. She figures the ring will bake into the earth so hard over time that it will become part of the Sonoran Desert itself long after she's gone. Maybe a hundred years from now, or a thousand, or longer, someone will uncover it and question why on earth that ring with a ruby the size of a penny had come to be buried in that spot. So be it. Let them wonder.

RUBY GLANCES OUT THE WINDOW every five minutes, watching for the full moon to rise over the lip of the Santa Catalinas. Tonight the miners will descend on Jericho and spill their pay on women and drink and gambling. Every payday, Silver Tip shuts down for forty-eight hours, enough time for miners to get a month's worth of shenanigans into two days and spend all their hard-earned dough right here in town. Soon, streets will crawl with every manner of man, guttural Germanic languages mixed with Irish lilts and enough booze to fill an ocean. Knifings and gunfights, too, over money or a woman. Lines at the bottom of Judd's stairs for visits with the upstairs girls. And a tent city that pops up overnight, rows and rows of canvas tents perched behind Judd's along Deadman's Alley and in every nook and cranny in Jericho. Every month, Ruby has to chase tenters off her property with a broomstick. She takes in paying customers only.

Last night, Ruby checked her calendar for the thirtieth time this month and washed her underclothes. Can a woman love a man as much as Ruby loves The Preacher? She aches for him the minute he leaves and aches for the whole month until he arrives, blessedly, again. Tonight, the rains have vanished, but the sky is still black-and-blue at the edges. Ruby doubles down on the kneading, her hands flying to finish the dough. Fletcher is out and Virgil and Sam are long asleep. Fifteen minutes later, Ruby hears the familiar set of raps on the window. Her heart judders.

"Perce!" Ruby opens the back door and a giant of a man sweeps Ruby up and spins her around.

"How's my Ruby Girl?"

"A sight better than I was a few minutes ago." They brush lips. "In now, with you, before we've got an audience." Ruby pushes Perce gently over the threshold and closes the door behind her. "I've missed you, Preacher Man."

Perce turns toward Ruby and squeezes her again. "I've missed you more, Ruby Girl. Like coming to an oasis in a drought, seeing you here." He kisses her deeply, right there in Ruby's kitchen.

Ruby leads Perce to the kitchen table. The kitchen is spanking clean tonight, no unwashed crocks or tableware in the sink, no crumbs on the planked wooden floor. She runs her hands over Perce's shoulders as he sits. He covers her slender hands with his own.

Ruby takes the coffee boiler off the range and pours a mug of coffee for Perce and another for herself. "Whiskey?"

He nods.

Fourteen, Ruby was, when Willie gave Ruby her first sip of whiskey. In Abilene, it was—or was it Amarillo? No matter. She has loved whiskey ever since, maybe as much as her pop. She pours a jigger into both mugs and sits opposite him, palms down on the table. Perce pats her hand and she melts in the warmth of his.

"Before," she colors, "you know . . ." She squeezes Perce's hand. "Tell me. How much did you miss me?"

"If a clock could cry, that's how much. Rather I had a whole month with you and a few hours away, instead of the other way around. I have an idea to change that. But before I lay out my plan, can a poor man please have a piece of that Ruby Pie? I'm aching for anything that's not bread, bacon, and beans."

Ruby jumps up. "Sorry. Of course." She cuts a generous slice of pastry and hands the plate to Perce. Is that the front door opening? She puts her fingers to her lips and goes through the dining room toward the parlor. She can't be seen with Perce. He really should be on the back porch or squirreled in her room already. If someone's come in, Ruby will have to redirect him so Perce gets wind of the danger. No, no one is here. She retraces her steps to the kitchen and sits. "What's new at the mine?"

"Bad dealings, if you ask me. Not that I aim to say anything. Do my job. Stay low. Get paid. Come see you. But too many men like me go missing." He shakes his head. "Your turn. Tell me about this inn of yours. Can't match that tale you told me last month."

"Which one?"

"Those rail bulls. Imagine wanting to put a spur up here like it's New York City or something."

"Like that will ever happen. Although I'd buy the first ticket." Ruby mimics handing Perce an imaginary receipt. "Have you ever been to San Francisco?"

Perce shakes his head.

"First place I'd like to go, if I ever get a day off. But that's as likely as beds making themselves." She sips her whiskey-laced coffee. "Since I've seen you last? Ranchers, prospectors, couple of Indian agents. One made my skin crawl. Oh! Had a couple of crooked land agents here last week. Couldn't trust a word they said, Jericho this and Jericho that. Like it's the best thing since the goddamn Garden of Eden." Ruby pictures Perce naked, his hands under her hips and mouth buried in her vulva, and that first roll-roll-rolling wave of pleasure.

"Ruby?"

"Sorry, my mind was on other things. Where was I?"

"Garden of Eden."

"Yes, right. I had to watch those bastards like hawks, way they got to drinking. I cut them off, I did. They were none too pleased with that. And you won't believe this, Perce. They wanted to buy the roadhouse right out from under me." Ruby slaps the table. "'Put in a desert resort,' they said. Have you ever heard hogwash the likes of that? A resort in the middle of the goddamn desert? I wonder about people sometimes."

Perce takes her hand again. "I worry about you here on your own with riff-raff like that coming through. So here's the plan I've hatched. You need help around this place, Ruby Girl. It's plain as day. You could always hire a girl to help with the washing. But there's upkeep." He points to peeling paint on the ceiling. "Thought I could ditch the mine and live here. In the shed out back, maybe. Help out. Watch the place. Do all the things you don't have the time and energy to do. And I could be with you. Every day."

"Every night, you mean." Ruby draws in a sharp breath. "Damn it, Perce. If I didn't think anyone would be on to us, maybe. The whole town is peering down as it is." She motions out the window. "Bet some busybodies saw you come in. You can't sneeze in Jericho without rousing suspicion. As soon as one person suspected, or squealed . . ."

"We'd be careful, Ruby Girl. All on the up and up as far as anyone is concerned." His face turns glum. "You might think this is sudden thinking. But it's not. Another colored has gone missing."

"Another one?"

"Three now. I don't purpose to be the fourth."

"I can't pay mine wages, Perce. Room and board, yes. And a couple of dollars a week. But, do you really think . . .?"

"I think it's the best idea I've had in a long time."

"I'd hate to put Wink out."

Ruby hears footsteps on the back stoop and straightens up. She pushes her chair away from Perce.

Fletcher bursts into the kitchen with two friends in tow. "What in the Sam Hill?"

"Fletcher, boys," Ruby says.

"Get the hell out of here, whoever you are," Fletcher yells at Perce.

Perce doesn't flinch.

"Fletcher!" Ruby says. "Where are your manners?" She pulls herself up, places her palms on the weathered table, and stares down her son. He used to be so sweet. Ruby only comes up to Fletcher's shoulders now. He's got a tuft of peach fuzz on his chin and a thin line of strawberry down on his upper lip. His hands are as large as Willie's were.

"Mr. Washington here is my guest," she says. "Sharing a cup of coffee is all."

Fletcher leans over Ruby, and sneers. His breath smells of whiskey. "Don't pay heed to the segregation laws, Ma?

I could have you arrested." He turns to Perce. "I've seen you up at the mine, haven't I? Once the bosses hear of this, you'd better see your ass out of this town."

Fletcher's friends laugh.

Ruby doesn't take her eye off Fletcher. "You're a disgrace." She turns to Perce. "I'm afraid you'll have to take your leave, Mr. Washington. I apologize for my son's rude behavior." She glares at Fletcher.

Perce stands. "Obliged for the coffee, Miz Fortune. Boys." He tips his hat and heads through the dining room, his long oilcoat swaying behind him.

Ruby whips her head around and grabs Fletcher's arm. "Who the hell do you think you are, Fletcher? The sheriff?"

Fletcher's friends lower their heads, pick at their nails, anything but watch Ruby upbraid Fletcher in front of them. She hears the front door close and stalls for time. "You boys, listen to me. Fletcher here can get worked up. Comes naturally by it. But just because you see two people sharing a cup of coffee doesn't translate into goddamn Sodom and Gomorrah."

Fletcher wrangles his arm out of Ruby's grasp. "After him," he says.

His friends look from one to the other, shrug, and push out the back door.

"You disgust me," Fletcher says. "Pig trough of a woman, going after a colored." He shakes his head. "You murdered my pa for the likes of him?"

"Watch your goddamn mouth, Fletcher. If I could wrangle you, I'd wash that filthy mouth of yours out with soap."

"Wash out your own goddamn mouth first, Ma. Who do you think I learned from?"

FEBRUARY 21, 1905
JERICHO, ARIZONA TERRITORY

"Where the hell are you?" Fletcher bellows from the kitchen.

Boys of that age can be so hot-headed. A couple of years ago, Fletcher's older brother Clayton lit out of town without much of a warning and Ruby misses him every day.

"My feet are itching to get out of Jericho, Ma," Clay said. That's it.

"Where . . . will you go?" Ruby almost swallowed her tongue.

"Don't know. Maybe Colorado. I'll be back someday. You've got a houseful of boys to keep you company 'til then."

Someday, that's a word Ruby banks on.

Ruby doesn't answer Fletcher right away, let him fume. She jabs a broom handle under the kitchen stoop to pry loose a large wasp's nest wedged underneath the porch. A wasp buzzes and pelts Ruby's forearm. She lobs the broom handle and plows through the kitchen door, holding her left wrist. Grabbing a damp towel, Ruby applies it to the nasty welt. *Stupid, going after wasps like that.* She swings around then to face Fletcher.

"What's got into you? Going off like a firecracker about the smallest thing, like your pop, like Clay. It's a wonder you haven't been fired yet from that job of yours."

Fletcher takes a mug from the sideboard and fills it with coffee. Ruby waits for it, the torrent of words.

"You say I'm no better than my pop. Well, you're no better than your ma."

"You leave my ma out of it."

Ruby was a mother four times in as many years, and no rest in between. She rattles off the boys' birthdates in her head to get her mind off Fletcher's outburst:

Willard George, III: September 9, 1888
Clayton Roy: August 12, 1889
Fletcher James: June 8, 1890
Virgil Case: March 29, 1891

And then her caboose, born on one of the hottest days on record in April.

Samuel Finis: April 22, 1895

"Watch your mouth, young man." Ruby balls her fist, relaxes it. "I won't have anyone—least of all you—talking crap about my mother."

"Everyone knows she was a whore."

Ruby stiffens. "And how does 'everyone' know this?"

"Judd told me. Used to be one of his girls."

"That's horseshit, Fletcher. Judd would probably say Queen Victoria was 'one of his girls' if he thought it would bring a laugh. My mother never set foot in Jericho."

"Maybe that's how your pop knew her to begin with. One of *his* many whores."

"I remind you who you're talking to, young man."

"No other mother . . ."

"Don't you start on that again."

"I know what I saw last night, and it isn't right."

"His name is . . ."

"I don't care what his name is."

". . . The Preacher."

"He ain't no preacher, Ma. What the hell is wrong with you?"

"What did I say about watching your language, Fletcher? And might I remind you my doings are no one else's business."

"Everyone knows what you're up to, Ma. You killed our pa and got away with it. Probably sharing the sheets with whatever his name is back then."

"How dare you!" This time, Ruby raises her fist, but stops herself. Her armpits are damp. "I didn't know The Preacher until . . . well, it's none of your goddamn business. It was years after your pa. And there's nothing going on. Next time . . ."

"There won't be a next time," Fletcher says.

"I thought I raised you better." Ruby unflexes her fist. "I killed your pa for good reason, and I'm not sorry about it. What he did to me, Fletch, I could take. But what he did to you and your brothers, that I couldn't stomach. Even Virgil, with the palsy no less. And Sam, hardly talking. That was the last straw. Your pa beat the voice right out of him. Given enough time and enough drink—or any reason— your pa would've killed us all."

"Still no reason to whore around for all the world to see." Fletcher puts his head in his hands and shakes it back and forth.

Ruby puts her hand on Fletcher's shoulder. He shrugs her off.

"I'm not whoring around at all, Fletcher. I was simply

sharing a cup of coffee and nosing about the doings up at Silver Tip. There are mines going under all up and down the Catalinas. If that mine goes belly up, Jericho will dry up in five seconds flat. And that would be disastrous for us."

"Why don't you ask me about the mine? I'm up there every day, hauling enough water to break a camel's back. Or ask the mine boss. You seem to know him pretty well. Paid you off, word is. Don't know what you did for that."

Ruby scowls. "Jimmy Bugg doesn't know the word 'honest' from Adam. I prefer to ask someone else who works up there to get an honest answer."

"There are plenty of others to ask."

"Sleeping it off behind Judd's, I reckon. And half of them—or more—don't know The Queen's English. Mr. Washington . . ."

"I don't care a damn about Mr. Washington, or whatever his name is. Nobody uses their given names up there." Fletcher pushes the chair out with a screech, wood on wood. "I'm not staying around to be witness to any more of it, Ma. I'm embarrassed to be your son. Won't be long and you'll see my backside headed out of this hellhole."

Ruby sighs and backs away, her bottom up against the sideboard. *Embarrassed?* "Suit yourself, Fletcher. Can't stop you, even if you've got a good paying job and friends and a roof over your head. Clay up and left, not much older than you, and for no good reason whatsoever."

"He had his reasons."

"'My feet are itching to get out of Jericho,' he said. That's all he said to me . . ."

Where are you, Clay? Safe? Well-fed? Loved?

". . . but we did get that letter once, though. From Colorado."

"You won't be getting any letters from me. Ma. Ever. I can't get far enough away from Jericho. Or from you."

SAME NIGHT

"He says he's going to leave. Just like Clayton." Ruby rocks on Divina's wide front porch. "Chasing them away, I am."

"That's nonsense, Pip. Boys—well, most of them anyway—need to get away from their mommas come this time. It's only natural."

"I suppose. All high and mighty, Fletcher is. Like I should award him for pissing in a tin can." Ruby picks at her fingernail. "I should probably blame myself. And curse I didn't have a girl."

"Count your blessings there. Girls are nothing but trouble and heartache."

"And you know this, how?"

"Damn it, Pip. You can be so . . . short-sighted. Think on it. I've been minding you since the day you came to Jericho, five days old and mad at the world." Divina reaches over and pats Ruby's shoulder. "And still mad at it, far as I can tell. Even though you're not my flesh and blood, you might as well be. Which brings me to . . ."

"What?" Ruby's voice is still clipped. Why should she take it out on Divina, when she's mad at Fletcher? *Stop it, Ruby, stop it.*

"Hard not to see how happy you are after you see that fella of yours. Although it will bring you nothing more than heartache and trouble."

Ruby relaxes her shoulders. "Sorry for being so touchy, Divina. Fletcher suspects, and now he's told his cronies. I'm afraid for Perce."

"Ah, that's his name. Always tips his hat when he passes, like he knows me. Or was taught right by his momma. And I've seen the way you look at him, and the way he looks at you."

"How? Where?"

"I came by the other night on my way home from . . . well, never mind where I was. Saw you two in the kitchen. Thought to come in, but then thought better of it. There's only one thing you can do about it, Pip. And you know what it is."

"Why can't a body be happy?"

"That's stuff for plays and novels. Don't get that kind of happiness on the near side of Hell." Divina shakes her head. "Here, have some tea." She pours a tall glass of cool tea from a weepy pitcher on the table between them and hands it to Ruby.

"But . . ." Ruby takes a sip and places the glass on the small table between the rockers.

"It's the truth, Pip. Name one person we know who's lucky in love. Not a one of us."

"Maybe because everyone loves someone who loves someone else."

"Made Shakespeare rich, or so Wink says."

"With that man I'm happier than I've ever been, Divina."

"Let him go, Pip. Hell will freeze over before a white woman can take up with a colored." Divina sips her tea and dabs her mouth. "Keep up your carrying on, and you'll get sloppy. Someone else will see you. Next thing you'll be weeping by the hanging tree and coming to me for condolences. Much as I hate to say it, Pip, it's your heart or his head. One of you is going to pay. Now get on home before you're tomorrow's bad news."

It's dark as Ruby walks swiftly down Jefferson, her head swimming. *Let him go? How?* Two men steal down Brewer's Alley, noses headed for an alehouse. Voices then, loud, outside of The Empire, and the next thing, a firearm discharges in the air. Ruby tenses. Dogs and vermin slither as Ruby hurries across the street away from the shots. Overhead, a comet streaks through the inky sky above Jericho. Ruby stops for a moment in the shadow of the bank to watch the ball of light race past stars.

As she passes Burton's shop windows, someone wrenches her arm. Ruby tries to bat at her assailant, but the hulk of a man pushes her roughly up against the plate glass.

"Well, well, well. Mrs. Fortune." Jimmy Bugg breathes in close to Ruby's face. He's laced with liquor. "Looks like Lady Luck is shining on me tonight."

"Get your filthy hands off of me," Ruby seethes.

"Don't order me, Ruby Fortune."

"You . . ."

"Shut it. Now. Any word from you and I might not be so nice." He pulls Ruby around to the side of Burton's store and elbows her up to the wooden siding under the large Cream of Wheat mural. He leans in and puts pressure on her chest.

"What you did, it's criminal," Bugg says. "Stealing right from under our noses."

"I did nothing of the sort."

"I checked the signature on that so-called will of yours. Doesn't match."

"I don't know what you're talking about."

"Oh, you know very well what I'm talking about. You forged that signature. Stole the mine away from us."

"I got what was my share fair and square." Ruby wishes then she had her pistol. *Finish the job.*

"Don't come near me again, Jimmy Bugg. First thing tomorrow, you'll wish you were in Omaha or St. Louis. I'll have your head for this. Or worse."

"You don't scare me, Mrs. Fortune. I could have my way with you. Or worse."

"You bastard. You and Willie Fortune and the rest of you. That mine was a failing operation from the start. You had no idea how to make it profitable."

Ruby notices Bugg's boots. They used to belong to Willie Fortune. There is no mistaking them, turquoise with steel tips. *How did he get ahold of those?*

"Jesus. You have no blazing idea, do you? We had it made in spades, the largest glory hole in the whole of Arizona Territory. Big money came through that operation when Willie Fortune was still alive, and it weren't all silver."

Ruby wrenches her arm out of Bugg's grasp.

He glares at her. "Damn it to hell. You cost us our future." He starts at her again, but she dodges him. "With one bullet, and that no-good signature of yours, you wrecked it all. This is on you, Ruby. And I don't mean for you to forget it."

"Get the hell out of my sight," she says.

He shrugs. "You haven't seen the last of me." He crosses Jefferson, his gait uneven, and ducks behind Judd's. She follows him at a safe distance. He staggers through the tent city behind the tavern. Ruby sidles up to the side of Judd's and watches him as he weaves between canvas tents. He stops in front of a large tent and kicks off Willie's boots.

Ruby hurries home then, pours a shot of whiskey, and sits on the back stoop. The welt on her arm has risen like yeast. It's then she remembers the wasps. They are silent tonight. She lights off the porch and goes out to the shed. Wink is sawing logs on his burlap mat, blanket off to the side. She covers Wink with his filthy coverlet and rummages quietly for a shovel and a sack. She tiptoes out of the shed and returns to the porch. With deft strokes, she purses the open sack around the nest, dislodges it, and carefully transfers it into the rough burlap. Setting it down gently, she cinches the top tight.

Ruby steals across Jefferson again. The burlap is now abuzz with angry wasps. She grips the bundle by the neck with gloved hands and keeps it away from her body. She can't afford to be stung again.

Nearly fifty tents have blossomed overnight between Judd's and Deadman's Alley. A few men linger outside tents, smoking and talking low. One man takes a piss right outside his bivouac and ducks back in, boots still on. Ruby hears Old Judd shut the tavern door and bolt it. She creeps along the wall so he doesn't see her and crouches under the stairs behind the tavern. Would those wasps shut up? Old Judd clods up the stairs above her, mumbling.

A loud clattering raises the hair on the back of Ruby's neck. "Shit!" he yells. Legs, arms, torso, twist as Old Judd bangs down the stairs. Ruby freezes. He lands on the ground at the base of the stairs and rubs his head. If he were sober, he'd be looking right at her, and he'd have a piece to say. But Old Judd gets hammered when the miners come to town, each one of them buying the barkeep a drink in exchange for his hospitality. He gets up to mount the stairs again. It's almost comical, watching him sway from one foot to the other and grabbing for the stair rail. Hell, if anyone's sober between here and the Silver Tip Mine, pigs could fly with their tails forward. Even the barkeep is past his limit.

Ruby waits for an opening, and then takes her chance. She skulks between canvases until she is certain she has reached Bugg's tent. Those are definitely his boots—Willie's boots, steel toes and all—outside the tent flap. Other than loud snoring, there is no other movement from inside.

Ruby glances both ways. No one is paying her any attention. Even if she is seen, she wouldn't be the first woman to sneak into a man's tent on payday. In one swift motion, she loosens the tent flap and checks to make certain it's Bugg inside. It is, in all his glory. She stifles a snort, loosens the drawstring, and tosses the burlap in, wasps and all.

FEBRUARY 22, 1905
JERICHO, ARIZONA TERRITORY

"Sheldon! Wait up!" Ruby hurries across Jefferson, her hands full. Sheldon Sloane is untying his horse in front of the post office. She catches her breath. "Off to Tucson, then?"

"Just heading out. Interviewing for a deputy. What's got into your britches? A bug?"

"Poor choice of words, Sheldon. Jimmy Bugg is onto me. Staked me out last night by Burton's. Was a bit rough."

"How rough?" Sheldon bristles.

"Pushed me up against the wall. Had a little talking to me. Looks like our—my—scheme is unraveling."

"That's all? Nothing more?"

"Nothing more. But I could've used a companion."

Sheldon touches Ruby's arm. "Just wait until I get my hands on him."

"He might be scarce today."

"What were you doing out late? You should know better on payday."

"Was up at Divina's. Time got away from me. Not like I haven't walked in Jericho after dark by myself before."

"Without a piece? Not like it used to be, Ruby. Better think twice about being out after dark again without one with scoundrels like Bugg in town."

"I fixed him good, Sheldon."

"How?"

"Let's just say I don't think he'll mess with me again anytime soon."

"Whatever it is you did or said—and I don't even know if I can imagine, although it might be humorous to guess—I'd advise you to stick close to home these next few nights. Don't give him a second chance. I can't keep vigil tonight like I did after Willie's funeral for those three nights." His brow creases. "Or was it four?"

"Four?"

"A man's got to do what a man's got to do, is all. Thought you were a bit kittenish that first night and I didn't want trouble. I didn't have much to worry about, though. By the time Bugg and his boys rambled up the hill, a pygmy goat could have warded them off. Talk about soused. I played a little buckshot hopscotch with them and they hightailed it out of sight."

"Did you say 'kittenish', Sheldon? When in God's name have I ever been 'kittenish'?" Ruby shakes her head. "Virgil said you caught up with the thugs who left the chicken at the schoolhouse."

"Did, yes. Got a tip from Judd, of all people." Sheldon snorts. "Wonders never cease. I guess two fellas were bragging about it. They're in the slammer now. Good thing I'll be gone tonight. They might not fare too well on my watch."

"Miss Stern will sleep better knowing it. Have you told her?"

"I have. But I don't have anyone to look in on those good-for-nothings tonight, one more reason it's time I hired a deputy. Can't take a piss without something going on here. One look at Tombstone and you know what I mean."

Three loud blasts pierce the desert air.

Ruby shades her eyes and looks up the mountainside toward the mine. "Damn it." *Perce. Not Perce.*

In less than a minute, Tom Tillis bursts out the front door of the livery and motions for two men standing outside to follow him down the alley toward the corral.

"I'll fetch Swendsen before I head to Tucson," Sheldon says. "Let's just hope this one still has a pulse."

"Damn that mine," Ruby says. "How many deaths this month? Six?" *Please, no no no, not Perce. How many times can I bargain with God?*

"More, if my sources are correct. Although some poor sods never make it to town. Tillis, Doc, they do big business on account of accidents."

Tillis careens out from the alley with his wagon and six-mule hitch, one of the two hired hands beside him on the bench seat.

Ruby hands Sheldon a small cake wrapped in brown paper. "Take this to Vi, will you? And don't you go eating it yourself."

Sheldon tips his hat. "I'm off then."

Ruby takes the post office steps one at a time. If only her legs were longer. She pushes through the door with a small grunt. "Hey, Virge."

"Ma." Virgil turns from the corkboard where he's pinning up a new wanted poster. His left leg drags behind. He overcompensates with his right, listing from side to side like a sailor on a rocking ship.

"Did you hear the blast?"

"I did. It will be a couple of hours before we have any news."

Ruby takes in a huge breath and lets it out slowly. Nothing to do but wait.

"Mail's just in," Virge says. He goes behind the counter and hands Ruby a postcard with familiar scrawl.

She flips the postcard over.

Ruby—
Sending up a girl on the Monday stage. When are you coming to town next?
—Vi

Ruby puts the postcard in her pocket. "See you at supper, Virge."

"Ma." He picks up the newest Horatio Alger, *Finding a Fortune*, and cracks it open. That boy devours those books. Ruby chuckles at the title.

As Ruby thrusts the door open, she all but collides with Margaret Stern on the threshold. Margaret loses her balance and tries to break her fall by grabbing onto the doorframe. She falters, her reticule bouncing down the steps.

A couple of roughs whistles as Margaret fumbles to stand.

"Miss Stern!" Ruby says. She reaches a hand toward the teacher. "Go home to your mommas, boys," Ruby yells to the men. "Haven't seen a woman's ankle before?" She swears under her breath.

"Thank you," Margaret says. "I didn't expect . . ."

"I'm sorry, Miss Stern. I might not care for you much, but I care for those louts a shitload less. And I don't wish you any harm. I don't."

"FOR PITY'S SAKE!" RUBY SAYS. She wipes her hand on her apron. "You look a sight."

Sam stands on the kitchen stoop. His elbow is bleeding and face streaked with dirt. For a ten-year-old, he's getting tall, knobby knees and skinny thighs. His blond hair is stringy and matted with sweat.

"I don't know how-all you get into these scrapes out there, Sam, but if I didn't know better, I'd think you were raised by a she-wolf."

Sam brushes dirt from his trousers. He signs "n" and "o."

Progress, Ruby thinks. *Next I'll teach him y-e-s.* "Now, not a step closer, young man. You stay right where you are. Don't even think about coming in with those filthy britches on." Ruby stands in the kitchen doorway, arms crossed. "With Wink, were you?"

Sam nods. He tugs on Ruby's sleeve.

"What is it, son? Hungry?"

He nods.

"Go on, wash up at the pump. I'll get a bandage and some vittles. Later, we'll work on more letters." *Y-E-S.*

Wink ambles into the yard, clutching something bulky under his soiled coat. "Won't believe what we found today, Miss Ruby." He unloads the haul onto the ground outside the kitchen stoop.

Ruby gasps. Women's bloomers. Three pair. They look all too familiar. "What the hell?"

"Never seen such a thing," Wink says. "Hanging off a cactus, just back there." He points to a spot beyond the back fence.

Ruby fingers the edge of one pair. "They're mine, Wink."

Wink looks skeptical.

"And I didn't put them there, if that's what you're wondering."

"Blew off the line, maybe?"

"I don't hang these outside."

"You can't think what I'm thinking, can you, Miss Ruby? That someone's been in your drawers?" He colors. "Your bureau drawers, I'm meaning."

Later that night, after going through the whole alphabet with Sam, hands contorted to make way for words, Ruby sits down to answer Vi. Before she writes, she checks her bureau drawer. She gets the shivers again. Who has been in her room? And why? And when? She shakes it off and sits at her compact writing desk and scratches out a two-cent postcard.

Vi—
Thanks, I'll look for the girl. And I'll be down soon, don't get your knuckles in a knot.
—Ruby

FEBRUARY 27, 1905
JERICHO, ARIZONA TERRITORY

The next stage from Tucson empties out, but there's no girl. No woman, even. Ruby walks back to the inn and flops on her bed. Where could she be? Vi said a girl would be up on the next stage. Had Ruby read that right? She thrashes through papers on her desk but can't find Vi's latest. In frustration, she grabs all the contents of her bureau drawer yet again, laying bloomers and slips and chemises out one by one on her bed. The underthings are hers, alright, the ones that Wink and Sam found in the desert. She blames herself for not noticing three pairs gone missing. But she does have a drawer full of them. She might skimp on butter sometimes, but fancy lace drawers? Never.

Hundreds of guests have been in and out of Jericho Inn since she opened in 1900. Ruby can remember every one of them. She's had her share of unsavory men in and out of the place, that's for sure. Some more than once. But no one except Perce has ever been in her bedroom. Not even the boys. It can't be Perce. No. So who got into her dresser?

Ruby hears Sheldon's booming voice in the parlor. He comes through the dining room and into the kitchen and stands near Ruby's bedroom doorway, hat in hand. "Just read the report, Ruby. Sorry to broach a delicate subject, but I've got to ask who's had access to your bedroom. And I'm going to need to see the evidence." Ruby shoos Sheldon back toward the parlor. He sinks into the sofa and fingers the shawl draped over the back.

Ruby appears with three sets of bloomers in her hand. "I've been over it a hundred times." She hands Sheldon her knickers like they're pieces of forbidden fruit, dodging Sheldon's question. "Not that it's locked, mind you."

"You'll be rethinking that." Sheldon fingers the finery. "Hmm . . . lacy."

"Do your job, Sheldon."

"There's some crazy people in this world, Ruby." He hands the underclothes back to Ruby.

"Amen. Coffee?"

"Thanks."

Ruby heads to the kitchen to get coffee on and returns to the parlor. "Maybe we're looking at this wrong, Sheldon. What if it was a woman? Someone desperate?"

"Perhaps. How certain are you the, *um uh*, duds are yours?"

"A hundred percent."

"But why would she raid your dresser and leave your drawers out to dry, right behind your place?"

"That's why you're the sheriff, not me, Sheldon."

"I'll be the laughing stock of Jericho if townsfolk get wind I'm in hot pursuit of a bloomers thief."

"Like I said, Sheldon. Do your job."

Ruby goes through to the kitchen again and returns with two mugs. "I'm plumb out of ideas. And I'm in a knot over why Vi's girl wasn't on the stage. I'm needing help here."

"I'm offering."

"Not that kind of help. And where would you find the time, between all your sheriff-ing and tax collecting and going to Tucson? Let alone beating down the doors with Judd's girls."

"If you'd do me the honor, I'd give up other girls today and never go back."

"I'm not here on earth to be your savior, Sheldon."

Loud voices, heavy footsteps puncture the night.

"Whoremongers!" someone yells.

Fletcher?

"The whole lot of you. You'll pay for this, damn it." It's Fletcher, alright.

Sheldon jumps from the couch to confront Fletcher, who bursts through the front door, still cussing.

Loud laughter follows.

Sheldon puts out his arm to steady the boy, but Fletcher bats him away. Ruby rises and goes to Fletcher, but he avoids her, too. He is clearly drunk.

"You should arrest them, Sheriff. They stole my girl." Fletcher weaves across the parlor, leans over, and vomits on the couch.

"Fletcher!"

The boy slumps over, his face in his own vomitus.

Ruby bangs out the inn door. "Get the hell out of here, all of you."

"We were just having a little fun," one of them says.

Sheldon towers over Ruby as he marches out onto the veranda. "Did you hear the lady? Scram this minute if you know what's good for you."

The boys scatter.

Ruby brushes past Sheldon and back into the parlor. She cradles Fletcher's head. He's crying now. "They held me down, Ma. Did the deed with my girl, all of them, with me watching." He sobs into his soiled shirtsleeve. Ruby didn't know Fletcher even had a girl.

"What girl?"

"One of Judd's."

"Judd's?"

"Yeah, Ma."

Sheldon goes through to the kitchen and returns with a handful of damp rags. Wordlessly, Sheldon and Ruby mop up vomit, the stench vile.

Ruby wipes Fletcher's face and hair. "Let's get you to bed now, Fletch. We'll talk about it in the morning."

Fletcher allows Ruby to guide him to the sleeping room off the parlor. The other boys don't stir. Ruby tucks Fletcher in bed, clothes and boots still on.

"Well, that's another day in the books," Ruby says as she emerges from the boys' room. Sheldon sits and slurps his now-cold coffee.

"Not easy raising boys," Sheldon says. "My ma always had me mind my manners. A body forgets sometimes."

Ruby sits next to Sheldon to avoid the wet spot at the other end of the couch. She'll have to order in more vinegar tomorrow to help with the smell. She folds her legs under her skirt and slurps her coffee, too. "My pop always slurped his coffee. Doesn't bother me any."

"Stuff of legends, your pop."

"I miss him like yesterday's fresh cream," Ruby says. "I talk to him, you know. Up at the cemetery."

"I wish I could talk you into . . ."

"Well, you can't. So stop up that bottle."

"We could . . ."

"Yes, we could. And don't think for a minute we wouldn't lop one another's heads off along the way."

"Maybe. But the getting to that point would be half the fun." Sheldon winks at Ruby.

"Depends who got to the other one first, Sheldon Sloane. I don't think Mrs. Sloane—*God rest her soul*—met with the blunt end of a pistol."

"You've got a point, Ruby. No, Charlotte came to a nasty end. Cholera." He bites his lip. "At the end,"—he stops for a second—"she was downright delirious. I hardly recognized her. My own wife." Sheldon stops again, his eyes focused on a dark patch on the ceiling. "Left a hole, she did. Right here." He taps his chest.

Ruby reaches over to touch Sheldon's arm.

Sheldon swirls the end of his coffee and gulps it. "Enough of that talk." He stands, straightens his vest, and tugs on his trousers. "But, if you don't mind me saying, Ruby, Charlotte never wore knickers like yours."

MARCH 20, 1905
JERICHO, ARIZONA TERRITORY

Holed up in Ruby's tiny bedroom in the soft hours before dawn, Ruby lies in Perce's arms, his dark body streaked with sweat.

"Perce?"

"Don't say it again. Nothing can keep me away from you, Ruby Girl." He curls her head under the crook of his arm and strokes her shoulder.

"I mean it, Perce."

"You don't sound too convincing."

Ruby sits up and swings her legs over the side of the bed. She throws her robe over her shoulders and cinches the waist. "I don't know what else to say. We can never be together, proper like." Ruby picks up a heavy catalogue from the small table next to the bed. "Ever wish you could order up a new life out of the Sears & Roebuck catalogue? 'New Life, see page 138.'" She shakes her head. "I'm saving up for the boys for Christmas."

"Already? It's only March."

"Can't ever be too early." Ruby flops back on the bed and props thick pillows behind her back. Perce sits up, a stained white sheet covering his legs and pelvis. Ruby flips through pages and points. "A bat and glove for Sam . . ." She runs her finger down the page. "Sixty-five cents plus $2.50. And balls of course. A buck apiece." Ruby flips to another page. "And an autoharp for Virgil. Another $1.75. Let's see. That's . . ." She does mental calculations. "About eight bucks. Not like I have eight bucks to spare, but I won't disappoint my boys. Not at goddamn Christmas."

Ruby turns the page and smiles.

"What is it, Ruby Girl?"

"I've always wanted one of these." Perce leans over and squints. Ruby points to a melon-shaped stringed instrument.

"A mandolin?"

Ruby looks past Perce to a spot somewhere only she can see. It unravels in her memory, as if she is there, standing inches from the performer in Big Burl's traveling show.

"Slovo was his name. Tall and thin. Wore shiny black trousers and a blouse with billowy sleeves embroidered with colorful flowers. And a funny little black hat with a feather in it. I would sneak up behind him when he was playing and sit behind the bench, close my eyes, and just listen. It was like nothing I heard before or since."

Ruby turns to look at Perce. "You should have heard it, Perce. The most beautiful tunes. Not ones my pop sang. Songs from somewhere else." She smiles from a place deep inside, as if the memory has burst through the scrim of where-all-things-go-to-hide-away to burble up to the surface. Her face is alive, hands in motion.

"That mandolin sung itself, Perce. It made the sweetest sound a body ever heard. If I could play the mandolin like that, I'd die happy." Ruby hums.

"Don't know that one."

"It's called, 'Janicka's Melody.'"

"Who's Janicka?"

"Slovo's sweetheart. Said he wrote it for her." She hums again. "Wonder what it would be like to have a song named after me. What it would sound like."

"It would be loud," Perce laughs. "Brassy. Bold."

Ruby bats at him. "Last time I'll let you into my thoughts, Mr. Preacher Man."

"I'm just pulling your leg, Ruby Girl. If a song were ever written about you, no one would forget it."

Ruby tenses. Are those footsteps outside her window? Or is she imagining it? She motions to Perce. "Under the bed," she says under her breath. She pulls the curtain back. The Santa Catalinas are waking to light. Ruby peers right and left and then down. She gasps. A bloodied hog's head lies directly under her window, steam rising from its nostrils and severed neck.

Ruby grabs her pistol. "Don't move," she whispers as she closes the bedroom door behind her. She crosses the kitchen and unlatches the door. No one is in the yard. She steps onto the back stoop and jams on her boots. When she rounds the back corner of the inn, a lanky coyote circles the hog's head. That will save her the trouble of disposing of it. But who left it there? And why?

Ruby locks the kitchen door and returns to her room. She latches that door, too.

"What is it, Ruby?" Perce is no longer under the bed.

"Too horrid for words. They find us here and who knows what they'll do to us, Perce. To you, mostly. Fletcher, his friends, they see you, and . . ." She shakes involuntarily. "You know the outcome. I've got to be rid of you, but I can't."

"I'll be careful, Ruby Girl. I've been in more scrapes than a nine-lived cat."

Ruby peeks out her bedroom curtain. The hind end of the coyote is trotting out the back of her property, its jaws clenched on the bloodied hog's head. A trail of blood splatters the desert floor. She lets the curtain go. Who? Why?

"Now come here, you beautiful woman." Perce comes up behind Ruby and peels her robe from her shoulders.

"I can't." *You need to go, Perce*, she thinks. *Before something happens that we both regret.*

"You can, and you will, that's what you said to me once." He guides her back to the mussed bed and lowers her onto the sheets. He bends to kiss the base of her neck and slides in next to Ruby on the narrow bed. "We've got more loving up to do."

Ruby sighs. Within minutes, she forgets the hog's head, the coyote, the sun, even.

MARCH 23, 1905
JERICHO, ARIZONA TERRITORY

Ninety-five degrees. Ninety-eight. Edging in on a hundred and three, hotter than a burnt boot. Snow in the high country melting fast. Ruby steps into the cold stream, red boots and all. Surrounded by bare palo verde, leggy ocotillo, and weedy brittlebush, the creek outside Jericho riffles over mica-tinged boulders, its braided channels flowing now with no indication that it's dry nine months of the year. From a distance, the creek looks like a river of copper; up close, the water is clear, its bottom mottled with sand and glinting rock. Sometimes you can't trust your own eyes.

Sometimes you have to. Last night, Ruby pored over her ledgers. Her eyes saw everything in black and white, no question about it. This inn-keeping business is a losing proposition, but she's too proud to admit it to anyone else.

Sam balances on stepping-stones and angles his arms out sideways as he picks his way across the *arroyo*. He loses his footing and steps in the creek; a second later, he is back on the slippery rocks playing catch as catch can with the creek. He signs to Ruby, "o" and "k," fist with a hole and then second and third fingers in a V with the thumb tucked between them. Ruby signs back and strides through ankle-high water and raises silt from the creek bed. As soon as she reaches the far side, the creek runs clear again. Ruby's mouth and tongue are dry and gritty. She dips her hand into the flow and cups a mouthful of cool creek water. Sam comes up beside her.

When she raises her head, Ruby is at eye-level with a bobcat not twenty yards away. She puts her arm out instinctively to stop Sam and stares the cat down until it slinks away. "Don't worry about cats, Sam. You can stare them down every time."

Ruby and Sam sift in dirt and sand for arrowheads, bits of pottery, colored rocks. There were Indian camps here, not thirty years ago. Last time they were here, Sam found a button from a soldier's coat stamped with a palmetto tree and Latin, a remnant of an army man who ran Indians off their land.

Ruby encourages Sam to keep everything, like she does. When you've lived on the traveling circuit, you tend to want to hold on to things of value, things that mean something to you. But Ruby's penchant for hoarding pales in comparison to Wink, so there you go. "One man's junk is another's man's treasure," Wink says. That's not Shakespeare as far as Ruby knows, but she can't be sure.

Ruby hunts for rocks and gems along the water's edge and pockets a piece of fool's gold to add to her stash of desert souvenirs that travelers can take home or worry their idle hands with if they're off the drink. Interesting rocks like this keep lodgers from taking other items from the hotel, towels and curtains and paintings right off the wall.

Not long after she opened Jericho Inn, one of the upstairs rooms was cleaned out, right down to bedding and rugs. If she ever has the opportunity to visit a Mr. and Mrs. Joseph T. Richards of Chicago, she expects she will be able to identify the décor of their parlor or bedroom, although she doubts Mr. and Mrs. Richards are actually man and wife, or live in Chicago at all.

Ruby plucks a small geode from beside a larger rock and fingers its rough edges. "Let you in on a little secret, Sam. You can't judge something from the outside alone. Inside of this ugly rock is the most gorgeous gem you'll ever see." She hands the rock to Sam. "I heard you can go to university to study rocks now. Imagine that. Rocks. Well, we all find a way to make our way in the world. You will too, Sam. You'll find your place." She pockets a piece of rose-colored quartz. "In the meantime, you could work for the Burtons, stocking, taking in freight, that sort of thing. Nothing that needs words."

The sun slashes across the desert like a knife. Ruby and Sam watch red-tailed hawks dip and fight in the air just above. When their pockets are full, they turn back toward Jericho. Away from the creek, the desert is still brown, all the way to the jagged ridge that separates mountain and sky.

After supper, Ruby sits on the back stoop nursing a whiskey-laced cup of tea.

Lengthening shadows take on animate qualities in the cracks and fissures of Oldfather Peak. One silhouette turns from the face of a dog to a fish to a pig, a nasty reminder of the hog's head outside her window. *Who? Why?* She knows why. Perce. Just not who . . .

A kettle of nighthawks swiftly darts and dances and dives above Ruby's head, as they feed on insects at twilight. Bats intermingle with the nighthawks, wings beating faster than hearts. She looks past them at the rose-colored mountains. One gash looks like her own face did once, after Willie took a razor strop to her. She doesn't think of Willie

much anymore, but you never know when something—
simple as a shadow—will trigger a nasty memory.

Ruby scoops up her skirt and heads inside. When will
the rains come to drench the desert green? On the flats,
there's nothing green in sight, not even in the kitchen, not
a potholder or a tea towel or an apron, not wallpaper even.
Just brown, brown, brown everywhere, inside and out, and
old, like dirt.

MARCH 24, 1905
JERICHO, ARIZONA TERRITORY

"Hey, Virge."

"Ma. Give me a minute. Mail's just in." Virgil stands behind the narrow cage at the Jericho Post Office and adjusts his wire-rimmed spectacles. He holds a letter up to light. It's addressed in a large, flowery scrawl to Judd Turpin, Jericho, A.T. Clearly, there's cash inside. Virgil puts that one aside.

Ruby shakes her head. "That how you swell your wages?"

Virgil colors. "Does nothing get by you, Ma?"

"I've wondered." She peers over the counter. "Like those new shoes."

"Judd gets plenty."

At precisely 12:10 p.m., Margaret Stern comes through the door. You could time your watch by it. Three times per week the mail arrives, on the Tucson to Mammoth run with stops in Catalina, Jericho, Oracle, American Flag, Southern Belle, and Willow Springs before horses collapse at the end of the line. Although mail delivery is at times uncertain, the schoolmarm is there at noon Monday, Wednesday, and Friday, without fail.

"Up to the 'F's, Miss Stern," Virgil says.

"I'll wait." Margaret Stern smooths her brown leather gloves and brown wool skirt. It's March, and temperatures this year are already hovering at a hundred. But Stern's attire never changes. Fall, winter, spring, summer, Margaret wears brown: brown cloak, brown skirt, brown vest, brown boots, brown gloves, brown hat. Only the hint of cream flowers out at her neck, where her blouse peeks through. She has divested of her solemn cloak today, it being this hot. Margaret removes her specs from an eyeglass ring pinned to her vest and wipes them with a cloth. A stray wisp of hair falls across her narrow face, at once attractive and harsh, as if she can't make up her mind who she is.

"Good day, Miss Stern," Ruby says.

"And to you, Mrs. Fortune." Margaret busies herself with her spectacles.

"Up to the 'N's now," Virgil says, slotting bills and postcards and letters into boxes behind him beneath twin photographs of President Theodore Roosevelt and Jericho's current postmaster, Harold M. Cleaver. "Nothing today, I'm afraid," he says, as he finishes the stack of mail. "Perhaps next time."

"Thank you, Virgil." Margaret pulls on her gloves. "Until then." It's the same conversation every time, and still no letter.

Sheldon Sloane clatters into the post office just as Margaret goes to pull the door open.

"Miss Stern."

"Mr. Sloane."

Sheldon holds the door until Margaret passes. "It's going to be a scorcher," he says.

"Is it?" Margaret descends the steps to the dusty street.

Sheldon turns to Virgil and shakes his head. "I don't understand that woman."

Virgil places his hands on the counter to steady them. He pushes a thick stack of mail toward the sheriff. "You know what Ma says."

They all answer in unison, Virgil, Sheldon, and Ruby. "Don't even try."

"About my mail, Virge?" Ruby asks.

"I'll bring it over later. I'm really only up to the 'N's, but there's never a letter for Miss Stern, so I just said that." He continues slotting letters into cubicles, holding each one up before filing.

Through the dust, three men ride up Jefferson from the west. They stop in front of the post office, dismount, and tie their horses to posts. Two of the men remain outside; the taller of the two lights a cigar.

The door bangs open.

"How can I help you?" Virgil, ever the salesman, asks the short man who enters. "If it's stamps you're after, they run two cents. A postal box'll run you fifty cents a month, but we've got a waiting list. A dollar a month and I'll find you one."

Sheldon motions to Ruby. They walk to the single shelf on the western wall. Sheldon keeps one eye trained on the stranger.

"Can send a telegraph, if you like," Virgil says. "Or make out a money order. What's your pleasure, sir?"

"Not here for the mail. Where can a man find a cheap roadhouse in this town?"

"Got any room tonight, Ma?"

"Sure do. Come on over, sir, we're across the street, couple of doors up." Ruby tilts her head toward the middle of town. "Two-story shingled affair begging for a new coat of paint. Big porch. On the right. You'll see the sign. Jeri-cho Inn. I'll be back in a quarter hour."

"Any other choices?" the man asks. He is dressed like a solicitor gone rogue, as if he hasn't bathed in days.

"Maybe Judd's," Sheldon says. He elbows Ruby.

"Judd's?"

"Best saloon in town. And best girls." He needles Ruby again.

She rolls her eyes. "Really, Sheldon."

"What, may I ask, are three fellas like you doing in here in Jericho?" Sheldon asks as he glances out the post office window to the men lingering outside. "Ten-day miners?"

"Squires—the tall one there—he's an Indian agent. Met up with him in Tucson and thought we'd ride north together. Protection, you might say."

Ruby glances out the window toward the agent. He wears a long black frock coat and a large hat. He turns just then and she averts her eyes. He looks like a sneak.

"For a price, you mean," Sheldon says.

"Everything's got a price, mister," the stranger says. "You the sheriff?"

Sheldon nods. "One and the same." He picks his teeth with the edge of a letter and doesn't take his eye off the stranger.

"My partner and I might be interested in a few days' work."

Virgil motions to the far wall. "Silver Tip might be hiring. Check the classifieds."

"What is it that you do, exactly?" Sheldon asks. By now, he has gathered up his mail.

"Little bit of this, little bit of that," the stranger answers.

Sheldon points next door. "Well, if you're looking for quick cash, try the livery."

"Thanks, Sheriff." He turns to leave and addresses

Virgil. "Be seeing you around, son." He tips his hat to Ruby. "Might be over."

Sheldon guides Ruby toward the door. "The two grifters there, they're probably harmless. The Indian agent, though. Don't like the looks of him."

Sheldon opens the heavy post office door and stands in the doorway. It's equally warm outside as in. He casts a long shadow on the wooden floor. "You take care of yourself, Virgil. And your ma here. I'm off to Tucson again, be back the day after tomorrow. This business of trying to find a deputy is getting tiresome."

THAT NIGHT, THE TALLEST OF the three lodgers stretches his legs out onto the low table between the sofa and the fireplace at Jericho Inn. He tilts his head back and exhales a halo of smoke. The other two, one noticeably shorter than the other, argue over cards.

Ruby sweeps through the parlor and gathers dirtied glasses. Virgil limps through the sitting area and enters the small bedroom off to the left. "'Night, Virge. And I'll be saying my good nights to you fellas, too," Ruby says. "Breakfast's at eight."

"You wouldn't know where we might find some ladies?" the shorter man asks.

"None to be had here, if that's what's you're asking. No lady guests, either," she says. "So don't go getting any ideas."

"That sheriff fella suggested Judd's," the taller man says. "Why don't you boys head over there?" He motions toward the door. "I'll help the little lady with the mess and be right behind you."

"That's no concern of yours," Ruby says. *Little lady, really? Again?* "Been doing this for years without as much as a lick of help. If you boys are headed to Judd's, bring your key. About to lock up now." The two other men crash out the door, still arguing.

"Just thought you might want some company," the taller man says.

"Not needed," Ruby says. She uses her rear to push open the parlor door and heads for the kitchen through the dining room, now set for breakfast. Depositing dirty glasses on the counter, Ruby wipes her hands on a towel.

A strong hand grabs her shoulder. "Jerusalem!" Ruby jumps. She turns to see the tall man bumped up behind her. "Get your hands off me," she says.

"I'm in the mood for some company."

Ruby shoves his hand away. "Won't have none of that here." She tries to wrench away, but he pins her to the counter.

"On your knees," he says.

Ruby glares at him through slit-like eyes.

"Wouldn't want something happening to your boy, the gimpy one, would you? Saw that he works the post office alone."

"You filthy cur." Ruby claws at the man's shirtsleeves. "Step back and we'll forget this conversation ever happened."

He tightens his grip on Ruby's shoulders. "I said, on your knees." He slaps Ruby square across the face.

Stunned, Ruby dabs her face. Her lip is bleeding and her face stings. "Damn you."

The man shoves Ruby to her knees as he opens his trousers. "You know what to do. We'll call it a deal. Nothing will happen to your boy."

Ruby is squeezed now between the man's legs and the cabinet. Unable to budge, she glares up at him. "You wouldn't dare."

"Wouldn't I? I hear your sheriff friend is out of town."

Ruby scowls.

"Do we have a deal?" The man leers over her. "Wouldn't want to read about your boy in the papers."

Ruby doesn't budge.

"I said now, whore." He cuffs the top of Ruby's head.

Ruby takes his member in her hands and stifles the urge to jerk it from his body.

"Wasn't looking for a hand job." He shoves his pelvis toward her face.

Afterwards, liquid spilling from the sides of her mouth, Ruby slumps, her backside against the cabinet. The man buttons his trousers and steps back. "You've done that before."

Why is Sheldon always in Tucson at the wrong time?

"We'll keep this little secret to ourselves," the tall man says. "Don't want the boys in on it." He hitches up his trousers. Then he bends down toward Ruby and whispers. "I'm thinking about changing the terms of our agreement. Meet me tomorrow after breakfast in my room."

"You said . . ."

"I said I'll see you tomorrow after breakfast. In my room. Under Squires, Jake Squires. Your boy will be off to work by then, I suspect. Don't come and I'll send my boys over to the post office to finish the job."

Squires bangs out the back door, whistling. Ruby, by now sprawled out on the kitchen floor, begins to shake, more with anger than fear. She rises to her knees, gags, and spits on the floor. She steadies herself on the lip of the dry sink, slugs a mouthful of water straight from the pitcher, and spits again, this time into the sink. She rushes to her bedroom and grabs her pistol. She hears the kitchen door creak open and braces for another assault. This time, Squires won't be so lucky. She rounds the corner with the pistol cocked, the front of her shirtwaist still wet and stained.

"Miss Ruby!" Wink stands at the kitchen door. "What in heavens?"

Ruby lowers the gun and hobbles to the door. "Sorry, Wink. I was looking for—"

"The one just come out through the back door? Tall?"
Ruby nods.

"Just say the word and I'll go for the sheriff."

"He's out of town, Wink. I'll have to sort this one out
myself."

"Get yourself to bed now, Miss Ruby. I'll keep watch
tonight."

During the night, Ruby wakes to the sound of a door
opening. Her heart jammers. *God in Heaven, if you're there,
I beg you, not Squires again.* She sits up, grabs her derringer,
and braces for the door to crack open. No one comes in.
Maybe a guest going out or coming in from the outhouse?
She really needs a lock on her bedroom door. She doesn't
sleep a minute all night.

At breakfast, Ruby avoids eye contact with Squires.
She replenishes breakfast rolls and scrambled eggs on the
buffet, refills coffee cups, and clears plates. She forces a
smile to the other guests and bustles between the kitchen
and dining room, lingering by the sideboard until she hears
the diners clearing out.

When she peeks into the dining room, it's empty. She
finishes the clearing up and stacks dirty dishes and cups
in the sink. There's no time for washing up. She checks
the boys' bedroom; Virgil has left and Sam has gone off
to school. The upstairs guests have retreated back to their
rooms and the parlor is eerily quiet. The mantel clock ticks
inexorably toward 9 a.m.

Ruby checks the register, even though she's certain of
what she'll find. It's right there, in large scrawl, J. Squires,
registered in Room #2. She reaches for the key, her hand
trembling. *No*, she thinks, *no*. She returns the key to the hook.

Ruby hefts a basketful of dishcloths and rags and heads
out the kitchen door. She bleached them twice in a bucket
after cleaning up the rest of Squires' mess. Ruby pegs out

the washing, her mouth full of clothespins. She keeps her eyes trained on the kitchen door.

"Did you lose track of time?" a voice says. Ruby feels the sharp edge of a knife at her back.

What the hell?

"We had an agreement, Mrs. Fortune."

"There's nothing I agree with you on, Mr. Squires." Ruby whips around and kicks Squires in the crotch, clothespins flying out of her mouth. Squires doubles over and lunges for her. Ruby runs toward the shed. There is sure to be a shovel handy. Just as Ruby grabs for one, Squires pushes her hard from behind, sending her sprawling into hay and dirt.

Ruby scrambles toward the back of the shed on hands and knees and attempts to get a handhold on the back wall. Squires catches her and shoves her against the wall. He pushes up her skirt from behind and rips at her drawers. Ruby yells and he puts his hand over her mouth. With his free hand, he fumbles with his trousers and shoves his member into Ruby's warm flesh.

"Whore." As he begins to pant, a sudden *wham crack* like a splitting log at the end of an ax. A gush of blood and slime pours over Ruby's head and blouse, red everywhere. He slumps forward. She screams and turns toward the open shed door. Through a mass of red, she sees a figure retreat. Squires slides, limp arms and legs, onto the shed floor. Ruby gags as she steps over him and stumbles toward the light outside.

VIRGIL MEANT TO TELL RUBY RIGHT away, but didn't until later, about that morning one of the men who had just spent the night at Jericho Inn burst into the post office, his crony keeping watch at the door, not the tall one, but the other shorter one. Virgil lowered the book he was reading and put a used envelope in as a placeholder. He snapped the book shut and put it aside.

"Last chance to make today's mail," Virgil said.

"Hands up, young man," the man whispered, brandishing a pistol.

Virgil raised trembling hands above his head. He had to pee.

"Open your cash drawer. Hand it over, all of it."

Virgil lowered his hands and reached for the drawer.

"Don't pull a fast one on me. You show a piece and you're done for."

"No firearms here," Virgil said, his voice shaky.

"Hurry it up, runt. I don't like waiting."

Virgil's hands trembled as he grabbed bills from the cash drawer. He laid them on the counter in a heap.

"Is that all? Coins, too."

Virgil scooped all the coins into his palm. One clattered to the floor.

"Don't go after that one," the man said. "Keep it. My tip." The man swept all the coins into a leather purse and stuffed the bills inside. "Like I said, be seeing you around." He slammed the door behind him.

Virgil came out from behind the counter and locked the door. His chest was tight.

When he was convinced the thieves didn't aim to return, he went back behind the counter. He bent down to retrieve the coin he dropped, as well as the bills his shaking hands let fall to the floor. Of the fourteen dollars he took in that day, he salvaged more than half.

Virgil placed the remaining cash and coin in a worn pouch and took his coat from the hat tree behind the counter. He locked the post office and walked up Jefferson toward the bank, looking back over his shoulder to see if anyone was following him.

"I knew I'd get a talking to," he told Ruby. "But no one was killed over it. And Uncle Sam got his share, even if I did have to make up the difference from my wages."

No one was killed over it? What you don't know, Virge.

"MISS RUBY?" WINK KNOCKS at the kitchen door.

Ruby sits at the kitchen table, a cup of tea cold in front of her.

"Miss Ruby?"

She shakes her head. "I'm sorry, Wink, come in." She starts to rise.

"Sit, sit. I've come to see how you're faring. After . . ."

She looks at Wink with expressionless eyes. He nods and shuffles toward the table. A dark red stain covers his sleeve. He smells like rust.

"You?" Ruby exhales. "I couldn't see anything except . . ."

"Don't waste another breath on that good-for-nothing. He's done for."

A breath catches in her throat. "What? Where?"

"The less you know, the better," Wink says. "As the Bard says, 'We are often happier in our ignorance than in our knowledge.' Trust me, here, Miss Ruby. You don't want to know." He takes her small hand in his filthy one. The warmth burns her skin, and somewhere deeper.

MARCH 27, 1905
TUCSON, ARIZONA TERRITORY

"Watch it, lady!" A burly man, all chaps and chaw (and wearing one of the meanest scowls Ruby has ever seen), barrels into her at the corner of Congress and Stone and no, she's not pleased. Her parcel falls onto the dusty boardwalk but did the lout stop? No.

"Swine!" she barks after him. "Watch where *you're* going, mister!" She bends to pick up the package. "Sometimes I hate this town," she mutters.

Divina pats Ruby's arm. "I'd have said something stronger."

"Ox?"

"Goddamn ox."

Ruby snorts. "Goddamn ox!" she yells in the direction the man went. Two other men walking toward the women step off the boardwalk into the street to avoid her. Ruby wipes the package with her bare hands, her skirt now covered in dust. In contrast to Divina's dark outfit (always a dark outfit), Ruby wears white today, top to toe, and forgoes gloves. Inside the box that clattered to the ground is another new white blouse from Madame Eaves. She can't keep them clean, but so it goes. Three more blouses like it (in addition to another special box, something she's saved for at the expense of, well, everything) will be delivered tomorrow morning before she and Divina head back to Jericho.

Ruby and Divina pass storefront after storefront: Sylvester W. Purgell, Attorney; Columbus Grill Room; Harry A. Drachman Shoe Co. Ruby eyes a soft red hat in the window of Bonanza General Store. It would match her red boots and red gloves perfectly. Maybe next time.

Divina whistles through her teeth. "To think you can get everything you need under one roof. We can thank the railroad for that."

Up the steps of the opulent Santa Rita Hotel and into the lobby and Ruby whistles through her teeth. *That chandelier!* Ruby and Divina freshen up in their handsomely appointed room (Ruby fingers the curtains, running her hand along the lower edge, *real lace*, an inch or more wide, *imagine*) before the women head for Merchant's Café for lunch, where, for twenty-five cents, they enjoy fried oysters and oyster bisque.

"Have you ever? Oysters?!" Divina asks, as the women slurp their soup with oversized spoons. The bustling dining room is crowded with merchants and salesmen, cowmen and rail bulls, women in pairs. Divina tips her bowl to scoop out the last of her soup.

Ruby nods, spoon mid-way to her mouth. "Sometimes I love this town."

Divina laughs. "I know you do. Look! Take a gander at Miss High-and-Mighty over there, in that outrageous hat."

Ruby looks over her shoulder.

"Not that way, Pip. Behind your other shoulder."

Ruby cranes her neck the other way to see a voluptuous young woman seated near a large gilt-edged mirror.

Dressed more for the theater than lunch, with a hat nearly two feet tall and sporting feathers, the woman pays more attention to her own reflection than to her suitor, who is pathetically trying to gain her attention.

"He won't be seeing her bloomers anytime soon," Ruby says. "Poor sod."

"What I'd do for someone like that young buck to see my bloomers," Divina says.

"That can be arranged," Ruby says.

"Don't think I haven't thought of it. Men do it all the time, take a woman on the side. Why not women? Take a man on the side? Now there's an idea."

"Wouldn't I love to be a fly on the wall in that room. Maybe I'll bankroll you."

"Like you have a penny to waste. Wait, is that the new governor? I believe it's John Henry Kibbey himself!"

A group of men escorts a portly man to a table in the center of the room. A beautiful young woman is at his side. Ruby strains her neck to see him but soon turns her attention back to the meal. When they've had their fill of oysters and finished gossiping about everyone in the room (and there is plenty to gossip about), Divina and Ruby walk toward the Santa Rita, still tittering.

Was that really his wife, do you think? Not in a million years! Let's *hope* it was his daughter. *Look at that one, will you?* Which one? *That one, with the bulge in his trousers.* You are wicked, Divina. *Mmm-hmm, don't I know it, Pip, and you're not far behind.* They elbow each other as they stroll through the hotel lobby and then take the stairs. Divina, winded, stretches out on the bed's white-coverlet while Ruby flips the electric light switch on and off.

"Will you quit that, Pip? I need forty winks."

Ruby pees in the new-fangled water closet and washes her hands under the faucet, hot and cold taps marked with a capital "H" and "C." *If ever!* She tries to relax on the bed next to Divina, but she is too restless. She writes a hasty note, tiptoes out of the hotel room, and closes the door softly behind her. She straightens her wide-brimmed straw hat on the landing before she descends the stairs.

Few people are out in the noonday heat. Ruby leaves the downtown area and wanders through a Mexican *barrio*. She envies women in loose white shifts as they gather laundry off long, droopy lines, their animated chatter filling the stifling afternoon air. Ruby is tempted to duck into a Mexican *tendajon*, but stands instead in the shade of an acacia tree, rubbing an itch on her back against the gnarled bark.

The new University of Arizona is only a mile away, and though Ruby would like to take in the broad expanse of such a campus of learning, the walk is too far in this weather. But to think Virgil or Sam could go to university, become a lawyer or an accountant or a doctor. Is Jericho, with its riff-raff of the world, only thirty-some-odd miles away? Might as well be as far away as the moon.

Ruby avoids a streetcar on Fourth Avenue. In her haste—and not looking to her right after stepping out of the streetcar's way—she barely dodges an automobile barreling up the street. *What a waste of money! When you can have a horse!*

Ruby checks her pocket watch. She wishes for a horse, so famished she is on the way back to the hotel. She walks from awning to awning to avoid the sun and dabs her forehead with a handkerchief. Although she's tempted by the smells from a Chinese kitchen, that would never do, so in the end she decides on the Hotel San Augustine for supper. One cannot be too careful with foreign food. Some of them eat dogs and horses, after all.

Seated with Divina in the plush dining room two hours later, Ruby runs her finger down the hotel's extravagant menu: Prime Rib Roast, Kansas City Beef au Jus, Suckling

Pig with Dressing. Peach Meringue Pie. That is something Ruby can never attempt, a meringue. It would fall flat in five seconds in the Jericho heat. One day she will have an icebox. And ice. There are two ice plants in Tucson now. But how to transport it without melting? Therein lies the miracle.

The high-ceilinged dining room is full tonight—railroad men, ranchers in their Sunday best, fashionable shop owners and their more fashionable wives, courting couples. Large potted plants grace each corner of the pink-wallpapered room. Original oil paintings hang from long wires descending from crown moulding. The din of serving trays, utensils, laughter, and conversation, all this fills the room, which is cooled by two large overhead fans, their blades making lazy loops around domed lights.

Ruby orders Kansas City beef, fifty cents for the full meal, the same as she charges guests for her midday dinner. After another cup of oyster bisque and a plate of sliced tomatoes, queen olives, and spiced pickles, the entrée arrives, heaped with mashed potatoes, green beans, and baked pumpkin. Divina has ordered pork with all the side dishes, and finishes with hot mince pie and coffee. At the last moment, Ruby skips the meringue in favor of chocolate ice cream and orders café noir.

"Yes, sometimes I love this town." Ruby pushes her chair back and wishes for a cigarette. She hasn't had one in years, not since the carnival days, but you never lose that craving, just one . . .

Night slides silently over day, pitch dark now at seven o'clock, as the women walk arm-in-arm on the short block back to the Santa Rita. Two men approach on the boardwalk, one short and bandy and the other tall and stout. Ruby thinks the second one might be considered handsome, if not for a huge paunch that sags south of his belt buckle.

"Pardon me, ma'am. You wouldn't want to share an

evening with a like-minded soul?" The stouter and larger of the two directs his comment to Divina.

"Out of my sight," Divina bellows. She waves her cane at the man and hits his sizeable paunch. "You're not the sort I have in mind."

The other man, undeterred, sidles up to Ruby. His hat sits askew over his pock-marked face. "Aw, c'mon. Saw you coming out of the San Augustine. For fifty cents each, you could come out even. Like we bought you dinner, but a whole lot more fun. We have rooms at . . ."

"You've come barking up the wrong tree," Ruby says.

"Have we?" The larger man jostles Divina and she nearly loses her balance. She bats her cane at him again.

"Didn't you hear me the first time?" Ruby draws her pistol from her belt. "Maybe you've heard of Ruby Fortune, Girl Wonder?" She waves the pistol at the men. "No? Well, even if you haven't, you don't want to run into her. Might have those tiny cocks of yours shot off." She aims the pistol below their belts.

"Sorry for the bother, ma'am," the first rough says, his hands in the air. His friend has already slunk away into an alley.

"Like I said. Men are bastards, Pip."

"Don't I know it."

Divina snores all night, so Ruby sleeps fitfully. She rises early to pack and wakes Divina at seven. After a breakfast of steak and eggs, hotcakes, hashbrowns, and coffee, Ruby checks her watch. The stage to Jericho leaves at noon.

"We best be off for Vi's," she says to Divina.

"Got the cake?" Divina asks.

"I do," Ruby answers. They shuffle their bags and boxes down the narrow hotel stairs and leave their goods behind the front desk with instructions for the desk manager to be on the lookout for Ruby's remaining deliveries.

Especially the one for Virgil. "Be sure to put that one aside in a safe place," she tells the bleary-eyed clerk. "We'll be back at eleven and won't have God's one minute to waste tracking it down."

Ruby and Divina head down Broadway toward the busy depot. Directly next door to the station, there's a neat sign over an arched entryway: VIOLA'S BOARDING HOUSE.

"Sight for these tired eyes, you two. Come in, come in." If Vi is a hundred pounds drenched, Ruby isn't convinced. Vi is dressed tip to toe in black, with an impossibly tiny waist. Seventy she must be by now, or older.

She takes the cake from Ruby and sets it aside. Vi sits at the edge of a small divan, her bird-like hands animated. "Now, where should we begin?" She motions for Ruby and Divina to sit on larger davenport opposite and taps her cane on the floor three times. "Mattie! Three glasses of iced tea!"

"I've got more to tell you than the day has hours," Ruby says.

"Tell me first what you've done here in the Old Pueblo. I don't get out as much as I used to, damn this hip." She pats her side.

"Wish you could have joined us at the San Augustine," Divina says. "That pie alone was worth fifty cents." Divina adjusts herself on the davenport, folds of fabric bunching under her.

"The San Augustine . . . now that would be a treat."

"Too bad we didn't have enough time go to out to Elysian Grove this time," Divina says. "The gardens, the boat rides, the tea house . . ."

"And the ice cream," Ruby says.

"Bring the boys next time, Ruby," Vi says. "Virgil would love it. And Sam. The shooting gallery, the zoo, the horseraces . . ."

"Is it true they're jockeyed by monkeys?" Divina asks. Vi nods.

"What next?" Ruby marvels. "If I bring the boys, they'll never want to leave."

The serving girl deposits a tray on a narrow table to Vi's left. Three tall glasses of iced tea sweat in the heat. "Anything else, ma'am?"

Vi glances at the hall clock. "It's almost time for my usual." Vi hands Ruby and Divina each a glass. "Care for a biscuit?" She doesn't take one for herself. She settles deeper into the divan then, crosses her legs, and lights a thin cigarette with gnarled hands. Her frosted glass sits full on the table, drops of perspiration coursing down the sides of the glass. "And what else have you two been up to?"

Ruby doesn't mention the roughs. "Like a buying spree?"

"Can't help yourself?" Vi asks. Her eyebrows arch.

"Left a few hats and gloves on the shelves." She thrusts her chest out and fingers the trim on her starched white collar. "Ordered up four of these from Madame Eaves. Cost me a small fortune. Although why I keep doing it is beyond me." Ruby doesn't mention that buying new blouses is straining her budget. "Can't keep a white one clean for five minutes in Jericho. Maybe I'll start wearing black, like you."

Vi snorts. Ruby doesn't know if Vi is referring to white blouses in general or Madame Eaves in particular or that Ruby wants to dress like her.

Ruby smooths her white skirt and loosens the top button of her new blouse. "How can you stand wearing black, Vi?"

"It's expected."

"Price of being a woman," Divina says. "Corsets, camisoles, chemises, bloomers, petticoats, stockings . . ."

"And that's before you add what God and all can see," Vi says. "Blouses, like your new one there, skirts, belts, vests, jackets, hats, boots. It's a racket, women's wear. Twice as expensive as men's wear. Why? Because they can get away with it. Look at Mexican women. Simple white shifts and sandals. They've got it right."

"Or your girls, wandering around in lingerie," Ruby says.

"And you wonder why I chose this line of work?" Vi asks.

"I thought it was . . ."

"The lingerie, Ruby, the lingerie."

"And I ordered three new pair just yesterday. French fashion."

Vi's eyebrows arch again.

"Speaking of, have I got a story for you. But first, I want to know about that girl of yours," Ruby says.

"What of her?"

"So I go to meet the stage on the day you said, and boy, am I hot under the collar, Vi. Land agents, fancy men, drummers, they all get off and there's not a girl in sight. And not a one of the others come calling to help with the sheets."

"What the hell? No girl?" Vi throws her hands in the air. "Saw her off on the stage myself. Gave her a bundle of cash, too, to get back on the right foot."

Now Ruby snorts. "That was your first mistake."

"My first? Damn it. Should have learned a few hundred mistakes ago I can't trust a soul." Vi shakes her head. "I'll send another girl up, Ruby. Even if I have to deliver her myself. Now what is it you were going to tell me? Something about lingerie?"

Ruby recounts the tale of Wink's find in the desert. "And the sheriff had the gall to ask who had been in my bedroom."

"No one has the right to ask you that, least of all a man."

"Goddamn right about that. I told him so, in so many words. Although I wouldn't mind him in my bedroom, just once."

"Just once?" Divina asks, stifling a snort.

Mattie returns with three short glasses, an amber ewer, and a teaspoon. She places the tray on a low table between the divan and the davenport.

"Just what the doctor ordered." Vi pours a generous amount of liqueur into three glasses. She picks one up and swills the golden liquid. Ruby thinks of laudanum. "Honey, vinegar, and whiskey," Vi says. "Good for what ails you." Vi hands a glass to Ruby and to Divina before taking hers down in a single gulp.

"Damn, that's good," Vi says. "I'll take whiskey over a man any day." Vi pats the spot next to her on the divan. "Come sit by me, will you, Ruby? But watch my hip, it's acting up on me."

Ruby squeezes in next to Vi.

"So tell me about the boys," Vi says.

"Proud of Virgil, I am. He runs that post office so well the postmaster just stops in twice a day. I'll bet my hat Virgil takes over before he's twenty."

"And Sam? That boy talking yet?"

Ruby shakes her head. "I blame myself for that. But he's learning sign language. It's like a secret code between us." She signs "I love you."

"What's that you say?"

"I love you."

"Show me."

Ruby bends Vi's gnarled third and fourth fingers down.

"Well, I'll be. I love you, too, Ruby, God knows. But don't you go blaming yourself for every damn thing. Gets you nowhere." Vi pokes at Ruby's midsection. "You're awfully skinny."

"Who's talking?"

"If Skinny here had her eyes in straight, she'd take up with that sheriff," Divina says. She turns to Vi and puts her hand to her mouth as if she's whispering. "The one

Ruby mentioned earlier she wouldn't mind having in her bedroom." Divina clucks her tongue. "Bet that one doesn't disappoint beneath the trousers."

Ruby slugs her whiskey concoction in one swallow, like Vi. Then she picks up Divina's glass and slugs that one, too.

"Speaking of trousers," Vi says, "send my regards to that old German sonofabitch up at the way station. Tell him I miss him." She pats Ruby's knee absentmindedly, her fragile fingers bony and translucent. "It's so good to see you, Ruby. Doesn't matter how many girls pass through these doors, God as my witness, I miss your momma the most." She bends her third and fourth fingers into the warm air, eyes misty.

MARCH 29, 1905
JERICHO, ARIZONA TERRITORY

Ruby removes a cake from the oven with two large mitts she fashioned from an old horse blanket. She's prepping for a houseful tonight. The inn was closed all week while Ruby made the trip to Tucson. No one needs to know the real god-ugly reason. And she's still getting over Fletcher high-tailing it out of town while she was gone. Not even a note.

"Happy Birthday, Virge," Ruby says. She's babied Virge, yes. You don't have a lame child and not do so, if you've got a momma's heart. Still, it's hard to let go. He's fourteen now. Clayton and Fletcher took off not long past that age, so she knows it's not far off, Virgil wanting to spread his wings. But never would be too soon for Virgil to leave. She won't have it.

"You can dig into this cake later. First, I'm making your favorite supper." Ruby flips the oven door shut with her elbow and hip. "Chicken, mashed potatoes, all the fixings."

Virgil slurps coffee. Smiles. Roger is curled up under his feet waiting for scraps.

"I've invited half the town, hope you don't mind."

"Ma!"

"No 'Ma'-ing me, young man. You only have a birthday once a year and I aim to see this one come and go in fine style. You only turn fourteen once."

Sam finishes his oatmeal and scrapes his bowl. He reaches for another nickel and balances it on an already high stack beside his place at the small table. It wobbles before righting itself.

Virgil reaches across the table to topple the stack.

"Don't be like Fletcher. Did either of you see him leave? Tell me."

The boys shake their heads.

"He didn't even say goodbye?"

Again, no.

"I'm seeing to it that you two don't up and leave, ever."

"I'm not going anywhere, Ma," Virgil says. "I've got a good job right here."

Sam looks up with hooded eyes.

"And that goes for you, too, little mister," Ruby says.

A thunderous boom shakes the earth.

"Damn, that one was loud," Ruby says. "Hope they're hitting pay dirt today." She doesn't mention the possibility of bodies mangled in the mine. *You've got to get out of here, Perce. If you don't end up hung for sleeping with me, you're gonna end up dead up at that mine.*

"You alright, Ma?" Virge asks.

Ruby can't get the image of Perce out of her mind. She shakes her head no, then yes. "Sorry, boys, don't what came over me. Now go fetch me some water, Sam. And you, Virge, run up to Mr. Burton's for me, will you? Put a sack of pota-toes and a pound of butter on my tab. Check if they have fresh cream while you're at it. But first, can you reach that crock for me up there? Yes, that one. Damn if I'm short."

Virgil hands Ruby the crock and reaches into his vest pocket. "Forgot to tell you, Ma. This came for you." He hands a letter to Ruby.

Ruby takes one look at the return address—Chicago— and puts the letter in her apron pocket. "Here, Roger." She tosses the last of the bacon to the dog. "Now get on with it, boys. I've got more to do than a mule today. Dinner won't cook itself."

RUBY'S TABLE IS FULL. SHE RARELY does a head count of dinner guests. Doesn't make sense. Someone you thought was a sure thing begs out; another you didn't expect shows up in a tie.

Tonight, for posterity's sake, she surveys her table, the crowd crammed around it loud and boisterous, the way she likes it. Virgil, Sam, Divina, Sheldon, and Wink, bathed and dressed for the occasion in an oversized suit. Surprisingly, Margaret Stern has joined them, along with shopkeepers Harvey and Mae Burton and their two daughters, and the new preacher Charles Dowd and his prim wife, trying hard not to show she's in the family way. The Dowds' twelve-year-old daughter Elizabeth picks at the corner of her plate. One of her eyes wanders, so you never know which one to focus on.

Doc Swendsen sent his regrets. A hard labor up the street has kept him tied up for hours. Ruby will save a plate for him, in case he shows later. She didn't get a response from Dog Webber other than "on deadline," his usual excuse. Hell, he might show up, you just never know. There are enough chairs. Ruby has learned from years and years of serving up that the walls will hold them all.

Ruby has set the table with her best linen and silver and china and stemware, her first purchases when she opened the inn in 1900. She passes platters heaped with browned chicken and bowls of steaming potatoes, beets, and peas. Everyone has wine tonight, even the children.

Talk, talk, talk, and not limited to the thermometer, mercury ninety-five in the shade. Ruby fans her face with a plate and shoos Roger out of the dining room. She's wearing one of her new white blouses and a comfortable suede split skirt. Once she sits, maybe she'll kick off her boots.

Wink leans in toward Divina. The sheriff holds court at the far end of table, telling a story of when he first came to Jericho. Sam teaches the Burton girls the signed alphabet. Laughter, tinkling of cutlery, more wine. *Where is Fletcher by now?*

Wink's hands fly as he converses with Divina. In polite company, he might be too close, but Divina nods as he rambles on. She leans on her fleshy elbow and bends her head toward him.

"How is it that you know your Shakespeare?" Divina asks.

"Looks can be deceiving, my dear." Wink gazes at Divina like the bloom is still on the rose, although both are nearing sixty. "University of Chicago," he says. "Theatrics. 'All the world's a stage and all the men and women merely players.'"

"*As You Like It*," Margaret Stern says.

"Act 2, Scene 7."

"What brought you to Jericho?" Margaret asks.

"Ah, my dear lady," Wink says. "'The course of true love never did run smooth.'"

"*A Midsummer Night's Dream*," Margaret says.

Wink nods. "Touché. What this town needs is a playhouse. Do you agree, Miss Stern?"

"A grand idea. Musicales, theatricals, forums . . ."

"And dances!" Wink beams.

"A playhouse would smarten up this town," Divina says. "That, and a library. Even Jerome has a playhouse and a library. And we don't want to be bested by Jerome, or anywhere, for that matter."

"You must be a mind reader, Miss Sunday," Margaret says.

"Palm reader, Miss Stern," Divina says. "If I could read peoples' minds, I'd be a whole heck of a lot richer."

Harvey Burton pipes up. "Put women in charge and we'll have a maypole at the center of town."

"Honestly, Harvey," Mae Burton says.

Margaret ignores Burton. "What do you say, Mrs. Burton? And you, Mrs. Dowd? We could form a chapter of the Arizona Federation of Woman's Clubs right here in Jericho."

"Sign me up," Mae Burton says.

Mrs. Dowd looks to her lap.

"We're here for another purpose," Reverend Dowd says.

"Good luck with that," Sheldon says. "You'll be lucky to have a half dozen in the pews every Sunday, yourselves included. We can't keep a preacher here more than a year. I say we start a petition for a library, right here tonight. Ruby, do you have a pen?"

"I'm glad to hear your interests run deeper than law and order," Margaret says.

"His interests run deep over at Judd's," Harvey Burton laughs.

The preacher's wife blanches.

"You'll hold your tongue right there, Burton," Sheldon says.

"Did you hear there's a colored woman at Judd's now?" Mae interrupts. "Don't know what this world is coming to. Or why anyone would want to cavort with coloreds." She glances at Ruby.

Harvey Burton stabs a large piece of chicken. "Keep your thoughts to yourself, Mae. For once." He turns back to Miss Stern. "The sheriff here is the master of vigilante justice. There's no 'law and order' in these parts."

"Beg your pardon, Burton," Sheldon answers. "Order comes before the law every time. Horse thieving, cattle rustling, claim jumping—they all require swift justice."

Burton barrels on. "Where do you stand on turf wars, Sheriff? Can't keep sheep ranchers and cattlemen in the same room at the tavern, or there's bound to be a fight. It's a battle for grass and water every day. Stupid animals don't know the difference. Heard you favor the cowmen. Now's your chance to set the record straight, seeing as I'm partial to mutton men."

"We'll take up this conversation another time, Burton. This is a young man's birthday party tonight."

"Heard we're getting a new deputy," Mae Burton breaks in. "Isn't that right, Sheriff?"

"News travels fast in this town, Mrs. Burton." Sheldon steers the conversation away from her husband. "Bart Gallagher's his name, big guy, not one to mess with. Just arrived from Kansas City. Took a while to find the right fit, but I knew as soon as I laid eyes on him. Hired him on the spot. But I told him to enjoy Tucson for a week and not get himself shot. He'll be here next Wednesday."

"Ruby, we have to get to Tucson again soon," Divina says. She mops up her gravy with a heel of bread. "I could enjoy myself there for a week myself. Maybe more if I had Bart Gallagher as company."

The minister's wife by now has her hanky pressed up to her nose. Her cross-eyed daughter stares at Divina like she's just opened a banned book.

Ruby bites her lip and stifles a laugh.

"What's the talk of statehood in Tucson?" Miss Stern asks.

"We were otherwise engaged, weren't we, Ruby?"

Again, Ruby bites down a laugh.

"No way in hell will anyone agree to that hare-brained idea," Sheldon says. "Joint statehood with New Mexico? Not a chance. Might be 1910, 1920—who knows—before Arizona becomes a state. Last hold outs we are here." He pounds the table.

"And proud of it," Ruby says. She places refilled platters on the table.

"A body could starve here, Ruby," Sheldon says.

"Isn't this what you have for supper most nights?"

"If it doesn't come out of a can, I haven't met it."

"That's a poor way to ask for an invitation more often."

"Just the truth, ma'am."

Ruby comes up behind Sheldon and whispers in his ear. "You're lucky you didn't come to supper a couple of weeks back, Sheldon. Two guests swore they had food poisoning, but I think it was a trick to get a free meal. So don't go trying that one on me."

"Let me see that hand of yours." Divina takes Wink's hand and arches her eyebrows. Wink relaxes in Divina's grip like a schoolboy. "First, I need to decipher the lines. This one here," she touches Wink's upturned palm, "is the heart line . . ."

Ruby finally sits and kicks off her boots. She takes the last of the chicken from the platter and slathers it with oily gravy. By now, the tablecloth is stained with wine and the noise level borders on cacophony. Ruby wouldn't have it any other way.

Between bites, Ruby turns to Reverend Dowd. "Of the San Francisco Dowds, did I hear you say? Divina and I aim to get to San Francisco as soon as we rustle up enough money."

"And time," Divina nods. "Why is it you left there, Reverend?"

"I didn't exactly choose it, ma'am. Were sent here because—"

"Let's let the guests enjoy their supper," his wife interrupts.

"I hope you know what you're in for here," Burton says. "There's not a more wicked town you could've landed in. I've heard it said the Lord destroyed Jericho. Well, He'll never get away with that here."

"Hold your tongue, Burton," Sheldon says.

"That'll be the day," Mae Burton says.

"Jericho has burned twice already," Sheldon says. "And rebuilt finer than before each time. If you mean, sir, that Jericho is indestructible, I'll agree with you there."

Ruby goes into the kitchen and bursts out a half-minute later, leading into the dining room with her backside out of the swinging doors. Who has swiped a piece from the cake? She turns the plate around so the missing piece doesn't show as she enters the dining room, candles blinking from the top of it. "Happy Birthday, Virgil!" She leans down to whisper into Virge's ear. "Don't know who dug into this, but I have an idea." She looks at Sam, who is still busy signing with the Burton girls.

Everyone around the table claps and cheers. "Here's to you, Virgil!" "Happy Birthday, Virge!" "Make a wish!"

Virgil blows out the fourteen candles in one big exhale.

"What did you wish for?" one of the Burton girls asks.

"Ain't supposed to tell," her sister answers. "If you do, it won't come true."

"Aren't," Margaret Stern says. "You *aren't* supposed to tell."

"Hogwash," Ruby says. "You girls probably think St. Nicholas comes round each year. Down the chimney."

The Burton girls look at each other, and then at Mae.

"Doesn't do any good lying to children."

The girls look at each other and then to their mother, their eyes wide.

"And we don't need to keep our birthday wishes secret," Ruby says. "Do tell, Virge. Let's spread a little good news around once."

Virgil stands, his hands steadied on the table. "I've been thinking, Ma. About what's been going on here lately at Jericho Inn."

SAME NIGHT

Ruby freezes. Does Virgil know about Wink? And Squires? Ruby glances over at Wink, but he's enamored of Divina. She counts her blessings that Wink swung that shovel just when he did. She won't see Jake Squire's backside again but she doesn't want God and all to know about it. *What did Wink do with him, anyway?* Ruby was too embarrassed to tell Sheldon about the encounter, but Squires' cronies are wanted for armed robbery now and it wouldn't behoove them to backtrack to Jericho while Sheldon's on watch and a new deputy on the way. Let them rot in another town's lockup. Filth. Rats. Stench. And keep this secret hers and Wink's alone.

"No need to get all anxious-like, Ma. I've got a good idea—maybe a wish, I don't know—but I wished for it just now."

Everyone around the table looks to Ruby, waiting for her reply.

"I'm listening."

Virgil plows in again. "Everyone's heard of the Acadia Ranch up in Oracle." The majority of the guests at the table nods. "A 'health resort,' they call it," Virgil continues. "People come from all over the United States to seek a cure for what ails them. Now, I'm not saying we cater to invalids only. I've seen catalogues advertising new spa resorts."

"Here, in Arizona Territory?" Mae Burton asks.

Virgil stammers, takes a breath. "Especially here. You might be surprised what comes through the post office. I read everything. I say we remodel Jericho Inn and take in a different clientele. No more riff-raff. Could get a heap more for the rooms, too."

Everyone's eyes are trained on Ruby. "A spa resort, you say? What makes it different than an inn? We've got great vittles here."

Murmurs and nods.

Virgil takes a brochure from under his plate. He holds up the colored tri-fold and waves it in the air. "The Catalina Hotel. In Tucson. 'Focusing on the needs of the most discerning traveler.'" He looks over the top of his spectacles at his mother. "And look." He points at the brochure. "A swimming pool. A golf course. Riding stables, too. Take city folk up into the mountains on horseback and they'll pay double."

"Big business, hunting," Harvey Burton says. He mimics taking a shot. "Like goddamn Teddy Roosevelt."

Sheldon nods. "Bighorn sheep, mountain lion, javelina."

"And don't forget quail," Burton says. "You can bag a couple dozen in no time."

Ruby is still stuck on the idea of a swimming pool. "A swimming pool? In the desert?"

"I'm with you on this one, Pip," Divina says. "Dig a hole in the desert and pour water in it, it'll just seep right back from where it came from. Sounds like a losing proposition to me."

"Sometimes we've got to look with a new set of eyes," Virgil says.

Ruby could hug Virgil right then and there, but she doesn't want to embarrass him. "Pass it over, the pamp'let."

"Golf?" Sheldon interrupts. "Gets in your blood, people say. Like an addiction."

"Hitting a ball with a stick?" Ruby laughs. "Sounds like a waste of time to me."

"It's called a club, Ma," Virgil says. "Played all over the world. Even some ladies play."

"Hmmm," Ruby says. "After last weekend . . ." She catches herself.

"What happened last weekend?" Sheldon asks.

"Let's just say, maybe it's time for some changes around here. I suppose you'll be having me change the name of the place. 'The Miracle' or some such."

"Nobody says you need to change the name, Ruby," Sheldon says. "Hell's Roadhouse is a fine name." He winks.

Ruby waves her silver cake server at Sheldon, shaking her head and suppressing a laugh. "Enough of that talk for now." She slices into the three-layer cake. "Let's dig into Virgil's cake here before it goes all weepy on us. Seems someone," she again looks at Sam, "couldn't help himself to a bite . . ."

Ruby plates a large slice for Virgil and places it in front of him. She bends and slips a small package from her apron pocket into his lap. "A little something I picked up for you in Tucson." Won't he love the engraved pocket watch? As she straightens, a large hand squeezes her backside. She bolts upright and turns to see Harvey Burton grinning at her.

"Okay everyone, time to sing to the birthday boy." Ruby taps a fork to an empty glass, drawing everyone's attention to Virgil. Mostly off-key, the group sings the familiar rendition. As the guests finish the chorus, Ruby rumples

Virgil's shaggy red hair and bends close to his ear. "Happy Birthday, Virge. I think you've got a grand idea." She jabs Harvey Burton in the thigh with the fork.

"Yikes!"

"Sorry, Harvey. Must've slipped out of my hand."

AFTER THE LAST OF THE GUESTS leaves, Ruby holds Sheldon back. "I think I know who pilfered my duds."

Sheldon's eyebrows arch. "Do you, now. Maybe I'll take another cup of coffee, if you're offering."

Ruby goes through to the kitchen.

"Mr. Sloane?" Ruby hears Virgil say. She keeps her ear to the door.

"I've need of a pistol."

"Why, may I ask?" Sheldon responds.

"Had a situation at the post office. Same fella that came in a few days back. Took seven dollars off me in the middle of the day."

"Stocky guy looking for work? With two others outside?"

"Yup. But only two of them. Not the tall one."

"Curious. Wonder where he's gone to."

Ruby's blood runs cold. *What do they know? Anything?*

"Beats me. Saw him the night before—the three of them stayed here at the inn—but I didn't see him after breakfast."

Nor will you ever see him again, thank God.

"I'll keep my eye out. But I should tell you, Virgil. It's against the law to carry a piece on the job."

"I'm well aware of that. Won't stop me, though."

Ruby backs into the dining room with two mugs. "Here you go, sir." She hands Sheldon the mug. "Virgil?"

"No thanks, Ma, I think I'll turn in."

It's then Ruby realizes her hands are shaking. She ties them behind her back.

"See you tomorrow, Virgil," Sheldon says. "We'll take up this conversation then. I'll stop by the post office. For tonight, happy birthday, son."

Sheldon and Ruby sit at the cluttered table.

"What were you and Virgil talking about?"

"Can't a fella have a man-to-man without you barging into all the details?"

"As long as you're not leading him down the pathway to Hell."

"That I would never do, and you know it, Ruby. Those boys of yours are like . . ."

"Don't go there, Sheldon."

Sheldon turns to Ruby. "Would you be quiet for one minute, woman?"

They drink coffee in silence.

"So, you were saying. You know who stole your duds?"

"Never mind, Sheldon. Maybe I jumped to conclusions, but I'm suspicious of everyone right about now. Even you."

Sheldon drains his mug. "Wasn't me, Ruby. Although those bloomers of yours were mighty fine. I have other intentions about seeing them."

"When Hell freezes over, you mean?"

"I can wait that long." Sheldon pats his middle. "That was quite the meal, Ruby. Widower like me . . ."

"Don't be giving me widower eyes, Sheldon. Might work for other women, but not here."

Sheldon stands. "You can't take a compliment? God, you infuriate me sometimes." He picks up his hat, tips it at her, and heads for the front door. His footfalls blend into the night.

Ruby sits still for a moment and then hurries to the porch. "Sheldon!" she calls after him, but it bounces off his back.

APRIL 3, 1905
JERICHO, ARIZONA TERRITORY

Ruby turns the unopened letter over and over in her hand. Five days she's had it now. The all-too familiar address is all the more reason not to unseal it.

Ruby hears footsteps on the porch and quickly tucks the letter back into her pocket. A portly woman barges through the door, a thinner friend in tow. Ruby does a double take. *What in heaven's name?*

"Sisters of the Order of Disorder," the bigger woman laughs. She has whiskers around her large mouth. Other than her lively wide-set eyes and prominent nose, the rest of her head is covered with a wimple. She extends her hand. "Sister Mary Lamb, from St. Joseph of Carondelet. And this is Sister Mary Theresa, although I call her 'The Other Mary.' We are all Marys." Her voice, deep-set for a woman, is nevertheless warm and welcoming.

The other woman nods. She is as thin as the other woman is broad, with a delightfully pretty face, what Ruby can see of it.

"Come in, come in," Ruby says. "From St. Mary's Hospital? Tucson?"

"Affiliated, yes."

"You good sisters do more for Tucson than a fly in a currant pie." Ruby motions to the well-stocked bar. "Help yourself, ladies. Supper and liquor is included in your lodging, a dollar a night each. Breakfast is fifty cents extra if you're not staying the week."

"Ah," Mary Lamb says. "I see you're a shrewd businesswoman." She pours two generous shots of whiskey into a short glass and hands the tumbler to The Other Mary. Then she dispenses one for herself, a three-fingered shot from where Ruby stands. "We'll make good on that arrangement."

Rare as chicken fricassee on a cattle ranch that Ruby gets solo female guests. These women—are they really sisters? Ruby doesn't judge. If women like the company of other women, that's their business.

The nuns settle into one of the plush damask green sofas facing the massive fireplace.

Ruby opens the register. She thinks back to the time President Teddy Roosevelt swaggered up the stairs of Jericho Inn back in '03, eighty degrees and a sky blue as an ocean. Roosevelt took up four lines when he signed his name in the oversized register, and then he called for a mint julep. Ruby had never heard of such a thing.

Sister Mary Lamb's deep purr brings Ruby back to the present. "We will just trouble you for one night, Mrs. . . .?"

"Fortune. Ruby Fortune. Raised right here in Jericho."

Mary Lamb gulps the last of her drink and pours another. "It's mighty fine to come across such a reputable establishment in a town such as this. Am I to presume there is a Mr. Fortune?"

"Not anymore."

"I see." Mary Lamb laughs, a deep, rumbling from her abdomen. "But nothing in the Lord's wide domain surprises me. To our rooms, then. After a short nap, we'll avail ourselves of your little town. You do have a surplus of taverns here in Jericho?"

"Taverns? Why, there's eight, ten, maybe more. Closest one is Judd's. What interest do you"—what should she call them, 'ladies'?—"have with a tavern?"

"Everyone inquires about that. In Bisbee . . ." The Other Mary pipes in.

"Shush now, Mary Theresa. I doubt Mrs. Fortune here is interested in our latest escapade."

"On the contrary, I'm fascinated."

"In Bisbee," The Other Mary continues, ignoring her companion. "We squeezed every last nickel out of townsfolk for our hospital and our orphanage."

"Ever see anyone say no to a nun?" Mary Lamb booms. Her laugh reverberates through the room. "Didn't think so. After our respite, you can point the way. We'll start with—what did you say the name was?"

"Judd's."

A knock on the kitchen door. "Halooo. Miss Ruby?"

"Excuse me for a moment," Ruby says.

"'Neither a borrower nor a lender be,'" Wink says, as Ruby approaches the screen door. "*Hamlet*. Act 1, Scene 3."

"What can I get you, Wink?"

"Sorry to trouble you, but I thought you might have some use for these." He reaches into his pack and pulls out a stack of rags. "Dumped by the rubbish pile."

Ruby takes the handful of tattered cloths. "Can always find use for these. Thank you, Wink. At least it's not, you know."

"Women's duds?"

"Mmm-hmm." Ruby turns to the sideboard and wraps up a slice a pie. "Tit for tat."

Wink smiles, his yellowed teeth marked with stain. "'If music be the food of love, play on.'"

"What play?"

"*Twelfth Night*."

"Don't know that one." Truth is, Ruby has never heard of any of them.

"That's my favorite of all." Wink's hands fly in front of his seldom-washed face. "Raucous adventure. Thrilling intrigue. Masked identity. Don't let anyone tell you the Bard is dry."

"Maybe one day I'll read one of those plays of yours."

"In time, Miss Ruby, in time. When you have use for them."

Like that's going to happen anytime soon.

"READY?" RUBY PULLS ON HER red gloves. She grabs her hat and opens the front door. Sister Mary Lamb and The Other Mary look less refreshed than Ruby would have thought after their three-hour rest. She can't imagine living beneath that dark habit, cowl, and wimple in Arizona heat.

"My son, Virgil, works at the post office." From her yard, Ruby points to the brick structure across the street. "And . . ." Ruby stops short and puts her hand out instinctively to block the nuns from coming another step. "Don't move." Ruby pulls her pistol from her waistband and shoots a curled rattler not two feet from where the women stand. The snake wriggles and goes still, its tail still rattling.

"My God, Mrs. Fortune," Mary Lamb says. The Other Mary blanches.

"God's got nothing to do with it." Ruby finds a stout stick and lifts the lifeless snake. "I was a lady sharpshooter in my day. Years of practice." She deposits the dead snake on the far side of the fence near the property line. "Now, where was I?"

As the women walk up Jefferson, Ruby points out other landmarks. They skirt horses and burros, freighters and wagons. The Other Mary keeps her head low, looking for snakes.

At the top of the rise, the women stop for a breath. Ruby motions toward the tavern across the street. "Best of luck to you," she says. "Hope you clean them out."

"Damn right about that," Mary Lamb says.

Ruby reaches into her inner vest pocket. "Here's five dollars to get you started. I'm an orphan, too."

"Very generous of you, Ruby Fortune of Jericho."

Ruby watches the nuns cross the street and enter the saloon. What she'd give to see these two in action. Ruby used to accompany Big Burl to Judd's when she was a girl. Saw more there than any nickelodeon. And went after Willie there more times than she can count. But she hasn't been back to Judd's since Willie died. Old Judd and Willie were tight, and she doesn't want to cross him. She has enough trouble with Jimmy Bugg around.

"'Afternoon, Ruby," Harvey Burton says as Ruby enters the general store. "Who're your friends?"

"Not friends. Lodgers. From St. Mary's in Tucson."

"The hospital?"

"Yes. Raising funds for their orphanage there."

"In a saloon?"

"Best place to pass the hat, they say. No one says no to the kind sisters."

"One looks bigger than a house. Maybe that's why. Wouldn't want to cross her."

"Bark worse than her bite," Ruby says. "And funny, I might add. The younger one plays it meek, but I'm sure she's just as cunning. Doe eyes, she has, like she's seducing you."

"A nun? Seducing?" Burton laughs. "This I need to see. Mae! Come out front, will you? Need to go out for minute."

"Bring your wallet, Harvey," Ruby says.

Burton pats his vest. "Noted." He barges out the door of the general store and heads toward the tavern.

Mae Burton comes out from behind the large wooden counter filled with penny candy and nickel sundries. "Mrs. Fortune! What can I get for you today? A nice leg of mutton came in just this morning."

Mutton, now there's a specialty. Quail and rabbit Ruby can get any day. Or venison. But mutton, yes, that will be a treat for the traveling sisters when they return from their venture to Jericho's saloons. She can't wait to hear all about it.

"Shall I put it on your account?" Mae asks. "It seems Mr. Burton is intent on spending all our profits today."

"And add another pound of butter and some corn meal."

"Done. Oh, and take a few calendars. April, already, can you believe it? We've got more calendars than we know what to do with. Tuck them into your guest rooms."

Ruby hurries home, the leg of mutton under her arm. As she approaches the inn, Ruby sees a young woman standing on the porch shading her eyes.

"Can I help you?"

The girl turns to face Ruby.

Ruby's heart lurches in her chest. A large welt flowers under the girl's eye, which is swollen shut. The girl can't be more than sixteen, maybe even younger than when Willie started thrashing her.

"Who did this to you?"

The girl lowers her hand. "A fella."

"Who? Where?"

"Doesn't matter."

"Did you just arrive in Jericho?"

"Vi sent me. Told me to find Ruby Fortune."

Ruby nods. "About time. What are we doing wasting daylight?" Ruby takes the girl's elbow and steers her into the inn.

"And you are?"

"Penny."

"Well, Penny Whatever-Your-Name-Is. Let's get a cold cloth on that eye of yours and we can talk it out over tea." Ruby guides Penny across the parlor, through the dining room, and into the kitchen. "Let's just say I've had my share of blackened eyes."

"You were . . ."

"No. But my momma worked the line. At Vi's. I was born there." Ruby dabs the younger woman's eye. "Have I shocked you? I've been known to do that without even trying. Can't count the number of times I looked a sight like you. But I need the help here, Penny. That's where you come in."

"Judd'll be looking for me within the hour."

"Judd? What the hell does Judd have to do with it? Did he do this to you?"

The girl nods. "I stayed there the last few nights, getting up my courage to come see you. He said I owed him all my wages for his hospitality. I fought him for it."

"Judd can go piss on himself," Ruby says. "He's got it out for me, too, but for different reasons. He wouldn't dare cross me in my own home. Sit here while I fetch another cloth."

"You're Fletcher's ma?" the girl asks.

Ruby stops and turns to the girl. "You know my boy?"

"In a backwards way. I've seen to his pals the last couple of nights. Judd won't have boys up in the rooms. But you can always make two bits on the side. More if there's more than one of them."

"Seems you've been busy." Ruby places the cool rag over the girl's eye again. She thinks of the Jarrett brothers, Leroy and Lorne. What ever became of them? Not that she didn't enjoy their company . . .

Penny bites her bottom lip. "Not saying I didn't like them, although they were a bit fumbling."

"A bit young, I might add."

Penny looks around the kitchen. "What kind of help are you needing here, ma'am?"

"Not in the way you're accustomed." Ruby wonders if hiring Penny is a good idea after all. Does she know the difference between a stew pot and braising pan? Flour from saleratus? "Where's your family, anyway?"

"Kansas. Clamped onto a fella coming west when I was fifteen. Last I saw him, he was heading out of Jerome on a fast horse. Not because of me. He might've killed a man, I'm not sure, but I suspect it. You hear everything in the trade. Made my way in Jerome for a few months until an older gentleman—I guess you'd call him a gentleman, he didn't hit me, at least—brought me to Tucson. The money's steadier there, he said. And the clientele isn't as rough."

"I can't offer you the same wages, but I can offer room, board, and two dollars a week if you're a hard worker. But there won't be any shenanigans. I mean it. I've got two boys here." Ruby shoots Penny a sly eye. "Young boys."

Penny dabs her eye again. "It's just that I don't know how much I'll be able to do, being in the family way."

There are ways to prevent it these days, Ruby thinks, *but that's water under the bridge now.* She needs the help. And there'll be time to teach the girl about pennyroyal later. Ruby washes out the rag, wrings it, and hands it back to the girl. "You're welcome to stay until the baby comes. And you can keep all your wages." Ruby stands over the seated girl, hands on her hips. "What I'd like to know is why the hell didn't you come here straight away?"

Penny lowers the cloth and looks up at Ruby. "Heard from the stage driver that you're not exactly roses."

"Hmph. Guess not. But don't worry about Judd coming after you. I'll take care of him."

RUBY ARRIVES AT JUDD'S Tavern in time to see the backside of the nuns heading up Brewer's Alley. She ditches her plan to confront Old Judd—yet—and tails Sister Mary Lamb and The Other Mary to The Empire. From her vantage point, Ruby watches Mary Lamb talking expressively to the barkeep, her head and hands animated.

The barkeep rings a bell at the end of the long mahogany bar. The din inside the saloon quiets.

"Gentlemen!"

A titter of guffaws.

"You, Frommer! And you, too, Chamberlain. All you chaps. Open your purses now, and give the good sisters a generous portion of your wages. The Good Book says to help orphans and widows—"

"We do our best with the widows!" one man shouts. Grimy men with soiled hats and scuffed boots hiked up on the long brass foot rail try, without success, not to spit chaw as they laugh.

"—as I was saying," the barkeep says, "see that all your wages don't go down a clap hole."

Sister Mary Lamb's bosom butts so close to patrons as she works the long bar that men would need a battering ram to elude her. Into her hand go coins, bills, nuggets. Sister Mary Theresa works tables, her pleading eyes and outstretched hands melting men's resolve.

When they emerge, Sister Mary Lamb is sweating profusely.

"Well done," Ruby says.

"Why, Mrs. Fortune!" The Other Mary says. "We weren't expecting you."

"Couldn't miss out," Ruby says. "Let's head to The Imperial next. After that, Dodson's. If you're needing an extra hand, I'll help collect. Why, we've got six, eight more watering holes to hit before the afternoon is out. Nothing I like better than parting a man from his money for a good cause."

"Really, Dog? Again?" Ruby bangs through the door of the *Jericho Courier-Journal*.

"Thanks to you, that inn of yours never fails to deliver the best fodder for this old rag, Ruby." Dog Webber waves the newspaper over his head. "Can't not print it."

Webber's collar might have been white once, maybe during Cleveland's first administration; his boots dirty his already-cluttered desk. Scraps of paper, piles of old newspapers, and stacks of books cover the top. Ruby can't see an inch of wood underneath. An oversized camera perches atop the mess.

Webber takes a long pull on his cigar. "I'll publish anything that moves here in Hellicho, like it or not. Like the time that camel wandered through town. Or about that lady stagecoach robber."

Ruby flips through the four-page newspaper. "That was news, Dog. A camel in the middle of the goddamn

Sonoran Desert. And that lady fugitive? That was news. But me? Again? Who the hell cares?"

"It's news, Ruby. Bona fide news. And sells more papers, people wanting to know exactly what goes on over there at that Jericho Inn of yours. No offense, mind you." Dog shuffles his boots. A book crashes to the floor, but he makes no attempt to retrieve it. "Folks have been talking, Ruby. About you taking on one of Judd's girls. Wondering if you're giving him competition."

"Bunch of busybodies. Who's gotten to you? Mrs. Burton? Mrs. Dowd? For all I care." Ruby straightens a pile of notebooks at the edge of Dog's desk and leans against the corner. "Judd's girl has a story, yes. But why is it everyone's business? She's mending her ways, if you're hankering to know. Hasn't had a visitor since I took her in. You can print that if you want to. Straight from the horse's mouth."

The notebooks clatter to the floor. Ruby bends to gather them.

"Leave them be, Ruby."

"How can you find anything in this mess?"

"Got a system. Might not work for the next man, but works for me. If I don't use a tip right away, I put it aside." He waves his hand around the office. "If I need it, I know it's here, somewhere."

"That's what filing boxes are for, you old cur."

"Are you offering? Saw you arranging my notebooks."

"Like I have time for that. Or anything. I've got to get back." Ruby tosses the newspaper onto Webber's cluttered desk. She bends her back to get a kink out. "I wish you'd leave me and Jericho Inn out of the paper. Got enough people talk about me as it is." She opens the newspaper office door and waits for the tinkling bell to stop. "But let me tell you, Dog. If the walls of that inn could talk, I could write a goddamn novel."

"HOW DO, PIP?" DIVINA RISES slowly from the waist and leans on her cane. Overnight, she's come to look like an old woman, fingers sprouting out at different angles, her pointer finger veering off from the top knuckle at an angle that Ruby remembers from school as obtuse. It's not like Divina to have her yard in weeds.

"Let me help," Ruby says. She shifts the newspaper from one arm to the other. The paper is damp from her sweat. She still can't believe the house she and Big Burl lived in next door is now gone, struck by lightning and burned back in '01, not long after she opened Jericho Inn. There's not a trace of it left.

"In a minute." Divina pecks Ruby on the cheek. "Come on in, have some refreshment. I'll take you up on your offer in just a bit."

Ruby follows Divina up the wide steps of the familiar adobe. *I need to get my arse up here more often.*

"Sit," Divina says. Ruby rests on a comfortable rocker next to the front door and fans her face with the newspaper, glad to be in the shade. Divina clatters into the house and returns with two glasses of cool tea. "Three sugars." She hands Ruby a tall glass. "And look what else I have." Divina holds out a peach, and hands it to Ruby along with a sharp knife, small plate, and faded tea towel. "Do you remember that time Big Sue had so many peaches we had peach pie for breakfast and dinner and supper, too? Palisade, Colorado, if I remember right."

Ruby stops slicing the peach, the knife midway into the juicy flesh.

"Can't say that I do," Ruby says. "Don't know if it's because my head got knocked so many times or if I plain don't remember."

"You remember Stick? Slovo?"

"Stick was a pervert."

"Not the only one. The jugglers in the Grinnell show? They would hump anything that moved. Like those Jarrett boys."

"I liked them."

Divina laughs. "Bet you did. You were what, fourteen?"

"Told them I was sixteen."

"Telling tales, like your pop. Speaking of the old sonofabitch, do you remember the first time we sold out two shows? Denver, it was. Your pop scooped you up and tossed you in the air so high I thought my breath would never come again."

"He did that all the time. I remember that, even if the rest of it is a little hazy. It's like everything after he passed on happened to another person. Like my life belonged to someone else."

Ruby carves the peach into eight sections and wipes her hand on the towel. She passes the plate to Divina. "It was good for a while with Willie, but then it seeped in, bad stuff, until it was all bad."

Divina fingers the peach and bites into the blushing pulp. "Since your pop's been gone, I guess most of it is worth forgetting." She passes the plate back to Ruby. "But if you ever want to know about anything, Pip, just let me know . . ." Divina's voice trails off. Then she sits up a little straighter. "What I mean to say, Pip, is I've got a memory that can't erase a single moment, no matter how hard I try. Some might call it a blessing. Not me. I call up a memory and it's as if I'm living it all over again. The good parts are worth the re-living. But the others, like the night your pop died, well, Pip, let's just say forgetting is the better end of the deal."

Ruby changes the subject abruptly. "I asked if I could help." She drains the end of the tea. A few sugar granules trace up the side of the empty glass.

"Not just yet. Let's sit a spell." Divina sighs. "A spell. Now that's one of the oddest requests I ever got. Always someone wanting me to help them find a husband, talk to a dead mother or sister. Mothers, mostly. Like I could. But if someone believes in something hard enough, they think it'll come true. Your pop always said that. Ironic."

Ruby wishes for more tea. Her throat is parched. But she doesn't want to bother Divina. The older woman's breathing is labored, even sitting. Ruby puts down the glass after licking the last of the sugar from the rim.

"Want to tell my fortune again?" Ruby asks. "Because according to the paper, I'm bound for the underworld." Ruby rustles the newspaper at Divina.

"I read all about it," Divina says. "Who would have ever thought?"

"Did you see the headline? *Local innkeeper houses lady outlaws.* I would think Dog would know better. I wouldn't hide any outlaw, lady or not. I've had my fair share, good paying customers, most of them. But conceal them? Never. They looked legitimate to me. I gave them five dollars myself for their cause."

"Seems you were taken, like most of Jericho." Divina picks up her copy of the *Courier-Journal.*

Eight of our hamlet's ten watering holes were hit this week by a set of con-women posing as itinerant nuns. Only George Murphy, owner and proprietor of Murphy's Bar, and Jack Simms, of The Axe and Pail, escaped the escapade. Those who didn't include Dodson's, The Empire, Hole In the Wall, The Imperial, Judd's Tavern, Last Call, The Pig Sty, and Stanford's.

Upon further investigation, the two women involved in the heist have no affiliation to St. Joseph of Carondelet, according to a spokeswoman for the hospital and *orphanage in Tucson. At last account, the fleet-footed felons fleeced the fine people of Jericho for upwards of $1,900.*

"It'll be old news by tomorrow, Pip."

"Who do you think they were?"

"Clever," Divina laughs. "You best watch your wallet next time someone comes begging. But I must admit, this is a new trick. Nuns."

Ruby scowls. "I don't know why Webber didn't lead with *Baffled businessmen buffaloed by bandits*. Why lay it all on me?"

"Good one, Pip. But Webber couldn't run that headline because he knows men can't stand the fact they've been swindled," Divina answers. "And certainly not by a woman. Let alone two of them." She takes a long swig of cool tea. "Better to blame you for housing them than take responsibility themselves. Granted, nuns in a saloon are not something you'd normally see in plain daylight in Jericho. A man with a stump leg? A freighter barreling down a group of schoolboys? A drunken brawl? Sure. But not women bandits."

"If they were women, after all," Ruby says. "Now that I think about it, Sister Mary Lamb's voice . . ." Ruby trails off, shaking her head. "After the third or fourth stop, I headed back to the inn to get supper on. I had that whole roast mutton and all the fixings and no nuns. They never came back. I ended up inviting Wink in and sent word up to Judd's. Had a tableful of strangers by the time the night was over and no leftovers."

"Thanks for the invite, Pip. Sorry I didn't make it. Had a bit of indigestion. Didn't sit right with me. Now come in. Let me see that tiny hand of yours."

THIRTEEN, RUBY WAS, THE FIRST and only time Divina read her palm. Divina had been reluctant, but acquiesced to stop Ruby's hounding her. Ruby sat rapt as Divina pulled her long sheer veil over her heavily rouged cheeks and lips. A chill sped down her spine as the two sat across a small table from one another on that hot Texas night long ago. Divina held Ruby's hand, as if her palm had all the answers.

"What is it?"

"Shush, Pip. It's time for you to be silent. For once."

Divina bent closer and squinted. She traced the four lines on Ruby's hand, three parallel lines and one cross-hatched line trisecting the others.

"The top line is your heart line," she said. "The one below is your head line. This one here"—she traced the long arcing groove in Ruby's hand—"is your life line. That one is long and open."

Ruby exhaled. "Whew."

"But here"—Divina ran her smooth finger over the top groove—"there will be trouble ahead, Pip. Perhaps soon."

"But . . ."

"No buts. This is something you will have to weather alone."

Ruby stared at Divina. "You're awfully puzzling."

"What I'm trying to say is follow your heart."

It is the best—and the worst—advice Ruby has ever gotten.

RUBY HOLDS THE DOOR FOR Divina. They enter the cool, dark parlor. Divina shuffles to her chair and sits opposite Ruby at a small table. There is no veil anymore.

"Do you remember what I told you that night? About following your heart?"

"I've made some bad choices."

"We all have, Pip. Speaking of, what's happening with that man of yours?"

"I keep telling him I can't see him anymore."

"Glad to hear it, for the both of you. If someone had been able to tell my fortune—really tell it, not some mumbo-jumbo—I would have hated what I saw," Divina says. "It's the devil's curse to get old, Pip. Those that died young had the right idea. Now give me your left hand," Divina says.

"I thought you read my right hand last time."

"I did. That's the one that you're born with. The left hand tells a different story." Divina holds Ruby's left hand in hers and squints. Her finger shakes as she traces the four lines on Ruby's left palm.

"See, Pip, it's different." She pokes at Ruby's life line. "Look at your right hand. The life line is smooth and unbroken. But here, on the left, there's a jagged break."

Ruby looks at both hands side by side. "That doesn't help."

"It does if you learn from it."

"What do you mean by that?"

"None of us knows what's going to happen, even an hour from now. You could be run down by a wagon or stabbed in the back. Hear from an old lover or meet a new one. Which brings me to this: let's make good on that promise and get ourselves to San Francisco before the year is out. See that ocean with our own eyes." Divina puts her hand on Ruby's. "I've got enough saved up for the two of us."

"You do?"

"I do, Pip. Plenty. Was just waiting for the right time to tell you."

"Before we talk anymore about that, there's something I've got to get off my chest." Ruby reaches into her pocket.

"Which is?"

"I got a letter. From Willie's sister."

APRIL 6, 1905
JERICHO, ARIZONA TERRITORY

As the sun arcs toward the horizon, Ruby stomps her boots to ward off snakes just awoken from their winter slumber, takes a swig from her canteen, and jumps off the back porch of Jericho Inn. A cloud of dirt dusts her ankles and calves; the hem of her split skirt balloons out and snaps back to slap her shins. A quail family scurries away, eight or ten babies dashing and darting after their parents. Penny is finishing up in the kitchen tonight. The girl is working out nicely. Ruby has set her up on the ground floor and given her more responsibilities as the weeks go by. Doc Swendsen says she's "healthy as a goddamn horse." There never was a baby. *Oh, the lies we tell . . .*

Ruby strides around the inn and pauses at the edge of her property. Turn right up Jefferson, you're a sinner or a saint. Or dead. Turn left, you're headed out of Jericho toward Tucson or Globe.

Back when Ruby was a girl, when she and Big Burl were home long enough from the hard life to rest their bones in

Jericho, Big Burl warned Ruby that if she stepped an inch outside of town on her own he'd have her hide, *so help him God*. Like he believed in God? Not a chance. But the way he said it drove enough fear into Ruby that she never did it. Those days, a whole town parented its own, where's Jesse or who's seen Mirabelle or where-the-devil is that slip of a rascal, Ruby? If Big Burl couldn't find her, he'd only have to heft himself to the crossroads, and there'd she be, standing under that ancient saguaro daring to defy him, singing the sun down or peppering the old cactus with buckshot. She felt safe there, at the edge of being good and being bad.

When Ruby came back to Jericho for good with Willie, their passel of boys in tow, she stood at this very intersection more times than the saguaro has arms deciding whether or not to light out of town for good. If it weren't for Clayton or Fletcher or Virgil or Sam, Ruby would've walked barefoot if she had to, north or south—heck, she would have walked east over the mountains or straight west, swallowing the sun, anything to get away from Willie Fortune. Her boys were all that tethered her here.

The sun has by now winked behind the horizon, stepping back for twelve hours before coming up again tomorrow with a vengeance. Ruby takes another slug from her canteen. Even though she's ridden out of Jericho a hundred times or more, she's never walked. What's stopping her tonight is the same thing that's stopped her every time before. No, Clayton isn't here, and neither is Fletcher. But she's still got Virgil, tender as a newborn lamb (although he's sprouting tawny peach fuzz in all the boy places). And then there's Sam.

Ruby couldn't have handled another son, no matter what Scripture says about God not giving a body more than it can handle. Tonight, Ruby is full up, and tempted to keep walking. She can't afford to keep the inn open much longer. And she misses a man in her bed. Once a month with Perce is not nearly enough, and she's all knotted up inside. She needs to tell him to get packing, once and for all, if she knows what's good for him. Even if it's the last thing she wants to do.

How about south? Tucson she loves. Or hates. Depends why she goes there. Sometimes she wishes she could stay a bit longer in town, but every time she's there she can't high tail it out of Tucson fast enough, counting miles on Oracle Road like Sam counts his nickels until she's back in Jericho. Could that stopover at that dirt hole halfway from Tucson to Jericho be any more tedious? *Home, home, home*, Ruby wills the stage driver. *Water your horses, yes, sure. Pay your fee. Smoke. Take a piss. But can we just get on?*

The town of Globe, now that's a different story. Globe, Ruby loves, although she hasn't been there in ages. It's the memory of Globe she loves. She pulled off her most impressive, never-to-be-repeated trick there, and no matter how many times she tried to replicate it, she never bested it, ninety-eight out of a hundred glass balls shattered to thunderous applause. Ruby still pictures it, riding full speed around the arena, colors blurring, ears burning, dust in her eyes and ears and mouth and heart swelled to twice its size with the fullness of it all. She loved that fringed skirt and that turquoise blouse. And still has the red boots.

If only she could recall experiences like Divina and puncture that scrim of memory viscerally, every time, every memory. Ruby has snippets like that. Sometimes she's reminded of a time that can never be recaptured but it's so vibrant—*so real*—that she has to blink to know where she is, still in a saddle rounding the showground for one last lap or standing in the middle of a coach road inhaling dirt.

Ruby crosses the road. She stops midway, smack in the middle of the byway. The stage doesn't run at night so anyone coming into Jericho at this hour is either a drifter or an outlaw. Ruby has seen her share of both, one of them newly in the ground, and two that took her—and most of Jericho—for fools.

Ruby takes out her derringer and fires off pot shots at the saguaro for old time's sake. Reloads and fires again. Loiters in the middle of the road until the stars appear. Soon, the night sky is awash with stars. She points to Polaris and traces her finger to the Big Dipper, sipping up the sky.

No, Ruby won't be going north or south tonight. Children have a way of doing that to a body. Even when they're grown, a piece of yourself walks around outside of you and you just can't let go. Other things, yes. Other people, too. But not your kin. Ruby would live in a shack and eat beetles if she had to, to protect them. They may leave her, but she'll never leave them. Not ever. Even when someone was thrashing the living daylights out of her. Or maybe more so because of it.

But she's ready to get away for a spell. See that ocean with her own eyes. She'll count the days now that Divina says she has enough tucked away for the both of them. That's a good thing, because Ruby can hardly make ends meet; she might have never gotten to San Francisco at this rate.

The desert has chilled off quickly. Ruby trudges uphill toward Jericho Inn, past the hanging tree, the livery, the post office, her back to possibility beckoning at the cross-roads. A few windows of the roadhouse are backlit with oil lamps. How is it she will ever pay for more oil?

In the distance, she hears the faint *hoo-hoo-hooooo* of an owl. She tightens her fringed shawl around her narrow shoulders and shivers. Somebody's died, that's what the owl call means at this time of night, doesn't it?

APRIL 7, 1905
JERICHO, ARIZONA TERRITORY

"Ruby! Open up!"

Ruby hears Sheldon banging on the kitchen door. The parlor clock has just chimed 6 a.m. as Ruby hurries to kick open the screen door, her hands covered with flour.

"Sheldon, what the devil?"

"It's Divina, Ruby. I'm sorry to be the one to tell you. She must have passed in the night."

Ruby slumps against the doorframe. "You mean . . ."

"Afraid so. Doc Swendsen sent me. Her heart must've given out. He was riding by and saw her slumped on the porch. Thought you should know before anyone else."

"But I was just there night before last," Ruby says. "She was . . . no, no, Sheldon, tell me it's not true."

"Can't lie, Ruby. Do you want to see her, before . . .?"

Ruby stares past Sheldon to the desert. "What do you think?" *Divina? Gone?* She shakes involuntarily, her head, her shoulders, her torso. *What in the hell am I going to do without you? Divina!*

The coffee pot boils. *Breakfast. Damn it, damn it. Penny, I have to wake Penny. She's going to have to get breakfast on quick.*

Ruby wipes flour from her shaking hands and yanks off her apron. "Help yourself to coffee, Sheldon. I'll be right back." She goes through the dining room like a woman blind and raps on the door of Room #1.

"Penny!" She hears a shuffle and murmur of voices. "Penny, open up!"

Penny opens the door a crack. "Ma'am?"

Ruby wedges her foot against the doorjamb.

"Please, ma'am." Penny pushes back against Ruby's boot.

"What the hell is going on here, Penny?"

The girl glances back over her shoulder and then back to Ruby. "I've had a visitor."

Ruby seethes. "We had an arrangement, Penny." She squints toward the bed. Charles Dowd? In his drawers? "Damn it to high heaven, is that you, Reverend?" Ruby pushes into the room. "God may be looking down on you in shame right now, but Divina's dead and I don't intend to let her meet her maker without a proper introduction, so you best be getting dressed and getting your worthless bones up to her place before I do."

Dowd blanches and fumbles with his clothing. "God bless her soul."

Ruby jabs her finger in Penny's face. "And, as for you, young lady, if I find you here when I return, you'll be sorry you ever met me."

"Don't go blowing your top, Ruby. It's only the parson."

"Don't talk back to me, damn it. I want you out, Penny. Today! There's nothing more to say."

"Why? Where will I go?"

"That's not my concern," Ruby says. "You make your

bed, you lie in it. There's plenty of other towns in need of your services." Ruby turns away and Penny slams the door shut.

Ruby yells through the closed door. "I mean it, Penny. Today." Back in the kitchen, Ruby shakes her head. "As if I don't have enough troubles for one day, Sheldon. The parson with Penny. Wait just a minute while I get my hat."

Sheldon supports Ruby as they trudge up the steep grade of Jefferson Street, the sun a gold sliver crawling up and over the Santa Catalinas. Ruby blinks back tears. *What am I going to do without you?* she thinks again.

As they pass the cemetery, Ruby stops for a breath. "Why, Divina wasn't even sixty, Sheldon. She never talked her age, but she couldn't have been more than fifty-seven, fifty-eight. About the same age as my pop." She takes another breath before continuing on. "She loved him, you know."

"Stubborn fool, he must've been, not to see it." He turns to Ruby. "Like you've been blind to . . ."

"Stop your talk right there, Sheldon. I'm not blind. Just not suited for you."

"I beg to differ, Ruby."

Ruby doesn't answer. When they reach Divina's gate, the sun has punched over the rim of the Catalinas. It's going to be another scorcher. She pats Swendsen's mare tied out front and pushes the gate open. "This is no time to be talking sweet, Sheldon. We've got a burying to do."

THE NEXT NIGHT, IT'S A PARADE of grief, all of Jericho come to dinner. But not Penny.

Ruby rolls up the sleeves of the black bombazine for some relief from the heat. God, how she hates this dress. She wears nothing underneath. If only she could simply wear whatever the hell she wants to, whenever she wants to. Wearing black is so . . . tiring. When the parson and his wife arrive, the very pregnant Mrs. Dowd thrusts a sad excuse for a bouquet into Ruby's hands, the parson not meeting Ruby's eyes.

"Divina is in a better place now," Mrs. Dowd says.

Ruby doubts that. She has trouble enough holding her tongue all through supper watching the not-so-good reverend handing out platitudes, his devoted wife at his side. *Just yesterday* . . . Ruby won't hold her tongue next time.

There is enough food leftover to feed all of Jericho twice over, everyone bringing something for the repast. Sheldon stays until Ruby shoos him out with a playful swat on the rear. He returns the favor and steals a quick kiss to her cheek.

"Get out, you scoundrel," she says.

"Sure you don't want me to stay?"

"How many ways are there to spell 'no', Sheldon?"

"Tell me again."

Ruby takes her time with the washing up. Wink is the last to darken the kitchen door, near eight o'clock and pitch black in the desert. The light of the moon casts weak shadows over cacti.

"Where have you been? I looked for you out back. Come on in and have a bite. I have leftovers for a week."

Wink shuffles to the kitchen table. He needs a bath. "I was up at Divina's place. Hoping she'd come out on the porch one more time."

"I know what you mean, Wink. That we will never see her again . . ." Ruby sets a plate in front of Wink. He eats without talking, the fork scraping the plate with each mouthful. When he finishes, he wipes his mouth with a napkin and fumbles in his coat pocket. He hands Ruby a small parcel wrapped in twine. "For you, Miss Ruby. I hoped to give it to Miss Divina one day."

Ruby tenses. She can't touch the package. "I don't know what to say, Wink."

"Oh, it isn't what it looks like, Miss Ruby. I'm not after your hand. There's enough fellas in line ahead of me. Like the one you just sent packing."

Ruby relaxes her shoulders.

"I don't have anyone else to give it to," Wink says. "And it shouldn't go to waste. It's a garnet, will match your gloves. I'd be honored if you wore it now and again. Although I suspect you'd rather have a ruby." He shoves the parcel toward Ruby.

Ruby looks at the box. "Actually no, Wink. I had a ruby once and never liked it. A garnet, though. That's an extravagance."

"My mother was mighty proud of that ring," Wink says. "She bought it with her own money in Chicago after my father died. Said if she didn't get a ring from her own husband she'd damn well buy one for herself."

"I like her already, Wink." Ruby settles on the chair across the table from Wink and unties the twine. "It's beautiful."

"Time someone wore it, if Divina can't."

"I know you loved her." Ruby fits the garnet onto the fourth finger of her right hand. "Are you sure, Wink? That I should have it? You could sell it—"

"Am right sure, Miss Ruby."

Ruby twirls the ring and looks up at the moon through the kitchen window. "You know, Wink, Divina loved my pop and he never took any notice of her. Why is it people always love the one that doesn't notice? Seems to be a lot of wasted heartache in this world on account of it."

"'O brawling love! O loving hate!'"

"Shakespeare again?"

"*Romeo and Juliet*." Wink leans in toward Ruby. "What about the sheriff?"

"It's just that . . ."

"'O brawling love! O loving hate!'" Wink recites again.

"Matches aren't made in heaven, Wink. Only in novels. Now let me dish up some pie for you."

Wink again eats in silence as Ruby sips another mug of black coffee.

"Hear that, Ruby?"

Ruby leans her head, straining to hear muffled voices. She opens the kitchen door and holds it for Wink. They sit on the bottom step, backs against the step above and legs splayed on the ground.

Laughter tinkles from somewhere out of sight, and then silence.

"What do you think they're saying to one another?" Ruby asks.

"He who has ears will always hear it," Wink says. "I think it's the sound of love echoing off the Catalinas tonight, Miss Ruby." His hands dance in front of his face. 'Love sought is good; but given unsought is better.' That's from *Twelfth Night*."

Ruby follows Wink's gaze to where it ends somewhere at the lip of the mountains. She nudges Wink. "Can't say as I'm not jealous." *Perce. I miss Perce tonight.*

"Jealousy never got anyone anywhere, Ruby. Better to drown your sorrows in drink. A bottle, now there's a friend. Never judges you or tells you off. Never talks behind your back or crosses you." Wink takes a pull on a bottle of cheap rye. "Care to join me, Miss Ruby?"

"Don't mind if I do, Wink. Pass it over. I'm thinking tonight's a night to get utterly scammered." Ruby takes a long swig.

"We could write some poetry tonight, in Divina's honor," Wink says. "Conjure up the Bard himself." Wink raises his grizzled face to the moon. "From Eden's bower, was a flower, Miss Divina Sunday," he starts.

Wink smells nothing like a flower, but Ruby ignores it. She tips the bottle again, hands it back to Wink, and adds to the rhyme. "Down to Hell, and just as well, eternal goddamn one way." Ruby collapses in laughter, her torso shaking.

"That's mighty good, Miss Ruby. Divina would have had a good laugh at that one."

Ruby heaves and doubles over, her laughter soon descending to quaking sobs.

Wink reaches for Ruby, but pulls his hand back. Another minute, he risks it. "Shh, now, Miss Ruby. Divina wouldn't want you bawling over her."

Still Ruby sobs. *Divina. Pop.*

"'Give sorrow words,' Miss Ruby. '"The grief that does not speak knits up the o'er wrought heart and bids it break.' From *Macbeth*." Wink pulls Ruby to the crook under his arm and Ruby rests her head on Wink's shoulder. "Divina was as tough as they come," he says. "Ever seen her cry?"

Ruby rubs her eyes. "Come to think of it, Wink, no." She flails her hand. "Give me that bottle again, you old fool." Her breath is shallow and her words halting. "You're right about one thing, at least. There never was a better friend than this."

Ruby has, by now, had enough to drink that Wink's stench doesn't bother her. Before she takes another pull, she raises the bottle toward the mountain peaks. "To Miss Divina Sunday. Best ma a girl could ever have." Ruby slugs a mouthful and wipes her eyes with her sleeve. "I swear I'll make it up to you, Divina. I'll go to San Francisco. See that goddamn ocean for the both of us."

SHELDON STEPS OVER THE threshold an hour later. "I got your note."

Ruby stumbles headlong into Sheldon's arms and buries her head in his chest.

"Do you mean . . .?"

Ruby nods.

Sheldon whistles. "I've been waiting a long time for this day, Ruby." He rubs her back the way Perce does, gentle yet firm.

Later, they lie together in Ruby's bed, legs and arms entwined.

Sheldon kisses the end of Ruby's upturned nose. "I've loved you since the first time I saw you, arguing in broad daylight with that good-for-nothing you called a husband. That day you put him out of his misery, I wanted to scoop you up right there in your parlor, take you home. Now's my chance, if you'll have me."

Ruby twirls her hair. "I want to love you, Sheldon. But I don't think I'm suited for marriage." Her voice is slurred from drink.

"I'll be the judge of that."

"That's the trouble. I'm judge and jury." Again, her words slur, coming out sounding like "zhudge and zhury." "Verdict is, I don't know that I can."

"Was it . . . ?"

"Are you kidding?" Ruby bats at Sheldon's chest. She nuzzles in his chest hair and runs her fingers up and down his torso. "If that's all there was to it, and none of the rest of it—mend your socks, make your bed, iron your goddamn shirts—I'd be your girl, money on the table."

Ruby is quiet for a moment, her tongue heavy and full. She tries to form words, but they come out jumbled. "Hell, I'm more than I can handle. Let alone saddle myself to someone else." *Except Perce.* "You're better off without me, Sheldon. Too many demons in my head."

"Give it time, Ruby."

Ruby head swings back and forth. The room spins. "Can't shake them, Sheldon."

"Shush up, woman, will you? Let a man enjoy himself for one night before you go off and spoil it." Sheldon tweaks her nose and kisses it again. "Arguing in bed, even. You're your own worst enemy. You know that, don't you?"

Ruby closes her eyes. "You won't let me forget it, I'm guessing."

"No, ma'am." Sheldon takes Ruby's face in his hands. "You are the most exasperating woman I have ever met. Makes me love you even more." He kisses her deeply.

"Sheldon . . ."

"Shush. Not another peep from you. Tonight—for once—I get the last word." Sheldon grazes Ruby's neck, shoulder, and collarbone. He places his hands around her narrow back and hips and moves his mouth down to her breasts.

Ruby holds Sheldon's head and massages his hair, at first gently, and then more urgently. She strokes his neck and shoulders roughly and pushes him back against the mattress. Climbing over his lean and weathered body, Ruby arches her back, her thighs taut, hair wild, and desire far from quenched.

APRIL 10, 1905
JERICHO, ARIZONA TERRITORY

Vi—

Bad news travels fast in this territory, so I'm guessing you've heard about Divina. Or else I'm sorry to be the bearer of bad news. First my pop and now Divina. Life is goddamn unfair sometimes. Don't you even think about dying.

—Ruby

Ruby posts the letter at the post office and continues straight up Jefferson. She ignores catcalls from outside Judd's, darts up Lower Gulch, and continues the back way up through town on Upper Gulch. Ruby catches her breath on the incline. She's not as hale as usual.

At the crest of the hill, past the cemetery, Ruby turns left into the schoolyard. It's four-thirty, and pupils have left for the day. She crosses the dirt yard toward the schoolhouse steps and stops to take another breath. She's recovered—barely—from her three-day hangover by now, but her mouth is still cotton dry. Damn that she didn't bring a canteen. She can't recollect being on a bender like that, but Divina was worth it. And so was Sheldon Sloane. Although she hasn't seen Perce yet. *What will I say? And how?*

"Miss Stern?" Ruby pokes her head into the one-room schoolhouse.

Margaret is sweeping with a thin straw broom, her tight bun loose at the edges.

"Mrs. . . ."

"For God's sake, Margaret, call me Ruby. We are the only two respectable women in town, except for Mrs. Burton and Mrs. Dowd, poor thing, the parson's wife. Can you imagine being married to the likes of him?"

Margaret replaces the broom and tidies her hair. "Have you come about Sam? His arithmetic is much improved." She straightens her severe skirt. "Although his spelling could use some work."

"Actually, it's not about any of the boys. Not this time. It's about Sheldon. Mr. Sloane."

"What about Mr. Sloane?"

"It's a delicate subject."

Margaret cocks her head. "And?"

"It's just that he's, well, lonely. Troubled, he's been, since his missus passed, and I think he has eyes for you."

"Nonsense," Margaret says. "If he has eyes for anyone, it's for you. A blind ox can see that."

"After I shot my husband? Ask yourself, what kind of rogue this side of Hell would take up with someone like me?"

"You have a point, there . . . Ruby."

Ruby sits at one of the desks, her fingers tracing a line on the carved top. "I was never a good student, Margaret. Knew my McGuffey's well enough, and could recite like nobody's business. Was made for the stage, my pop said.

We were on the road most of my growing up. So while I might not know much about book learning, I certainly recognize a good match when I see one. You and Sheldon would make a handsome pair."

Margaret takes in a deep breath, holds it, and then lets it out in a long whistling exhale. "I . . . I have my sights set on another."

"Who? Certainly not the bank manager?"

"No, no one from Jericho."

"Ah, I see. From . . .?"

"Iowa. Des Moines. But it's been two years since I've had a letter." She turns toward her desk. "Although why I am telling you this is beyond me."

Ruby rises. "Why not? I've had my heart broken more times than most. I wonder why we women don't talk about it more frankly."

"That might be easy for you to say, being more—shall we say—experienced."

"Divina pined for my pop for her whole life and he never saw her. Really saw her. Right in front of him, she was, since he was a young man. Her whole life wasted on the love of a man she could never have. And he's the one who missed out."

Divina. What am I going to do without you?

Ruby stares out the schoolhouse window at the Catalinas and then pulls her attention back to Margaret.

"Now, I'm not saying we can be friends, although there've been unlikelier pairs. But woman-to-woman, Sheldon Sloane is as good as they come. We've got what? Fifty years on this earth? Sixty, if we're lucky? Hell, we're halfway to that now, Margaret, you and me. What prospects can I hope for? You, on the other hand, have an opportunity right in front of you that you'd be a goddamn fool to squander."

"I'm not convinced . . ."

"What more evidence do you need? You're one of only two women—me being the other—in God knows how many miles who doesn't make a living off not being hitched."

"Ruby!"

"Say it isn't true, Margaret. There's a good man out there and I'll do whatever it takes to see he's pinned down."

"It's just that . . ."

"What?"

"I'm still waiting for a letter." Margaret fiddles with her hands. "Oh, I get the occasional missive from my maiden aunts in Ohio, but the one I've been waiting for would be postmarked Des Moines, where I first boarded as a schoolteacher in 1902." Her eyes mist. "I remember his scrawl like it's my own; I've got a receipt on onion-thin paper that creases and cracks every time I look at it."

A receipt? That's all? Not a note, or a letter?

Ruby clears her throat. "Were you ever intimate with this Mr. Whatever-His-Name-Is?"

"Heavens, no. His name was Calhoun. Robert Calhoun. He was the superintendent."

"Married?"

Margaret nods. "But his wife was frail. He paid me a good amount of attention."

"Be that as it may, Margaret, two years without a letter says more than any letter might say."

"I've heard that mail is often delayed. Or lost."

"Make all the excuses in the world, Margaret. If someone wants to find you, they will go to the ends of the earth to do so. And a married man? No. No letter on his behalf is coming to Jericho. Ever."

Margaret sinks on to a hard bench and hangs her head. "I've known since the day I left Iowa that there'd never be a letter. The two I wrote him were never answered. But I never gave up hoping he'd change his mind."

"Look around. Make the best of it. Sheldon Sloane is the best horse you could ever bet on. I daresay you would grow to enjoy his company, in and out of the bedroom."

Margaret's face reddens.

"It's true, Margaret. Don't think I haven't thought about it. More than once." She feels her cheeks heating up with the lie. She's been with Sheldon three nights in a row. "But I've got to be true to myself."

"What do you mean?"

"My heart belongs to someone else. Someone I'll never have. Sounds like Shakespeare, doesn't it? Not that I couldn't grow to love Sheldon, but it would be under the wrong pretenses. Being with a good man but in love with another. I couldn't live with myself."

"I wonder if I'm in love with Mr. Calhoun or the idea of it."

"Then what are you waiting for?"

"I couldn't. Not before marriage, anyway," Margaret stammers.

"Really, Margaret. It's 1905. No one's going to tar and feather you." Ruby puts her hand on Margaret's shoulder. The schoolteacher tenses at the touch. Ruby doesn't remove her hand. "If you can look at yourself in the mirror every morning, regardless of what you've done or felt or said, and you can live with yourself, you're the only one you have to account to. No one else. Except God, if you believe that horseshit."

"Don't you believe?"

"It's not that I don't want to. I just can't trust in a God who looks the other way while someone knocks the life out of you, or your kids. So I stopped believing a long time ago."

"Maybe you're stronger because of it, what you went through . . ."

"Oh, I'm stronger alright, Margaret. Just don't know why I had to learn it that way." Ruby opens her arms. "Come here." Ruby gathers Margaret into an embrace. Margaret softens and sighs. Light slants into the class-room, dust motes hovering in the air. Ruby rubs Margaret's back in slow, deliberate strokes. After a full minute, Ruby releases her grasp and smiles up at Margaret, a full half-foot taller. "See, that wasn't hard, was it?" Margaret dabs her eyes with her sleeve, shakes her head, *no*.

"Just wait, Margaret. There's heaven on this earth wait-ing a few blocks down the hill, in scuffed boots and with an even more scuffed heart. Like yours."

Ruby hurries downhill past tailor, bakery, laundry. Tavern, tavern, tavern. Nods and gossip, dirt and dung. *Ruby. Sheriff. Fine day. It is.* Outside Judd's, Willa, sweeping the boardwalk, a large bruise on her forearm.

Ruby stops. "Damn it, Willa. Again? Why the hell do you stay with that bastard?"

Willa pauses, rests on the broom handle. "Ruby."

"Did you hear me?"

"What choice do I have? Married to him. And I'm not as handy with a pistol as you are."

"You can divorce him."

"I don't want to divorce."

"He'll never change, Willa."

Willa shrugs.

"Do you have family? Anywhere you can go?" Ruby asks. She realizes she doesn't know the half about people she sees every day.

Willa shakes her head. "Even if I did, I still love the old bastard."

Ruby glances inside Judd's. Is that Penny behind the bar? "That girl there?" Ruby asks. "Have you hired her on?"

Willa turns to look inside the tavern. "Penny? Yes, she's helping out. Judd's taken a shine to her."

Ruby touches Willa's arm. "Think about what I've said, Willa. There's life after. After the bruises, I mean. And tell Penny that Ruby wants to talk to her."

THAT NIGHT, RUBY CAN'T SLEEP. She argues with herself until she's done with words. She dresses, pulls on her boots, and steals out the back door. Halfway across Washington Street, between Burton's and the sheriff's office, Ruby almost turns around. But she doesn't. She avoids a couple of roughs well past sobriety, rounds the back of the jail, and stands outside Sheldon's room until her heart almost knocks on the door by itself.

After three short raps, Sheldon opens the latch. He pulls Ruby in and shuts the door behind them.

APRIL 11, 1905
JERICHO, ARIZONA TERRITORY

Ruby awakens to a sickly, acrid smell. She's back from Sheldon's, must be one or two in the morning by now by the slight chill in the desert air. She throws on her robe and runs to the window to see a ball of flame engulfing the general store next door. Ruby rushes to the back porch to see fingers of fire lick the edges of her property.

Divina! she thinks, *I've got to get to Divina.* And then remembers Divina is gone.

Grasses, already consumed in flame, jump from clump to clump before her eyes. A few minutes more, and the fire will be at her door. With a houseful of guests! Shouts, men, horses appear. A line of townspeople forms a bucket brigade. Jericho's lone pump wagon rounds the corner and men spool out to spray water on the blaze.

Ruby hurries to the boys' room to rouse them. She gathers every bucket, pot, and pitcher, the ones she can reach, and throws them on the table. Virgil and Sam rush into the kitchen, Sam rubbing sleep from his eyes. Virgil pushes the back door open to observe the fire engulfing Burton's.

"Quick, Virgil. Now. Nothing we can do for Burton. But we need to drench the outer walls and the ground, to keep the fire away. Sam, you go roust Wink."

Virgil mans the pump while Ruby and Sam run back and forth from the pump to the perimeter of the inn to dump precious water onto the burning desert. Wink helps, his steps slower than Ruby's or the boys'. By now, guests are huddled on the second-floor balcony. A woman screams. Ruby watches Burton's store disappear in front of her eyes, the last of the roof timbers crashing into the center of the inferno. The fire has now jumped the road, but the bank is unharmed, being stone. Up the south side of Jefferson, house upon house pops with flame. If it crosses Jefferson, Judd's and the church will be next.

Ruby can't worry about anything else now except saving the roadhouse. Back, forth, heavy buckets. Embers settle in Ruby's hair and singe her robe. The foundation. The root cellar. The porch. *Why aren't the guests helping?*

"M-more, Virgil! Watch out Sam!"

Kittens, ever huddling beneath her back porch, mew and scatter into the desert. Ruby trips on debris, once falling. Up again, more water, never enough water. A coyote howl. Hair plastered to neck and shoulders. Elbows black. Shoulders cracking in their sockets.

Is there anything more frightening than fire? The way it licks and jumps in reds and oranges and sickly yellows? *Quick, quick, quick, no time to spare.*

Ruby trades places with Virgil. *No, we can't stop yet, no.* When her arms go numb from pumping, she rests for a split-second, holding her hanky to her nose to avoid smoke and embers and looks up for the first time in an hour.

Her robe is now beyond repair. She wipes her forehead. Who sweats at midnight? Half of Jericho is burning again. Up, down, pump. Up, down, again. Wink takes over for a moment to give Ruby respite. She heaves bucket after bucket and screams toward the boys. "There, Virgil! Over there, Sam!"

Bloody guests.

When Ruby realizes it's up to her, she takes over at the pump again. Ruby can't feel her arms, but still she pumps. How many times will Jericho burn? It's enough to make a body give up and not bother trying. But there they are, shadows of townspeople trying to save Harvey Burton's store with Mae Burton wailing outside. Ruby takes up the pump again, up, down, up, until she can't feel anything, inside or out.

Later, clustered in the smoky kitchen with her sons and red-eyed guests, Ruby wraps her arms around a smudge-faced Sam. "You'd best be back to your rooms," Ruby says. "Although we could have used your help."

"We won't be staying here a moment longer," one of the guests says. "Best arrange a rig to take us back to Tucson right away."

"And we'll be expecting a full refund," another says.

"All of you. Please. Not to worry, you'll get a refund. There's nothing to do now. Try to get some shut-eye. I'll sort it out in the morning."

Virgil enters the kitchen with a full bucket. Ruby reaches for the pail. "Here, Sam. Drink."

"What is everyone going to do, Ma?" Virgil asks.

"Rebuild, of course."

"You know what the Bible says about that, Ma. 'Cursed before the Lord is the one who undertakes to rebuild this city, Jericho.' Maybe let's go to Tucson, or find Clayton or Fletcher, move there."

"We will do no such thing, Virgil. Jericho is my home, and has been since I was five days old. It's burned before. Twice. If the Lord wanted to curse Jericho for once and for all, he could think of another way. One more time in ashes isn't going to make a damn bit of difference. We just double down, rebuild. In brick next time, if we're smart. And if God is so intent on demolishing this place, why is the church still standing? Answer me that one, Virgil."

"I'm heading there now."

"Take Sam. I'll be right behind you."

Ten minutes later, Ruby hitches her skirt above the ankles and wades through soot on the way to Jericho's house of worship. Trouble in Jericho and townsfolk gather there first before they take refuge at the taverns. A spooked horse runs by. Ruby steps over charred debris, smashed glass. Burton's lot lays in ruin, much of the wreckage now on Ruby's property. The bucket brigade has moved on now up Jefferson, where an inferno still envelops the south side of the street. It's as bright as day in the dead of night.

A lone figure comes down the middle of Jefferson Street. Ruby would know that silhouette anywhere. She runs toward him, dodging hot timbers. Perce puts down a large rucksack amid charred debris and sweeps Ruby into his arms. A slow rumble of sobs starts in Ruby's belly and climbs up her chest and throat. "Its . . . too . . . awful . . ."

"Shh, Ruby. I'm here."

Ruby quakes. Has she realized before this moment how much she's missed Perce? That she wants Perce in her bed every night, not Sheldon? No matter what it takes?

"The Lord doesn't put anything in our path we can't conquer," Perce says. "You can see the fire from camp. Whole ton of men hightailed it down here to help. My only thought was for my Ruby Girl."

They walk toward the church amid a sea of charred faces.

Virgil stands at the church door, half inside and half out. Inside, sooty faces huddle in pews. From the front of the church, Harvey Burton booms to the crowd. "We have our work cut out for us." People nod, murmur. "And we need to find the perpetrator." More nods.

As Ruby and Perce approach the vestibule, Virgil holds out his hands. "Not a good idea, Ma."

"Let us in, Virge. It's no night for deciding who can or can't come into the church tonight. Mr. Washington is a preacher anyway."

"Plus, we know one another," Perce says. "Don't we?" He motions to his rucksack.

Virgil drops his hands to let Ruby and Perce enter the church. As they pass, Virgil and Perce nod to each other.

All heads turn as they enter.

"Wait one minute, here," Burton says. "We won't be having no darkie here." He rushes towards Perce from the front of the small church.

"He's the one!" One of Fletcher's friends balls his fists and shakes it. "I saw him!"

A huge bear of a man blocks townspeople from storming the doorway. "Miz Fortune, isn't it? Burt Gallagher. Been meaning to make your acquaintance. But you best be on your way. And you, too, partner," he says to Perce. "We've had enough trouble in Jericho for one night. Don't need any more."

"Where's the sheriff?" Ruby asks.

"On Upper Gulch. I'm in charge down here, Miz Fortune. And I say it's time for your friend here to leave."

Ruby steers Perce away from the church door and back across the street toward the roadhouse. "Bastards."

Sheldon barrels down Jefferson, his face streaked with soot. Ruby flags him down.

"How bad, Sheldon?"

"You don't want to know." He nods to Perce. "Mr. . . .?"

"Washington. Perce Washington." Perce extends his hand. Sheldon shakes it.

"Mr. Washington came down from the mine to help," Ruby says. "But it seems his help isn't wanted."

"Everyone's hot tonight, Ruby." Sheldon faces Perce. "Talk is a colored started the fire. You know anything about that?"

"Says who?" Ruby interrupts.

"Heard it at The Empire. Man up there said he saw a colored torch Burton's."

"You know that's not necessarily true."

Sheldon again addresses Perce. "I'm not saying you've got a thing to do with this fire, Mr. Washington, but best to stay out of everyone's way tonight. You, too, Ruby." Sheldon tips his hat. He coughs into a handkerchief and proceeds toward the church.

Smoke is so thick that Ruby can't see past the cross-roads, except for an eerie orange glow toward the Santa Catalina Mountains. And the stench! Ruby and Perce hurry to the back end of the hotel. When she is sure no one is still in the kitchen, she motions for Perce to come in. "Quick, now."

Ruby hastens Perce into her bedroom and closes the door. Perce leans Ruby against the door and embraces her, his breath mixed with soot that lingers in the air. Ruby melts into the embrace. She will never succumb to Sheldon again. Perce leads Ruby to the bed and sits beside her, covering her small blackened hands with his large black ones. He rubs her knuckles and pulls her close.

Ruby cradles her head. "Who? Who would have done this?"

"I have an idea. And it wasn't me."

"Who?"

"I'd put money on Jimmy Bugg. Everyone knows he has a grudge against coloreds. Probably started the rumor himself."

"I never did tell you . . ."

"Tell me what?"

She thinks of Sheldon, but stuffs it away. Every woman has her secrets, even from those she loves best. ". . . how Jimmy Bugg roughed me up."

Perce's eyes narrow. "When?" His fists clench.

"It doesn't matter now. If I had told you when it happened, you would have been swinging from the hanging tree long before now. Going after a mine boss? I've told you before, Perce, and I'm afraid this is the last time. You have got to put Jericho behind you. There are jobs to be had on the railroad. Get the hell out of Arizona Territory before Fletcher's friends catch up with you. Or anyone else."

Perce rustles in his knapsack and hands Ruby an odd-shaped package. "For you."

Ruby turns the heavy package over and places it on her lap. "What? It's not even my birthday."

Perce holds Ruby's face in his hands and kisses her. "When is your birthday, Ruby Girl?" he whispers.

Ruby opens her eyes. "July the first, or so Miss Viola says. She's the . . ."

"Everyone in earshot of Tucson knows who Miss Viola is."

"I was born there. My momma was one of her girls. Vi sent word to my pop, said I couldn't be anyone else's on account of the voice I got."

Perce slaps his knee. "Well, if that doesn't beat all." He stares at Ruby. "Come to think on it, you look a little bit like Vi, has anyone ever told you that?"

"Shush, Perce. I've got guests. Unhappy guests, I might add."

"Well, go on. Open it."

Ruby loosens the twine and undoes the brown paper, one fold at a time. When the wrapper falls away, she gasps. "For me?" She picks up the neck of the instrument and its strings shiver. "A mandolin?"

"You said you wanted one."

"I never thought . . ."

"Well, Perce never forgets. I sent off for it as soon as you told me you wanted one. Virgil's been holding it at the post office for me. Had to pay extra for that. Your boy's a right entrepreneur. I picked it up a few days ago on the sly, met Virgil after dark. Thought if I was in town, I'd surprise you. I rapped on your window, but you didn't answer."

Because I was with Sheldon, Ruby thinks. Her stomach sours. She sits and positions the mandolin on her lap and strums. A discordant jumble of notes fills the air. She strums again. "That's the prettiest sound I ever heard," she says. "And it isn't even a song."

"You take your time with it, Ruby Girl. Make a song or don't make a song. Heck, it's pretty just looking at it. Like you."

Ruby gets up and puts the mandolin down on the chair. She circles behind Perce and puts her arms around him, her face buried in his hair.

"I love you, Perce," she says. "More than any man on earth." She nuzzles there, drinking in contentment. "I figure I've got to tell you before it's too late."

Perce turns and burrows his head into Ruby's breasts. "It's never too late, Ruby Girl. Never too late."

A loud bang on the kitchen door disrupts their embrace.

"We know he's in there, Ruby." Harvey Burton. Ruby puts her fingers to her lips and motions for Perce to get under the bed.

"Hold on, Harvey," Ruby calls. "Be right there." She closes the bedroom door behind her and opens the kitchen door. A group of men stands by Burton. They carry lit torches.

"There's been enough trouble here tonight, fellas. Don't need anyone coming close to the roadhouse with goddamn torches after half the town has gone to Hell."

"We know he's in there. That colored," Burton says. "Talk is he started the fire."

"That's hogwash, Harvey, and you know it."

"We want to ask him a couple of questions."

"The hell you do."

"Someone saw you crossing the road with him, Ruby. Don't make a liar of me."

"So you did. And that's where we parted ways. He's headed out of town."

"I don't believe you."

"Don't you?" Ruby says. "He's probably five miles north of town by now, on his way to Globe."

"At night?"

"Best time for a colored man to get about, so I've heard."

"Why is he in such a hurry to get out of town, then? If he didn't start the fire?"

"Maybe because of men like you, Harvey."

"Let us in," one of the men yells.

"I will do no such thing, gentlemen. I have a house full of paying guests and a great mess to attend to. You boys go cool off at Judd's. I'm sure he's open. There's no colored man here. Never has been."

"That's not what Fletcher said," Harvey says.

"Fletcher's got his head up his arse," Ruby says. "Took off to see if he could find it."

"You best be telling the truth, Ruby."

SAME NIGHT

"Shh, not another word." Ruby opens the doors of the root cellar and pushes Perce inside. "They saw you coming over to my place. Burton and a few others. I've sent them on a wild goose chase. Told them you were headed to Globe. You stay quiet and as soon as I'm certain they won't be back, I'll rap on the door. You need to be out of here before the sun even thinks of coming up."

"Come with me, Ruby."

Come with me, come with me, come with me. Perce should know better. Why do men ask the impossible of women? But it doesn't mean the words don't rattle one after the other inside her head. Ruby waits in her bedroom, the clock marking a steady *tick tock tick*. Ten minutes. Fifteen. A half hour. Ruby lies on her back and follows a crack in the ceiling to where it meets the wall. Paint peels in blisters and there's soot everywhere. She hears a rodent scurry in the walls. When Ruby is fairly certain Burton won't return tonight, she steals outside and knocks on the cellar door. "Wait for me at the old mine. Esperanza. I'll be there as soon as I can." Perce disappears southeast in the desert, silent as a cat.

When night begins to wake from slumber, Ruby creaks the back door of the roadhouse closed and crosses Jefferson. The blaze has abated, but a lingering glow hovers over town, like a halo. As Ruby crosses the street, she sees lights still on at Judd's, long past legal curfew. It's a safe bet all of Jericho's menfolk are deep into their cups by now.

In and out of silvery shafts of light, Ruby creeps through the alley to the back of the livery. She feels her way along rough walls, hitting her shin on a crate. She noses down the stable wing until she finds the stall she's looking for, nudges the door open, and sidles up to Swendsen's mare. The mare nickers.

"Just you and me, Maisie." Ruby strokes the mare's head and grabs tack from the back wall. Ruby whispers to the horse as she saddles her, and quickly leads her out the still-open door. If the sawbones needs the mare tonight, he's out of luck.

The moon is sliced neatly in half, like an apple. Into the night Ruby rides, counting off miles as horse and rider pick their way toward the scuttled mine. The desert offers itself up, eerie and consoling, illuminated by the moon. Wild saguaro arms reach toward heaven and cholla branches prick the night. Ugly, the desert is often called. Told that enough times, a body might believe it. Might. Well, sometimes it's enough—sometimes it's best—to be a desert.

Ruby swivels to check that no one is tailing her. She's given false information, buying time for Perce to get as far away as he can on two long legs. As she nears the Esperanza Mine, a big cat scurries from a boulder. It bounds away, consumed by the night. Ruby tethers the mare to a post near the mine entrance. "I'll be back in the blink of an eye." She scours the area. No sign of the cat.

Like in a children's tale, Ruby passes through the narrow door of the now shuttered operation. If her pop were reading the Brothers Grimm to her, this is where she might expect to encounter an ogre or a colony of wild beasts. She would likely starve or be subject to a spell. The ending might not be pleasant, and would serve as a warning for other girls: Don't tempt danger. You might not come out alive.

Ruby sees black. Smells damp. Hears a faint creak of earth shifting, like an old man, and a steady *drip drip drip* from somewhere in the dark cavern. She feels her way past the opening, hands on damp walls, as she breathes in metallic air. With a thud, the door shuts behind her. Her heart jolts in her chest. She smacks her head on the low ceiling and is glad she's still wearing a hat.

"Perce? You here?" Ruby times the silence and calls out again, this time a little louder. "Perce! Where are you?" She scrapes her leg against a discarded piece of mine equipment and jumps. Her shin is already bruised from bumping into the crate at the livery. Now it's bleeding.

A shuffle, then a touch. Hair prickles her neck.

"Not so loud, Ruby. The devil can hear you in here." Perce lights the stub of a candle that flickers off damp mine walls.

Ruby's breath catches in her throat. "They're going to kill you, Perce. Burton and his mob. String you up on the hanging tree. Probably tonight." Her voice falters. "You've got to get to Tucson and hop a train. And never use the name Preacher again. Or Washington. You can be traced to names like that."

"Shush, now. No one's gonna catch up with me, Ruby Girl. I've got a back pocket name. Headman Brown. 'From Tennessee.' That'll throw them off. I can talk Tennessee. Easy. Preacher, he gets left behind here with you."

Ruby rummages in her satchel and hands Perce a lumpy bundle. "I brought you some vittles and a change of clothes. Sorry if they don't fit right. They're ones Fletcher left behind. And, here." She reaches into her vest pocket. "All I can spare."

"I don't want your money, Ruby. It's you I want." Perce grabs Ruby's collar and kisses her hard. Her rump is up against the damp mine walls. She returns Perce's ardor and clings to him. Low moans echo in the darkness.

Ruby untangles herself from Perce's arms. "I've got to get back to Jericho before anyone notices I'm gone. Or the mare. Took Doc Swendsen's horse without asking. And I'm running on borrowed time. But your clock is running faster than mine, Perce. Damn that my father could live with an Apache woman and no one cared a piss about that. But I'm seen with you and it's over. For both of us. What were we thinking?"

Ruby rubs her eyes. She doesn't want Perce to see they're welling up. "Get out of this hellhole and head for Tucson. Hide out during the day and find your way into town after dark. The Golden State Limited leaves just before midnight. You'll be in San Francisco the day after that."

"Just one more kiss, Ruby Girl."

"Damn it, Perce."

Ruby hears the mare whinny. She needs to get her back unharmed. Quick.

"It's time, Perce." Ruby pats Perce's chest. "You take care of yourself, you hear?"

Perce straightens up. His head scrapes the ceiling of the mine. "This old preacher man knows how to take care of himself. But who's gonna take care of my Ruby Girl?"

"I can take care of myself, Perce." *But why can't we . . .*

He pulls Ruby in again. Her groin is still wet. She loses herself in a passionate kiss and then wrenches away and points her finger at Perce's chest. "Now listen to me, Preacher. I don't ever want to see you again, you hear me?" Her fingers thrum his chest like a drum.

Perce takes her hand. "You can't mean that, Ruby Girl."

Ruby pulls her hand away. "Don't come to Jericho ever again."

"Words like that hurt the worst coming from the ones you love most." Perce releases Ruby. He takes her hand and kisses it. "I don't believe you mean it."

Ruby runs her fingers along the fringe of his vest. It's all she can do not to leave everything behind and follow him. *Come with me, come with me, come with me.*

Perce shoulders the knapsack and pulls his hat low. "Hoped I'd never have to say these words to you." He looks back over his shoulder. "Goodbye, Ruby Girl."

The mine door clangs shut. Ruby leans back against the damp black walls, sobbing. If the mine shattered into rubble and buried her whole right there, right then, it · wouldn't cover her grief by half.

What have I done?

Ruby screams, from somewhere low in her gut. It echoes off the mine walls. All she sees, all she feels, all she knows, is black.

Sorrow seeps in then,

drip

drip

drip

"Red-handed." Sheldon bounds around the corner of the roadhouse, his voice booming.

Ruby's heart judders. Has someone intercepted Perce? Or worse? She puts down her washing and takes a clothes-pin from her mouth. Her eyes remain red-rimmed as the night of the fire, and not from the blistering sun, although it suits her to let everyone think that. It's been a week since the fire. A week since she sent Perce packing with no plans to see him again. A week since she's gone to Sheldon's bed.

"What the hell?"

"Burton. He must've set the fire."

"To his own store?"

"Motive is everything, Ruby. I couldn't sleep thinking on it. Man's always in debt. And just took out insurance on the store, after ten years of scraping by without it." Sheldon snaps his fingers. "All of sudden, it clicked. When I went to investigate, I got more than I bargained for. Look what I found." Sheldon tips the box he's carrying so Ruby can peer inside. "Found these bloomers in Burton's chifferobe, singed by the fire. Stash we found would have shamed a whore."

"You mean . . ."

"In all sizes and shapes, I might add."

"Not Mae's?"

"Certainly not. She was as surprised as we were. And swore at him like a mad cowhand. Words I never heard come from a woman. Not even you."

Ruby thinks back to the day Burton lurked near her bedroom door, his hands stuffed into his trouser pockets.

"Suspect he took yours, the ones Wink found," Sheldon says. "Right off the line. Probably ordered crates of them from the Sears & Roebuck, too, or from the drummers. All I know is he could have opened up a ladies shop instead of that grocery of his."

"Or maybe he took them from my bedroom."

"What the devil?"

"Saw him coming out of my room a few months back, was mad as a hornet but didn't think much of it after. Said he was looking for me. Seems like he was looking for something else."

"Damn."

"Seen it before, Sheldon. There were some oddballs in the carnival. Stick, for one. This once, I had just had my pie—I got an extra slice of pie every night, Big Sue, our cook, she never denied me—and the tall man—Stick was his name—he pinched my behind. Right under my skirt. I think he would've taken those drawers right off if I'd let him. He was right handy."

"Did he . . ."

"No, not me. But he had his hands all over other girls, and not just Big Sue, his sweetheart."

"Takes all kinds, Ruby. Me? If I were to have a collection, it wouldn't be undergarments."

"Maybe a bottle," Ruby says. "Never met a shot of hooch I didn't like." She motions toward the inn. "Come in a minute, won't you?"

Sheldon and Ruby pass through the kitchen. Ruby takes two mugs from the sideboard and pours coffee, still warm on the stove. Even though it's been a week, the smell of smoke still pervades the kitchen. Ruby has wrung out rag after rag scrubbing soot. Still the stench lingers. There won't be any guests coming her way soon. Ruby nods to Sheldon and they head to the parlor. Sheldon sinks into the large couch, his long legs in front of him.

"Boy, do I wish Divina were here. She would love all this."

"You miss her."

"Bad."

Ruby uncorks a bottle of whiskey and pours a liberal amount into her mug. "You, Sheriff?"

Sheldon puts up his hand. "It's what, 10 a.m., Ruby? Can't say as I never have a nip on duty. But I make sure it's past noon." He clears his throat. "I've been waiting for an excuse to come see you, anyway. There've been no knocks on my door these last seven nights."

"You've been counting?"

"I have."

"I'm not coming by again, Sheldon."

"Can I ask why?"

"You can ask until Kingdom Come, but you won't get an answer. I just can't."

"You have another fella?"

"I do."

Sheldon drops his eyes. "This is going to kill me, Ruby."

"You'll never see him."

"And how is that possible in this town? You're not making any sense, Ruby."

"Let me lay it out square for you." Ruby places her palms on the table. "I'm in it up to here"—she motions to her neck—"with someone I can't be with, this side of Hell, anyway."

Sheldon puts down his mug. "Mr. Washington?"

Ruby nods.

Sheldon whistles.

"He's gone, Sheldon. Lit out of town the night of the fire. But it's not fair to you to keep coming to your bed."

"I can live with it."

"I can't, Sheldon. I've told too many lies in my life and I'm coming clean here with you. I don't love you."

"You like me well enough."

"And that will never change."

"If you change your mind . . ."

"You'll be the first to know."

Sheldon drains his mug. "I just don't understand you, Ruby." He unfolds himself from the divan. "If I can, I'll stop by again later and take you up on your offer."

Ruby looks at Sheldon sideways. Like a day off the drink, just making it to the next day, Ruby is weaning herself off Sheldon.

"For the whiskey, Ruby."

A few minutes later, Ruby checks her pride at the door and walks to Judd's. Confound that Penny. Hadn't Ruby told Willa to have the girl come by? But has she? No. She's as stubborn as Ruby.

Ruby peers around the back of Burton's—the very place Bugg rammed her up against the siding. She gauges blackened boards and broken windows and sidesteps a heap of trash outside the back door. Only a corner of the Cream of Wheat mural is visible. Sam won't get a job after school here anytime soon.

Ruby continues across Jefferson. A wagon swerves

to avoid a pack of stray dogs, raising a fog of dust. Ruby coughs. She picks her way through the street, skirting dung. Two men sit outside the tavern, one whittling and the other playing a mouth harp. The whittler takes his knife and picks at his teeth. The harmonica player nods his head, but doesn't tip his hat.

"Ma'am," the whittler says.

Neither of them stands.

Ruby sweeps past the men into the dim interior of the tavern. Just the smell transports her back to the last time she was inside Judd's, looking for Willie, the day before she took up her pistol. It smells as sour as she remembers it, sweat and beer and dirt and men all mixed together.

Ruby approaches the bar. "Penny?"

The young woman gives Ruby the sly eye.

"I want to talk to you."

"I ain't got anything to say. Least of all, sorry."

"It's me that's sorry, Penny."

The barmaid puts down her cloth. "Well, that's a surprise."

"I'm sorry for throwing you out." Ruby clears her throat. "It's not like I haven't had an indiscretion or two."

"I'm not coming back, if that's what you're asking."

"Noted. But the door is open, Penny. That's all I've come to say. I made a mistake tossing you out. If you're ever needing a job, come on over. Or just come on over and have a glass of cool tea sometime. We're not so unalike, you and me."

On the way back to the inn, Ruby darts past the charred remains of Burton's General Store. Mae is gleaning through debris, her shop apron blackened.

"Heard about Harvey up and leaving," Ruby says. "I'm sorry to hear it."

"Are you? I'm not. Harvey was no businessman. And a worthless husband."

"Well, that would explain it. Sheldon thinks Harvey set the fire. Harvey is probably in Tucson now collecting on that insurance."

"Everyone says the fire was started by that colored, the one you carry on with."

Ruby heart almost stops. "I don't know what you're talking about."

"You most certainly do. And I'm sure Dog Webber would be interested."

"That's blackmail, Mae."

"That's business, Ruby."

"You wouldn't dare."

"Wouldn't I? Speaking of Sheldon, I have something on Sheldon and you, too. Saw him coming out of your place the morning after you dispatched your husband. Quite early, I might add. And you've been going to his place nights. I'm not a night owl for nothing."

"It's nothing, Mae."

"You can't prove it."

"Maybe not. But I have something on Harvey. He's a cheat and a thief. And I have a sneaking suspicion he"— *or you*, she thinks—"may have left a rather unsavory item under my window. Not too many other people *dispatching* hogs in this town."

Mae looks away.

I knew it.

"Won't find me chasing that swine," Mae says, avoiding Ruby's accusation. "The shop is in my name. Insurance, too." Mae smiles wryly. "Not born yesterday."

"*You* set the fire?" Ruby cocks her head to the side. *After just telling me Perce set it? And risking all of Jericho?*

"That's for the law to decide," Mae says. "I have my livelihood to think of. And my girls. And my reputation."

"What do you want from me, Mae?"

"Now we're getting to the heart of the matter. A little extra cash might keep me from talking."

"The same goes for me, Mae. I've got as much on you as you've got on me."

APRIL 18, 1905
JERICHO, ARIZONA TERRITORY

Ruby jumps when Virgil sneaks up behind her and taps her on the shoulder. "Virge! You almost made me lose my breakfast."

"Sorry, Ma. Am heading out."

"Have a good day, son." Ruby hands Virgil a packet of dried meats and cheeses, a rind of bread, and three carrots for his dinner break.

"I've been thinking, Ma . . ."

"About?"

"Making a fresh start."

Ruby puts her arm around Virgil. "Your birthday wish?"

"Everyone in Jericho is rebuilding. Even Mae Burton."

Mae's words of yesterday grind at Ruby. She rolls her head from side to side. Her neck is tight. Will Mae really go to Dog and spill the beans? For all of Jericho to read?

"Why not us, Ma? We can rebuild, and better."

Ruby doesn't answer right away. Then she nods, at first imperceptibly, and then more vigorously. "I'd have to ask

Sheldon for another loan. He's been helping me keep this place afloat after a few bank loans."

"He knows you're good for it."

Ruby pecks Virgil on the cheek.

"Ma!"

"You're right about this, Virge. We're in frightful need of some new beginnings around here."

"C'MON, SAM." RUBY KICKS RED dirt as she and Sam shoulder their canteens and head toward the desert with Roger. Sam is just home from school and Wink is passed out. There are no guests, so she has all the time in the world today. So what if they have scraps for supper?

They pass stunted trees and clumps of bunchgrass, both starting to green. Scat lines the pathway: bobcat, kit fox, coatimundi. Ruby hears a rattle, and motions for Sam and Roger to stop. Crouching, Ruby takes a handful of gravel and scatters it in the direction of the rattler. From the corner of her eye, she sees the snake slither away. She motions Sam to follow again. Roger stays close to Sam's heels.

"There's so much you don't learn at school, but don't tell Miss Stern I said so."

Sam smiles wryly.

"Look around. This is a good a classroom as any. Take that saguaro. It's likely a hundred years old. And has never moved, Sam. Just grew where it sprung up, prickly and useful at once, and shelter to insects and birds. Tells me this, we don't need to go to the ends of the earth to do good. Can do that right here, in Jericho."

Ruby points to the sky. "Clouds?" Ruby balls her fists. "Some days they bunch together so tight they burst . . ." She uncurls her fingers. ". . . and everything goes to Hell in a hand basket, floods and mud and stains you can never get out, no matter how hard you try. Tells me we're not in control, Sam. Never have been, never will be."

Ruby's split skirt chafes her thighs. She sits on a nearby boulder and drinks from her canteen. Sam sits on another boulder not far away. Ruby swipes her mouth and lowers her canteen so Roger can slurp from it.

A cactus wren chirps from a nearby mesquite, then darts away.

"The wren, the thrasher, the dove? Think about it, Sam. They have everything they need right here. Tells me I ought to be content. That's the hardest lesson to learn."

Ruby bends over to meet Sam eye to eye. Soon, he'll be as tall as she is. He's already as tan, with the same yellow hair, although his is straight as a teetotaler to her curls. "You'll learn these things on your own time," she says. "And a heap more if you're paying attention. I reckon you're old enough to walk in the desert by yourself now. But keep Jericho in your sights, especially if you're not with me or Wink. See to it you keep close by, you hear?"

Sam nods.

"I've got one more thing to tell you." Ruby spreads her split skirt to get air circulating. "Your pop used to sing to me, before he got mean. When I start to think of the bad times, I sing this to myself to help me feel better. He made up some of the words, you'll see. But it's not just a song about me, Sam. It's about this desert. A rose underneath all the thorns."

Ruby begins, her alto voice strong and clear.

There's a yellow rose in Texas I'm going down to see . . .

THE NEXT DAY, SAM DOESN'T come home for the midday meal, and still isn't home by supper. Ruby tries not to let it get the better of her. He's just late, right? Or lost time with Wink?

By the time supper is ready, Ruby knows something's amiss. Sam would never miss a meal, let alone two. And she saw Wink an hour earlier heading to the livery. If Sam isn't with Wink, where can he be? Did he even go to school today?

Ruby gets a rush of cold blood in her veins and her eyes bulge. She knows exactly where Sam is. He is somewhere out in that desert that she just herself told him he could wander in alone. Ruby's eyes dart across the landscape. No sign of him.

Ruby tamps the stove's burners off and covers the iron pots. She rips off her apron, grabs her hat, and sprints across the street toward the sheriff's office. She bangs in without a greeting. "It's Sam."

"Sam?" Sheldon looks up from his reports and removes his glasses.

I didn't even know he wore glasses . . .

"Missing. Since this morning. Skipped dinner. Didn't show for supper. Thought he might be with Wink, but . . ." She sets her mouth. "Damn it, Sheldon, get off your arse and help me."

"Don't 'damn it' me, Ruby. Of course, I'll help. Now gather yourself and let's be smart about this."

News travels faster than a cat in heat in a town like Jericho. Within an hour, townspeople have joined the search. Doc Swendsen and Sheldon ride ahead through desert underbrush. Ruby and Margaret Stern follow on foot. Virgil limps behind Ruby but Roger sprints ahead. Dog Webber wields his ungainly camera and strides past Virgil and the women.

"Sam! Sam!" Ruby's words echo in the desert air. She feels like she can't take in enough breath. "Damn it, Margaret. I told Sam just yesterday that he could explore the desert on his own. I don't know whether to be glad he heeded my advice or mad as hell that he did."

"I wondered why he wasn't at school today."

"Wish I had known that earlier, but it's not your fault, Margaret."

"Where do you think he's headed?" Margaret asks.

Ruby stops to think. "The pools. He loves it there."

The women run toward the foothills southeast of Jericho. They dodge cholla and sagebrush as they cover dry, cracked terrain. All around, they hear others yelling for Sam fanned out over a wide swath of the desert. Even Old Judd and Willa join the search. Ruby spots Tom Tillis and his crew a quarter-mile away in a wagon. Is that Wink with them? But no Mae Burton, damn her.

Ruby and Margaret pause before the last incline. The steep trail winds through mesquite and brittlebush, yellow with flower.

"We'll find him, Ruby." Margaret squeezes Ruby's hand.

Ruby can't find words to answer. Her throat is choked with dust and despair. If something has happened to Sam, it's her fault. It's all her fault, Willie dying, Sam not talking, now this. She loosens her hand and starts to run up the trail, her skirt catching on acacia thorns. Sweat drips in the crevice between her breasts and perspiration stains her underarms. Where is he?

In the near distance, Ruby hears Roger yowl. She stops for a second to ascertain where the bark emanates from.

"This way, Margaret!"

When they reach the pools, Roger is still yowling. Ruby lets out a blood-curdling scream. Sam's crumpled body lies beside the stream behind a boulder the size of Arizona Territory itself. His tawny hair is matted with blood.

"Doc! Quick! Over here!" Margaret waves her hands above her head.

Ruby rushes to Sam and kneels. She places her head on his cool body and detects a shallow breath. "Sam!" she says, and gently turns his face. It is stained red.

Sam's eyes flicker as Ruby cradles him to her chest. "Oh, Sam," she murmurs.

Sheldon and Doc Swendsen gallop toward the pools. Swendsen grabs his medicine kit and dismounts while Sheldon ties the horses to a mesquite.

"This is all my doing," Ruby cries. "I told him he was old enough to be out in the desert alone."

"Let's reserve blame for later, after we get this boy back home," Sheldon says. He crouches by Ruby's side.

Willa has beat her husband up the incline. "Can I help?" Willa asks. "I had nurse's training. In the war."

Other loud voices ring out down the trail. A crowd gathers around the unconscious boy, his clothing torn and bloodied. Margaret kneels on the other side of Ruby. She props Ruby up as she holds Sam. Sheldon removes his hat and wipes his forehead. He offers an arm around Ruby, his hand brushing Margaret's. She doesn't pull away.

"Anyone have water?" Swendsen asks. He puts his head to Sam's chest.

Old Judd offers a canteen. Swendsen tears off his vest and unbuttons his shirt. He peels it off and soaks it, then applies the cool garment to Sam's forehead. After a swift examination, Swendsen, in an undershirt now, picks up the boy and gently carries him down the trail. "Looks like a big cat might have roughed him up a bit, but he'll come through. Not named Fortune for nothing."

Margaret picks up Swendsen's vest and hands it to Sheldon. They follow Swendsen to the base of the trail. By now, Tom Tillis and two helpers have arrived with a livery wagon.

"Easy now," Swendsen says. Tillis assists Swendsen in lifting Sam into the wagon bed, where Wink sits, his hat in his hands.

"Take my place, Ruby." Wink steps down from the wagon and helps Ruby up.

"Roger!" she calls. The dog races to Ruby's side.

"I'll take care of him, Ruby," Wink says. "You get along now."

The wagon hurtles off toward Swendsen's surgery where Doc makes a poultice of kerosene, turpentine, and lard. He soaks a wool cloth in the mix and places the dressing on Sam's chest.

"Will he . . . ?"

"He'll come through just fine, Ruby. Probably came upon a cat and she swiped at him before running away. The boy will be scared more than he'll be hurt. Might not go out into the desert by his lonesome anytime soon."

Sam's eyes flicker open. He seems disoriented at first. Ruby takes his hand and he signs an "o" and a "k." She signs back.

Supper! Ruby thinks. *And those guests who just arrived without a reservation!* "Rest up, Sam. I'll be back in the wink of an eye."

"Better that he's in his own bed." Swendsen takes a shirt from a peg on the surgery wall and puts it on over his bloodied undershirt. He carries Sam to the inn, with Ruby following.

"Thanks, Doc," Ruby says. "I can take it from here." Ruby puts Sam to bed and then hurries toward the dining room, hoping the guests have helped themselves to the supper she left in the kitchen when she fled so abruptly. Ruby enters the dining room, hot and sweaty, to find her new guests sitting at the dining table enjoying the last of their meal.

"I hope you don't mind that I took the liberty of utilizing the kitchen." A large housewife from Prescott who is accompanying her husband while he scouts out property in Jericho stands at the far end of the table, Ruby's apron barely filling out the woman's portly frame.

"Snooping in the kitchen, you might say," her husband adds. On the table, chicken, potato salad, fresh peas.

Ruby exhales. "There'll be no charge for your stay, of course. My treat. And don't see to the washing up."

"There are two people at it already back there," the woman's husband says. "The sheriff and the school teacher."

Ruby goes through to the kitchen. Margaret, in another of Ruby's aprons, is elbow-deep in dishwater. Sheldon takes a dish from Margaret and dries it with a tea towel.

"Sheldon, Margaret, I don't know what to say."

"Go get cleaned up, Ruby," Sheldon says. "We saved you a plate."

Ruby closes the bedroom door behind her. She strips and washes her body with a sponge. Her tummy sags. She looks at herself sideways in the mirror and sucks in her midsection. It is covered with stretch marks. Why has she not noticed this before? She dresses and sits on the edge of her bed. *Sam . . . oh Sam . . .*

Back in the kitchen, she pours a cup of tea. She's not hungry.

"Anything else we can do for you tonight?" Margaret asks. She hangs Ruby's apron on a hook and dries her hands on a towel.

"You've done plenty to help. Go on, you two." *Maybe something good came of this day, after all.*

Sheldon whispers something to Ruby.

"Bugg?"

He nods. "Bad doings at the mine. Going to Yuma for it."

Ruby whistles. "Well, I'll be." *Yes, something good came of this day, alright.* She pushes out the kitchen door and sits on the back stoop under a near-full moon, alone.

At least, Sam is safe. Ruby won't let him out of her sight for a good long while. She thinks of Clayton and Fletcher, wonders where they are. Even though they made fun of

Virgil and didn't pay much attention to Sam, Ruby is convinced they would have led the search today, long legs striding through desert brush and strong arms carrying Sam home between them. They are brothers, after all.

Hadn't Clayton said he'd be back someday? Although 'someday' isn't yet. But what can Ruby do? He saw how Willie treated her, and Clayton received the most thrashings of all the boys, being the oldest to survive. Who wouldn't want to leave the place where those memories smolder? Ruby holds out hope Clayton will show up on her porch one day and lift her off the ground. And Fletcher? He was once the dearest child, but the wounds of his harsh words linger fresh as the day he said them. He'll be back too, won't he? Isn't family stronger than words?

Virgil, on the other hand, is as comfortable as an old slipper. Ruby doesn't take him for granted, but knows he'll never leave Jericho. Even if he is to find a missus.

But if she had lost Sam today, Ruby would have fallen into a gaping hole of grief so deep she would never have been able to claw out. Over time, it may have dissolved until the boulder of sadness rubbled into specks of dirt finer than sea salt, but by that time she would have gone stark raving mad from it all, stumbling in the desert looking for her youngest son like the lost sheep of the Bible until her tongue parched dry and every last ounce of energy a body could rustle up withered like a shriveled leaf.

Who is she kidding? No, if Sam had died in the desert today, Ruby would have gone to the exact place she found him and curled into a ball so tight that the yawning hole of heartache would have had no choice but to have its fill of her right then and there. There wouldn't have been the need to prolong the agony any longer. One bullet is all it takes.

Virgil would have been left with the sorting out of it all. People don't give Virgil credit. Well, Ruby does. Virgil could run the hotel and the post office and the saloon all at once. And maybe the store and the mine, while he was at it. Hell, he could be senator, or even president, given the chance.

But Sam is safe and Ruby is breathing and Virgil will open the post office at 9 a.m. sharp, like he's done every day since Harold M. Cleaver gave him the job, and he'll likely do the same for forty years to come, like clockwork.

ONE YEAR LATER
APRIL 18, 1906
JERICHO, ARIZONA TERRITORY

Ruby clasps Virgil's hand. It's bigger than hers now. A large sign picketed in the ground in front of the newly-remodeled hotel reads THE MIRACLE. Ruby will never refer to the inn as a roadhouse again.

"You were right, Virge. The perfect name. Didn't Wink do a swell job on the sign?"

Ruby and Virgil walk the perimeter of the hotel, painted white now from eaves to foundation. Each floor has two new water closets, no more outhouse. A telephone sits in the parlor, waiting for the new exchange. The front verandah and the back porch are fortified. But what Ruby is most excited about is the new icehouse, adjacent to the kitchen.

Ruby and Virgil cross the large flagstone patio to the edge of the three-hole golf course carved into the back plot, the flattest place in Jericho.

"Still think it's a waste of time," Ruby says.

"You'll thank me for it, Ma. That, and the tennis court." He motions to a tidy dirt court off to the right. "One day, we'll put in a pool."

"That will be the day, Virge. I'll be working until I'm a hundred and ten to pay this off as it is—"

"The bank?"

"And Sheldon. Again. But it's worth it, by God, it's worth it." Ruby strides to the riding stables between the hotel and the new Burton's General Store. A large paddock holds a stallion, a gelding, and two mares. The large black stallion has a white diamond on his forehead and a white snip on his muzzle; the gelding is at least fifteen hands high, a handsome buckskin with a thick, dark mane. A palomino mare with a white blaze on her nose cozies up to the fence. The other, a stunning bay, shies away as Ruby enters the corral.

"Hello, Sunny." Ruby greets the palomino, strokes her neck. Sunny lowers her head and Ruby rests her forehead against the mare's. The bay, tentative, whinnies. "Shh, it's alright, girl." Ruby reaches for Lady and strokes her as well. Clucking for the gelding, Ruby waits for the large horse to nicker. "Fine boy, aren't you." Bright nudges his face toward Ruby; she finds that sweet spot under his mane and scratches there. Is he favoring one foot? She'll keep an eye out. The stallion paws the ground. He's the only one tethered. "One minute, Jake." She nuzzles the gelding again and turns toward the stallion with a hand outstretched. "I didn't forget about you." How could she forget that name? Blow job, knife in the back, shovel? Faster than a deacon takes up a collection will Ruby find a new name for Jake. *George, now there's a fine name. Like my pop.*

"Here, George." In her hand, a lump of sugar, like Big Burl used to give her when she was learning to talk. Ruby scratches the stallion's forehead as he lowers his head to smell her hand. His warm lips snatch the lump and leave Ruby's hand wet.

Back in the kitchen, Ruby takes a pitcher of water from the new icebox and pours a glass. The new icehouse is only steps away, lined with large stones and drain hole for blocked ice to melt. Now if she can only figure out how to make ice in the desert instead of ordering it in large blocks from Tucson, she'll be a rich woman.

She won't have paying customers until next week so Ruby invites her usual guests to supper. Sheldon, Doc, Wink, Virgil, and Sam are already here. She has yet to invite Mae Burton. Neither Mae nor Ruby has made good on their threat to out the other. It's an uneasy silence, like either of them could pull the trigger on it at any time.

Margaret arrives, giving Ruby a brief hug. A hugger, Ruby is not, but she did institute it, that day in the schoolroom. They've gotten into the habit. Margaret is wearing white today, a change from her usual brown. Ruby remarks that it becomes her.

Dog arrives late, his hat askew. It looks like he hasn't changed clothes in a week. He barges into the dining room, a notebook in his hand. "Big quake in San Francisco," he says. "News just in on the telegraph."

Gasps, all eyes riveted on the newshawk.

"Early reports say the city is flattened."

"My God," Swendsen says.

"Tell us more, Dog," Sheldon says.

Webber reads from a notepad. "This from the *Call-Chronicle-Examiner*: 'Earthquake and Fire: San Francisco in Ruins.'"

Margaret gasps and reaches out instinctively to touch Ruby's arm.

Dog keeps reading. "And this from *The Evening Times*: 'A Thousand Persons Reported to be Dead. City is in

Flames . . . Firemen Helpless . . .Water Mains Burst, Leaving Buildings at Fire's Mercy . . .'" He looks up over his spectacles. *"The San Jose Mercury and Herald* says it all: 'San Francisco Annihilated.'"

Dog shakes his head. "Gone. The whole city."

Ruby's face goes cold. *Perce.* Maybe he's in Stockton or Sacramento. That's far enough from San Francisco, isn't it? *But please, please, don't be in San Francisco.*

"When will you have more news, Dog?" Swendsen asks.

"Maybe later tonight. I've got to get back to the telegraph."

"Come, sit a minute, Dog. Food's going cold," Ruby says.

"You aren't the first one to command this old Dog to sit, Ruby."

"Good one, Dog."

"We've had enough trouble here in Jericho, nearly burned to the ground three times now," Wink says.

Damn Mae.

"My money's on Burton setting that fire himself," Sheldon says. "The way he lit out of town."

What you don't know, Sheldon . . .

He continues, seemingly unaware of Ruby's furrowed forehead. "Although it's quite the handsome shop Mae Burton has there, now. I don't know how she does it without a husband."

Ruby glares at Sheldon. "Give a woman credit."

"Not you I'm talking about, Ruby."

Ruby's face softens, but just a bit. "She won't be on her own for long, that's my bet. Husbands are easy to come by, if you have enough money."

"Ruby . . ." Margaret says.

"Don't be 'Ruby'-ing me, Margaret. That woman is a conniver. She'll have a new man in that new shop before you can skin a cat."

"If there's a new man in town," Dog says, "I'll notice."

"And write him up?" Margaret asks. "Regardless of whether it's true?"

Dog places his hands over his heart. "Dagger, Miss Stern. Straight to my heart."

"Am I right? Not everything we read in the *Courier-Journal* is true?"

"I've been known to find a way to get everything worth reading in Hellicho into the paper."

"Have I told you how much I loathe you, Dog?" Ruby sticks her tongue out. That man can get her all riled up in no time.

Dog snickers. "You love me, Ruby. I know it."

"Don't go getting your hopes up."

For tonight's menu, Ruby has pulled out all the stops: Pork roast with mint jelly, potatoes, cabbage salad, carrots, and applesauce. Restaurant style, Ruby dishes up from the sideboard and serves. She doesn't have much of an appetite. Thank goodness her boys do. They are skinny as rails.

"Last supper here, you might say," Ruby says. "First guests to The Miracle coming Tuesday, a couple from Philadelphia, a rancher's wife and her sister, and a mother and daughter from Memphis."

"Tennessee?" Swendsen asks.

"Virgil put a notice in every paper east of the Mississippi," Ruby says. She smiles at her son. "'All-inclusive resort prices.' What is it that you said, Virgil? 'The most attractive spa in the Southwest for Health, Pleasure, Food, and Company.'"

Sheldon whistles. "Spa?"

Virgil answers. "I wrote, 'If you are looking to book a week, month, or season for rest and recuperation, look no further than to The Miracle, Arizona Territory's newest resort spa.'"

"Well, what do you know. You're a genius, Virgil,"

Sheldon says. "Your ma here can charge resort prices. Pay me back faster."

"Twenty-five dollars a week for rooms now, meals included. And liquor on the side," Ruby says.

"Thought you said, 'all inclusive,'" Sheldon says.

"Read it again, Virge. About the most attractive spa in the Southwest for . . ."

"'. . . Health, Pleasure, Food, and Company.'"

"See, Sheldon. It doesn't say anything about 'Drink.'"

Sheldon winks at Ruby. "More for you then."

"Money or drink?"

"Both."

"Some might call that highway robbery," Sheldon says.

"Hmph," Ruby says. "I call it smart."

"Are you worried at all about guests coming with consumption, Ruby? Like up at Acadia Ranch?" Margaret asks.

"Acadia Ranch has tent houses for lungers. If we get too many of them, we might build a row of tent houses out back. With patios, mind you. All looking at the Catalinas. Doc Swendsen could make house calls each day for an added fee, couldn't you, Doc."

"Good idea, Ruby," Swendsen nods.

"Best be careful, though," Margaret says. "And you too, Doc. This consumption is highly contagious, I hear."

"Of course, we'll be careful. I boil all the sheets and towels in between customers, and it's not like we're sharing sheets with them."

"I've an idea, Ruby," Dog says.

"And?" Ruby arches her eyebrows.

"Give you a year's free advertising for all the dirt you've provided me over the years."

"I haven't given you any dirt!"

"The what-all that goes on at your roadhouse—"

"Inn."

"—inn, yes. That's what I'm talking about."

"Sold a lot of papers writing me up."

"High time for some tit for tat. I'll write to all the Arizona papers. You'll need a steady clientele of locals—Tucsonans, especially—to keep you afloat in the hot months. We can tout the good Jericho air, and it's cooler here than down Tucson way. 'Good for whatever ails you,' I'll say."

"Have I told you how much I love you, Dog?" She winks at the gruff newspaperman.

"Told you so."

"When they taste your cooking . . ." Wink begins. ". . . and that pie, they'll be back."

"From your mouth to God's ears."

"Fortune right under your feet here, Ruby," Sheldon says. "Pun intended." He turns toward Virgil. "Should think of printing up postcards, son, like The Mountain View does. Send them all over the territory. Give the Neals up in Oracle a run for their money. Your take? The Miracle is closer to Tucson by eight miles and has the newest and best amenities, not the least of which is your mother, right here. Best damn cook in Arizona Territory."

"I like your thinking," Ruby says. She loads up heaping portions of Ruby Pie and saves the last piece for herself. She pours a last round of coffee, sets the coffeepot on the sideboard, and snitches a piece of crust. "Time for a tour before we get any more bad news."

Webber pushes his chair back from the table and loosens his belt. "Back to it."

Chairs scrape away from the table and Roger noses underneath to snoop for scraps.

"Now, go on. All of you," Ruby says. "At your own pace. Upstairs, downstairs, out back. I'll get nightcaps."

Sheldon brushes Ruby's arm as he heads for the parlor. "I'm proud of you, Ruby."

Ruby gets on her tiptoes to kiss his cheek. "Couldn't have done it without you, mister. Again. And I'll pay you back, Sheldon. Every penny. Even if it kills me."

THE NIGHT DARKENS AND GUESTS depart one by one, until it's just Ruby, Sheldon, and Margaret on the back patio under the great canopy of stars. Sheldon's arm is casually draped over the back of Margaret's chair. *Don't think I don't notice*, Ruby smiles to herself. After a third nightcap, she bids Sheldon and Margaret goodnight as they leave together. Is her plan working? Even if it's taken a damn long time? Ruby has herself to blame for that, lapsing twice over the past year—or three times, if you count the time Ruby and Sheldon met at the pools and made love on a boulder under the stars, their passion feral.

Under the full moon, Ruby thinks of Perce. If only she could take Perce by the arm and walk him around The Miracle. Show him all the improvements she's made to the inn and the property. *Oooh* and *aaah* over the new kitchen, the icehouse, the rooms. Laugh over the fact that yes, you can put in a resort in the middle of the goddamn Arizonan desert and yes, they will come. If only things were different, Perce beside Ruby with his arm draped over her chair, casual talk, laughter. Fingers entwined on liquor-laced nights like this. And then, slow dancing under the moon, his hands on the small of her back, the promise of ecstasy. But that's like asking a lizard to sing.

As Ruby settles beneath her covers, she takes her hand to herself. It's damn lonely in that hole in Ruby's heart. No warm dimple in the bed. No one to share secrets with, or laughs. No one to jabber with about who-said-what-and-when. Ruby has fought the loneliness in any way she could. She has screamed from her guts, railed, broken down in sobs to rock a rowboat. She's gone numb with it, slapped herself into getting used to it, to learn to carry it, because, at the bottom of it, there's no other way around it.

Ruby's hand moves faster until she arches her back in the darkness. *What does Shakespeare say about this*, she thinks, *this pain of love?* The ache is so real she cries out, but the night doesn't answer, it never does, does it?

JUNE 26, 1906
JERICHO, ARIZONA TERRITORY

"More lungers?" Virgil asks.

"Don't be vulgar, Virgil." Ruby says.

"But you said . . ."

"Doesn't mean you can. But yes, you're right, I won't use that term again."

Ruby folds another set of white sheets, crisp from drying in the summer sun. "All I know is that this disease isn't something that quack Pinkham's Vegetable Compound claims it can cure. I hear doctors try everything, purging, vomiting, bleeding." She needs to see Doc Swendsen soon. She's starting to cough up blood. Not every day, but often enough.

Ruby adds the folded sheets to a growing pile. "Help me here, Virge." She tosses a stack of towels toward him.

Virgil folds towels with precision. "I didn't mean to say it isn't serious, Ma."

"These folks don't have much to look forward to, Virge. The Miracle is a respite, a balm, sunshine and hearty meals and exercise, if they're able. Make them think they're getting better." *Will I get better? Ever?*

"Trouble is, you don't know when your time's up," Virgil says. "I can't stop thinking about San Francisco."

Perce, where are you, Perce?

"Which is why we need to make hay while the sun shines, as the old saying goes, Virge. And, while we're at it, build a couple of tent houses out back and charge the hell for them."

BY OCTOBER, RUBY FIGURES the hotel will turn a handsome profit. She pays careful attention to her ledgers and does the figures. Especially if she adds those tent houses.

Every Monday, another group of guests is off. There's more stained sheets than ever before, but the money's good. Tuberculosis is lucrative. People come out by train now to take in the dry desert air. Some stay for two weeks, or three. Ruby's had guests from points north and east who looked five minutes from death. After a stay in the desert air, they leave a sight hardier, swearing they'll be back for a longer visit next year. The Miracle is living up to its name.

Not to be outdone by The Mountain View in Oracle, The Shangri-La in Globe, or The Catalina in Tucson, The Miracle is a bargain by comparison. That's the secret, lure guests in with lower prices and then add to the tab. Booze is now charged by the glass, with receipts adding up nightly. Virgil tends bar at night, regaling guests with stories of bygone lodgers, especially Teddy Roosevelt.

"And this once, we had a couple of traveling nuns . . ." Virgil says.

Ears perk up.

"Nuns?" one of the lodgers asks.

". . . and I got taken along with the rest of Jericho!" Ruby laughs along with her guests as Virgil recounts the story. "You should have seen them," Ruby adds. "Hustling patrons at all the saloons. 'For the orphanage,' they said. Took off with nearly two grand."

Thanks to Dog Webber, Tucsonans are beating down the doors: territorial legislators, university professors, wealthy businessmen. It's ten degrees cooler here in Jericho in the summers, and Ruby lowers her rates for Arizonans. Word is out in high circles that Ruby's got a plum address. And the best pie.

Tucson councilman John Winston is on the register tonight (he signed his full name with his signature flourish, the "J" and "W" twice the size of the other letters). Accompanying him is a woman. Ruby calls her Mrs. Winston. Last month the councilman brought a different companion. Ruby called her Mrs. Winston, too. One of them could be. Or the next one. *You never know*, she tells herself. When you've been fooled by a pair of counterfeit nuns, of all things, you learn things aren't always what they seem.

Tucson botanist Dr. William Austin Cannon and his painter wife are also here, registered for a full week. Cannon takes to the desert at dawn with a knapsack and isn't back until supper. He ranges the foothills of Mount Lemmon, rising to more than nine thousand feet in the distance. Lemmon's wide tabletop is unremarkable at first glance, like the desert. Cannon's wife sets her easel up in the early afternoon under an umbrella and takes her time with brushes and oils as she paints landscapes. Ruby offers tea and sweets. The woman, stout and severe, declines as she paints.

After supper, Ruby serves another round of coffee. "Tell me, Dr. Cannon, what exactly it is you do there at your scientific research station?"

"In a nutshell?" Cannon wipes his trim moustache with a napkin. "We study deserts and catalogue their species. The Carnegie Foundation funds my research, here and in North Africa and in Australia." He goes on, using words Ruby has never heard of: "transpiration" and "morphology." To Ruby, cacti are spiky and a nuisance, except in spring, when they're briefly splendid.

"Good luck with that!" Winston says. "I cannot imagine why anyone would bother cataloguing desert plants."

"You underestimate the desert, sir," Cannon says. "This is absolutely the finest place to work that could be possibly found. So many species, as you move up the mountain."

"Lemmon?" Ruby asks.

Cannon nods. "Did you know, sir"—he looks directly at Winston now—"that from desert floor to mountain top there may be more species of plants here in this little slice of the desert than in all the southwest?"

That shuts Winston up.

"And you, Mrs. Cannon. You sell your paintings, I presume?" Ruby asks. "I might be in the market."

"A woman painter?" Winston shakes his head. "Next you'll be wanting to run for the territorial legislature."

"And a damn sight better we'll all be when that happens," Mrs. Cannon replies.

That shuts Winston up again.

It's guests like this who swell Ruby's coffers. If she's going to run the most lucrative resort in all the territory, she has to put up with the Winstons of the world.

"WILLA!" RUBY AND MARGARET turn when Willa walks by, covering her blackened eye. Ruby and Margaret have been standing in front of the post office long past time that

Ruby should be back to fix supper for guests. "What the devil happened?" Ruby asks.

At that moment, Mae Burton arrives at the post office, her hands full of envelopes. The women gather around Willa, whose eye freshly oozes.

"It's nothing," Willa says.

"Hogwash," Ruby says. "You can't fool anyone in this town. Not us, anyway."

"How long are you going to put up with Judd's nonsense?" Mae asks. "Come stay with me, Willa. I've got the lodgings and I can use help at the store."

"I don't know if I can . . ."

"Of course you can," Ruby says. "Or stay with me. God knows I could use help, too."

"Or me," Margaret says. "You could keep house, cook, clean."

"Seems we've got a bidding war going on here," Ruby says.

"Why would you do this for me?" Willa asks.

"Because we've been in your shoes, one way or the other, all of us," Ruby says. "Take Margaret here, heart broken to pieces years ago." She turns to Margaret. "Hope I'm not spilling secrets out of school." She points to Mae. "And Mae, here, husband left her high and dry." Ruby takes Willa's arm. "And me, well, I've had both those things happen to me, and worse. We women have to stick together in this town. Don't you agree, Mae?"

Mae nods.

With that exchange, Ruby decides not to finger Mae Burton for the fire so Mae's accusatory story about Ruby taking up with Perce won't see the pages of the *Jericho Courier-Journal*. A truce they've sealed, without words.

"Come with me right now, Willa, as soon as I drop these letters off," Mae says. "You won't go back to Judd tonight."

"My offer still holds," Ruby says.

"Mine, too," Margaret adds.

Before bed, Ruby takes the mandolin from its place on her bureau and strums it. If you're going to play the mandolin, you've got to pick it up. Start from somewhere. Note by note. That's how she learned to talk, word by word, like her pop used to say, feeding her lumps of sugar. An hour later, Ruby's fingers are plumb sore, but she's picked out a simple tune, nothing like Slovo, but no one is there to listen, so there are no snickers about her expertise, or lack of it.

Ruby puts the mandolin away, dreaming of Perce. *Damn, do I miss you.*

Ruby will visit San Francisco once the city is up and running again, which it will be, like Jerome and Bisbee and Jericho, and every town that's met ruin and rises from the ashes, only better. Divina has left her a hefty inheritance and she owes Divina far more than she ever could repay. That ocean is waiting.

And maybe Perce.

AUGUST 9, 1906
JERICHO, ARIZONA TERRITORY

Margaret, a better athlete than Ruby knew, lowers her racquet and meets Ruby at the net.

"One more set, and then I've got to head in and start supper." Ruby wipes her forehead with her sweat-stained blouse. She's glad to stop, her breathing comes difficult now.

Margaret's white blouse doesn't show a lick of perspiration. And in this heat. "Good set, Ruby. How about we call it a draw, one set to one? I have an, erm, engagement tonight."

Ruby curls her lips into a smile. "An engagement, now."

"Sheldon is coming for supper. At my place."

The women walk arm in arm back to the patio. Ruby squeezes Margaret's hand. "About time. In that case, I have something for you. Wait here." Ruby ducks inside and returns with a small package wrapped in brown paper. She hands it to Margaret. "I've been saving this for you for a long time."

"Shall I open it here?"

"It's not for prying eyes, if you get my meaning. Open it at home." Ruby laughs. "Oh, hell, come into the kitchen. Open it here."

Margaret stands at Ruby's kitchen table and unfolds the package. She gasps.

"Why, Ruby!"

"Can't be wearing old drawers."

"Where did you get these?" Margaret fingers the black lace trim. "I've never seen anything so lovely."

"Tucson. Not that I think Mr. Sloane will see them tonight, mind you."

Margaret colors. "I would think not."

"Let's just say that men appreciate the finer things when it comes to a lady. Even if he doesn't see them, you know you're wearing them. Gives you confidence. Might even say power."

"Power?"

"Women rule the world, Margaret. My pop's old Apache lady friend told me that. Although I often doubt it. But if I don't know anything else, I know this. You can bring a man to his knees with even a hint of lace."

"I've never been known to have easy virtue."

"Virtue be damned, Margaret. Better to regret what you've done than what you haven't."

After dark, Ruby sits on the front porch sipping whiskey neat. Town is jumping tonight, Judd's doors swinging open faster than a grasshopper in a chicken coop. Two men, smoking, walk past the inn and cross Jefferson toward the livery. The lip of Oldfather Peak glows under the moonlight. A shot rings out from somewhere up Jefferson and then a fast horse, minus a rider. A dust devil swirls in the middle of the street, gone as fast as it appeared. Shouts dissipate in the distance, then a clanging of pots and pans. That's Sheldon's signal that he's needed.

But, according to Margaret's plans, Sheldon is otherwise engaged tonight. Ruby doesn't want to think too much about it, or in too much detail, so she goes about chores, straightening the kitchen, the parlor, the dining room.

Put your boots on, Ruby. No.

She rearranges her stemware and cutlery, stacks and restacks plates.

You know you want to. No, Ruby.

After she scrubs out the sink, she sits on the back porch as the moon rises over the hem of the mountains, humming, and hoping against hope that *by just about now* Margaret's black lacy drawers are down around her ankles and she's crying out for all to hear, the *rise rise rise* exploding, the best damn man in all of Jericho hammering her home.

AUGUST 15, 1906
JERICHO, ARIZONA TERRITORY

In a balloon of dust, Charley Paulson's new coach pulls up in front of The Miracle. "Whoa," he calls, as six horses jangle to a stop. Ruby squints. *Company? Today?* Her boarders left Monday and she's not expecting new guests until next Tuesday. She's taken a week off for summer cleaning, and does The Miracle need it. Sure, a man might arrive on horseback unannounced and if she's got a room ready, she might put him up. But why Paulson? Today? Ruby wipes her greasy hands on her apron and unties it. She tosses it over the sideboard and straightens her hair. Not exactly company clothes, a split skirt and blouse. And not her go-to-meeting boots.

Two men and a dainty woman rise from seats behind the driver. The woman offers a gloved hand to one of the men as she steps out of the wagon. She wears a slim black suit, frilled blouse, and buttoned boots. Ruby has never seen a hat so large on a woman so small.

Ruby steps off the porch. "Paulson! Wasn't expecting you today." She approaches the trio beside the wagon. "And you are?"

"Arnold Bruebecker, ma'am," the taller of the two men replies as he tips his hat. "And my partner, James Rumsen."

Both men wear city suits, no boots. The second man tips his hat, Sunday best manners here in Jericho. The small woman doesn't look to be more than twenty and holds her reticule to her breastbone like it contains a breakable item.

"And may I introduce Miss Hattie Fortune."

Fortune. Ruby's blood runs cold. Fists. Blackened eyes. Hands at her throat. And the letter she never answered. Never even opened.

"Can we bother you for a glass of cool tea?" Bruebecker asks. "That's a hell of a drive from Tucson."

"Pardon me, Mr. Bruebecker," Ruby stammers. "Of course, come in."

"I'll be off," Paulson says. "See you Monday."

"Monday? I've got a full house until then," Ruby lies.

"These folks said they had a reservation."

Ruby looks at Bruebecker.

"You didn't get our telegram?" he asks. "Three rooms for the remainder of the week?"

Ruby shakes her head. "'Fraid not. I take boarders by the week, Tuesday to Monday, except for special circumstances."

"Which is why we are here," Hattie says, as she moves toward the shade of the porch. "Special circumstances."

Ruby's mind spins. She'll have to explain why she lied that she's full up.

Virgil, late to the post office after the noon meal, lopes down the wide front steps of the inn. "Miss." He tips his hat toward the young woman. His eyes linger on her.

"Why the doleful face, Virge?" Ruby whispers as he passes. "Oh, never mind." He's almost sixteen, she reminds herself. Not many young women of courting age in Jericho except the parson's daughter, Elizabeth. And Elizabeth doesn't won't *will never* look or dress the likes of Miss Hattie Fortune.

"Come in, please." Ruby disappears to the kitchen and returns with three tall glasses of iced tea and hands the frosted glasses to her new guests. "What do I owe the honor of your company?" If she only opened the letter she might know, *damn it all.*

Hattie Fortune sips the iced tea and dabs at her mouth. "We've got a conundrum, ma'am," Hattie says. She nods to Bruebecker, who reaches into his valise to procure a document. "It wasn't until yesterday when we arrived in Tucson that we learned of Willard's death."

"Willard?" Ruby asks.

"My brother, Mrs. Fortune.'

"Which brings us to the conundrum," Rumsen interrupts. "Willard's father, Mr. Willard Fortune, Sr., left all his assets and worldly goods to his only son, Willard Fortune, Jr., with the caveat that he care for Miss Fortune." He motions to Hattie, who is fanning herself with an oversized white fan. "We tried without success to reach Willard, and now we know why our letters were returned unopened. It seems he's been dead for seven years, and no one thought to contact his father or his sister."

"That can't be," Ruby says. "I was under the impression that father and son had had a falling out. From what my husband"—Ruby winces as she says this—"told me, he never expected to be named an heir to his father's estate."

"Perhaps if Mr. Fortune, Sr. had known of his son's death, he might have made other arrangements. Until his last day, he hoped for reconciliation. And now we have come to find out . . ."

"And just yesterday," Mr. Rumsen interrupts.

". . . that not only is Mr. Fortune, Jr. dead, he came to an all too gruesome end," Bruebecker says.

"At your hand, we understand," Hattie says. She looks condescendingly at Ruby.

Ruby doesn't break eye contact. When Hattie looks away, Ruby goes on. "When did Mr. Fortune, Sr.—Willie's father—pass on?"

"Are you attempting to deflect the conversation, Mrs. Fortune?"

Sweat forms under Ruby's collar. It itches. "The judge declared it a clear case of self-defense." She brushes hair off her neck.

"We'll speak with the authorities ourselves to ascertain that fact," Rumsen says. "Because under Illinois law, if Mr. Fortune, Jr. is now deceased, the estate entire would go to you, with the understanding that you would take Miss Fortune on as your ward."

Hattie continues to fan her pale face. "I won't agree to that," she says.

Will I ever be free of Willie Fortune? And now his sister? Ruby stands. "Nor will I, Miss Fortune, so we agree on that. You'll have to give me a moment to freshen up a room for Miss Fortune here. I will then attend to your rooms, gentlemen."

"So you do have vacancies? Is this another one of your falsehoods?" Bruebecker asks.

"I've told no falsehoods. I have vacancies because the inn is closed for a week for summer cleaning. No boarders until Tuesday. But I will make an exception for you."

"Why was my letter never answered, Mrs. Fortune?" Hattie presses Ruby. "I waited and waited until my waiting held out. Now we have come to find . . ."

"My husband"—again Ruby cringes to say it—"your brother, that is, was a most disagreeable man. I am sorry I did not respond to your letter. I never opened it, truth be told. There was nothing to say. Except that he was dead."

THERE ARE ONLY SEVEN AT SUPPER: Bruebecker, Rumsen, Hattie, Sam, Virgil, Sheldon, and Ruby. Ruby thought it prudent not to invite Wink tonight. And certainly not the parson. Virgil is love-struck by Hattie and Sam's manners could use improvement. The roast is tough and the vegetables burnt. Ruby's heart wasn't into cooking today. Even the conversation lags.

Three loud knocks on the hotel door interrupt the awkward silence.

"If you'll excuse me." Ruby exits the dining room and opens the door to the inn. "Dog?"

"Sheldon here?"

"He is."

"Big dust up at Judd's. Swendsen's attending. Guy knifed in the belly. Doesn't look good. And the other one's got a slash on his thigh from here to here." Dog motions with his hand, groin to knee.

"Come on through."

Ruby leads Dog through the parlor toward the dining room. When they enter, the men stand.

"Hate to interrupt your supper, but we're needing the sheriff."

"What's the trouble?" Sheldon asks.

"Rather not go into the details in present company. There's trouble up at Judd's. Two guys down, in a bad way."

Hattie blanches and puts her hanky to her mouth. Virgil can't keep his eyes off the young woman. Sam steals a bun from Virgil's plate.

"Excuse me Ruby, Miss Fortune, gentlemen." Sheldon follows the newspaperman.

Sam scrapes his chair and disappears out through the kitchen, bun in hand. The back door slams.

"Well, I never," Rumsen says. "What kind of a town is this?"

"One that we'll not be sorry to leave behind," Bruebecker answers.

Virgil still cannot take his eyes off Hattie, who is paler than before.

That leaves five at the table (if you discount the aging dog by Ruby's feet): a distressed young woman, a heartsick teen, two glowering businessmen, and Ruby, who, for maybe the first time in her life, has nothing to say.

"KEEP YOUR DAMN MONEY." Ruby stands at the door of Hattie's guest room and glares at the young woman, who she wishes would disappear like a spider under a rock.

Hattie winces. "Must you?"

"Must I what? Watch my damn mouth? Or tell you the truth?" Ruby's eyes narrow. "You've got nothing to fear from me, Miss Fortune. I don't want you here any more than you want to be here. And, speaking of truth, there is something you need to know."

A vertical ridge lines Hattie's pale forehead, between her eyes.

"Your dear departed brother beat the life out of me more times than I can count," Ruby says. "Suffocated me once, held a gun to my head on many occasions. It was down to him or me when I did what I had to do."

Hattie looks away and shakes her head. "I have a hard time believing you, Mrs. Fortune. Willard was never violent at home."

"I hear your father didn't spare the rod."

"With Willard, no. He thought it in Willard's best interest."

"Willard—Willie—came by it naturally, then. And not only me. The boys, too. Not just a larruping if they deserved it. I mean bloodied noses and broken arms. For the smallest reason. Sometimes no reason at all."

"Even Virgil?"

"Yes, especially Virgil, on account of his palsy. Willie took any excuse to cuff Virgil, like Virge can help his condition. Born with it, he was."

"He seems like a sweet young man."

"Not too many people in your life you'll meet like Virgil. As honest as they come." *If you overlook that he pilfers from letters, but who can blame him on those wages?* "Seeing your brother take it out on Virgil time and time again about broke my heart. And Sam. Hardly walking and Willie'd pick on him, taunt him even, until Sam would explode in anger. That gave Willie the right to box his ears? To trip him? To take him behind the shed and whup him with a belt?"

Hattie looks away.

"Like your father did to Willie, too many times to count, by his estimation. Which is why he lit out of Chicago and never looked back. Never thought he'd hear from your father again. Which is why this situation is so ironic."

"I don't know what to say."

"I want nothing to do with your father, your brother, or you, Miss Fortune," Ruby says. "That's why you can keep your damn money. I don't want a single nickel of it."

"I thought we were in for a fight. There are always uses for money." Hattie looks out the window and waves her pale arm. "Grass, perhaps, or a swimming pool. This place is . . . lacking." She feigns disgust.

Ruby scowls. "Has anyone ever told you you're unbearable?"

"That's harsh."

"I've heard that before." Ruby peers at Hattie, her brows furrowed. "Let me be very frank with you, Miss Fortune. I'm done fighting. Unless someone comes after my boys. Or my hotel. We used to have a she-bear in the traveling show. She fought for her cubs; maimed a man because of it. Well, I could do more than maim. Over my dead body, I'd advise you not to come after either one. So you pick. The money is yours for the taking. And then you and I never have to cross paths again."

Hattie looks straight at Ruby. "Is it true? That you killed Willard in cold blood?"

"Are you deaf, Miss Fortune? I've told you I killed Willie in self-defense, as your two solicitors will verify with the court." Ruby turns to leave. "I'm not sorry he's gone. A bastard, he was, that brother of yours."

And I'm free from him, at last.

AUGUST 18, 1906
JERICHO, ARIZONA TERRITORY

Hattie Fortune leaves behind a wake of dust, a handkerchief, and a broken heart. Dust Ruby deals with every day, it gets in all the wrong places. The handkerchief will find good use, you can always use a hanky. As for a broken heart, that's beyond Ruby's purview; Virgil's in a pucker that he'll have to deal with on his own.

Ruby strips beds and attacks laundry. She soaks and rinses and soaks again, scrubs, suds, and scalds her hands raw. Finally, the wash all on the line now, sheets and pillow sleeves and coverlets. And a dainty lace hanky, left behind, fluttering in the desert wind like a flag of surrender. It will be crisp in less than a half hour in this weather. Ruby will think twice about giving the hanky to Virgil as a keepsake. It's his goddamn aunt, after all.

By late the next afternoon, another set of travelers arrives ready for baths after the long trip from Tucson. It never ends, being an innkeeper. And Ruby didn't get half of what she had hoped to do in terms of summer cleaning because of Hattie's unannounced visit. She wonders if she made the right choice, rejecting the Fortune inheritance. Then she reminds herself, *yes*.

Sam meanders out of the inn. Ruby cocks her head and motions to him. "Shh. Look." Ruby points to the top of a saguaro just yards from where they stand. A striking purplish-black bird perches on the top of the multi-armed cactus. "Like a chameleon, changing colors to blend in. Phainopepla. Don't ask me to spell it."

Ruby lowers her voice so as not to disturb the preening bird, its *too-eet, too-eet, cheet cheet cheet* sounding like the strumming of love. The desert is drab compared to the bird, its shimmering wings trembling. When the crested flier leaves its perch atop the cactus, the air is empty, minus the trill. Ruby breathes in, and her throat itches. She removes clothespins from her mouth and takes a swig from the tin drum canteen slung over her shoulder and hands it to Sam.

"Give me a minute," Ruby says. She pops remaining clothespins into a cloth sack pegged to the clothesline. "Looks like a good day for shade." Ruby heads into the kitchen. A few minutes later, she emerges with a small sack and a full canteen. "C'mon Sam. Day's a-wasting." Roger, deep in slumber under the back porch, doesn't stir.

Ruby strides on the cracked desert floor, Sam just behind her. No Roger today. Sam chases a roadrunner and plays hide-and-seek behind a cholla, once prickling himself. He doesn't say a word as he picks the prickly ball from his arm but his mouth forms a perfect "O".

Sweat beads down her neck as Ruby gulps water. She dribbles water down the crevice in her blouse. "Just another mile, Sam. Then we'll be lolly-gagging like a couple of hobos."

Ruby sponges sweat from her forehead with her sleeve. "Never be too busy to take care of yourself. Remember that, will you? Took me long enough to learn it. You can have all the book learning in the world and be as dumb as a doorpost if you don't learn that." She looks Sam in the eye. "I don't know how much time I've got left on this earth, so I want to be sure you've heard me."

JUST YESTERDAY, RUBY WALKED with purpose toward the crossroads and turned left into Doc Swendsen's surgery. Her appointment was at two. On the way back to the inn, Ruby caught sight of herself in Burton's plate glass window. She pretended to look at the bushels of produce and displays of dry goods. Her reflection frightened her, usually full cheeks shrunken, eyes dulled. She lifted a finger to her cheek.

"Ruby?"

Ruby recognized the reflection in the window. "Sheldon, I didn't hear you."

"Too busy looking at those bolts of fabric, I suspect." He motioned toward the goods. "Or maybe those other notions."

"A shovel, maybe, Sheldon. Or a broom. What I've got serves, until it doesn't."

"That reminds me of a funny thing my ma used to say. She would take me into the bath by the ear and say, 'You're a sorry sight, Sheldon, until you aren't.'"

"Where was that?" Ruby suddenly realized she doesn't know a thing about Sheldon's past. Never asked, and he never offered.

"North Carolina. The day I left, I told my ma I was going to get as far away from my pa as I could get."

"That's what Fletcher said to me when he lit out of town."

"I bet I came farther. And hated him more."

Too late, Ruby wondered what else she didn't know about him.

SAM OPENS HIS MOUTH IN response to Ruby, and for a split-second Ruby thinks he's going to say something. She waits, but he doesn't speak. "Now look at me, Sam."

He returns her gaze.

"It's a sign of respect to look people in the eye," Ruby says. "Don't stare through them. Another word to the wise: pick your friends wisely. The opposite is also true. Always know who your enemies are. There are people out there who pose as friends, and before you know it, they stab you in the back."

Sam looks down.

"Look up, Sam."

He looks at Ruby again.

"This is the most important, son. No matter what, do the right thing every time, even if it costs you. Especially if it costs you. Now go ahead."

Ruby stops at the edge of the now-dry creek and shimmies out of her skirt. Sam is already stripped to the waist and tugging on his belt. He plows into the shade of a desert willow and emerges in his underdrawers with a smile that could light up the sky.

"Turn around," Ruby says. Sam turns toward the mountains but peeks back over his shoulder. "I said turn around, young man. You're a rogue, just like Fletcher." Ruby rips off her soaked blouse and steps into the shade in her damp chemise and bloomers. She doesn't own a new-fangled bath suit. "I'm going to have my hands full with you, I can see that, Sam. And once you find your voice again, I'll bet you'll have plenty to say."

They sprawl in the shade under the willows. A cool breeze flows down the canyon from the high country. Sam falls asleep. Ruby, cooler now, relives the past few days in her mind. Did she really give up all that money? She could have laid sod around The Miracle. Or put in a swimming pool. Live a comfortable existence, likely enough to pay Sheldon back for the hefty loan. But how steep is that price to pay? No, she's happy she didn't take it.

When the sun starts its creep down past the high mark, Ruby scrambles out of the shade and dons her blouse and skirt. She pulls on her boots and stamps them on the hard-pan. "Bet you can't catch me."

Sam runs past as Ruby cinches her belt. He doesn't wear a shirt.

"Race you back," Ruby yells. She stops to pick up Sam's shirt, which has fallen in the dirt. He hasn't noticed that he's dropped it.

On the run back to Jericho, Ruby sidesteps bones and debris as she follows her son. His lean arms pump the desert air as his body zigzags through desert underbrush. How long his legs have become, like his brothers. Ruby doesn't try to overtake him. Probably couldn't now, her breath is labored.

You can see Jericho for miles out in the desert, buildings sprouting at odd angles on all its terraced ledges. If there is room for one more structure in town, Ruby doesn't know where it could fit. All the spaces are used up. One earthquake is all it would take to topple Jericho. One never knows when.

Ruby's body tingles as the sun licks sweat from her skin. She douses her head with the last of the canteen's water and sprints to catch up to Sam as they near The Miracle. Her hair flies behind her, a mass of gold. It dries within minutes, as if the sun itself has settled in it, and stayed.

41

SEPTEMBER 10, 1906
JERICHO, ARIZONA TERRITORY

Guests come and go and Ruby's bank account swells. She has to pinch herself, the numbers are so good. The Miracle is certainly living up to its name.

A Mrs. R. Conklin and her daughter arrive on the Tuesday coach. Also on the shuttle from Tucson is a couple from Delaware and a single man, who has trouble descending from the wagon. Charley Paulson helps the man down the last step and unloads luggage.

"In the parlor, Charley," Ruby says.

Paulson grimaces.

Ruby takes the freighter aside. "New prices, new services," she says. "I'm not getting any younger and don't have the help I used to." She coughs into a hanky. It's red.

Paulson hefts trunks and suitcases inside the front door of the inn. It takes him four trips up and down the wide front steps of The Miracle. "That'll be four dollars extra, ma'am."

"On top of the passengers' fees?"

"New services, new prices."

Ruby flicks her thumb at him.

"Come in," she motions to her guests as she ushers them into the parlor. No one sits.

"Have a seat, Mr. . . . ?"

"Redoubt. Chalmers Redoubt."

"I'll be back for you shortly, Mr. Redoubt." Ruby walks Mrs. Conklin and her daughter and the Delaware couple to their upstairs rooms. "Freshen up and I'll have those bags up to you in no time." Ruby stops on the stairway and catches her breath. She hurries to the parlor where Redoubt waits, reclined now on the sofa.

"Mr. Redoubt, here, let me." Ruby takes the man's satchel and leads him to Room #3, now called "The Conquistador."

"Is there anything I can get for you?" she asks.

"A good lie down is in order."

"Make yourself at home. Water is on the bedstead and extra pillows in the armoire. Dinner's at noon. If you sleep through, I'll save you a plate." Ruby fluffs up two large pillows on the bed and motions to the chamber pot beneath the bed. She doesn't mention golf or tennis or horses. One look at him, and anyone can see he is not long for this world; consumption has rendered him nearly weightless as a feather. "After a spell, come sit on the patio," Ruby says. "No one in Jericho has a view like ours."

"I'll avail myself of the bed for now, Mrs. Fortune. The journey was quite taxing. It's a long way from Cincinnati. And no one warned me about the dust." He shakes a mantle of filth from his clothing onto the newly swept carpet and coughs into a stained hanky.

"It is a desert, after all," Ruby says. "Give yourself a day or two. The sunshine, the warmth, the views, that's what people remember."

"And your pie, according to the brochures."

"Yes, my pie. Now, if you'll excuse me, is there anything else until dinnertime?"

"Can you help me off with my jacket?"

Ruby peels the jacket from Redoubt's narrow shoulders. He winces. Ruby drapes the garment on the back of the chair and pulls back the coverlet on the bed. "Have a good rest, Mr. Redoubt. Until I see you again."

Ruby checks her watch. It's nearly ten-thirty. She closes the guest room door behind her and bangs into the kitchen. She pins her hair up and grabs her apron. Her hands fly as she readies lamb roast, salted boiled potatoes, radish salad, and asparagus. She sets the table, pours water, and gets coffee to boil. Two pies cool on the kitchen table. She rests for ten minutes with a glass of cool tea. A few minutes to noon, she knocks on all the guest doors. "Dinner's almost on."

Mrs. Conklin and her daughter arrive first, taking places at the far end of the table. The Delaware couple arrives next and sits at the far side of the long table. Mr. Redoubt does not show.

"Haven't had such an intimate group in ever so long," Ruby says. She serves the meal family style and leaves the guests to eat. "No need to clear your places."

The Conklins retire to their room after the noon meal and the other couple takes to the patio, where the woman fans herself incessantly and her husband sinks his nose deep into a book, his spectacles nearly touching the pages.

Ruby heaps leftovers onto a plate for Mr. Redoubt and finishes washing up. She peeks her head out the kitchen door but doesn't get the guests' attention. Ruby walks out to the patio and clears her throat. The man raises his head from his book. His wife has now dropped off to sleep.

"I won't be long," Ruby says. "I'll be to town and back within an hour. Help yourself to tea on the kitchen sideboard. You'll find extra slices of pie there, as well."

The Conklins and the Delawareans come to supper and sit in the exact spots they chose for dinner. Still the guests do not speak to one another. Again, no Mr. Redoubt. After supper, Ruby knocks on Redoubt's door, a plate of cold food in her hand.

There is no reply.

Ruby puts the plate of food down and tries the door. It is unlatched. "Mr. Redoubt?" she whispers, as she nudges the door open.

The body in the bed is as still as the night. Ruby advances slowly, watching for the rise and fall of the coverlet. "Mr. Redoubt," she says again, this time louder. Mr. Redoubt doesn't answer, and never will again, no matter how loud Ruby calls for him.

Even before she reaches the edge of the bed, Ruby knows Chalmers Redoubt is dead. She drags the bedside chair close to the man and sits. For ten minutes, she stays by his side. It's the least you can do for a body, sit by while his spirit leaves the room for the netherworld. When the curtain flutters, Ruby rises from the chair and covers the slight man with a sheet. She places her hands on his head and offers as much of a prayer as she remembers, not that it will do him any good. But it won't do him harm, that's what Ruby tells herself. It won't do him any harm.

"SHELDON?" RUBY KNOCKS on Sheldon's door behind the jail.

A minute later, Sheldon opens the door, half dressed. Ruby sees his mussed bed inside.

"Ruby? What is it?"

"I haven't come for . . ."

"I've been meaning to tell you . . ."

"I know, Sheldon. And I'm glad for both of you. I'm sorry for the interruption but I need you for a different matter. Please come over quick. And bring Doc with you."

Doc Swendsen and Sheldon remove the body at midnight. Ruby doesn't want to upset her guests or her sons. She rummages through Redoubt's satchel and finds no identification, as if he knew he wanted to die, and came here to do it. And he didn't even have her pie before he left the world behind.

"What will you do with him?" Ruby asks. She holds the door for the men. They pass through and load the shrouded corpse into Swendsen's cart.

"Anatomy," Swendsen says. "The fate of anyone who isn't claimed before a charity burial."

"Please don't tell Dog about this," Ruby says. "I won't have another customer."

"Our secret," Doc says. "The undertaker and I have an understanding on this; he won't tell a soul. I pay his tab at The Axe and Pail."

Swendsen covers Redoubt's corpse with burlap sackcloth. "What did you say his name was, Ruby? I put it in my register under initials only. To help me remember."

"I've had more people register with aliases than moths to flame. You just don't know who to trust. He gave his name as Redoubt. Chalmers Redoubt."

"Like a fortress?" Sheldon asks.

Ruby shrugs her shoulders. She doubts the man's name was Redoubt. Or Chalmers. But who knows? Ruby took enough guff from Willie when she chose the name Fletcher for her third-born son. "Clayton is a strong name," he had said, "but Fletcher? Sounds like a sodomite." Willie had pranced around the tent like a fairy. "Why not John? Or Robert? Give a boy a real name."

"The name Fletcher means arrow-maker. That a boy-name enough for you?" Ruby put her hands on her hips and thrust her chin out. "I birth a child, I name him. You go on, try to birth a child of your own, Willie Fortune. You can name him whatever you goddamn please." And so Fletcher it was.

Doc wipes his hands on his long coat and shakes Sheldon's hand. "I should know a sight more about tuberculosis by tomorrow, thanks to Mr. Redoubt, or whatever his name is. I'd wager his lungs are shriveled to the size of a pea." Swendsen looks at Ruby. "At the end, that is, not until . . ."

Ruby shoots Swendsen a dirty look. This fact she does not want to know. "And where do you fit into this, Sheldon?" Ruby asks. "Being the sheriff and all."

Sheldon lights a cigarette and leans against the wagon, his long leg crossed. He tilts his head up and exhales, that face she knows so well outlined against the dark night sky. "What body?"

SEPTEMBER 24, 1906
JERICHO, ARIZONA TERRITORY

First the sore throat, then the fever. Soon the diarrhea.
"Is it . . . ?"

"Quit that talk right now, young man. Doc says it's
likely a mild case of the influenza. Plenty of bed rest and
water should have you up in no time."

"You sure, Ma?"

"When have you ever had reason to doubt me, Virgil?
I talk plain as day, whether you like it or not. If you had
tuberculosis, you'd have noticed signs long before yesterday. Fatigue. Night sweats. Loss of appetite. And coughing
up blood. You don't fit the bill, Virge. It's not tuberculosis."

"I've got it bad."

"I'll get you some mustard salve."

Ruby calls Willa in to attend to Virgil as Ruby deals
with laundry, cooking, baking, and needs of guests. *One
dead guest is one too many.*

Ruby doesn't have much time for walking or playing
the mandolin. Lodgers never used to ask for changes of

sheets mid-week or special modifications to the menu. She has to pay through the nose for fresh produce at Mae Burton's new store, where prices have rocketed sky high.

When Ruby complained to Mae, she was met with a rare nod of agreement. "Did you lower your prices when you opened that new inn of yours?" Ruby bit her tongue. *Guilty.* "I've worked my tail off to get this place up and running," Mae said. "I suspect you know a thing or two about that."

"The store is looking good, Mae." *Why remain enemies?* But it doesn't hurt to keep tabs, just in case. Ruby swears she sees Dog Webber coming out of Mae's late at night. Something is up there. Ruby is dead tired herself, operating on four hours' sleep per night, the reason she can't miss Webber stealing away from Mae's at 3 a.m. Next, there'll be a wedding, and Dog Webber can put his feet up more often. Husbands are easy to come by when you have the money, Ruby said so herself, with Webber in the room. *Well, why shouldn't everyone be afforded happiness?*

Ruby checks to see that all the guests have retired for the night. She peeks into Virgil and Sam's room and sees that her youngest is fast asleep. She sits at the edge of Virgil's bed and strokes his warm forehead.

"Feeling any better?"

"Not much."

Ruby wrings out a cloth from the washstand next to the bed and mops Virgil's face, neck, and arms.

"I can do that, Ma."

"I know you can. But I'm your momma."

Virgil sighs and closes his eyes.

"I do think you're on the mend, Virge."

"Hope so. I'm tired of being tired."

Ruby replaces the cloth and wipes her hands dry on her skirt. "Is there anything you've ever wanted to ask me?" She holds her breath. "Anything about . . ."

"Why did you do it, Ma?"

Ruby touches Virgil's forehead. *Do you know how much I love you, Virgil?*

"I had to, Virge. He would have killed us all." She strokes his head. "Someone else might have hightailed it out of here afterwards, but I couldn't. And I won't. Ever. I'll never leave Sam. Or you. Not for more than a few days, maybe, to go to Tucson. Or a few weeks, if I ever get to San Francisco . . ."

Will I ever get to San Francisco?

"Thanks to your idea, Virge, we really have something here now, don't we? All of us?"

"Don't spend all those hours reading trade catalogues and brochures and almanacs for nothing, Ma. And there's something else—"

"What are you taking about? Still pining after Miss Fortune? She's your aunt, for God's sake, Virge. Put that away."

"I know, Ma, though there aren't any girls in Jericho the likes of her. What I've been thinking about is going to college."

Ruby stiffens. "We can talk about that in a year or two, Virge. You're set at the post office. Plus, if anything happens to me, you'll have to take over The Miracle."

"No thanks, Ma. Clay and Fletch left, and I aim to follow them."

"I don't want to lose you, too, Virge. Not yet."

"I've already sent off for catalogues."

No, please, no.

"Well, when they arrive, you just tuck them away somewhere. There's a nice girl out there for you, somewhere. Maybe right here."

"Who?"

Ruby thinks. *Not the upstairs girls.* "There's the parson's girl."

"I don't think so, Ma. She's a bookworm."

"And what's wrong with books?"

"Nothing, Ma. It's just her eyes, they're crossed."

"And who are you to go off on someone not looking like all the others?" Ruby is sorry she's said it as soon as the words fly out of her mouth. "Sorry, Virge. That was uncalled for. I'm not saying Elizabeth or not Elizabeth. Just don't discount what's right in front of you. Could save a heap of trouble and time. And heartache. Now get some sleep. Tomorrow, you'll feel better, mark my words."

Who am I to hold my boys back?

"Did you send for the university in Tucson?"

"I did, Ma."

"Well, let's talk about those catalogues when they come."

As Ruby closes the boys' bedroom door, a small mouse scurries under the divan. Ruby opens the front door of the hotel and chases the rodent out. She closes the door as quietly as she can, given the hour. She's full up tonight, and has to get to bed herself. As she tiptoes to her bedroom, she thanks her lucky stars that Virgil is on the mend and still at home.

Ruby can't be having bodies removed at midnight. The next one would likely have identification or a companion, a wife or husband or child. If anyone finds out that guests have died at The Miracle—especially of tuberculosis—Ruby won't see another customer.

Ruby goes to Judd's the next morning to find Harold Cleaver already in his cups. Willa is behind the bar, washing glasses. Her stay at Mae's lasted two days before she was back. *Some women never learn.*

"It's Virgil," Ruby says. "He's ill."

The postmaster worries his drink. He checks his watch. "Can't have Virgil missing work, Mrs. Fortune."

"Well, I can't have him dying, Mr. Cleaver."

Cleaver blanches. "Do you mean . . ."

"No. Don't think it's serious—and Doc has seconded that. But Virgil looks like death warmed over. A couple of days of rest should do it."

Cleaver stammers. "I'll give him until next Monday. But count this as his one and only week off of the year." He gathers up his hat and leaves by the tavern's back door.

"You won't be sorry, Mr. Cleaver," Ruby calls after him. "You'll never find a better employee in all of Arizona Territory. And I mean that."

Willa bends over the bar, her generous cleavage in full sight. "He'll be right as rain in no time. You can trust me on that."

Ruby hopes Willa is right. And hopes that Virgil never gets a wild hair to go to Chicago, or anywhere, for that matter.

Old Judd ambles into the tavern through the back door.

"I've got some business with you, Judd," Ruby says.

"What's your pleasure?" he asks. He reaches for a whiskey bottle.

"Not drinking," Ruby says. "I get to say this stone cold sober. You are a bastard, Judd."

He steps back, mocking offense. "Not like I haven't heard that before."

"I mean it, Judd. Knock off of Willa. I'm thinking of giving her shooting lessons."

RUBY COUGHS INTO HER HANKY. It's still red. She stuffs it into her pocket and sets out to do the wash. Halfway through, she sits. Coughs again. More blood. Doc Swendsen has already told her to take it easy (easy for him to say). Loss of appetite isn't new to Ruby. During the years Willie was thrashing her, she rarely thought about food. Back then, she wondered if she'd make it through the day.

Ruby nips at piecrust crumbs, sips coffee. Wipes the roast pan clean with a heel of bread. Swipes the last of the butter onto her finger. When was the last time she sat down for a real meal? Fatigue climbs into her bones every hour until she collapses in bed at night. She can't afford to lose any more weight. But the night sweats are the worst, and now they're no longer about Willie Fortune.

Each night, Ruby places a towel over her pillow. She's gone through two pillow sleeves already this week and can't afford to throw away another. There are already too many guests dirtying her sheets and towels. Ruby soaks stained linens in cold water, rubs them with saleratus, rinses them. Often, there's still a faint tinge of pink on cleaned sheets. So Ruby puts the stained side of the linens at the foot of the beds in the ground floor rooms. Men aren't so particular.

Ruby can't risk discolored sheets in the upper floor rooms, even if the guests are tubercular. They are paying resort prices, the lucky ones. Those that can't afford to stay at The Miracle or The Mountain View, or don't have connections to the sanitarium in Tucson, find themselves in "Tentville" north of town. Dog Webber wrote about them just last week in the *Courier-Journal*.

Row upon row of white tents dot the otherwise drab landscape, and loud hacking can be heard throughout the night. Tents can be purchased for eighty dollars or rented for fifteen dollars per month. It is a grim sight to see human wraiths open tent flaps to hail farmers, milkmen, and butchers peddling their supplies to a community near dead. One would think these poor souls would rather be at home, wherever that might be, but they have come for the cure to the dreaded disease that thus far eludes them.

Ruby sits at the kitchen table and laboriously fills out orders for more sets of sheets from the Sears & Roebuck catalogue. She's turned a profit, but there's always more to buy than she's budgeted for. Sheldon is generous, but she can't go on wearing out her welcome on his bank account. *Collecting taxes must pay off*, she thinks. And winning poker hands. And kickbacks and payoffs, too, she can only imagine. She really has no idea where all Sheldon's money comes from. Maybe he makes it.

"You'd do it for me, if the tables were turned," Sheldon says. "This inn of yours is the best thing to happen to this town. Like Teddy Roosevelt said."

"I'm not disagreeing, but I don't want to overstep."

"You? Overstep?"

"I do love you, Sheldon."

"I know you do."

SAME NIGHT

Could there be just a few more hours each day? Ruby is wrung out, but there's that bright spot, Virgil improving. If there were two of her, or three, that might be enough to keep up with the demands of running the hotel. Willa won't come work for her fulltime, but how about Penny? *Who still hasn't come calling.* Maybe Ruby will hire some of Judd's upstairs girls to get them out of harm's way. *Like my poor momma . . .* She puts her head on the table and nods off.

A loud banging on the back door awakens her. She rousts and straightens her skirt, checks her hair. When she opens the back screen, her heart lurches.

"Mr. Bugg."

"Thought I'd never come back? Finish what I started? And there's that little business about wasps."

"I have no idea what you're talking about," Ruby says. Her feet are cemented to the spot. "What is it that you want?"

"What's rightfully mine."

Roger growls.

Bugg pushes past Ruby into the kitchen, kicks at Roger, and drags a chair over the wood floor. "What do you think I want?"

"You come barging in here. You tell me."

"Your hotel."

"Bastard." Ruby stands with her hands on the back of a kitchen chair. "You'll have to kill me for it."

"That can be arranged." Bugg fingers his six-shooter. "But there's another way." He sits across from where Ruby is standing. "I've had a long year to think about it locked up at Yuma."

"Gave me pleasure every day thinking about it."

Bugg places his dirty hands on the table. His eyes bore through Ruby.

She shifts, uncomfortable under his gaze.

He clears his throat. "Marry me, Ruby. Then we both get what we want."

Ruby's eyes widen. "Marry you? How romantic." She shakes her head and whistles. "You could have your pick of any woman. I clearly recall you saying you didn't have the inclination."

"That long in a lockup does funny things to you. It's not like we'd be the first to share the sheets that didn't get off on the right foot."

"Mr. Bugg . . ."

"Jimmy."

"I think not, Mr. Bugg."

"What can I do to change your mind? I know a thing or two about making an operation succeed." Bugg's large hands are folded on the tabletop. They are no cleaner than when Ruby sat across from him in the mine office all those years ago.

"There's nothing you can do to change my mind," she says.

"I'd hate to kill you."

Stop, Ruby, think.

"Wait." Going into her bedroom, Ruby stands with her back against the closed door. Her hands shake. When her heart slows, she opens the top drawer of her bureau and rummages through her underthings. The thick envelope is wedged into the back of the drawer behind bloomers and chemises. She fingers the packet and takes it out of the drawer. She sits at her small desk and hastily writes an addendum, folds it, and tucks it into the envelope.

Ruby re-enters the kitchen and tosses the heavy packet on the table.

"And this is?"

"The deed. To The Miracle. You can have it after I pass. Of natural causes only."

"Very tricky, Ruby. You think of everything." Bugg leans across the table, opens the envelope, and unfolds the deed.

"Sign here," Ruby says. She hands Bugg a pen.

Jimmy Bugg takes the pen and signs with a large hand. He blows on the ink as it dries.

"And here." Ruby places the single sheet of paper in front of Bugg. "A guarantee that you'll make an allowance for my boys."

"I still don't understand this sudden change of heart."

Ruby pulls out her hanky and waves in front of Bugg. "I'm ill, Mr. Bugg. No one knows. Nor will they. I've got tuberculosis."

"Tuberculosis?"

Ruby nods.

"Damn."

"I've been known to use stronger language than that when the situation warrants, Mr. Bugg. As you might recall."

"I don't know what to say."

"How about goddamn."

"Goddamn it, then. Goddamn it to Hell."

"More like it."

Ruby refolds the deed and places it in the envelope. She keeps the addendum. She will return it to her bureau drawer in an envelope clearly marked 'Sheldon Sloane.' If Jimmy Bugg bugs out on payment, Sheldon will know who to look for, and where, and why.

Bugg pockets the packet and stands. He places his large hands on the back of the kitchen chair and pushes it back in. "Well, I guess that's it. Although you surprise me. Not the way I thought this would turn out."

"Did you really think I would marry you?"

"No."

"Or you'd have the guts to kill me?"

He stammers. "No."

"Mr. Bugg?"

"Jimmy."

"Do I have your word?"

"You do, Ruby. I can call you Ruby, can't I?"

Ruby shrugs.

"Your boys will get their fair share. Although I could hold a grudge about the wasps. I'm allergic. Covered with hives, I was. For days."

Ruby ignores Bugg's last comment. "Ten percent of the hotel to each one of my four boys before you take ownership. You'll pay upfront. When the time comes." Ruby rises from the chair. She coughs into her hanky. It's red again.

Bugg recoils at sight of the hanky.

"You've saved me some trouble, Mr. Bugg."

"Jimmy."

"Yes. Jimmy."

"By how?"

"I didn't know who I'd will the hotel to and I want it to keep going long after I'm gone. No business man like you in Jericho." She tries to stuff her disingenuousness.

"You showing up tonight made it crystal clear. The Miracle will be yours, to do with it as you will, or must. After. But I have one request before you go. Don't come anywhere near me or the hotel until you hear."

"I can live with that." Bugg opens the screen door and turns back to look at Ruby. "I'm heading up to Jerome. You remember Red Callahan? Buck Torres? We've got a business venture going there." Bugg puts his hat on. "I'll keep an ear out. I hope it's not too soon."

"You and me, both."

"I meant it about marrying me." He bangs the kitchen door shut behind him.

Ruby lowers herself into the kitchen chair and lays her head on the table again. She breathes freely for the first time since Bugg startled her at the back door. Marry him? Not a chance in Hell.

And now her sons—all of them—are guaranteed an allowance. Bugg signed for it, right in front of Ruby tonight. Bugg, on the other hand, won't realize *until the time comes* that he now owes more than ten thousand to pay off Sheldon's loan. If she doesn't live to see that day, she can picture it, Bugg madder than he was about the wasps, and the sting much worse. A man doesn't like to be parted from his horse or his billfold or his pride. His pride, mostly. And by a woman.

Ruby laughs for the first time in ages, so hard she gets into a coughing fit. She can almost feel her lungs filling with fluid. But she can't help it. She got him good, that Jimmy Bugg, first, with the forged signature on Willie's fake will and again tonight with the signed deed to her heavily leveraged hotel. Sheldon will get a laugh out of this.

No, Ruby reminds herself, *I got that bastard three times, if you count the wasps.*

And then, coughing be damned, Ruby gets to laughing again until tears stream down her face onto the red-tinged hanky. But she's not sad. Not in the least. Just today, Doc Swendsen confirmed Ruby doesn't have tuberculosis at all.

"Walking pneumonia, desert fever, but not what we thought, Ruby. You'll probably outlive every last one of us."

DECEMBER 30, 1906
JERICHO, ARIZONA TERRITORY

The last of the guests has finally gone to bed. The piano arrived this week, and has already been put to good use, four-part harmony in the parlor just tonight. "Let's have us a *sang*," the Southern man twanged as he motioned to guests, who were languishing on couches nursing their third or fourth whiskey to toast the old year. A parlor filled with music, isn't that a thing? It might be years too late for Ruby to learn to play the piano, but maybe not. Maybe she'll sit down when no one's looking, plunk out a song, like she does on the mandolin. Or maybe Perce was right, some things are pretty enough just to look at.

Ruby kicks the screen door closed with her heel. The night air hangs fresh. She sits on the kitchen stoop sipping the dregs of her tea. It's past ten o'clock and dark as death, except for constellations that peek through wandering clouds, a belt here, a spear there.

Coyotes yip in the distance, and then comes an ear-piercing scream. Poor rabbit. Ruby had to shoot a coyote that lurked near the back stoop just this morning. Coming after ever-present kittens, she suspects. Forget the mournful face, coyotes are thieves, scavengers, all. Sometimes you have to look a scoundrel in the face. Assess the situation. Pull the trigger.

Ruby steps off the stoop and raises a cloud of rust-colored dust, although it's too dark to see it settle in any other color but ink. Her back aches, so she leans backward from the waist to get the kink out. Only the faintest coyote yip now, then nothing. It's a wonder there are any coyotes left after the fall hunting season; there are bounties on coyote, wolf, wildcat, sheep, and bear. Even javelina.

For old time's sake, Ruby ambles up Jefferson toward Divina's old place. On Brewer's Alley, men range in and out of saloons, hats low, drowning sorrows nickel by nickel. Wait until tomorrow, New Year's Eve. Ruby winds up the rise past Margaret's. Sheldon's horse. *Yes.* There better be a wedding in the offing soon, or she'll have some strong words with Sheldon.

Ruby opens Divina's rusted gate; its yaw grates her ears like bad chalk. Ruby peers inside Divina's house. It's even messier than the last day Divina drew breath. Critters have taken up residence, packrats and cockroaches and mice. Ruby wipes the dust-smeared window with her fist. Divina's fortune-telling table is still there, dusty and void.

"Behind all those potions and tarot cards and veils, I thought it was only Jean Parker Purdue," Ruby says. "All those miracles? Thought they were shams. Couldn't have been more wrong. I should have put more stake into it. And into you." Ruby coughs. The blood is less frequent now. "Someone told me once you don't miss something until it's gone. Well, I goddamn miss you, Divina. I've come to tell you I'm going to buy that ticket. Go to San Francisco. Run into that sea with all my clothes on and not give a dead rat what anyone says about it. And find Perce, if it's the last thing I do."

Ruby sits in the rocking chair on the porch, its back fitting the curve of her spine like a familiar hand. She hasn't dared fix up Divina's old place even though it's been a couple of years now. She doesn't want to take away any of the memories. Townsfolk say the old place is haunted. So what if people think Divina's ghost lives there now. Who's to say it doesn't? A slight draught blows through, and Ruby shivers. She rocks there, back, *creak*, forth, *creak* for the shy part of a half hour, talking like Divina's right there, tut-tutting.

"So yesterday," she starts, "Virgil comes home and waves a letter in the air over my head. 'From Fletcher!' he yells. About wet my pants. I jumped and jumped until I snatched it from his hands. Let me tell you, if I read that letter twenty times, I read it two hundred times. Turns out, Fletch's been staying with Clayton up in Durango and thought I'd want to know he's found himself a lady. 'A lady,' he said! Said he'd write soon again because this Letty of his is expecting a little one come November. When they can scrape up enough dough, they'll come to Jericho, maybe next summer. You can bet your last dollar I aim to have them stay. All of them. Imagine, Divina. *A baby. Isn't that a miracle?*"

LATE THAT NIGHT, THE MOON climbs in Ruby's kitchen window. If only there would be that familiar knock. But too many months—twenty-one of them, to be exact—have gone by, and she did tell Perce not to come back. Sometimes women say one thing and mean another. Maybe men should spend as much time trying to understand women as they do cleaning a gun or talking politics or drinking until dawn. Of course, she didn't mean it.

Come back, come back, come back. We can make it, some way, can't we? Even if we never touch each other again?

It's unusually cold tonight, a ring around the moon. In the Sonoran Desert, that signals snow. It's almost midnight when Ruby pulls on a wrap and goes out to the shed. Huddled up against the door of the shed, Wink lies unmoving, an empty bottle on his lap.

"Wink!" Ruby bends closer to see if he's breathing. A slight exhale assures her. "Wink!" she says again, this time louder. Her pulse quickens as she shakes his shoulder.

Wink stirs, his eyes rheumy. "Miss Ruby?" He tips his hat back from over his eyes.

"Get up, Wink. It's too cold outside tonight."

"I wouldn't want to trouble you . . ."

"It's no trouble, come on now." She helps the drunken man to his feet. "We'll get you some coffee and a warm room for the night."

"I can't ever pay you, Ruby," he slurs.

"You pay me in all kinds of other ways, Wink. Helping me about the place. Not that I don't notice. Wood doesn't stack itself. Weeds don't pick themselves. And there have been no pack rats under the porch lately." She offers Wink her hand. "And don't think I don't notice the way you are with Sam. Few people in this hellhole pay him any mind. Besides, The Miracle is bringing in receipts to make a lady blush. I'm thinking of building you a little house of your own. Right here on the property. What do you think of that idea?" Ruby guides Wink up the kitchen stoop and sits him on a hard-backed chair in the kitchen. "I'll get coffee on."

"'The fool doth think he is wise . . .'"

"Your friend Shakespeare again?"

"From *As You Like It* . . . 'but the wise man knows himself to be a fool.'"

"Enough of that nonsense, Wink. There's not a man half as wise as you in all of Jericho. Even fools can see that."

"Maybe because of the bottle."

"No, you crazy old coot. It's not because of the bottle. It's the poets, they know how to speak what most of us cannot."

After the coffee has boiled, Ruby sets a steaming cup in front of Wink. He reaches for the mug with shaking hands. "How's Virgil getting on?"

"Better every day. We dodged a bullet there." Ruby draws in a sharp breath. If she's going to ask him, better inquire when he's drunk. Might not remember that way. "I've got a question for you, Wink. About your Bard."

"Well, let's see." Wink scratches his bearded chin. "Born 1564, Stratford-Upon-Avon. Wrote thirty-nine plays, a hundred fifty-odd sonnets . . ." Wink's voice is garbled. "Had a wife, Anne Hathaway. Three children, two girls and a boy. Although the boy died. Of the plague. Shakespeare never got over it."

Ruby tops off her coffee. "No one escapes heartache, Wink." She sits opposite him at the table. "I'm not digging for Mr. Shakespeare's life history. I want to know what he says about love."

Wink smiles at Ruby over the top of his mug. He is now missing one of his front teeth. What scrapes has he been in now? Then he starts to laugh. "How long is the night, Miss Ruby?"

Ruby gets up to feed more kindling to the stove and shuts the kitchen door tightly against the cold. "Would you look at that, Wink? Snow."

Wink hobbles to the door. "Haven't seen snow here in years. Back in Chicago, that's another matter. One of the reasons I left, although not the main reason."

"A woman?"

Wink nods. His eyes tear up.

"Are you apt to tell me?"

"No, Miss Ruby."

"There's something else you've never told me about."

"Squires?"

"I need to know."

"He's under the shed." Wink cocks his head toward the shed where he spends most nights.

"What?"

"The truth, Miss Ruby. I buried him there, after I hit him with that shovel. Couldn't have an old gimp like me drag a man his size out in broad daylight, could you? Someone would have noticed, even in this town."

"You mean to tell me that man is buried here on my property?"

"Sorry, Miss Ruby. But you'll never hear from him again. Our secret."

"You can't go back out there tonight, Wink. Or any night. You'll stay right here at The Miracle until we build your new cabin."

"And why would you do that for me, Miss Ruby?"

"Why do any of us do anything, Wink? Because I want to. Because it's the right thing to do."

Ruby gives Wink the key to Room #2 ("The Outlaw"), the very room Squires wanted her to meet him in the morning after he accosted her. *The irony*, she thinks. Ruby tiptoes back to the kitchen and opens the door softly. She puts on her boots and grabs a wrap. In the shed, Ruby finds a jug of kerosene. She thinks to pour it liberally around the shed and strike a match. But no, she doesn't want to set Jericho aflame for the fourth time. And there's a better idea: build a stone patio over the spot next to Wink's new cabin. They can have a laugh over that one when they put their feet up and knock back a few. Ruby replaces the kerosene on the shelf and emerges into the desert night, now shrouded white.

JANUARY 2, 1907
JERICHO, ARIZONA TERRITORY

Ruby steals away to her bedroom and flops on her bed. She slides her thumb under the seal and opens Vi's letter. Vi usually sends a postcard, which Ruby can read in the blink of an eye between meals and washing up or sitting on the crapper. But a letter, that's something she needs time to read. She's finally got ten minutes to herself before closing up the hotel for the night. Ruby smooths the crinkled stationery.

> *Ruby dear—*
> *1907. Can you believe it? I will be 79 years of age this year. When a body inches toward 80, she can say whatever it is she wants to and no longer give a fig what others think.*
>
> *Which is why it's long past time I told you.*

Told Ruby what?

Your momma loved your pop something fierce. Everyone did (I'm not telling you anything you don't already know, but this is God's honest truth: he loved you most of all).

Ruby presses her lips together. *Pop.*

Poor Divina had it the worst. She followed your pop to the ends of the earth, and look what that got her. But back to your momma. When she told me she aimed to keep Big Burl's baby, it caused quite the stir. We had words, as I recall. She was a stubborn one, your momma, like you. 'Call her Pip,' she said, just before she drifted away.

Ruby puts the letter down into her lap. Pip? How could Divina have known that? All these years Ruby thought Divina was pulling tricks out of her arse, the cards, the fortunes, the prophecy, all of it. Maybe it wasn't all a crock of horseshit, after all. She reads the next paragraph, in Vi's spider-like scrawl.

But I called you Ruby, to mark the beauty in your momma's dying. Because, you see, Ruby, your momma was my girl.

Ruby drops the letter to the floor. *Vi is my grandmother?* Ruby's hands tremble as she salvages the letter.

I know this will come as a shock, Ruby. I couldn't raise you, but Divina could. Simple as that. I hope you don't hate me for it. Or Divina. But now you know.

Chitters disturb Ruby's thoughts. Along the fencepost, grosbeak and cactus wren twit and flutter. In swoops a cardinal, red as a ruby, chasing other birds away.

> *Damn if my hands aren't all gnarled up, Ruby. I can't write two words together anymore. Come see me soon. I'm not going to live forever, you know.*
> *—Your Vi*

APRIL 19, 1907
JERICHO, ARIZONA TERRITORY

At dawn, it's quiet, as if there's a curtain between the living and the dead, like sleep, but longer. Winding through dust and brush of Jericho Cemetery, and avoiding the crooked pile of rocks that marks Willie Fortune's unceremonious leave of the world, Ruby reaches Big Burl's grave, one of only two large granite markers in a cemetery littered with rude wooden crosses and tilting cairns. The other granite headstone to the left of Big Burl's belongs to Divina, paid out of Ruby's pocket with the sum Divina left to her.

Ruby catches her breath. She is short-winded after walking up the long, hair-pinned rise. The desert fever, or whatever she has, is lingering. Ruby pauses first at Divina's grave and runs her hand over the rough granite. *We have a goddamn lot to talk about, Divina.* She pulls a handful of bunchgrass from in front of the stone.

To the right of Big Burl's massive grave is the tiny etched stone Ruby placed there so many years ago, the baby never far from Ruby's thoughts, although she never mentions his name. It's too painful.

Baby Willie
1888

Ruby picks seedpods and debris from around the empty grave. She would bring flowers if there were any flowers to bring. She clears a spot by her father's gravestone and scans for scorpions, rearranges her skirt with rough hands, and pulls her knees up to her chest, her red boots peeking out beneath.

"Did you know, too? About Vi? And Divina?"

The stones are silent. She knows Big Burl is listening, even to the rough parts, but he won't tell. The dead are good secret keepers, after all. Maybe if Ruby waits long enough and listens hard enough, she'll get an answer.

Something rustles in the brush. Ruby is always on high alert for snakes. She turns right and left, checks behind her. Nothing.

The sun edges over the Catalinas, the color of the wide sky nothing short of dazzling, corals and purples and oranges piercing the day. And that sound? A mourning dove? Yes, there, atop a towering spike thrust skyward from the heart of a century plant. Its haunting coo softens the air. Ruby exhales, as if she's been holding her breath for far too long.

Ruby feels a stirring, then, from somewhere deep, like an answer pushing up to the surface through rocks and dirt. What is it that burbles up inside her? And in the air around her? The clouds even? Is it a trick of the eye? Or the mind? It looks like the mountains are rising, too.

You think so, Pop? Yes?

It's alright, Ruby, yes, she hears. *Nothing ill will come of the telling of it. Go ahead. Word by word.*

Prickles rise on her neck. *Pop?*

I'm right here, Ruby.

And then it happens, in the blink of an eye. Something has shifted, like the rock stripped from the tomb. Ruby checks toward the sky again. The world is on fire.

In the empty post-dawn graveyard, Ruby jumps up, arms wide, embracing the blazing sky, not the same woman she was when she woke up this morning, or all the mornings spooling back years and years. It's as if the skin has peeled off her pain and guilt and shame and there she is, naked to the world, beautiful and singing.

Nothing ill will come of the telling of it. Go ahead. Word by word.

Stranger things have happened than hearing from the dead. But where will she start? Black and white? Night and day? Hate and love?

Hate, she thinks, *I know you well. You come in many sizes and shapes, like cast-off coats.* Give hate space to breathe and it multiplies and festers and dredges up memories that hurt far more than scars will ever, ever reveal. *Then again, love can come in disguise, too,* Ruby thinks: a nod of the head, a hand on your shoulder, a rare hug. A note. Pie left covered on the doorstep, still warm. Or that once, wrapped in brown paper and twine, a mandolin.

I'm done with hate, Ruby muses. *But I'm not done with love.*

Now, you might argue that love would be harder to find than a nugget on the street here in Jericho. Look again. Send word that you're hurting and everyone within earshot will be at your door, dragging frailties and flaws behind them. "There, there," they'll say, and nod, as they stuff into your hands hot dishes on chipped china or poor excuses for bouquets tied with scraps of string. They'll surround you like a fortress, guns drawn against whoever or whatever is coming at you.

And when you're grieving, tears poker-hot on your cheeks and face looking like Hell itself (and the rest of you feeling like it), they'll try to say all the right things at all the wrong times, doing the best they can under the worst of circumstances.

It's as natural as breathing, just the knowing of it.

47

APRIL 22, 1907
JERICHO, ARIZONA TERRITORY

The way Wink told it to Ruby, she could see it, hear it, *almost feel it*, as if she were there with Wink and Sam out in the desert. Feathered clouds obscured the sun, Wink told Ruby, leaving a long tail of wisps behind, "as if an afterthought," he said, and continued his story. *Don't the poets always say it best?*

"Take this old tin here," Wink said to Sam, as the older man bent over to pick up a rusted can. "We can hold onto grudges and anger and bitterness for just so long until it turns us nasty." He put the can into his soiled pack. "Anger like that starts to wear on a body. Time to let go."

Sam kicked a mesquite branch out of the way and came up shoulder to shoulder with the old man as they walked through the desert. Stretched across the trail ahead was a large bull snake lolling in the sun. Wink put out his arm. They watched the snake for any sign of movement.

"Well, would you look at that, Sam. The weather warms up and the desert exhales, and with it, snakes." They gave the bull snake a wide berth and tromped past with heavy footfalls. It curled slightly, but didn't move.

"Like the Garden of Eden." Wink paused. "And just as mystifying."

Sam looked puzzled.

"No matter how far we wander, there's no place so far as the soft folds of a woman's flesh . . . but I'm not talking about women today," Wink said, shaking his head vehemently. "That's a whole other subject for a whole other day. Give it a year, maybe two. What I'm talking about now is not knowing what the next day will bring—that's the gamble of life. We've got to look past the part we're afraid of, because if we don't, we're no better off than dead."

Wink scuffed a few steps and stopped. "'Out, out, brief candle!'"

Sam signed, *Shakespeare*?

"That's right, Sam. Best writer in the English language. Had something to say for everything." His long arm wrapped around Sam's bony shoulder as he gave the boy a squeeze.

"'To be, or not to be; that is the question.' *Hamlet*. Act 3, Scene 1."

Sam looked up at Wink with large brown eyes, signing, *What*?

"Can't always figure what your fingers are saying, chap, but from where I stand, you've got your whole life ahead of you like a long calendar." Wink mimicked turning page after page. "So I say let it go, Sam. Whatever it is that's got your tongue tied up in knots." Wink patted Sam again and started to quote another line, but thought better of it.

"Hard fact here: the past is over, Sam. No way to get it back. Everything dies. People, stars, even mountains." Wink slowed down and stopped. "I think it's time you knew the real story, Sam. Not just the bits and pieces part of it. Or what you saw."

Wink dusted off the top of a boulder. "Have a seat,

young squire." He motioned to the cleared spot. Sam sat, his back straight, feet touching the ground. He tossed his long blond hair out of his face. Wink parted his long swing coat and sat on the low boulder next to the boy. "You're old enough now." Wink looked toward the Santa Catalina Mountains, not making eye contact.

"Some say I talk in parables—that's a fancy name for stories, Sam—but don't let it be said that Theodore W. Inkman tells untruths." Wink turned toward Sam. "Here is the story, plain and simple."

Sam returned Wink's gaze, his eyes narrowed because of the sun.

"Your pa was right miserable to your ma," Wink started. "Some men—your pa in this case—think the world owes them something. Like they're better than their neighbor or their brother. When they don't get what they want, they take it out on those around them, usually the ones they're closest to. That's what happened with your ma. Your pa thought he could misuse your ma for no fault of hers. She took it and took it until she couldn't take it anymore. In the end, she was protecting you, Sam. You and your brothers."

Wink stopped and wiped spittle from his whiskered chin. "You might think your ma went too far—you saw it, after all, and that's a shame in anyone's book—but this world is better off in spades without men the likes of your pa."

Sam's eyes rimmed with tears.

Wink scratched his unkempt beard. "You can't change a thing, no matter how hard you try." He nodded. "Today is all we're promised, Sam. Tomorrow, well, that's too far ahead for this old fart to worry about." Wink stood and opened his arms. "We're either on *el camino de dios*—that's God's road, boy—or *el camino del diablo*, the devil's way. Either road, Sam, we make decisions, some good, some bad. That's what your ma did, some good choices and some not-so-good choices.

What she did wasn't so much for her, but for you boys. The way she tells it, it was especially for you."

Wink took Sam's chin in his grubby hand and looked the boy in the eye. "Understand?"

Sam swiped at his eyes and pushed Wink's arm away.

"Up he jumped then," Wink told Ruby afterward. "Grabbed his canteen and broke into a run, gangly legs sprinting over prickly pear and sagebrush on the way back to The Miracle. I yelled after him, 'Where're you going, young squire? We've got nickels to make while the sun shines!' but he didn't look back, Ruby. He didn't look back."

SAM LEAPS OVER THE BACK FENCE and lopes across the yard. He barges through the kitchen door, dirt crusted and sweaty and out of breath.

"Well, if it isn't the birthday boy. Twelve years old already." Ruby pulls Sam's birthday cake out the oven with new oven mitts and sets the pan on the counter. She plunges her warm hands into cool dishwater in the sink.

Sam drops his pack on the floor with a thud. Ruby, hands and forearms wet, turns to face her son. Sam stares at Ruby, hard, and then runs headlong toward his mother. Suds and water droplets fly in bone-dry desert air as Ruby envelops him.

"Thank you, Ma," Sam says, his voice stumbling over words. "For all of it."

Well, Ruby knows that twelve-year-old boys aren't keen about their mommas scooping them up like small fry, but with a cry from deeper in her gut than any sound that has come before, Ruby gathers that gangly man-boy of hers in her arms and bawls her living soul out, clutching her son, his hair, his shoulders, his back, her fingers squeezing out all the lost conversations. They stand there in the kitchen like that, chattering and crying, and chattering some more until the day runs late and Ruby's voice runs dry.

"Eighteen coming tonight, Sam," she croaks, when at last they sit side-by-side at the kitchen table drinking iced tea. "Nineteen, if Dog rousts that lazy arse of his and makes it in time." She hugs Sam tight again, like she never wants to let go, ever. "No matter, one way or the other. There's always room for more."

Ruby need not worry about her table, or about Sam's voice. Sam talks a blue streak at his birthday supper, to the delight of all present, even the crotchety Dog Webber who makes it after all, and who is now playfully interrogating Sam. *Speak up, boy; we all want to hear what's in that head of yours.* Wine glasses, plates, forks, knives, spoons, all of Jericho come, even Mae. *You can have a job at the store anytime*, she says to Sam. Margaret asking Sam to teach her to sign; "o" and "k" he signs to her. Virgil and Elizabeth, heads close, and Virgil egging Sam on. *About time you came clean, Sam, how you swiped that piece of my birthday cake hot out of the oven.* And then there's Sam's cake on the table, and twelve candles, and that familiar lusty chorus, *Happy Birthday to you, Sam!* Present after present, and Penny offering Sam the best gift of all: a bag full of nickels. *What will you buy with that, young man?* Sheldon asking, and Sam answering, *a Coca-Cola, sir.*

Ruby steals a look at Sheldon over the jabbering. He offers up a smile, raises a glass, and nods. "To you, Ruby," he mouths. And then everyone is clapping and Ruby is standing there, crying, in front of God and all creation, but what does she care? Fletcher's coming home, and maybe Clayton, too. Endings and beginnings. Babies. Forgiveness. Friends. And, according to Doc, she'll live longer than Jimmy Bugg anyway. Virgil squeezes Ruby's hand and Sam smiles like a cat that's snared a mouse and isn't he the clever one, the first shall be last and the last shall be first and all is well with the world, all of it.

When I burst out the kitchen door this morning, the world blazed red orange yellow white, colors so brilliant they could goddamn blind you, saguaro, totem, cholla, prickly pear—the whole lot of them—shoving fist-sized blossoms toward the rising sun.

I couldn't help myself. I raised my arms and yelled to the sky and the mountains and the desert whole. "Take that," I hollered, "all you rat bags, all you nay-sayers, all you *fools*!"

I don't care who heard me. But someone did, because the earth rumbled beneath my feet.

That you, Pop? Divina?

When I stamped my feet, I must have startled that roadrunner loping by. She swerved as she ran like a woman drunk, right left right, her long tail bouncing behind her. As I watched her run cockeyed through the desert, she raised her tail feather by an old saguaro and a glint caught my eye.

The ruby ring! Of course!

That got me to laughing so hard my innards hurt. Used to be, I hardly had a penny. But now? I can almost feel that old shovel in my hand, digging up that blasted ring. It's my ticket to . . . *everything*.

And the earth rumbled again, louder this time, the dead laughing. We hooted then, all of us, and there I was, six years old, riding on Pop's broad shoulders somewhere in the middle of Texas with my wild hair spilling out behind me and Pop bellowing in that great big voice of his, *Hold on, Ruby! Hold on!*

So I did now, didn't I? I held on, alright.

Heaven might not have me.

But I'm not afraid of Hell anymore.

AFTERWORD

This is a work of fiction. All of the characters leapt onto the page from a place deep within my soul and imagination, although I used Tucson artist Allen Polt's painting "The Girl With the Red Gloves" as my visual muse for the character Ruby Fortune. Ruby embodies the spirit of millions of women who have found the courage to speak up about past abuse and risen from it stronger. Any resemblance to anyone, living or dead, is unintentional, coincidental, speculative, or false.

Jericho is also completely fictional, placed between Tucson and Mammoth at the northern edge of the Santa Catalina Mining District, and molded in the image of other historic mining towns in Arizona, notably Jerome and Bisbee. President Theodore Roosevelt visited Arizona Territory in a great swing of western states and territories in 1903, so it is not beyond the realm of possibility that he would have visited a town like Jericho. Any errors concerning Arizona history, places, or historic personages belong to the author alone.

Big Burl and his Triple B Traveling Carnival and Wild West Show is based on a score of other outfits that attempted to rival Buffalo Bill Cody's iconic Wild West Show that flourished in the American West, and later nationally and internationally, in the late nineteenth century. Interestingly enough, Cody had a stake in a mine outside Oracle, Arizona just on the other side of what I call Oldfather Mountain and stayed at The Mountain View Hotel when he was in town.

A word about ethnic groups depicted in the novel. I have used late nineteenth century terminology as I wrote the manuscript. In no way do I condone the mistreatment, caricature, or condescension of Blacks, Hispanics, Asians, or Native Americans then or now.

As I embarked on this story, I was filled with questions. What would it take for a woman to survive in Arizona Territory on her own at the turn of the last century? Who would be her allies? Her adversaries? How would she provide for herself? What drove her? Who would she love? To what lengths would she go to protect her children? How could she be her own person in a man's world? And how could she survive horrific abuse intact?

These, and other questions, percolated for a few months until the day I asked myself if I had the courage to tell Ruby's story. That's when I sat down to write.

ACKNOWLEDGMENTS

Many thanks to a small cadre of readers for help shepherding *Hardland* to completion. The first round of thanks goes to my critique partners: Shelley Blanton-Stroud, Gretchen Cherington, and Debra Thomas. The next round of thanks goes to readers of the earliest draft of *Hardland*: Janis Daly, Jim Euchner, Michelle Ferrer, Vanessa Finch, Karen Jones, Lynn Hall, Aimee Smythe, my father, author Gerald F. Sweeney, and, in a later draft, dear friend Nancy Soderlund Tupper. I also want to thank those who helped fill in holes on everything from A to Z: Bob Anderson, William Ascarza, Court Hall, Lisa O'Brien, Richard Ohlenberg, Brian Smith, Barbara Steele, Chuck Sternberg, and Michele Anne Waite. And also to Edgar R. "Frosty" Potter, whose iconic book, "Cowboy Slang," taught me some dang colorful language used in the manuscript.

A million thanks to my husband, D. Michael Barclay, will never begin to express the gratitude I have for everything he does to support my writing life, including heavy lifting in the research department and the box-and-suitcase-carrying department. Deepest thanks go to my brilliant editor, Ellen Notbohm. I need to write a huge THANK YOU in chalk all over her neighborhood and hope it's imprinted on her heart, in every color of the rainbow.

In the production stage, I owe many thanks to my intrepid publisher, Brooke Warner, project manager Lauren Wise Wait, cover designer Julie Metz, and the whole team/sisterhood at She Writes Press for surrounding me as Ruby's story jumped onto the page. Also to proofreader Katrina Larsen Groen, and to my publicity team: Krista Soukup of Blue Cottage Agency, webmistress/newsletter editor Anji Verlaque, and social media manager Janis Daly for believing in *Hardland* and doing the hard work to get it out into the marketplace.

I would be remiss not to thank Ken Stern, editor and publisher of *The La Conner Weekly News* in La Conner, Washington, and Sally Cram, a friend from Soroptimist International of La Conner, Washington, who each bid on the opportunity to name two characters in *Hardland* at a fundraiser for La Conner Regional Library several years ago. The characters Margaret Stern and Mary Lam (with and without a 'b') honor their sisters.

In closing, I owe a debt of gratitude to Anne Vaughan Spilsbury, to whose memory this novel is dedicated. When I was a young woman, I spent countless hours sitting on a high stool in Anne Vaughan's cavernous kitchen at Bay Crest in Huntington, New York, where I downed frosty glasses of iced tea and words of wisdom as her hands flew to put together yet another meal for an ever-revolving door of company. Anne Vaughan modeled a life well lived and taught me firsthand about the cost and consequences of decisions.

In addition to raising a houseful of boys, Anne Vaughan spent her days as a tireless community activist with Family Service League, American Field Service, St. John's Episcopal

Church of Huntington, and other charities. With humor, loyalty, vitality, and love, Anne Vaughan gave and gave and gave of herself. Even when she burned the candle at both ends (which was more often than not!) and later, after she received a diagnosis that would eventually claim her life, there was never a day when a friend—or a stranger—wasn't welcomed to her love-filled table.

REFERENCES

Ascarza, William, *Images of America: Southeastern Arizona Mining Towns*, Arcadia Publishing, Charleston, S.C. 2011

Brown, Wynne, *More Than Petticoats: Remarkable Arizona Women*, TwoDot Press, Guilford, Conn. 2003

Cleere, Jan, *Levi's & Lace: Arizona Women Who Made History*, Rio Nuevo Publishing, Tucson, Ariz. 2011

Crutchfield, James A., ed., *The Way West: True Stories of the American Frontier*, Tom Doherty and Associates, N.Y. 2005

Cuming, Harry and Mary, *Yesterday's Tucson Today, Book 1*, West Press, Tucson, Ariz. 1994

Devine, David, *Historic Tales of Territorial Tucson 1854-1912*, The History Press, Charleston, S.C. 2020

Furnas, J.C., *The Americans: A Social History of the United States 1587-1914*, G. P. Putnam's Sons, N.Y. 1969

Gard, Wayne, *Frontier Justice*, University of Oklahoma Press, Norman, Okla. 1949

Lauer, Charles D., *Old West: Adventures in Arizona*, Golden West Publishers, Phoenix, Ariz. 1989

Reddin, Paul, *Wild West Shows*, University of Illinois Press, Urbana, Ill. 1999

Schlereth, Thomas J., *Victorian America: Transformations in Everyday Life*, Harper Collins, N.Y. 1992

Sonnichsen, C. L., *Tucson: The Life and Times of an American City*, University of Oklahoma Press, Norman, Okla. 1982

Trimble, Marshall, *Arizona*, Doubleday, Garden City, N.Y. 1977

Warren, Louis S., *Buffalo Bill's America: William Cody and The Wild West Show*, Vintage, N.Y. 2005

Zucker, Robert E., *Treasures of the Santa Catalina Mountains: Unraveling the Legends and the History of the Lost Mine, Lost City and Lost Mission*, BZB Publishing, Tucson, Ariz. 2014

QUESTIONS FOR DISCUSSON

1. There were a plethora of Wild West shows in the American West in the late nineteenth century and early twentieth centuries (the most notable example is Buffalo Bill Cody). How did these shows celebrate frontier life? How did they exploit it?

2. Some readers have said Ruby is as prickly as cacti, but also likeable. What are you able to overlook to like her?

3. What role did Big Burl have in his daughter Ruby's life? What about Divina and Vi?

4. Most characters possess both positive and negative traits. What negative traits does Ruby Fortune possess? What positive traits does Willie Fortune possess? Explain.

5. How did Willie's death affect all his sons differently? Clayton? Fletcher? Virgil? Sam? How do you cope with tragedy? Do you run from it or face it head on? Or is there another way you deal with raw emotions and the long-term effects of it?

6. Two of Ruby's sons—Virgil and Sam—have some form of disability. How does Ruby treat them? Advocate for them? Talk about how it would have been more difficult to raise a child with a disability more than 100 years ago.

7. What is Wink's role in the novel? How do the Shake-spearean quotes he offers fit in?

8. Margaret Stern acts as a thorn in Ruby's side and later as a confidante. How do both women—and their rela-tionship—change in the arc of the story?

9. One in three women experiences domestic violence in her lifetime, often at the hands of a family member, friend, or spouse. How has the topic of domestic violence come out from the shadows over the past 100 years? What do you see as the solution to this issue?

10. In murder investigations today, there is an in-depth inquiry, media attention, a jury trial, and possible prison sentence. How does Ruby escape all this? Do you think this is right or wrong? And how do Sheldon Sloane's feelings for Ruby affect his judgment?

11. In what other ways is "frontier justice" exercised in the novel?

12. If you met Ruby today, what advice do you think she would give you?

ABOUT THE AUTHOR

Award-winning author Ashley E. Sweeney was born in New York and graduated from Wheaton College in Norton, Massachusetts. Her multiple awards include the New Mexico-Arizona Book Award, Nancy Pearl Book Award, Independent Publisher Book Award, Next Generation Indie Book Award, and Arizona Authors Association Literary Award; she has also been a finalist for the Western Fictioneers Peacemaker Award, Sarton Women's Book Award, and WILLA Literary Award for Historical Fiction (twice), among others. Ashley lives and writes in the Pacific Northwest and Tucson. *Hardland* is her third novel.

Author photo © Justin Haugen

SELECTED TITLES FROM SHE WRITES PRESS

She Writes Press is an independent publishing company founded to serve women writers everywhere. Visit us at www.shewritespress.com.

Answer Creek by Ashley E. Sweeney. $16.95, 978-1-63152-844-6. Starvation. Desperation. Madness. As the Donner Party treks west on the Oregon–California Trail, one young woman risks everything—values, faith, reputation, and every last coin sewn into the hem of her skirt—for the mirage of a better life in California.

Eliza Waite by Ashley Sweeney. $16.95, 978-1-63152-058-7. When Eliza Waite chooses to leave a stagnant life in rural Washington State and join the masses traveling north to Alaska in 1898 during the tumultuous Klondike Gold Rush, she encounters challenges and successes in both business and love.

The Island of Worthy Boys by Connie Hertzberg Mayo. $16.95, 978-1-63152-001-3. In early-19th-century Boston, two adolescent boys escape arrest after accidentally killing a man by conning their way into an island school for boys—a perfect place to hide, as long as they can keep their web of lies from unraveling.

The Green Lace Corset by Jill G. Hall. $16.95, 978-1-63152-769-2. An artist buys a corset in a Flagstaff resale boutique and is forced to make the biggest decision of her life. A young midwestern woman is kidnapped on a train in 1885 and taken to the Wild West. Both women find the strength to overcome their fears and discover the true meaning of family—with a little push from a green lace corset.

The River by Starlight by Ellen Notbohm. $16.95, 978-1-63152-335-9. A frontier Montana couple's dreams of prosperity and family shatter in the face of an enigmatic post-partum illness of mind and body that exacts a terrible price. A tale of unthinkable loss, resilience, and redemption, based on true events.

Things Unsaid by Diana Y. Paul. $16.95, 978-1-63152-812-5. A family saga of three generations fighting over money and obligation—and a tale of survival, resilience, and recovery.